ALSO BY TRACY STERN

Longings

This I

by

Promise You

TRACY STERN

SIMON AND SCHUSTER

New York London Toronto Sydney Tokyo

SIMON AND SCHUSTER
Simon & Schuster Building
Rockefeller Center
1230 Avenue of the Americas
New York, New York 10020

This book is a work of fiction. Names, characters, places
and incidents are either the product of the author's
imagination or are used fictitiously. Any resemblance to
actual events or locales or persons, living or dead, is
entirely coincidental.

Copyright © 1990 by Tracy Stern

All rights reserved
including the right of reproduction
in whole or in part in any form.

SIMON AND SCHUSTER and colophon are registered
trademarks of Simon & Schuster Inc.

Designed by Laurie Jewell
Manufactured in the United States of America

1   3   5   7   9   10   8   6   4   2

Library of Congress Cataloging in Publication Data

Stern, Tracy.
This I promise you/by Tracy Stern.
p.   cm.
I. Title.
PS3569.T415T4   1990
813'.54—dc20   89-28085
CIP
ISBN 0-671-67348-3

For B.B., of course

Whatever is not taken from us remains with us.
It is the best part of ourselves.

Ce qu'on ne nous prenne pas nous reste,
c'est le meilleur de nous-même.

—Georges Braque

C H A P T E R

1

A SINGLE TEAR traveled slowly down the child's beautiful cheek. Its path tickled her, and with the back of her free hand she made one brisk movement and wiped it away. She continued her descent from the top of the enormous curved staircase. She took each step carefully, placing her small, delicate black patent leather Mary Jane squarely in the center of each wide, highly glossed tread of white statuary marble. At its broadest, the staircase was more than twelve feet across, but the young girl stayed very close to the ornately carved banister, a habit she had developed long ago when mastering the climb as a toddler. She ran the fingertips of her left hand in between each of the smooth marble spindles. They were icy cold. Her right hand was gently held by her governess, Margarethe.

Margarethe smiled down at the beautiful child she loved as if she were her own. At forty-two Margarethe had never married; she had found contentment enough in the work she had chosen. All of the happiness and security she needed had been provided by the generous Becker family.

From the first day of her arrival, Margarethe had felt at home with the warm, generous family. She loved living amidst the luxury and excitement of the grand hotel, the Waldhotel Becker. It was the fanciest and most exclusive resort in all of Germany. The famous hotel had been built during the last century by Ludwig Becker, the great-grandfather of Katharina, the child Margarethe was leading down the majestic staircase. Now the hotel was run by her grandfather, Karl-Gustav.

"Kati, are you all right, my little one?"

Kati looked up sweetly at the woman she both loved and respected. A woman whose job, indeed whose entire life, had been to discipline and to teach. She had always carried out both of those assignments in a spirit of kindness mixed with a good measure of tenderness and understanding. She could be a cross disciplinarian, but underneath it all she had a heart of gold. Her every action had the welfare of Katharina and her sister in mind.

"Yes, I'm fine, Nana. I hope Papa comes soon."

"He will be here very shortly," she assured her, summoning up her most confident tone of voice.

Katharina had been born almost two years to the day after her older sister. Margarethe had so loved the child immediately upon seeing her that, rather than complain about the added responsibility, or ask for additional staff to help her care for the newborn, she merely felt doubly blessed to have two beautiful children to look after.

In no time, Katharina grew to be her favorite of the two girls. She had only to hear her gurgling and laughing in her crib each day at dawn, to be greeted by her sweet-scented cheek as she bent over to kiss her good morning, and her day was off to a good start. On the other hand, the older sister always awakened with a dour, unhappy expression. A demanding child who tried the patience of both her parents and the ever-tolerant Margarethe, over the years Eva-Maria's disposition had only soured, despite, or perhaps in spite of the concerted efforts made by family members to improve it. Secretly, Margarethe had always felt that there was something evil, something sinister in the child's character. She prayed for her in church each Sunday. Eva-Maria had inherited her mother's flawless beauty: flaxen-colored hair that hung in thick, luxurious curls halfway down her back, perfectly proportioned facial features, and a pair of cornflower-blue eyes that would melt the heart and soul of even the most obstinate opponent. Now, at sixteen, her extraordinary physical beauty, long legs, slim hips, and tiny waist easily camouflaged a decidedly selfish personality. On more than one occasion Margarethe had seen her use her body in such a way with one of the porters or waiters in the hotel that clearly indicated she already knew the power of her feminine assets. Conversely, Kati, as she had been nicknamed at an early age, was a mirror image of her gentle father. Johannes Meier was an attractive, stocky man who had passed on his sandy hair and pale blue eyes to his younger daughter. Those eyes held a sparkle and warmth that years later would prove to be far more attractive and seductive than any pair of perfect breasts, or long, shapely legs. Kati's beauty was more classic than glamorous, the type of healthy good looks and refined features that in the future, when they were accentuated by clever makeup, would produce spectacular results. By far the child's most attractive trait was her delightful personality. She was constantly smiling. The smallest pleasures seemed to give her the greatest joy. Everyone who came in contact with her, from the lowliest kitchen aide to the fanciest and richest of European royalty, was touched by the girl's warmth. All agreed she was a delicious child to have around.

Karl-Gustav and his wife, Marianne, had worshiped their only daughter, Tilla. Their first child, a son, had died just a few days after birth. Peter, their second son, was born two years later and became Karl-Gustav's singular hope for an heir to carry on the family tradition at the grand hotel. But that hope was dashed when, at twenty-three, Peter was killed in the fight for the liberation of Paris.

Karl-Gustav had always secretly harbored the idea that Tilla would choose as her husband someone who would be able to take over the hotel when the time came. So it came as a great surprise to everyone, especially to her parents, when she married Johannes. A native of Stuttgart, Johannes was a quiet, unassuming man who was an accountant by trade. He seemed so sedate, and to some, almost boring in contrast to the princes, counts, and barons whom Tilla could have chosen. But Tilla was also a quiet, reserved girl who was uncomfortable with more dynamic, powerful men. She was painfully shy and seemed always to be trying to run out of the spotlight she found herself in as the attractive daughter of the outgoing, party-loving Karl-Gustav. Because Johannes shared the same desire for a simple life, they appeared to be a perfect match. He adapted beautifully to Tilla's life in the hotel: the constant flow of guests; the endless stream of questions, requests, complaints, occasional compliments; and the almost total lack of privacy. He kept to himself, concentrating on expanding his own business in the small accounting firm he established in town.

The guests who came to stay at the Waldhotel Becker, particularly the regular clientele who returned annually, were among the most discerning and demanding in the world. Karl-Gustav had described his best guest as one who "was rich and determined to make his dreams come true." He was thoroughly committed to making every wish a reality. So successful was he that it was rare for anyone to visit the hotel only once.

A stay at Becker's, even for only one night, was an experience not easily forgotten. Once guests entered the elegant, inviting granite building they were immediately transported to a magical enclave where temptation and luxury abounded. The Waldhotel was not a large hotel. It had only one hundred rooms, two restaurants, two bars, and a single *salon de thé*. The quality of the staff, the understated elegance of the furnishings in both the private apartments and public rooms, and the breathtaking beauty of the hotel's setting along the bank of the peaceful River Oos all combined to create an atmosphere that one dreamed of returning to time and time again.

"The finest hotel in Germany, perhaps in all the world."
"The Waldhotel Becker is the tops!"
"*Merci infiniment,* Karl-Gustav, for a delightful stay."
"Bravo, bravo for the Waldhotel, we will see you next year!"

Such was a sampling of the thousands of entries in the hotel's guest book. The author Gérard de Nerval had written, "One has to visit Switzerland, but one should live in Baden-Baden." Preferably, one assumed, in great luxury at the Waldhotel Becker. The signatures read like a Who's Who of statesmen, diplomats, presidents, kings, and those who merely enjoyed, appreciated, and could afford the good life.

As Europe's summer capital, Baden-Baden was a rich source of cultural, social, and sports activities. The beautiful landscape alone provided reason to visit. At one time in history the area had been sea, desert, glacier, and volcano. Now people traveled to Baden-Baden for many purposes, foremost among them the famous waters long claimed to contain therapeutic properties. The geological faults that ran between the Rhine Plain and the Black Forest really gave Baden-Baden its raison d'être, for they created the hot springs that originally attracted the Romans to the area two thousand years earlier. They built impressive baths of marble and polished green granite, some of which still remained. The springs were the hottest in Europe, reaching temperatures up to 156 degrees Fahrenheit, and are still going strong, pumping over 211,000 gallons per day filled with sodium and chloride ions and trace elements of other curative substances. People came to the various cure or *kur* clinics to bathe, drink, and inhale the steam of the precious substance. The waters were said to calm the digestive systems of those who had abused it through seasons of eating too much rich food.

The horse racing at Iffezheim in the springtime was another major draw. The first race had been held there in 1858, and its stables still boasted the most illustrious horses accompanied by world-famous trainers. The Grand Week of racing in September was regarded as one of the premier events on the European social calendar. With its tennis club, open since 1880, and the world-class casino providing its own kind of therapy year-round, Baden-Baden was perpetually "in season."

People visited Karl-Gustav Becker's hotel for a combination of calm, comfort, and cuisine. For the past forty-nine years he and his handpicked staff had strived to provide those very things. Karl-Gustav was the second generation of Beckers to operate the hotel. Lured by the promise of the waters to relieve his own painful arthritic condition, his father, Ludwig Becker, had moved the family across the Rhine from their home in Strasbourg. They had remained there ever since.

During World War II Baden-Baden was spared the destruction that devastated so much of the country when the French Army made Baden-Baden its German headquarters. Karl-Gustav served his homeland well from a distance as a member of the Free French. At the end of the war, they were in occupation not only of Baden-Baden but of much of the surrounding area as well. The Free French took over all the city had to offer—the baths, the casino—and of course, the hotels. After the war was over, many thousands of Karl-Gustav's countrymen remained in the region.

Through the decades, using his charm and connections, Karl-Gustav had managed to attract an extremely loyal clientele. For these select few, the Waldhotel was the only place to take their holidays.

Most of them made annual pilgrimages to the hotel and booked stays ranging from a week to more than three months at a time. They came from all over the world—French, Italians, Swedes, Americans, British, South Americans—dukes, lords, kings, and princes—anyone who appreciated and could afford the superlative services that were consistently offered at Becker's. No one would argue that the extraordinary popularity of the hotel was directly attributable to Karl-Gustav and his philosophy about how to run a world-class resort. His commitment to pleasing his guests was all-consuming, his attention to every detail relentless. A short walk across the lobby or through the dining room would elicit a terse memo noting countless points that needed to be attended to at once if his standards were to be maintained. Always there were details that a less discriminating eye would be sure to miss.

Karl-Gustav was a very special individual who catered to individuals. He had fostered an intimate relationship between his hotel and those who came to stay at Becker's, and he treasured every day of his existence in the beautiful home he had created primarily for the enjoyment of his guests.

Margarethe's eyes began to tear with her thoughts of him. Her memories swept her back to her first introduction to the legendary hotelier. She had been so terrified to meet him, this formidable Frenchman who was regarded almost as royalty in the region.

Margarethe had traveled that morning so long ago from Appenweier, her small hometown village only a few kilometers to the south of Baden-Baden. Appenweier was a quaint, provincial town. Its main square with only one bakery, one butcher, and one small dry goods store appeared today much as it had in the nineteenth century. But Baden-Baden, the idyllic city in the heart of Germany's Black Forest, was the bastion of the Becker family. Baden-Baden, with its elegant shops, wide boulevards, and glittering casino, was the city where Margarethe had always dreamed of living. Baden-Baden, with its cosmopolitan sophistication, was considered by many to be the easternmost city in France. Indeed she knew that many families, like Katharina's own great grandfather, had crossed over the border and settled there.

On that brilliantly sunny fall day over sixteen years ago Tilla had led her to the top of the very same staircase she was now coming down with Karl-Gustav's grandchild. She showed her into his private office. Margarethe had taken a deep breath and tried her hardest to appear calm. Her fears began to dissolve as he took her hand in his and smiled kindly.

"Why, you're trembling, Margarethe," he had said, immediately detecting her nervousness. He had addressed her with a warmth that would normally only exist after many years of acquaintance, a warmth that was extremely unusual for a Frenchman. At once she knew why he had been so successful with his hotel. He deserved his reputation as a man who made his guests feel at home. "Are you cold? Let us order you something hot to drink at once. Perhaps you'd also like some toast, or a sandwich?"

Of course, she politely refused. As nice as he seemed to be, her hands still shook. She was terrified of spilling something on the new dress she had saved so long for and had finally been able to buy only last week, just in time for this special occasion.

Karl-Gustav had insisted, and by the time the tea and delicate finger sandwiches arrived, she had begun to relax a little. She had never seen such a beautiful tea set, the silver pots gleaming brightly on the huge tray. They were etched ever so delicately in a Victorian floral pattern. Their handles were made of ivory. As she watched the floor waiter slowly fill the elegant china cups, she prayed silently to herself that Karl-Gustav would find her an acceptable governess for his new granddaughter. How she would love to come and live in the beautiful hotel!

So her very first meeting with Karl-Gustav had begun. Throughout the years his kindness and generosity had never lessened. Of course Margarethe was much closer to the family than the hotel servants, but she never lost sight of the fact that she was an employee and therefore replaceable. Still, she couldn't remember a time when Karl-Gustav's door had not been open to her. He had helped her when she had most needed it—only last year when her sister had been ill, he had paid all of the expenses for her to travel the one hundred forty-five kilometers up to Frankfurt to see a specialist. Six years ago when her own grandfather had died, he had sent flowers to the funeral and allowed her mother to come and stay in a lovely room in the hotel for several days with his compliments. He had done all of those things without question, and her grateful thank-you was all he ever expected in return. Oh yes, Karl-Gustav was a truly great gentleman. . . .

Now her eyes were brimming over, and she held Kati's hand a little tighter. She glanced at the regal portrait of the great man that hung on the wall below them.

One more step . . . another . . . almost as if they were in slow motion. . . .

The child's pace slowed even more as they reached the curve in the staircase that brought the main foyer into view. Suddenly Kati froze. She surveyed the activity below. It was a little after four o'clock in the afternoon, always a busy time in the reception area. Many of the guests were just returning to the hotel after a visit to the thermal baths, their skin glowing and radiant from the mineral-rich therapeutic waters. Others were coming in from riding or hiking through the resplendent Black Forest. The less energetic were back from a leisurely stroll through the charming town or along the river's edge.

Kati heard the sounds of a dozen foreign languages requesting their room keys from the receptionist. She recognized almost all of them—her command of French and English was equal to her native German. This year in school she was mastering Italian as well.

In the small dining room to the left of the foyer a pair of lovers lingered over a bottle of wine, their eyes locked and their hands clasped together across the table. They were enchanted only with each other and were totally oblivious to the activity surrounding them.

The concierge's desk, which her grandfather had always referred to as the "center of the universe," was secure with Dieter, one of the most senior members of the Waldhotel's staff. "Yes," Karl-Gustav would say, "it's the control station, the eye of the storm. If anything is out of sorts here," he would continue, "then the whole operation will be off kilter. But when everything is in order, ahh . . ."—he would pause, smile, and raise his hands toward the heavens in a gesture of thanks—"then the hotel will be like a skillfully conducted symphony, or a brilliantly constructed Swiss timepiece. A work of art!" he would exclaim.

Karl-Gustav had chosen his station masters with the care of a general selecting the men who would lead his troops into battle. Dieter was nearing sixty. He had manned the desk with the precision of a drill sergeant and the compassion of a saint for over a quarter of a century. Displayed proudly on the lapels of his meticulously pressed burgundy wool uniform were the discreet golden pins each formed by two crossed keys, the insignia of Les Clefs d'Or. They signified his membership in the international brotherhood of concierges, that select society that allows for the flow of information between concierges of world-class hotels.

Dieter was one of Kati's biggest fans. Like Margarethe, he had never found the time or inclination to marry and he treated the child as if she were his own. He played with her on his day off, and in the summer they went on outings to swim and fish in the nearby Lake Mummelsee. He had little tolerance for her older sister, finding her moody and spoiled, always demanding attention. There was no doubt in anyone's mind that Kati was the child he adored.

A grateful couple was standing in front of his desk, refolding a map of the local area on which Dieter had obviously indicated the quickest or most picturesque route to their desired destination. His every move was tailor-made to please the clientele. Like his friend and mentor, Dieter specialized in turning guests' dreams into realities. "That's what makes the job so satisfying," he would insist, "making the people happy, seeing them smile. It makes the other ninety-nine percent worth putting up with!" From his post in the lobby he was like the head umpire in a sports match. He spoke only when necessary, but he *saw* everything.

Straight ahead the grand salon was filled with people enjoying the traditional afternoon tea, a ritual the hotel provided with more style and opulence than any other resort in the forest. People planned their entire schedule during the weekends so that they could end up late in the day at the Waldhotel. Silver service carts dotted the antique-filled room, their contents elaborately yet tastefully displayed. Sandwiches of cucumber and watercress, ham, and smoked salmon were lined up like soldiers on one level of the cart. Scones, miniature eclairs, bite-size tarts in a variety of flavors—raspberry, lingonberry, blackberry, and strawberry—all baked with fruit hand-picked from the hotel's garden, were proudly offered to the guests. Normally restrained people's appetites soared, their self-control disappeared. Children's eyes grew wide with anticipation. Teas from around the globe were available to satisfy even the most sophisticated palate. All one had to do was peer into the highly polished mahogany tea caddy and point a finger in the direction of one of the twenty-six exotic blends—Formosa Oolong, Lapsang Souchong, Bohea, or Imperial Hyson—and minutes later they would be presented with a perfect afternoon libation.

"It's so busy today," Margarethe commented as she peered into the rooms, her words simply an attempt to keep some dialogue going with the child.

"Yes, yes, it is," Kati agreed politely, yet distantly. Clearly she was lost in her own private thoughts.

A little over an hour earlier Kati had been in the middle of her weekly session with Frau Bauer when she had looked up to see her mother signaling frantically to Margarethe.

On the second Tuesday of each month, at three o'clock, Kati and four of her schoolmates, plus Margarethe if she was not otherwise busy, would gather in a remote corner of the grand salon to await the arrival of Frau Bauer. In she would march, at precisely five minutes after three, pause momentarily at the entrance to the room, and then proceed directly to the waiting girls. For the next hour and a half, Frau Bauer would instruct the willing, eager students in the social graces of life. The sessions had begun in the fall of last year. Upon hearing about the classes, Tilla had immediately contacted the mothers of all the other girls and offered the use of the hotel for the lessons. What better, more appropriate setting than the salon of one of the most exclusive hotels in the world for their daughters to be instructed in the manners that would prepare them for a proper, refined lifestyle when they grew up and married? Of course, all of the mothers had agreed wholeheartedly, and the arrangements were made. The first several lessons had covered every detail of the art of the tea service—

the proper silver, the presentation, the amount of steeping time required to brew the most flavorful cup. Usually that topic was presented much later in the course, but Frau Bauer had rearranged the curriculum so that they could learn the tea service first and therefore be able to fully appreciate their surroundings during subsequent sessions. So, they had mastered the tea service, place settings, invitations, introductions, and other rules of etiquette absolutely vital for women married to important men.

Today's subject was ballroom dancing, and all of the points pertaining to that activity.

"Heidi, what do you say to a young man at the conclusion of a dance?"

At the sound of her name Heidi snapped to attention. Heidi was Kati's best friend. An intelligent, sweet, but oftentimes scatterbrained child, she always prided herself on being able to give the correct answers. Frau Bauer could be very stern with the girls, and none of them wished to be admonished in front of their peers. "I would thank him for a nice dance," replied the adorable child with red pigtails.

"Yes, that is correct," Frau Bauer agreed, "but only after he has walked you back to your table. Remember, girls, the young man is expected to take you back to exactly where you were seated. It is the *only* proper thing to do. You must insist on it," she added forcefully.

Frau Bauer took her task very seriously. The finest families in Germany had entrusted their daughters to her for years. Graduates of her rigorous courses were expected to portray the very essence of good manners.

Just as Frau Bauer was preparing to grill another of the students, Kati spotted her mother across the room, waving her hands wildly in an attempt to get Margarethe's attention. Margarethe had seen her at exactly the same moment as Kati, for they quickly glanced at each other before hurriedly excusing themselves and practically running the width of the room toward her.

Tilla continued flailing her arms wildly. Something was terribly wrong. Kati had never seen her mother look so frightened, so distraught, her skin pale as dust. Kati knew that she would never interrupt Frau Bauer's lessons for anything less than an emergency. Obviously she was panicked. Once Tilla was certain that Margarethe would follow, she turned abruptly and ran back up the grand staircase to the second floor.

That scene seemed like ages ago to Kati, so much had happened since then. She was astounded now as she watched from the stairs the many guests rushing to and fro, each of them preoccupied with his own activities. Her friends were exactly as she had left them, chatting happily and appearing as if there was nothing more important in the world than the number of steps in a waltz movement.

Kati's mind raced with the memories of what she had just seen. Her mother, standing at the top of the stairs, clutching the house telephone in one hand, pleading for help from the medical clinic next door to the hotel. Her other hand pointed in the direction of the open door to Karl-Gustav's study.

"Please, please send Dr. Mizner immediately," she cried. "Karl-Gustav is ill. Please, he must come at once."

The clinic's doctor arrived not more than two minutes after that, but it was already too late. Karl-Gustav had been dead for almost an hour before Tilla had run into his study to ask him for his approval of the itinerary she had prepared for a distinguished group of diplomats that were arriving from Brussels the following week. She was intensely studying the paper she was carrying, not bothering to look up. "Father, do you think the Consul General would prefer venison or duck, or should we offer a choice for the banquet?" she asked, never once lifting her eyes from her paper. When he didn't respond, at first she thought he hadn't heard her. He was bent over and appeared to be retieing one of his elegant, handmade English shoes. But after she had repeated her question several times with no response, she suddenly froze with the fear of what actually might have happened. She ran frantically to him, shaking his broad shoulders mercilessly. Her deepest fears were confirmed. Her dear, dear father would never hear her again.

Kati had fled past her mother into the wood-paneled library where she had spent so many happy nights with her grandfather, her Opalein. They would read or play together before Kati was sent upstairs to her bedroom on the third floor. Often he would tell her a funny story about one of the guests. It was always the best part of her day.

The smell of the blazing fire was familiar. The wood crackled occasionally, shooting out a spark. At first glance, everything looked normal to her. Then she saw him, slumped behind his desk, all bent over and looking very uncomfortable. He was such a large man that Tilla had been unable to move him, to prop up his massive chest. Kati ran to him and instinctively touched his hand. It was as cold as the marble spindle she was holding as she stood now on the staircase landing. The thought of it made her pull her hand back sharply, as if she had just been burned. The sudden action jerked both Kati and Margarethe out of their reveries.

Margarethe spoke first. "Dearest, do you want me to go and tell your friends that you will not rejoin them?"

"No, I will go," the little girl answered with firm resolve. As she spoke, out of the corner of her eye she saw her father push his way through the revolving glass doors and enter the hotel lobby. He glanced quickly up at them and waved in greeting before turning sharply and running down the long corridor toward the private elevator that would take him to the family apartments.

"He must be with your mother now, Kati," Margarethe said in an effort to console the child. She was still unsure how much Kati understood about what had just happened. Even though she was mature for her age, she was only fourteen. The tear on Kati's cheek had not escaped Margarethe's notice. Death was such a traumatic event to experience at any age. She worried about the young girl. But her questions were answered, and her worries temporarily put to rest moments later as the little girl released her hand and walked down among the guests, through the grand salon, and across the room to the corner where her friends sat. She stood waiting for a moment until all of their eyes were focused on her. With all of the composure and fortitude expected of a member of the Becker-Meier family she announced, "I am very sorry, Frau Bauer, but today's lesson must end now. You see, my grandfather has died, and I must go and be with my family now."

Not waiting for their responses, or their offers of condolence, she turned and walked quickly from the room, following her father's path to their private elevator. Somehow she knew, in her young heart, that after today things would never be quite the same again.

CHAPTER

2

"IT'S A BARBARIC and uncivilized custom, and I will not go!" screamed the girl at the top of her lungs.

"That, young lady, will be decided later, but what you will do immediately is lower your voice. Your visions of the world are of little interest to either the guests or the staff." Tilla spoke brusquely to her older daughter. She gave her a look that left little doubt about how she felt.

Why was the child always so difficult, so obstinate? And why did she insist on being so irascible, even now? It seemed that she fought her at every path.

Tilla was at the very end of her rope. The three days following her father's death had been among the most trying and painful of her life. She felt as if she were sinking, so many things weighed on her mind. There were thousands of details to attend to—each one was another small reminder of her loss and of the huge challenge of running the hotel that lay ahead of them. The last thing she needed right now was Eva-Maria's intolerable behavior.

Karl-Gustav's will specified that the hotel operation was not to be disturbed or disrupted in any way after his passing. "Everything must go on as usual," he had written on the cover of his last will and testament. "The utmost care must be taken so as not to disturb the peace and tranquility of those visiting the Waldhotel." Even in death, his main concern was for the comfort of his guests.

His request was proving difficult to honor, since Karl-Gustav had been acting as the hotel's resident manager as well as owner since Herr Hunt had retired last summer after fifteen years of service. Tilla and Johannes were relying heavily on Dieter to see them through, to keep things together, at least until after the funeral.

The funeral was the subject of Eva-Maria's outburst just now. Eva-Maria had rebelled against the family's strict Catholic values at an early age. She stopped going to Sunday school at seven and since that time had never shown any interest in returning to the Church.

"Eva, what are you doing?" Kati had asked her sister earlier in the day when she heard her talking on the phone to the stables.

"Shhhh," Eva-Maria had answered, cradling the receiver in her neck and covering the mouthpiece with her hand. "Yes, I'll be there to pick up Windward at one o'clock. Thanks."

"Eva, you can't ride today. It's the funeral," Kati reminded her, hoping beyond hope that she had just forgotten.

"I'm not going to any funeral," Eva-Maria replied with such force that Kati was taken aback. She was used to her sister's strong-willed ways, and this tone left little room for negotiation. Still she couldn't help trying to convince her otherwise.

"Not go?" she asked incredulously. "Not go to Opa's service? How can you even think of staying away? Didn't you love him?"

"Of course I loved him, I just don't believe in these archaic rituals. You don't have to do everything you're told to do, Kati. You have to make some decisions for yourself."

"I've made my decision," Kati answered adamantly. "I wouldn't miss going to the service for anything in the world. I loved Opa very much."

"Well then, go right ahead and go. But don't try to make me see it your way. I just don't."

Kati had tried her hardest. She knew her sister better than to continue to push her. It would only end in a horrible argument. Eva-Maria's mind was made up, and that was it. She turned from her room and headed toward her own, confused and hurt. More and more often she just didn't understand her sister at all.

Now Kati and Eva-Maria were in Tilla's dressing room watching their mother prepare for the service that would begin later in the morning. Kati was already dressed in a navy-blue lightweight wool jumper with white smocking on the bib. The crisp white blouse she wore underneath was trimmed with a delicate lace at the collar and cuffs. Her long hair was pulled back in Alice in Wonderland style and was fastened securely with a tortoise shell barrette—a present from her grandfather upon his return from a visit to Japan last year. It had become one of her favorite things from the moment she gently lifted it out of the beautiful red lacquer box tied with a black silk cord. "Oh, Opa, it's beautiful," she had cried with delight. "Just a *petit cadeau* for my little one. I'm pleased you like it," he had said, his rugged face smiling with pleasure. She thought it was even more special as she wore it today.

Tilla sat facing the mirror at her elegantly accessorized dressing table. She fastened a single strand of perfectly matched nine-millimeter pearls around her neck. They had been left to her by her mother, who had always insisted that a woman wasn't fully dressed without her pearls. They lay exquisitely on her black wool crepe Chanel dress. It was a simple, tailored style, very classic, with just the correct number of gold signature buttons on the sleeves and down the back. She had bought it in Paris last May, thinking it would serve as a good basic dress to wear on occasions that required a serious look. What she had had in mind were dinners at embassies, or semi-formal evenings at the hotel. Now, only six months later she was wearing it to the saddest and most unthinkable of all events. With the silver-handled brush that bore her monogram, she mechanically gathered her thick hair at the back of her head and wound it tightly into a chignon. The hat she would wear was still being steamed in the hotel laundry. After a frantic and exhaustive search earlier in the morning, her maid had found its enormous box buried in one of the dusty steamer trunks in the basement. Tilla had not worn it, or even seen it, since her mother Marianne's funeral ten years earlier.

Her hair complete, she shifted her puffy, red-rimmed eyes to Eva-Maria's reflection in the mirror. "Your grandfather would be very hurt to know that you did not attend his funeral," she said softly to her daughter. "It's really the least you could do for him after all the love he felt for you."

Eva-Maria turned her head quickly toward the mirror and met her mother's eyes. "Don't be silly, Mother. That's just the point, he'll never know. He can't know anything anymore, because he's dead, don't you understand? Dead! He can't hear anything, he can't feel anything! Nothing! And all of you getting dressed up like spooky characters, with all those black dresses, and going to the church—it's awful, it's barbaric!"

"Eva-Maria, stop it!" Kati screamed, seeing the pain streak

across her mother's face as the harshness of what she was saying hit her.

A sharp knock on the door interrupted the girl's furious outburst, and Suzanne, Tilla's personal maid, entered bearing the hat.

"I'm so sorry to have taken so long, Frau Meier," she said apologetically, "but I felt it must be perfect for Herr Becker's service," she added as she whirled the hat around on her hand, giving it one last thorough inspection. Only then did she present it to Tilla.

"It's not a problem, Suzanne, your timing is fine. We'll be leaving for the church in ten minutes."

"Oh, I'm so glad I didn't keep you. There, the hat looks just right. Good we found it in time among all of those trunks." Satisfied that the hat was perfectly positioned and comfortable on her mistress's head, Suzanne began to tidy up the dressing table. She scurried about collecting tissues, and replacing the lids on opened jars of makeup. Kati helped by matching loose lids with open bottles.

Sensing the tension in the room, Suzanne tried her best to make light conversation. "My, Kati, you surely look like a proper lady today. Your grandfather would have been very proud of you."

Continuing her search for out-of-place items, Suzanne spotted Eva-Maria perched on top of one of the dressers, attired in her riding habit. She had her boots on, and she was tapping herself lightly on the knees with a riding crop.

"Eva-Maria, may I help you with your dress? If your mother doesn't need me anymore, I could help you before I have to go and change. We don't have much time, so we'd better hurry."

"You needn't bother, Suzanne, I'm not going." With one last smack of her crop she got up and left the room.

Shock at the girl's impudence was written across Suzanne's cherubic face. Tilla looked helpless and profoundly confused. "I suppose each of us must remember Father in our own way, no matter how strange it seems," she said resignedly. Grabbing her gloves in one hand and Kati's hand in the other, she led her out into the hallway. Taking a deep breath during their last moments of privacy, she said calmly, "Come, sweetheart, we mustn't keep your father waiting."

. . .

The old parish church was only a short distance from the hotel. Bells rang out from its twin limestone towers. Their sounds echoed through the trees. As they exited the porte cochere, they could see streams of mourners coming from all directions heading for the service.

"There won't be enough room for all of the people," Johannes commented as he held Tilla's elbow and guided her gently through the crowd. "Everyone loved your father so much."

Tilla and Johannes nodded in recognition as they saw many of Karl-Gustav's oldest friends gathering for his last good-bye.

Kati followed her parents obediently to the first pew. She knew that her parents had been married here, and since her christening she had been inside the place of worship many times, but mostly on happy occasions, like the celebration of midnight mass on Christmas Eve or the weddings of family friends. Last year a couple staying at the hotel had been married here also and had asked her mother and father to be their witnesses. Kati had been included too; she had the honor of holding their rings on a velvet pillow. But she had never seen the church as full as it was on today's somber occasion. The pews filled to capacity as people squeezed together to allow one or two more friends to join them. Those who arrived just before the service began were forced to remain standing in the back.

The entire altar was covered with the overflow of floral arrangements that continued to arrive from all over Europe and as far away as California and Japan. Cascading down all sides of the gleaming casket were enormous multicolored dahlias from Karl-Gustav's garden. He and Marianne had planted the dahlia garden years ago in a local park that bordered the hotel property on the river side. Over the years it had given immense joy to both the natives and the visitors, and a visit to the garden when it began to bloom was a must for all guests. The representation of species was outstanding—over one hundred varieties had been painstakingly cultivated. Karl-Gustav had tended the garden himself every year, often with the help of Kati and Dieter. After Marianne's death, it became more and more of an all-consuming passion. He could often be found there early in the evening on warm summer nights when the embryonic blooms were just beginning to show. Now, for the first time anyone could remember,

Tilla had ordered the hotel gardeners to cut a quantity of all the species to cover his casket. They had waited until as late as possible this morning before carrying their trugs to the park and selecting the largest and most extraordinary blossoms. Dieter had led the men out and pointed to those he thought still looked the fullest even this late into the season. They were all concerned about picking only the very best for the man who had been so good to them, the man whom they had respected so much.

The previous evening all those who had been asked to speak at the service had gathered in Karl-Gustav's private dining room in his apartment on the third floor. The room was hardly ever used, for he generally preferred to take his meals downstairs among the guests. By dining there, he was always assured that the level of culinary perfection he demanded was being maintained. But Johannes and Tilla both felt it was more appropriate to have a quiet dinner upstairs to finalize the order of the eulogists and to thank old family friends for their willingness to participate.

After the dinner Kati and her parents sat together in the library in front of a roaring fire. Eva-Maria exited before dessert had been served in order to go to a movie.

Tilla stroked Kati's long honey-colored mane. "Tomorrow will be a very long day for all of us."

"I know, Mutti, everyone has been so sad, and so quiet since Opa died. I heard Elizabeth and Gabriele crying in the pantry today," she said, referring to two of the old-timers, floor maids who had been at Becker's for more than twenty years.

"Kati," her mother began, "you must know that everyone in the hotel, as well as so many of the people in town, loved your Opalein very much. He was respected by all those he came in contact with, whether they washed dishes in the kitchen or ran entire countries. He was a great humanitarian, and he lived a rich, full life. His death was quick and devoid of a great deal of pain, so Dr. Mizner assures us. Many people who have such a love of life are not given so much time to enjoy it. So tomorrow you must try to remember all of the goodness of your grandfather. He loved you so very much. You must think of all the wonderful times you had with him and what fun you had together."

Just then there was a soft knock at the door and Margarethe poked her head in through the large sliding doors.

Johannes beckoned her to enter. "Perfect timing, Margarethe. What Kati needs now is a warm bath and a good night's sleep." He kissed his younger daughter on the cheek and patted her off in the direction of Margarethe.

But sleep had eluded her last night, and today as Kati sat between her mother and father in the crowded church, made unbearably stuffy by all the mourners, all she could think of was her grandfather's contorted face, her wonderful Opalein's face, twisted in pain, his body bent forward in his leather study chair. She began to tremble. There was no doubt in her mind that at any second she would be ill. Right there, right in the church, in front of everyone. The heat, the sweet, sickening fragrance of all the flowers so close to them was suffocating her. She looked up at the sparkling casket. . . .

Her father must have sensed her queasiness, for he put his arm around her and pulled her closer to him. Despite her nausea, she was able to recognize the Lord Mayor of the City, an old friend of her grandfather's, take his place at the pulpit and prepare to speak.

The Lord Mayor was a brilliant orator. He was blessed with the uncanny ability to intersperse humor without losing any of his heartfelt sincerity, even on the most solemn of occasions. When he spoke of Karl-Gustav, the emotion came from his soul. His robust voice filled the church. Even those standing behind the very last row could hear his every word.

"I knew him for thirty years. He was a friend for every one of those thirty years. Our dear, departed friend was eighty years old, but he had the mind and the spirit of a much younger man. He was interested in everything. Only last month he was one of the first to stand in line to see what all the young people were making such a fuss about—this new movie *Help!* with those fellows called the Beatles. His curiosity and enthusiasm were contagious. All those around him benefited from his philosophy of life. Even though Germany was his adopted country, he served it with more passion than many of its native men. He was a great ambassador for Germany. When Queen Elizabeth II visited earlier this year, he was asked to receive her. . . . " and he continued on.

Kati tried to smile at the vision of her Opa watching the Beatles movie, tapping his custom-shod feet to the beat of their revolutionary music, but it took all of her power of concentration to fight another wave of nausea as it swept over her. Oh, the incense, the awful, overpowering scent. . . . She remembered the order of the eulogists from last night's dinner and realized that the Lord Mayor was among the very first. Oh, it would be so much longer before the service would end, and she could have some fresh air. Maybe Eva-Maria was right, maybe this was an old-fashioned, terrible ritual that no one should be forced to endure. She took a deep breath, inhaling more of the nauseating odors. How was she ever going to make it?

She closed her eyes tightly and tried to imagine being somewhere else, anyplace other than in the overheated church. But all she saw was the image of her grandfather's face. Opening her eyes quickly, her gaze stopped on one of the tall white candles burning brightly on the side of the altar. A beam of light filtered through the stained-glass windowpane and passed directly through its flame. It exploded into a kaleidoscope of colors. As she continued to stare at it, mesmerized by its beauty, she wondered if anyone else in the church was sharing the phenomenon, or if it was meant for her eyes only. The candle's flame flickered and the starburst jumped from place to place. Following its erratic path, her mind traveled back to a night many years before. She must have been only five or six years old at the time.

It was the night of the grand gala in celebration of a guest performance of the Paris Opera. They would perform in the town concert hall, which was an exact miniature of the Opera House in Paris. The hotel had been booked to capacity for well over a year, and on that very night it had never seemed so beautiful or magical as it did to the two small girls who sat upstairs on the balcony watching the activity in the courtyard and lobby below them. They were sitting on the fine Persian carpet, their thin, gawky legs dangling down through the spindles of the staircase railing.

"Look at that one, Eva," Kati squealed with delight as she pointed to the latest in a series of grand touring cars pulling up under the bright yellow canopy and depositing two more members of the world's high society who were gathering for the festivities. "I've never seen a car so big or so shiny, and look, they've brought their dogs!" Two small Belgian griffons jumped from the luxurious hunting-green leather seats and circled the car wildly. Their short back legs kicked out furiously as the wiry little animals chased each other at a fast clip. They only stood about eight inches high and couldn't have weighed more than four pounds wringing wet. The carriage masters on duty cornered the tiny, frisky beings and handed them over carefully to their elegant owner.

"I wish we could have dogs like that," Kati said wistfully, watching as their mistress carried the little creatures into the hotel. Tilla had forbidden the girls to have a dog, always insisting that it would be a source of complaint for the guests. But guests' dogs were always welcome at the Waldhotel, and many of them arrived with pets in tow. The hotel stocked three sizes of baskets for the canines. Each animal was provided with his own food and water bowl—a silver-plated affair with the famous Waldhotel logo engraved on the front. There was a steep charge for this special service, but no one had ever complained.

"I always have to go to Heidi's to play with Sheifly. But it's not the same."

Her sister, not interested in pets of any kind, promptly changed the subject. "What about all the carriages? I'll bet they borrowed every horse for miles around."

As part of the evening's entertainment, Karl-Gustav had arranged for those staying at the hotel to be transported by horse-drawn hansom to and from the concert hall. The floral wreaths that would decorate the horses' necks were being assembled in the back of the building and then stacked in the alleyway opposite the hotel's entrance. The pile now almost reached the windows on the second floor.

A constant procession of valets and floor maids carried the ladies' opulent evening gowns and the men's formal jackets back and forth from the pressing stations on each floor.

"There you are!" Margarethe's familiar voice reached them as she stood in the lobby, her head craned back, looking up to the balcony above. "I've been searching everywhere for you two!"

"I guess the party is ending before it even starts for us," Kati said disappointedly to her older sister. "It's already way past our bedtime."

"Long past," Margarethe agreed as she reached the top of the stairs and hurried the girls off toward their bedrooms.

Kneeling by the side of her bed, saying her nightly prayers, Kati heard the heavy tread of her grandfather as he walked down the long hallway. Even the padding of the thick Oriental carpets could not disguise his footsteps, his walk was so distinctive and powerful. She clasped her tiny hands together tightly and bowed her head. Her long golden hair, just brushed the requisite one hundred strokes by Margarethe, fell softly around her shoulders. "Lord keep us safe this night. Secure from all our fears. May angels guard us while we sleep till morning light appears. Amen." Her grandfather entered the room just as she was climbing in between the freshly laundered white sheets. Her face lit up when she saw him.

"Hello, my little one, I've come to tuck you in tonight. Your mother and father are busy dressing for the big event. So in you go now." He held back the plush down comforter and waited for her to hop up into the bed.

Kati saw that in one hand he was holding his large round key chain. Swinging from the circular ring were the enormous skeleton keys that opened the vault downstairs behind the concierge's desk. The lead key was almost as big as her tiny hand, with elaborate teeth cut out to fit the intricate lock on the main door. The key's metal surface was rusty with age, for the same vault had existed in the hotel ever since Kati's great-grandfather had first ordered it built for the hotel opening. Kati loved going into the big vault. Once the huge outside door was opened, it revealed the shiny solid-steel grate through which one could see all of the safety-deposit boxes. They varied in size, from very tiny, only about five inches square, to the large ones that were used for storing important papers or briefcases. But the small boxes were the ones that held such fascination for the little girl, for they almost always contained the sparkling jewels— diamonds and emeralds and rubies, and the ones she thought were the most beautiful of all—pearls. The jewelry owned by the hotel's clientele was among the most magnificent in the world. Tilla had explained all of this to her one day when they had gone into the safe to get her diamond-set brooch. It was a beautiful piece, constructed of three separate sprays of oak leaves and acorns, all made of diamonds and mounted on a gold fitting. Kati had seen bigger, fancier pieces of jewelry on many of the guests, but her mother had told her that she treasured the brooch more than any other thing because Kati's father had given it to her. Ever since that time Kati had been constantly on the lookout for another opportunity to visit the vault. Suddenly she realized the time was now.

"Oh, Opa, are you going to go into the vault?" she asked him, her eyes already pleading for the chance to accompany him.

"Yes, my little girl," he had said. "I've got to get all of the jewels out and deliver them to their owners. It's almost time for the big party to begin."

With that confirmation, the little girl sat upright in her bed, covers thrown back. She wore her most winning smile.

"Oh, let me go with you, please. I just want to see some of the beautiful things. Oh, please, Opa, I promise I'll come right back upstairs afterward."

Karl-Gustav knew that he had no time to take the little girl with him. If the jewelry was not delivered to the guests' rooms right on schedule, exactly at the time they had specified, the phone on Dieter's desk would be ringing off the hook. But as he looked into the pleading blue eyes of his favorite grandchild, he also knew he simply could not refuse her.

"Oh, all right, little one, but only for a minute. Then you must promise me that you'll come right back upstairs and get immediately back into this very bed. If you don't, I'll be in serious trouble with Margarethe, and I can't afford to allow that to happen. Is that clearly understood?"

With that fierce warning the child leaped out of bed and was already at the door. "Oh yes, Opa, I promise, I promise, I'll come right back, I will. It will be our secret. Let's go now!" She tugged at the sleeve of her grandfather's dinner jacket.

"Just a minute, young lady. Where do you think you're going without your house shoes and a warm robe? You can't appear in my lobby attired only in a nightgown. Remember, you are a lady."

"Okay, okay, I'll put them on," she reluctantly agreed, fearful that any distraction would shorten her time in the vault.

Seconds later she had both of her fuzzy, fur-lined slippers on and had grabbed her pink woolen robe from the foot of the bed. Her grandfather scooped her up and balanced her on his hip as he walked down the hallway.

"You're getting too big for me to carry, you know. Next year at this time you'll be too heavy, even for me."

"Never, Opa, I'll never be too big for you to carry me," she insisted, snuggling her head next to his and kissing him on the cheek.

Activity in the lobby was still frenetic when they crossed the marble floor to the vault. Dieter was frantically trying to locate a pair of size-11 evening shoes for a guest who had left his behind in London. Hundreds of bottles of the finest French champagne were being readied for the guests to drink when they returned from the opera. The carriages were beginning to queue up in front of the hotel. Even the horses were ready for the festivities now that they had been bedecked with their colorful wreaths. Everyone appeared to be working at double their normal speed as they scurried back and forth.

Karl-Gustav shifted the child to his other side. He juggled her there while he selected the largest key from among the many on his ring. The heavy metal door swung open slowly, and Kati's anticipation grew.

"Oh, Opa, are there lots of beautiful things here tonight?"

"Yes, I'm almost certain of it," he assured her. "Let's see here, I'll tell you exactly what we might find in just a minute." Always a shining example of French perfection and a good amount of adopted German efficiency after all of his years in the country, Karl-Gustav removed a listing of the jewels being stored in the vault that night. The myriad of columns indicated the name of the guest, their room number, the items entrusted to the vault, and the specific pieces that were to be delivered that evening. He perused the list quickly, his eyes stopping halfway down the page.

"Oh, Katharina," he said, "here, I think we may find something very special. Let's have a look, shall we?" His voice shared her enthusiasm. He realized it was a lot more fun doing this with Kati than doing it alone, even though he knew he would be late.

"Yes, Opa, please hurry, I can't wait!"

He walked to the side of the vault and searched for the number indicated on his sheet. After scanning row upon row, he finally located one of the medium-size boxes.

"Here it is, angel. Let's see what we've got here."

He used another, smaller key to unlock the selected box. Slowly he lifted the lid to reveal its contents. At first the only things Kati could see were about a dozen small black velvet bags. Each one had a number embroidered in gold thread right below its drawstring.

"Tonight the Duchess wants numbers fourteen, eighteen, and twenty-three," Karl-Gustav told the anxious child.

The largest pouch was number twenty-three. He carefully removed it from the box and knelt down next to the little girl.

"Can you guess what this one is?"

"Of course," she answered confidently. "It's a necklace." She smiled proudly at her grandfather, certain that she had answered correctly.

"No, little one," he replied, "I've really got a surprise for you. Go ahead," he urged, handing her the pouch, "open it and see for yourself."

Still convinced that it had to be a necklace, Kati took the bag from him and loosened the drawstring quickly. Inside was a burgundy leather box inscribed with the Cartier logo. Lifting the lid, she soon realized that, as always, her grandfather was right. She shrieked with delight when she saw what it really was.

"Oh, Opa, does it belong to a *real* princess?" she asked, for she had only seen princesses wearing little crowns such as this in the books her mother had shown her.

"No, not a princess, little one. This tiara belongs to a duchess . . . well, a type of duchess, you could say," he corrected himself, knowing he would be unable to fully and satisfactorily explain the entire story to the young child. "This tiara belongs to the Duchess of Windsor."

"Oh," she said. She wasn't sure if her mother had told her about that lady, but right at the moment she was too fascinated by the lovely object to care whom it belonged to. She just knew it was the most enchanting thing she had ever seen.

"It's very beautiful, Opa," she said, marveling at the number of diamonds in the precious jewel. She held the magnificent diadem above her head and lowered it onto her tiny head. The front of the tiara, made heavy by the quantity of stones, fell forward over her small face, covering her eyes.

Her grandfather began to laugh. "Here, Kati, let me help you," he offered, gently adjusting and trying to balance the weighty jewel on her head. "There you go, it's perfect now."

"Let me see, I want to see how I look!"

"You look lovely," he assured her, "wait just a minute and I'll go and find something so you may see for yourself."

Karl-Gustav stepped out of the vault and borrowed a small purse mirror from one of the female clerks at the exchange desk.

Of course, Kati was thrilled with her appearance in the tiara.

"I think it suits me very well, don't you, Opa?" she asked in her most sophisticated tone of voice.

"Yes, my little one," he agreed as he admired the beautiful young child wearing a piece of jewelry belonging to the woman for whom the King of England had given up the throne. He silently wished that a love that powerful, that all-consuming, would bless his granddaughter some day.

A glance at his pocket watch confirmed what he already suspected. If the deliveries of the jewels were not made soon, the complaints would start rolling in. But he couldn't take his eyes off the precious little girl.

"One day, Kati, you, too, will have beautiful things of your very own," he said, "beautiful necklaces and rings that you will wear on special nights like this."

"Oh, I hope so!" she said excitedly. "I feel so pretty with it on!"

The last vision of her daydream was the image of her grandfather, laden down with the many numbered velvet pouches, still juggling her on his hip, slowly closing the doors of the enormous vault and locking in the remaining valuables with the master key.

The organist was playing a reprise of the haunting, energetic *Symphonie Fantastique* by Berlioz, which had been one of Karl-Gustav's favorites. The loudness of the music, plus the weight of her father's hand on her shoulder, jolted Kati from her trancelike state. At first she thought the whole thing was a dream, but she soon realized it wasn't as the pallbearers slowly carried the flower-draped coffin down the aisle and outside to the waiting horse-drawn bier. Once all of the mourners had exited the church, the funeral cortege proceeded through the town square and down to the Promenade of Kings and Emperors—the Lichtentaler Allee—the path that ran by the edge of the River Oos, past the Waldhotel and the magnificent summer residences. Its name was more than justified by the stunning profusion of trees lining its sides—old oaks, young lindens, maples, poplars, cedars, and cypresses, plus the more exotic species of Japanese Emperor Paulownias, Australian gingkos, and Caucasian witch hazels. On its wide expanse, trees and shrubs from all five continents were represented. For centuries poets and artists had proclaimed it one of the most exquisite avenues in the world.

The normally serene river, oftentimes no more active than a country brook, was flowing heavily, its water level higher than it had been in years. The sound of the rushing current was like an outpouring of feeling for a man who had spent so many hours by its side and who had never tired of its beauty.

The assemblage stopped briefly in front of the Waldhotel Becker to allow those members of the hotel staff who, because of work schedules, were unable to attend the funeral, to pay their last respects. Dieter had, of course, put his second-in-command in charge so that he could be at the service. On the previous day he had organized the moving tribute. All of the employees, many of whom were like an extended family to Karl-Gustav, were gathered on the stairs leading out from the grand salon. Everyone had donned their most formal uniforms for the occasion. The floor maids had put on the freshly starched white caps that were required attire when royalty was in residence at the Waldhotel. The waiters were all in their swallow-tailed coats. The maîtres d'hôtel, the receptionists, the hall porters, and the valets all stood together in mourning, joined as a family. This was the saddest of all days for the staff of the Waldhotel Becker.

The hotel orchestra had set up on the wide expanse of perfectly manicured lawn that ran down to the edge of the river where they often entertained guests during the summer months. Once the horses had stopped, the strains of "As Time Goes By," the melody that Karl-

Gustav had requested open every elegant dinner dance the hotel had hosted for the last two decades, sounded. There were tears in nearly everyone's eyes, some cried openly, particularly those who had worked with the great hotelier the longest. Long after the procession had passed, Kati looked back to see them all standing exactly as they had been when the orchestra played the last notes of its final farewell.

Kati walked proudly at her mother's side, her head held high, for her thoughts had been made pleasant by her sweet reverie. She had missed every single word of the eulogies, but she was content with her own remembrances.

As the mourners slowly passed by the last of the formidable summer mansions that lined the banks of the unusually active river and headed for the cemetery only a half kilometer in the distance, the horses bearing the casket stopped abruptly, their attention distracted by the whinnying of another horse in the distance.

Those who could also hear the sound looked up on the hillside just in time to see the figure of a young girl turn her horse sharply and ride farther into the forest. Only Kati and her parents recognized the brilliant blue of Eva-Maria's woolen riding jacket.

At the cemetery the plot next to Marianne Becker had been prepared to receive her husband. He had visited her gravesite every Sunday afternoon for the past ten years, always bringing an offering of their precious dahlias when they were in bloom. Now he would join her at last.

As the final handful of earth was thrown into the grave, Karl-Gustav Becker's only surviving child cried softly in her own husband's arms. All at once she was overcome by the enormity of her loss, as well as the enormity of the task left to her. She thought of the future and of the burden now resting squarely on her shoulders. She thought of the past, of her two lost brothers, gone forever. César, named after her father's idol, the great Swiss hotelier César Ritz. He had had such hopes for his first son. He was devastated by the loss of the poor, pathetic anencephalic child who had survived for only five days after his birth. Everyone knew what a blessing it was that the brainless child died so soon, but the bereaved parents still grieved terribly for their loss. When Peter was born two years later, their hopes sprang anew. But Peter was lost also in the fight to liberate Paris from German occupation. Oh, her lovely brother. How she missed him so. Not a day passed when she did not think of him. After his death Tilla had wanted to become more involved in the hotel. At first she had tried to spend more time with her father, concentrating on learning one area at a time. But somehow she had never been able to devote as much time as she had planned. Even with Margarethe's help, raising Kati and Eva-Maria was a full-time job. There was always something else that demanded her time. So the years had passed and she had mastered very little of what she really had wanted to learn. And now, so suddenly, it was too late. Her chance to learn from the master was gone forever.

Her sobs became stronger as she leaned into Johannes's strong arms. She wondered if possibly her father had loved her too much, and now expected more of her than she was capable of delivering.

Kati stood by her mother's side, her eyes frozen as she stared into the open grave. She looked up when she heard Tilla start to speak. She strained to hear her, for her words were barely audible.

"Oh, dear Father, I promise I shall do whatever is in my power to carry on the tradition you have spent your entire life creating, no matter what it takes, no matter what the price," she whispered softly.

"I promise too," Kati added sweetly.

Tilla looked down into her daughter's lovely face and smiled. Unknowingly, Kati had just uttered the truest words of her young life.

Taking a deep breath and grasping the hands of Johannes and Kati, Tilla Becker-Meier slowly led her family away from the cemetery in the direction of the hotel. Their public ordeal was over; their private ordeal had only begun.

CHAPTER

3

THE MORNING after the funeral Tilla awoke early. Rays of muted sunlight were already peaking through the heavy damask curtains. Before he left for his office in town, Johannes had opened the tall, narrow French doors leading out to their terrace overlooking the river. Fresh, clean fall air wafted in intermittently in gentle breezes. Tilla listened for the sound of the river, but the only thing she could hear was the movement of the birds as they scattered about and the scraping of the dry autumn leaves brushing against the side of the building. It only confirmed that it wasn't her imagination yesterday that made it seem as if the river was roaring out of its bed. Today it was resting, having used up all its strength to say good-bye to one of its dearest friends.

She turned over onto her stomach and pulled the covers up tightly around her shoulders. If her thoughts about the river were true, she knew that it was the only thing that could afford to rest. Yesterday she had glanced briefly at the correspondence starting to pile up on Karl-Gustav's desk. The letters and requests would have to be answered almost immediately. Guests were waiting to hear if their favorite suite was available for two weeks in January, if the hotel could accommodate a christening celebration for seventy-five guests several weeks from now, and of course, all of the Christmas and New Year's parties that were traditionally held at the Waldhotel were awaiting confirmation. Tilla's mind raced with the list of things that had to be done at once. But all those things plus the mounting pile of countless minutiae would have to wait until later in the afternoon. In less than an hour Tilla had to preside over the daily staff meeting that her father had scheduled each morning at nine o'clock.

The heads of each of the departments were requested to attend. It gave them a forum in which to voice their concerns over issues and to share important information with others in the hotel.

She was very nervous, even though she knew every one of the people well. Some of them had known her since she was a young girl. Now she was faced with the prospect of trying to run the hotel, a place she had always regarded as her home. Her first job was to gain the confidence of each member of the staff. Forcing them to see her in a new light was going to be a Herculean task.

The girls stopped in to say good-bye on their way to school. Tilla had not spoken to Eva-Maria since her display of abhorrent behavior the day before.

"I won't be home tonight for dinner. I'm going to the movies," her daughter announced. Tilla started to mention the fact that she had just been to the movies two nights earlier, on the eve of her grandfather's funeral. Since there was only one theater in the small town, she couldn't imagine why she was supposedly going again. But she wisely decided to save all her strength for the challenges of the day ahead. Besides, the phone began to ring, and the girls were already late.

"Good luck today, Mutti," Kati cried out as they dashed from the room.

Tilla waved a kiss in thanks to her thoughtful child.

It was Dieter calling from downstairs. "I'm so sorry to disturb you, Frau Meier, but we've an early-morning situation here that will require your immediate presence."

Dieter was careful never to use the word "problem" when he was describing what was almost certainly a problem. Tilla could tell from his tone of voice that the cause of the "situation" was standing right in front of him, hovering over his desk.

"If you could stop by at my desk on your way to the meeting, it would be most appreciated."

"I'll be right down."

She dressed quickly in an elegant, lightweight wool day dress, applied one more coat of the vibrant red lipstick she always wore, took a last look in her dressing-table mirror, smiled her bravest, most confident smile, and hurriedly left the apartment.

The breakfast room was about half full. Many of the guests liked to get an early start on the day. Others, on most mornings over seventy percent, preferred to take their coffee and croissants leisurely, in the privacy of their rooms. They could read any one of a half dozen foreign newspapers they had requested, or just sit peacefully on their terrace, sipping the hotel's famous coffee and enjoying the serenity of the view, wrapped comfortably in the plush white terry robes provided daily by the hotel.

The activity in the lobby looked about normal for the time of day. Those with early-morning flights out of Frankfurt were requesting their cars and checking out. Sports enthusiasts were off to the courts or engaging in the newly popular sport of jogging.

A smartly dressed woman in a tailored suit sat in one of the chairs facing Dieter's desk. Tilla did not recognize her as a regular visitor. The woman had perched her Hermès handbag on top of the desk. Her hands were clutched tightly around the small leather handle. Tilla assumed the woman was the "situation."

Dieter spotted Tilla as she came into view on the staircase. He smiled politely and rolled his eyes in a manner that told her the whole story without uttering one word.

Tilla crossed the lobby at a solid, steady pace. When she was near the woman, she offered her hand in greeting.

"I'm Tilla Becker-Meier, I hope I can be of some help to you."

The woman turned her head in Tilla's direction, but made no motion to accept Tilla's outstretched hand. Her hands remained firmly clenched on the handle of the expensive bag. She squinted her eyes until they were only narrow slits in an otherwise unpleasant face.

"Only if you can find out who is responsible for stealing my earrings from our room this morning while we were having breakfast," she snapped.

Tilla was taken aback by the woman's accusation. Theft occurred in all hotels—even the most exclusive were certainly not exempt—but it had been years since she even remembered hearing of a reported incident at the Waldhotel. Dishonesty was the single quality for which Karl-Gustav had absolutely no tolerance.

She attempted to respond to the outrageous accusation as calmly as possible. "Well, perhaps if you could explain to me what happened, I will be able to help you."

The woman became hysterical. "I just told this man everything," she screamed and pointed at Dieter, "and the only thing he had to say was that I might have misplaced them and that we should take another look in the room. But I am telling you they are gone, gone, gone," she repeated, her voice rising an octave with every syllable. "Besides, who are you, anyway?" she demanded. "I would think that a problem of this magnitude would command the attention of the owner of this hotel, that, oh, what's his name, that German man, Karl something."

Tilla winced at the mention of her father. "Karl-Gustav Becker," she informed the ill-bred, ill-mannered woman. "Sadly, Herr Becker passed away three days ago. He was actually a Frenchman, not a German," she added, for what reason she wasn't entirely sure. The reality of what she had said hit her hard. It was the first time she had been forced to articulate the facts. She clutched the back of the chair in which the woman was sitting. Glancing down, she could see the white of her knuckles.

"I'm his daughter and I'm in charge of the hotel now." She was determined not to let the couple upset her. However, the woman was unaffected by Tilla's explanation. She continued her diatribe as if she hadn't heard a word that had been said. Other guests in the lobby stopped to see what all the commotion was about. They stared discreetly in the direction of the desk.

A pasty-faced gentleman standing by her side who appeared to be her husband tried to quiet her down. She wasn't interested.

"Oh, be quiet yourself, Harry. If it were up to you, we wouldn't even be reporting this!"

Tilla saw the head of the security department walk behind the reception area and motion to Dieter.

"Herr Rohr, may I see you for a moment over here, please?"

Dieter excused himself while the woman continued to repeat her story to the still-disbelieving Tilla.

Returning only seconds later wearing a confident look on his face, Dieter took his chair again. "Mrs. Wigman, you said that your earrings were pearls surrounded by diamonds, is that correct?"

"Yes," she snorted, "how many times must I repeat myself? I told you they were rather large, and I must say, almost perfect pearls, completely encircled by sizable round diamonds of great clarity. They were very, very valuable."

"I understand, Mrs. Wigman." Dieter slowly lifted his closed hand from underneath the desk. "Would these be your earrings? The pair that you just described?" He opened his palm to reveal a pair of modest earrings—small cultured pearls with just a tiny sparkle of a diamond on either side. Only someone with an extraordinary imagination would have described them as "important."

The woman's gasp was audible to both her husband and Tilla. For a split second she considered denying ownership of the paltry baubles, but she wisely decided against it, having to admit that she had been caught at her own game. Releasing her hold on the handbag, she reached out and grabbed the earrings from Dieter's hand. Still she remained unsatisfied.

"Now I suppose you're going to claim that they were in the room all the time."

"As a matter of fact," Dieter replied, now wishing to savor every minute of the incident, "they were in the soap dish in the bathroom. Perhaps you left them there last night before retiring. Our security department was able to find them for you. In any case, we are delighted that they have been located and returned to you."

Suddenly he was anxious to get the horrible woman and her unfortunate husband away from his desk so that he could get on with his day. Already this dreadful couple had delayed the start of Tilla's staff meeting.

"So are we, and we are sorry for the inconvenience we have caused you." At last the husband spoke. As he did, he took a firm hold of his wife's expensively clad arm and practically yanked her out of the chair.

Once the elevator door had shut, Dieter simply shook his head in a combination of disgust and amazement. After all the years he had spent in the business, he never ceased to be astounded at people's behavior. Especially their poor behavior. He made a mental note of the couple's name. The next time a telex arrived from London requesting a room for Mr. and Mrs. Harry Wigman, they would be informed that the hotel was booked to capacity. Never again would they be guests at the Waldhotel.

"At least one of them is capable of being embarrassed," was Tilla's only comment.

· · ·

Everyone was already seated and waiting patiently for Tilla when she walked into her father's office. She had hoped to arrive before everyone else and to have a few moments to herself to get organized, but the Wigman episode had delayed her. Karl-Gustav had rarely been late for this meeting. He felt that keeping people waiting showed no respect at all for their time.

"I'm so sorry," she offered as she rushed past all of the familiar faces. As she neared her father's desk, suddenly she realized that the only place left for her to sit was in his big leather chair. The last time she had seen it was when she had discovered his lifeless body there days earlier. Now she stared at the empty chair awaiting her. Momentarily she panicked. The reality of what she had to do struck hard. The desktop was piled high with papers. She couldn't remain standing, for she needed the surface of the desk on which to take copious notes. She had no choice but to sit in the chair. She was tempted to take the easiest way out, to turn back, to run from the room.

"Don't worry," she heard a reassuring voice call out. "We're happy to wait for you. We're all here to help."

She turned and saw the smiling, supportive faces of those responsible for running the Waldhotel. Their warmth gave her all the encouragement she needed. Still, for the duration of the meeting she sat hesitantly on the edge of the imposing chair.

The staff meeting that morning lasted almost an hour longer than usual, but it provided Tilla with a wealth of information about the operation of each of the departments. Every department head, from housekeeping to purchasing, was a professional in his or her own right. They practically ran the meeting for her, and each pledged to give her all of the support she would surely be needing in the days and months ahead. She left the room with a padful of notes, additional things that would have to be attended to very soon. Dieter walked with her down the hallway.

"Why wasn't Herr Klebe or one of his people at the meeting?" she asked. Herr Klebe ran the accounting department.

Dieter smiled at the question. "Didn't your father ever share his philosophy about the accountants with you?" he asked incredulously.

She shook her head.

"For all the years I can remember, accounting was never invited to those meetings. Karl-Gustav always said that he didn't need any 'numbers' men, as he used to call them, to tell him how the hotel was doing. He wisely realized the importance of having them on staff, but he only wanted to know how many dinners were served last night and how many beds were filled. He claimed his 'feelings' about the hotel at any given moment could tell him pretty accurately how the hotel was doing. What is uncanny is that he was almost always right."

Tilla shook her head again, this time in amazement. How long would it take her to get a "feel" for the hotel? For the hundreth time that week she thought about all the lost time, time that now could never be recaptured. She had concentrated on being a good wife and mother to her children, and for that she was not sorry. She only regretted that she had lost the chance to learn from her father. Now she would just have to work harder and longer, trying to make up for all of those years. She prayed that if she really applied herself it wouldn't be too long before she, too, could have a sense of the business. But in her heart Tilla remained a realist. The most experience she had ever had in the hotel was the planning of some of the menus, of course under the strict eye of their head chef, Franz Kellner. Nothing she had ever done was of great importance; deciding whether to serve fish or beef, broccoli or string beans at a gala was hardly the criterion on which great hotel traditions were founded.

She left Dieter to get on with his day and returned back upstairs to begin hers in earnest. Her father's office was empty and silent now. As she approached Karl-Gustav's wide mahogany desk for the second time that morning, she glanced up at the portrait of her grandfather, Ludwig Becker. It hung gracefully in its place over the mantle, which it had occupied for decades. The portrait always held a certain fascination for her and she never tired of looking at it. She could remember many nights as a child sitting on her father's lap and listening to stories of the famous Ludwig. Karl-Gustav had brought him to life for her with tales of his wild escapades. The painting was a remarkable oil of a man she had never had the joy of knowing. It portrayed the founder of the Waldhotel Becker in all his glory, dressed in the most elegant Edwardian finery. Nothing in his stately demeanor disclosed his humble origins as the eighth child of a hardworking French peasant farmer. Both his father and his father before him had earned a fair, modest living toiling the fertile Alsatian soil. They had raised plump, hearty geese to produce the area's well-known foie gras.

At an early age Ludwig left Marmoutier, his small village of less than five hundred people. He ventured out to expand his horizons and seek his fortune. He was fortunate enough to find work in Paris, first as a waiter and later as a restaurant manager. After stints at Voisin, the most fashionable eatery of its day, and the Savoy in London, he felt he had absorbed everything he needed to know about the hotel business. Finally the right opportunity presented itself and he was able to fulfill his lifelong dream with the creation of the Wald-hotel. From the very first day, when the awning over the porte cochere had been completed, the establishment had been a wild success. Unfortunately, the health of the hotel was much stronger than that of Ludwig, and little more than six years after opening its impressive doors he was dead. The reins were passed on to his eager, willing son, Karl-Gustav.

Tilla stood staring at the painting for a while longer, gathering strength to face the work ahead. It may just have been her imagination, but she thought his kind blue eyes gave her a vote of confidence. Imagination or not, it was exactly the signal she needed to bury the temptation to run out of the room and back to the privacy and security of her own apartment.

The first thing she did was remove the many silver-framed pictures from the corner of the desk. Over the years the collection had grown steadily. Karl-Gustav had refused to use the small side tables to house some of the treasured photos. Instead he insisted on keeping all of them in his full view, so that he might enjoy them while he worked. He preferred to stack up the continuing influx of papers rather than to eliminate some of his valued snapshots in an attempt to clear off some much-needed work space. Tilla could not bear to look at them just now. Even glancing at the pictures for a moment while she gently placed one frame on top of the other was more pain than she could stand. She had not really looked at many of the pictures in years: they had become so much a part of the room that she didn't pay any more attention to them than to the sofa or chairs.

A photo of Karl-Gustav and his exquisite bride, Marianne, on their wedding day, Karl-Gustav standing in the center of his beautiful dahlia garden, Karl-Gustav on the lawn of the hotel surrounded by his successful American visitors Henry Ford and William Vanderbilt, her wonderful brother Peter and Karl-Gustav on horseback, Peter in his military uniform, Tilla with the girls on a ski trip to St. Moritz—there were so many glorious memories. Memories of a lifetime filled with joy and success, plus a fair share of heartache and pain. Such a rich, full life. She stopped her tears before they clouded her vision.

Sitting lightly on the edge of the oversized chair, its dark brown leather cracked and dry from years of use, she was able for the first time to see the room from her father's vantage point. It was a small but comfortable space. Karl-Gustav didn't believe in giving "management" big offices. It only took away from having more space available for the comfort of the guests. The red-tufted sofa and roomy, comfortable chairs were the same ones Tilla had sat in as a little girl. The valuable hunting prints, elegantly framed and hung against the dark green walls, gave the room a decidedly masculine flavor. The soft light from the gleaming brass lamps and a continuously blazing fire enriched the room, making it warm and inviting.

She began separating the correspondence into piles. Those items needing immediate attention were placed smack in the center of the desk. Those that could wait for a few days were placed in a large folder. Requests that could be handled by specific departments were routed on to the department head. The last pile she created was for things that she had absolutely no idea what to do with. To her dismay this pile continued to grow, surpassing all the others in thickness. Don't panic, she kept repeating to herself every time she looked at the burgeoning stack. Don't panic, she would repeat again, this is only the first day, the first of many. There are lots of people around to help you, to delegate the work to . . . just don't panic. Try to resolve each letter, each piece of paper, one by one.

Once she had her fears firmly in check, Tilla began to relax a bit and started to cope with the masses of papers now neatly organized before her. The most pressing subject to be dealt with were the guests who were due to arrive during the coming week. From the way it appeared, the arrivals listing was exactly what Karl-Gustav had been working on when his fatal heart attack had violently and quickly squeezed the life from his veins.

The hotel was booked to capacity through the first of the new year. Many of the hotel's regular guests returned annually to spend the holidays in the warm and congenial family atmosphere of the Waldhotel. Indeed, many of the staff were like relations to those they had served so loyally for so many years. As she leafed through the arrival notices, she was amazed at the number of intimate details about the guests that were noted on almost every sheet, a system on which Karl-Gustav had always prided himself.

A specially constructed eight-foot-long bed had to be brought up from the basement storage area to accommodate the six-foot-seven Mr. Robert Gordon when he arrived on Wednesday from Zurich. For breakfast, Lady Arianne Hulde, who would be arriving on Saturday, ate only two small pieces of melba toast with a glass of freshly squeezed lemon juice—no coffee, no butter, no jam or marmalade—nothing else was to be on her tray or there would be unbearable abuse for the poor soul, the hall porter, who was destined to deliver her morning meal precisely at seven forty-five. Mr. and Mrs. Ramos were arriving from Buenos Aires with their four children, a nanny, and a maid. They had requested that their help be housed on the same floor as their suite, a difficult request to honor because the hotel rooms had been rearranged since it had become less and less common for people to travel with their own help. In fact, Karl-Gustav had noted that it was almost impossible to accommodate their request, but he had suggested that the chief engineer be called in to reconnect the *service privé* buttons located in the smaller rooms. The buttons, a throwback to the really super-luxurious days of the hotel, signaled the help in the rooms reserved for them on a lower floor. In most of the grand hotels the servants' rooms were located at the top of the building. At the Waldhotel many of the best views of the river and the forest beyond were from the charming rooms on the top floor, so Ludwig had made the architect alter his plans, relocating the help to the first floor. All of these special buttons had long ago been disconnected, but for a situation such as this it might be possible to reconnect the bells. "Call Herr Conrad," Karl-Gustav's note had said. "He's the only one around who was here when they were installed."

The Ramoses were arriving by train from Frankfurt and would need to be met at the station. It was further suggested that two drivers be dispatched, as Mrs. Ramos was known to travel quite heavily. It was noted on their card that on her last visit she had arrived with no less than twenty valises.

The eighty-four-year-old Alain Chopard, a devotee of the Wald-hotel for thirty years, would be arriving from Geneva that evening. For the next six weeks he would be taking the cure for his debilitating rheumatism at the clinic next door. Monsieur Chopard liked to eat his evening meal alone each night at eight. He preferred to be seated at a small table near the window overlooking the river. Karl-Gustav had advised the maître d'hôtel to reserve table number thirty-two for the duration of his stay. His precise note, written in crimson ink in his elegant hand, had also cautioned, "No children, noisy Italians, or tables of more than four nearby. Monsieur Chopard likes to dine without interruptions of any sort—and at his age he deserves nothing less!" It had apparently never occurred to Karl-Gustav that the man was his contemporary.

The list of the day's arrivals needed to be in the hands of thirty-five key members of the staff by noontime so that preparations could be made. They could also refresh their memories and be prepared to greet the guests by name when they encountered them during their stay.

Tilla continued to be astounded by the number and extent of details that had been noted on each guest's arrival sheet. What was most disturbing, however, was the realization that all of the infor-mation, the intimate details of the lives of their guests, were singularly contained in the mind of one of the great hoteliers of the world, her departed father. How would they ever, ever be able to maintain his impeccable standards if he had taken to his grave the very informa-tion they needed to carry on?

The purchasing department was the area most foreign to her. How could she possibly know if the eight-percent increase in the price of the special linen sheets that the hotel had used for years was justified? Karl-Gustav had demanded to know why the vegetable bills for the month of September were so much higher than last year's when the number of meals served was less. The answer that came back seemed reasonable to her, but how was she to be sure?

So engrossed was she in the immense variety and quantity of work that she was startled by Johannes's voice.

"I thought I might find you here," he said from the doorway. "You look every bit the executive in charge." He walked toward the desk and gave his wife an affectionate kiss on the cheek.

"What time is it?" was all she could ask, amazed that it was anywhere near time for lunch.

"Half past one."

"Oh, goodness, I had no idea it was so late, I'm sorry. Did you wait downstairs for me all this time?" Johannes always came back to the hotel to have lunch with Tilla and, in the past, with Karl-Gustav. The Waldhotel was only a short ten-minute walk from his office on the Sophienstrasse, Baden-Baden's main shopping and commercial street.

"No, I came about twelve-thirty, but immediately ran into Dieter. We spent some time together. There are some things that must be decided at once. Matters involving the staff. With the occupancy rate running so high through the first of the year, we need to add two floor maids and maybe one porter. Also, we've got to get a general manager in here as soon as we possibly can. Otherwise, things will become impossible. Don't you agree?"

She hesitated for a moment before responding to his question. "Well, Johannes, I'm not so certain that a general manager is the answer. After having had a brief look at all of the mail, all of the letters and requests, I'm not sure that just hiring someone cold, someone from the outside, let's say, is the right thing to do. After all, no matter who it is, they're not going to know all of the things that Father did. They won't know what the guests really need, what they enjoyed about their last stay, where they like to sit in the dining room, and all of the other special details that I'm finding out only he knew."

"So what is your suggestion, Tilla? I don't quite understand; what is it that you're recommending?"

She threw her hands up in despair. "Oh, Johannes, I really don't know either," she admitted aloud for the first time. "It's just that I don't think we ought to allow some stranger to come in here and run the hotel. I think we owe it to my father and to ourselves to at least try to take over and continue his success as best we can. It's my family's heritage, our history." She sighed. "Oh, if only Peter had lived, he could have taken over, he would have known exactly what to do." Her voice, earlier so confident, began to crack.

"Tilla, are you saying that *you* want to run the hotel? That *you* serve as general manager? Tilla, you are hardly qualified for that job. You've only had a very small amount of experience, and only in the banquet area. Management is a full-time, nonstop situation. Think of the girls. They need you." His voice suggested that she couldn't have dreamed up anything more ludicrous. His total rejection of the idea gave her the impetus to continue her argument.

"Well, it is exactly what I'm suggesting. And, very honestly, I was hoping that it was an idea you would embrace wholeheartedly. I was really hoping that you would—" He didn't allow her to finish.

"That I would what, Tilla? That I would leave my practice, to come and try to operate a business that I have no talent for, no skills for, and quite frankly, don't really have a tremendous amount of interest in? If I had any interest in running the hotel, I would have started a long time ago." The look on her face told him that he had hurt her deeply.

"Oh, Tilla, I'm sorry, really I am," he said, "but what you're talking about is out of the question. Do you know what you're say-ing? Have you given it enough thought? Today is only the first day. I think you'll feel differently after some time, after you realize exactly what the job entails."

"I'm well aware of what I'm saying, and I resent it terribly to hear you suggest that I can't do the work, or that we couldn't do it together. The girls will be fine. They have Margarethe. And I'm not going anywhere. I'll be here all the time. What you're really trying to say, underneath it all, is that no woman has ever been the head of a grand hotel. Isn't that what you mean?"

"No, it isn't," he insisted. But she understood him well enough to know better.

After the heated exchange, their lunch conversation was strained and tense. Tilla welcomed the many interruptions from several of the staff members. Already they seemed to realize that besides Dieter, she was the only person to whom they could bring their questions.

Johannes returned to his office, and Tilla returned to her father's desk. Her most welcome interruption came when Margarethe brought her a cup of tea and some cookies late in the afternoon.

"Oh, Margarethe, how thoughtful of you. A hot cup of tea is exactly what I need right now."

"I thought you might," she said, beaming at Tilla's warm response. Like Dieter, Margarethe took great pleasure in making others smile. "When you didn't come down earlier, I thought you might still be up here, working right through."

"You're so right. I could stay here all night and barely make a dent in this pile," Tilla replied, moving stacks of paper around to make room for the small teapot.

"You've really got your hands full," Margarethe agreed, surveying the enormous quantity of mail. She saw at one glance that Tilla had undertaken a huge responsibility, one that she was not certain she was capable of handling. At that very instant she realized she would have to work extra hard to keep not only Kati and Eva-Maria organized, but now their mother as well. As always, she met her new challenge with open arms.

Only when she became aware of the sound of Kati's footsteps running down the hallway did Tilla realize that it must be time for dinner.

Kati sailed past the doorway of Karl-Gustav's office at a fast clip, but she turned around immediately when she realized her mother was sitting at the desk.

"Hello, Mutti, how did it go today?" asked the out-of-breath, disheveled-looking teenager.

"Fine, sweetheart, how was school?"

"The usual, but I did get a good mark on my English test. The second highest in the class."

"Oh, I'm so proud of you!" Tilla praised her while she began to straighten out her school uniform and tried to make some sense of her tangled hair. Finally she just gave up and hugged her tightly.

"But the best thing happened after school. At Heidi's," she said, her eyes begging her mother to ask what she was practically bursting to tell her.

Tilla immediately put down the papers she was reading and gave her full attention to her daughter. "Oh, really? Well, tell me all about it."

Kati's eyes sparkled with excitement at the prospect of what she was about to say. "Frau Fichtl invited me to go skiing with them over Christmas. Oh, Mutti, it would be so much fun! Can I go? Please? Please say yes."

Tilla couldn't help smiling at the beautiful child. She was always astounded at the directness, the openness of children. When they wanted something, they simply asked—no hesitation, no prefaces—they just asked straight out. Kati still had that direct way of approaching things even though she was now a teenager. It was an appealing quality Tilla hoped she would retain into adulthood.

"Now, Kati, wait a minute, slow down, you can't possibly expect me to say yes without some more details. Sit down and start from the beginning. Tell me everything about the trip."

"Okay," said the happy child, so relieved not to have received a flat-out no right away. "Where should I start?"

"Well, how about where you are going to go?" her mother suggested.

"Oh, that's good," Kati agreed. "We'll be going to Gstaad. We'll take the train down to Zurich. There we'll meet Heidi's aunt and uncle, and we'll all go to the ski lodge together. Oh, doesn't it sound like fun? Heidi's going to take Scheifly with her. He loves the snow. I know it will be great."

Tilla was pleased that Kati was so enthusiastic. After the past week the trauma and the events surrounding her grandfather's funeral had been enough to trouble even the most well-adjusted child. Tilla had been terribly worried about her. Now she was glad to see that she was able to forget the pain of recent days. Or, if not totally forget it, at least not continue to mope around like her older sister. Eva-Maria had not been her normal, argumentative self since her outburst on the day of the funeral.

"When will you leave?"

Kati's face lit up even more brightly. She surmised by her mother's question that the trip was almost certainly a go.

"Not until the day after Christmas. So we'll be able to have Christmas together, like always." But the moment she said it, she realized it wouldn't be like always. This year would be very different without her grandfather. She saw the pain on her mother's face that the unintentional reminder had caused. "Oh, Mother, I'm so sorry," Kati cried. She ran to her mother and put her arms around her waist. "I didn't mean it to come out like that. I know it won't be the same without Opa. But we still all have each other. No one can take that away from us."

"I know you didn't mean it, sweetheart. I know you would never say anything to hurt me. It's just that, it's so true. . . . " Tilla closed her eyes in an effort to ward off the tears. She steeled herself against the urge to fall apart completely, to abandon the tedious task of going through the mail, to dismiss as fruitless the notion of trying to pull the hotel together. But one look at her daughter's precious face, and she had all her strength renewed twofold. "So, tell me the rest. You leave the day after Christmas and when do you come back? Do you spend New Year's there? I hear it is beautiful then. They have a big celebration on the mountain, complete with fireworks, and skiers in wonderful costumes."

"Yes, that's exactly what Heidi's mother said. She grew up near there, and every year her family would take she and her sister there."

"Not 'she and her sister,' 'her and her sister,' " corrected Tilla. She was a fanatic about proper grammar, in each of the several languages she spoke. She insisted on perfection from her children also.

"Yes, Mother," Kati agreed, but even the reprimand could not squash her enthusiasm. "So, it's all right, then, I can tell Heidi yes, I can go?"

Tilla gave it one more minute's reflection. The Fichtls were one of the oldest families in Baden-Baden. Heidi's father was the youngest generation in a long line of bankers and financially astute men. Her mother, Sonja, was a lovely Swiss woman who ran the most successful flower shop in town. Her creativity and talent were known throughout the area. The beautiful arrangements were easy to recognize because she always tied a multitude of brilliant-colored thin silk ribbons around the neck of the vase. They became her trademark. People called from as far away as Heidelberg to have one of her creations. Tilla had spoken with Sonja only two days ago. She had called to offer her family's condolences and to tell her that they were running a bit behind with the deliveries because of the immense number of extra orders that had come in for Karl-Gustav's funeral. Yes, Tilla liked Sonja Fichtl, and Heidi, their only child, was a lovely girl who had been Kati's best friend for a long time. Of course, she wasn't crazy about not having Kati home for the holidays. But this year, with all the challenges they would have to face to see the hotel through the season, she was almost glad for the opportunity not to have to worry about her. Her decision was made.

"Kati, I think it's a wonderful idea. Barring any serious opposition from your father, whom we can consult at dinner, I think you should plan on going, and having a terrific time."

"Oh, Mother, thank you." Kati screamed. She hugged Tilla tightly. "I can't wait. It's going to be the best fun!"

"I agree. I'm sure you'll also agree that it won't be much fun if we keep your father waiting much longer for dinner. I've already been late for one meal today," Tilla said, recalling her unpleasant conversation with Johannes. "We'd better go get dressed."

"I'll hurry, I promise. I'll be downstairs in just a few minutes," Kati said as she skipped out of the room.

Dinner passed quietly. To Kati's delight, her father agreed to the trip without any problem. He asked the usual questions, duplicates of those her mother had posed only an hour earlier. But she sensed that he was not totally involved in the conversation. His mind seemed to be far away. After they had finished discussing the trip, she noticed that little else was said, so Kati excused herself early, claiming she had lots of homework to finish. Tilla suspected the real reason was to have a long telephone talk with her holiday traveling companion.

In Tilla's mind, dinner was just another reminder of the enormous change in the hotel only a day after her father had been laid to rest. Before, every night when they ate in the hotel dining room, her father had sat in the corner chair at the corner table, where he had a full view of the spacious room. His eyes would constantly wander— from waiter to waiter, to the reservation podium, to the kitchen door —taking in every detail of the night's activity. He was like the director of a play, and all of the actors were aware of his presence. They were anxious to please, for they were well aware that their understudies waited patiently in the wings. But tonight the director was not there. All the actors were still in place, but a spark of motivation was missing. Tilla's senses were not finely tuned enough to determine what was not exactly right, what could be improved upon, what small nuances were amiss. She looked around just as she had observed her father doing for so many years, but she simply didn't see with the same eyes. For a brief moment she feared that the play might never be the same again.

"I've given a lot of thought to what we spoke about earlier."

For the second time that day Johannes's voice startled her. But at the same time his tone of voice was encouraging. Maybe he would agree to her idea after all. Her face brightened, and she smiled her most caring smile. "You have?"

"Yes, I thought about it all afternoon. As a matter of fact, I got very little of my own work done."

Now he sounded irritated. Her hopes began to fade. "Well, what do you think?"

"I still think it is a poor idea for you to try to run the hotel. Just look around you, Tilla. This is a huge organization, one that must run on schedule and right on target, or it might as well not run at all. It's an enormous responsibility, and one that I don't think you're equipped for. And I know that I'm not willing to give up my work in order to support your folly."

She bristled at the word. "It's hardly a *folly*, Johannes. If anything it's a gift, a blessing, and most importantly, it's my family's heritage. I still maintain that the least I can do is try to continue it."

But Johannes was adamant. Her continuing attempts to change his mind were met with growing resistance.

In their bed that night Tilla was cool to Johannes's intimate advances. Besides being more than slightly angry with him, she had a million other things on her mind, remnants of the long day's work. Her head was spinning with details. Would Jean-François, the sommelier, remember to stock the Gettys' favorite champagne? Would Lady Hulde's tray arrive exactly as scheduled? Would the guests like the new Christmas menu proposed by the chef? These were just a few of the questions that weighed heavily on her mind. She didn't even dare to turn her thoughts to the larger issues.

Johannes's breathing became steadier. As soon as she was certain he was sleeping deeply, she left the bed. Silently she crossed the room and entered her dressing area. With her warm woolen robe wrapped snugly around her and fleece-lined slippers on her feet, she quietly padded her way down the hall, past her sleeping daughters' bedrooms toward her father's office. It was just after one o'clock, and Dieter was taking a last-minute instruction up to one of the floor maids.

"If I don't tape it right on the door, she'll claim she never received it," he said, holding up the note. "What are you doing up at this hour, anyway, Frau Meier?"

"Just going in to look over a few more things," Tilla answered as they approached the office doorway.

"Well, if you insist, at least let me start a fire for you, to take the chill off the room."

At first she refused, but he was so quick and so efficient that a burning blaze had been started before she knew it. It did light up the room. "Well, now that that's done, sit down and have a cognac before you go," she offered.

"Thank you. I think I will." He poured two snifters full and handed one to Tilla. They sat in the large wing chairs facing the still-high flames. "It's been a long day for you. You must be exhausted. But I can understand and sympathize with your insomnia. It's overwhelming, isn't it?"

"More than I ever could have imagined, Dieter. But, you know, the time passed so quickly when I was working. I kept Johannes waiting for lunch, not even realizing that the entire morning had gone by. I was truly enjoying it. I loved opening the letters, finding out who was coming, who would be dining here next month, who will be celebrating their birthday or anniversary at our hotel. I loved reading all the reports, even knowing that so many decisions have to be made. I'm surprised that I became so interested so quickly. But it is clear that Johannes doesn't share my feelings. He doesn't even want to get involved. He wants us to hire a manager right away so that I can go back to being a full-time wife. But after today I'm not certain I can do that. I have this strong urge to really get involved, to try to continue the work that everyone, with my father at the helm, was trying to achieve." She looked at him, trying to read his thoughts. "Do you think I'm crazy?"

"Not in the least, Frau Meier," he answered at once. "In fact, I think if you're willing to keep it up, willing to learn from everyone here who has something to teach you, you can make it work."

"You do, you really do?" she said, perhaps too quickly.

"Yes, I don't see any reason why not. But it is a long road," he cautioned. "Your father is a nearly impossible act to follow."

"I know. My grandfather wasn't so forgettable either," she commented, looking up at the portrait. His eyes were still on her.

"Oh, he was something. He really put Baden-Baden on the map, you know, with his concept of making the spa, and the waters, not only therapeutic but luxurious as well. As silly as it seems these days, he was the one responsible for making sure that each room in the hotel had its own bath. Before his innovative thinking even the grandest hotels in Paris didn't have private baths in all the rooms. He was also responsible for the meticulous closet designs. Even today, many people still comment on the luxurious wardrobes here. Ludwig designed every one of them himself, with the help of your grandmother. Of course, some of the special-sized drawers, such as the narrow, deep one that used to hold women's artificial hairpieces, are no longer appropriate, but the guests still appreciate the extra space."

Tilla smiled at Dieter's charming story.

"Yes," he continued, "this town has much to be thankful to him for. He was crucial to its success. Just as you are going to be crucial to its continued success."

"Dieter, do you really believe we can do it?"

"I do, Frau Meier, and you know that you have my never-ending support at all times."

"That's one of the things I'm certain of," she assured him. "Now I'm going to get some work done." She seated herself in the chair, this time in a more comfortable, secure position with her legs tucked snugly under her, her robe wrapped tightly about her.

Dieter finished his cognac and got up to leave.

"Promise me you won't work too late. Tomorrow is another day, and in this business it is certain that you never, ever know what that might bring."

"I promise," she said, smiling at her strongest supporter. But she soon broke that promise. The pale light of morning was streaking through the windows as she tiptoed back to her bedroom and slid silently under the covers. She was sound asleep by her husband's side before he awoke.

CHAPTER

4

THE HOLIDAYS were a magical time in Baden-Baden. Those who were fortunate enough to live there year-round and were able to experience each of the twelve months agreed almost unanimously that December was the most glorious one. Those who disagreed were almost always inveterate golfers whose game was temporarily halted by the thick coating of pure white snow across their sacred course. By Christmas Day the tops of the majestic firs and pines were almost always tipped in white. The hiking trails of the summer months became streaked with the tracks of cross-country skis. A spectacular ride on the Merkur cable car to the region's highest point had lines longer than those leading into the casino on a Saturday night.

People bundled up in their warmest clothes for long strolls along the river. At night, mammoth portions of hearty German food were served, and a good percentage of the year's production of robust red wines from the surrounding vineyards was consumed. After these dinners, practically unable to move at a human pace, the diners often spent several more hours casually sipping Irish coffees or brandies and listening to music in front of a glowing fire at one of the many lively pubs.

Of course, the Waldhotel led the way and set the standards in this celebration. The staff worked practically all year to plan activities for the guests that were guaranteed to elicit a robust holiday spirit in even the most Scrooge-like individual. Its fantasy setting was made even more enchanting by the thousands of tiny fairy lights that decorated the trees near the river. Their reflection on the nearly frozen water brilliantly illuminated the path along the Lichtentaler Allee. Guests paraded through the lobby in the finest, most extravagant furs the world had to offer—Russian sable, mink, fisher, Canadian lynx, ermine, and stone marten were only a few of the many types on continuous display, gracing some of the most glamorous women in the world.

The Meiers had their traditional Christmas Day dinner in the hotel restaurant. Johannes complimented Tilla on the extravagant menu she and Chef Kellner had prepared. Each offering—pheasant, lamb, rabbit, or venison—was made to sound more delicious than the other. Everyone dressed in their finest holiday outfits. Kati looked sweeter and prettier than ever in a red velvet dress with black satin trim. She was a picture of femininity with her long tresses tied back gracefully with a lace ribbon. Eva-Maria insisted on sporting a new "fashionable" haircut she had seen in one of the British magazines. A revolutionary model named Twiggy was just coming on to the European scene, and Eva-Maria had decided at once to have her hair shorn in the same short, boyish style as fashion's latest golden girl. Only months before, she had singed her hair when the trend was to iron any wave out of one's tresses, creating perfectly straight hair that often resembled straw. Even Johannes, who rarely involved himself in discussions on the subject of fashion, commented that the newest hairstyle was a little severe. He said that quite frankly he thought it looked a bit silly. Eva-Maria was not upset by her father's comments. She operated on the theory that any attention was better than none, no matter how she got it. However, Tilla couldn't help but notice the admiring stares her older daughter attracted from the men in the dining room. Heads turned discreetly and followed the girl to their table in the corner. In spite of her trendy appearance, her extraordinary physical beauty came shining through.

Tilla tried not to dwell on the fact that the holidays were very different from all of those in her past. Still she couldn't help feeling a little melancholy and depressed. She missed Karl-Gustav's jolly laughter and Christmas spirit. As she walked through the lobby, not recognizing many of the guests by name, she knew that her father would have known most of them. He would have been able to add his own personal season's greeting. However, to her delight, the hotel was full and appeared to be running smoothly.

Only after Tilla and Johannes had returned from taking Kati to the train station for her trip to Switzerland did she have the slightest clue that all was not going as well as she had thought. Standing behind the reception desk searching frantically for a misplaced telex, she overheard the conversation of two smart-looking French couples while they were waiting for their final bill. They were obviously friends and had been staying at the hotel together.

"Did you enjoy the stay, Charles?" one man inquired of the other.

"Yes, I did. As usual, the baths were superb. Whether it's my imagination or they really do help, I don't know, but I certainly feel much better than when we left Paris last week."

"It's probably a combination," commented one of the wives, who was chicly dressed in a winter suit that Tilla recognized as part of the current Christian Dior collection. As she listened to their conversation, Tilla thought they were exactly the type of clientele the Waldhotel should attract. They were obviously moneyed, well-dressed, and if they had enjoyed their stay, they would tell all their friends about it once they returned home.

"My only disappointment was the hotel," said the other man. At this, Tilla dropped the papers in her hand and moved forward so that she could better hear every word they were saying.

"Really, why do you say that?" the man who had spoken first asked.

"Well, we were here two years ago and we had a wonderful time. It just seemed that the staff was much more organized then. Things worked a little more smoothly. Boom, boom, boom," he hit his fist against the counter. "They never once seemed to miss a beat. But this time, for example, when we ordered champagne to drink in our room on Christmas Eve, it arrived right on time, but they had brought red-wine glasses in which to serve it."

"Are you serious? Such a grand faux pas!" said Charles, an incredulous look on his face, as if his friend had just told him that the floor maid came naked to their room. Any self-respecting Frenchman found such a breach of etiquette a serious affront to his finely tuned sensibilities.

"Yes, I am serious. Can you believe it? *Incroyable!* Even an apprentice knows that one doesn't drink Dom Perignon from a balloon-shaped goblet. It may sound trivial, but it's just not the kind of thing one expects from a supposedly world-class hotel."

"You're right," the Dior-clad woman agreed.

"Mistakes like that are intolerable at prices like these," the man commented as he surveyed his bill and signed for payment. "Maybe next time we should try that other hotel down the street. A friend of mine has told me good things about it."

Tilla had heard enough. She quickly scribbled a note to the head of the floor service to check and see who had made the delivery to Room 313 on Christmas Eve. He would have to be reprimanded for his error. She also took the names and addresses of both the couples from the cashier. Later that afternoon she would write them a letter of apology. But she knew that it was probably already too late. Her father had once told her that a hotelier only gets one chance to impress and captivate his guests. He was no doubt correct, but she wanted to at least make an effort to try to reverse the damage.

After the incident in the lobby, Tilla began to see things with a different eye. She was constantly on the lookout for mistakes, errors that could cost them the hotel's most precious commodity—its reputation. She worked harder than ever, putting in an extraordinary number of hours during the week Kati was away. Johannes continued to go to his office every morning as usual. They had not discussed the staff situation any further. Everything finally came to a head two months later.

"Tilla, do you have any idea what's happening in the lobby at this very moment?" Johannes's voice was much sterner than she ever remembered hearing it. He stormed into the office and stood directly in front of her. His entire body seemed to be shaking. These days it was common practice for Tilla to continue working right up until lunchtime. Johannes still came home for lunch, but now he had to either call or come upstairs to pull her away from the monumental stacks of paper on the cluttered desk.

"Johannes, what is the problem?" she asked in an irritated tone. She had already had a tough morning—a long staff meeting followed by hundreds of interruptions. "Of course I don't know what's happening downstairs. I'm obviously up here. I'm certain that if I were needed, Dieter would call me."

"Dieter is only one person, and believe me, he's got his hands full right now."

"Well, I'm sure he can handle it. I have all the faith in the world in him," she insisted.

"Not this time," he countered. "This is a disaster. There is a man in the lobby, a man claiming to be the sultan of somewhere, I didn't catch the name of the country. Anyway, it doesn't matter. He is not traveling alone. He has an entourage of . . . oh, I would say at least fourteen people. They're all dressed in those traditional, flowing costumes. He claims that he wrote for reservations over a month ago, requesting adjoining rooms for all of these people. He says he asked to be met at the train station. He received a confirmation for the dates of the stay and was assured that he would be met. He is waving the telex in everyone's face to show that he is not mistaken about these things. However, he is here, not having been met at the station. Now he is being told there are no rooms available, let alone adjoining rooms. I just don't understand what has happened, and neither do any of the people who are in charge. In the meantime, while they are trying to straighten this mess out, he is causing untold trouble in the lobby. He is yelling so loudly you can probably hear him on the Sophienstrasse."

Tilla's face was the color of the white pieces of paper she had been reading. "Oh, God, oh no," she whispered.

"What did you say?" Johannes demanded. "I can't hear you. You don't know anything about this, do you?"

"I know everything about it," she answered in a shocked voice.

"Exactly what does that mean?"

"Johannes, stop yelling at me. I have enough going on here to choke a horse. I don't need you to make it even worse." She put her hands to her face and made no effort to stop the tears. "This is the worst thing. This is what I feared would happen someday. It's the nightmare that awakens me every morning. Oh, how could I be so forgetful?"

"Forgetful? Do you mean you knew this group was due to arrive?"

"Yes," she snapped, not for a second even attempting to conceal the irritation in her voice. "That's exactly what I mean. I received the

Sultan's letter over six weeks ago. I sent him a telex confirming his requests, and then I, I . . . oh, God, this just can't be—"

"You forgot to forward the information to reservations, is that it, Tilla?"

"Yes, yes, I remember doing it. Sending the telex, that is. Then I was called away, to the restaurant or somewhere for some other emergency, and I simply forgot to ever forward the paperwork." She began to search the desk frantically. "It's here somewhere," she said, patting the papers down, turning some over, moving some from one side of the desk to the other, "I know it's here."

"Well, it doesn't really matter now. The damage is done. They are here. All of them. In the lobby. Now. The only question that remains is whether or not the problem can be resolved. I must say, Tilla, it only points up the truth of what I have been attempting to tell you. You are doing too much, much too much. Situations like this only happen when one cannot handle everything he or she is trying to do."

" 'When one cannot handle . . .' " she said, repeating his words. "Johannes, you sound so officious. I'm not just someone, some stranger trying to run the hotel. It belongs to my family, and I'm your wife, not *someone!*"

"I'm glad that you still remember that much," he said.

"Oh, Johannes, please, I'm trying my hardest." Streams of mascara ran down her face where her tears had traveled. He was unmoved by her show of emotion. He had also just spoken some of the harshest words of their seventeen-year marriage.

Unfortunately, the Sultan crisis could only be solved by sending the entire party of eighteen people to the Europäischer Hof, a hotel of much less quality only a few blocks from the Waldhotel. They had the requisite number of adjoining rooms and were more than happy to accommodate the noisy, demanding crowd.

As the months passed, the hotel took more and more of Tilla's time. Her daily lunches with Johannes stopped almost completely. It was rare if they ate together more than once a week. The girls were occupied with school and other activities—Kati with her studies and

Eva-Maria with her riding and, of late—boys. They all ate together on most evenings, but the meals were anything but relaxed, as Tilla was constantly called away from the table to deal with one problem or another.

One late summer evening, after the girls had excused themselves from the table, Tilla and Johannes were left alone on the terrace. They had enjoyed a lovely meal outdoors under the spacious yellow-and-white-striped awning that extended out halfway across the perfectly manicured lawn. They savored the last of the long days that would too soon shorten, bringing darkness to the forest by four-thirty in the afternoon.

"Tilla, I've been thinking, let's go away for a few days. To Paris, or somewhere. Anywhere you like. Just for two or three days, an extended weekend. We haven't been anywhere for so long, and I think we need to get away and spend some time discussing the future."

Her first reaction was concern for the hotel. She had practically convinced herself that she had become an integral part of its operation. In fact, she had. But she saw before her the distinct, very real opportunity to create an even wider gap in their marriage if she were to refuse his offer.

She'd worry about the hotel after. She answered as if she hadn't another thought in the world except that of spending some precious time away with her husband.

"I'd love to go. When can we leave?"

They took an afternoon flight from Frankfurt to Paris the following Friday. Tilla left Dieter in control with strict instructions to call her at once if anything of importance happened. He had assured her that there was nothing for her to worry about. Pulling away from the hotel, she felt the same emotions she had experienced the first time she had left the girls alone with Margarethe for a few days. Like a child leaving home, Tilla craned her neck out the side window of the car and watched the hotel disappear from view as they turned out of the driveway.

. . .

"It's always good to come back here, isn't it?" Johannes asked Tilla once they had finally settled into their room at the Crillon. They had spent their wedding night and the first two days of their honeymoon in a room very similar to the one they now occupied.

"It is indeed," she agreed. Memories of those days together filled her thoughts as she unpacked her small weekend bag.

Johannes took her into his arms and kissed her in a way that told her he was sorry for all the problems of the last few months. She knew it was a very difficult thing for him to do, as he was not a terribly demonstrative man. He had always kept his emotions very much to himself.

She returned his embrace. Suddenly, feeling the strength of his arms around her—so familiar, yet so foreign to her because it had been so long—she was overcome with emotion. He kissed away her tears.

"I love you so very much, Tilla," Johannes offered in another unusual display of feeling. This proclamation, so long unsaid, brought forth another surge of tears.

"And I need you so much," Tilla countered. Her mouth was hungry for his. After so long, after so many late nights when she had fallen into bed next to him exhausted and concerned, it felt wonderful to be close to him again. Johannes's touch offered that special kind of intimacy shared only by a couple who have been together for a very long time. But its familiarity did not detract from its sensuality. They made love slowly, spending the rest of the afternoon gently becoming reacquainted with each other. When they awakened hours later, still wrapped in each other's arms, they were content to begin their rediscovery all over again.

During their stay they were blessed with mild temperatures and bright sunshine. Sitting at a café on Sunday, leisurely enjoying a *citron pressé* and watching the multitudes of people out for a walk, Johannes gently took her hand in his.

"I've made a decision."

Immediately her mind filled with the most horrible imaginings. For a few brief seconds she forgot their amorous carryings on only two days before. He's going to leave me, she thought. She was certain. That had to be it. Coming here was the easiest way for him to do it, so that he wouldn't have to tell me in the hotel, to save me the embarrassment of being humiliated before the employees. So I wouldn't fall apart in front of the girls. He's found another woman. He's been carrying on a mad, passionate affair while I've been running around trying to learn the hotel business. Who could it be? What did she look like? Someone in town? Someone from his office? Her rampant imagination, running wild and conjuring up visions of his mistress, was interrupted only when he continued to speak.

"I've decided to leave the firm and come and help you run the hotel."

"Oh, Johannes, it's the best possible news. I'm thrilled! Really I am," she repeated, in order to alleviate any doubt that might have shown on her face. His change of heart was something she had stopped hoping for long ago. Now that it had come at last, her happiness was tempered with fear. She took both of his hands in hers and squeezed them with delight. "Just think how wonderful it will be. We'll bring the hotel back to life. It can be just like before. I'm certain of it. Oh, I couldn't be happier." She had a moment's more hesitation. Her fears surfaced again. "Are you sure it's what you want to do?"

"Well, I made it clear that it wasn't what I wanted before. But now that I've seen you working so hard, for almost a year now, I have to admit that I've become more and more interested. The area you could probably use the most help in is the one I should be most familiar with, the financial. I know Herr Klebe is good, but he doesn't have a proprietor's perspective. I think I can contribute a lot in that area. Institute some tighter controls, put in some newer procedures."

"I couldn't agree with you more, darling. I'm so glad you want us to do this together."

"There's just one thing," he added. "I've thought about this as much as I've thought about the other, though, so please give me a chance to explain all of my reasons to you."

Again she was baffled as to what it might be.

"Okay, I'm listening," she said, taking a cautious sip of her bitter-lemon drink.

"I believe we need to hire a general manager—someone to look at the big picture, someone to pull everything together. A really skilled, seasoned professional. That will free you up to concentrate on the areas you've proven yourself to be best in—guest relations, catering, and banquets—and of course overseeing the restaurant. Those are the areas that are most important, and if we can get them up to speed, we can increase the profits enormously. The restaurant alone has such tremendous potential now that Kellner's got his staff in place. It could be a veritable gold mine."

His argument left her unconvinced. She still harbored so many fears about bringing someone new into the operation at such a high level, but she was too delighted with Johannes's change of heart to put up a fight. After all, he had been observing the business almost as an outsider. Maybe he was right after all. The bonds of their marriage had begun to disintegrate over the last months. They never had any time together. Johannes's joining the hotel would certainly solve that problem. They'd be together constantly. Agreeing to this one request was a small concession to make if it would help make their relationship strong again.

"Okay," she said, "but let's take our time finding exactly the right person. I don't care if we have to interview hundreds of candidates. It's better to get someone a month later who can handle the job than to hire someone quickly and have a disaster on our hands. Do you agree?"

"Couldn't agree more. We'll take our time until we find the most appropriate person, one who will do justice to the hotel. I'll talk to Heinrich and Charles as soon as we return and see how quickly I can extract myself from the firm. I think it shouldn't take more than a month or so. In the meantime, we can start contacting anyone who might be able to suggest some names."

"Yes, that's a good idea," she added, the last trace of hesitation gone from her voice. All of a sudden she was anxious to get home, anxious to see Dieter, the staff, everyone at the Waldhotel and to assure them that now, with Johannes overseeing the financial part of the hotel, she was certain that everything was going to be all right.

They returned from Paris late Sunday night, and Tilla was up with the first light preparing for the staff meeting.

"I have something wonderful to announce to all of you," she

told the department heads with the enthusiasm of a child. She could hardly contain her excitement and was so thrilled when her news was met with applause.

"It is good news, Tilla," Dieter agreed after everyone else had left the room. "I think it will make all the difference in the world to have Johannes here all the time, constantly riding on the numbers men. There's nothing like an owner to keep people on their toes."

"That's exactly what he said. The one thing I didn't tell the group, however, is that he's insisting that we hire a general manager right away. He feels it's the only way to get the hotel back on track. He's willing to interview many people, but I know he's anxious to get someone fairly quickly. Any suggestions?"

"Well, Tilla, I must admit that I agree with him. We do need someone at that level. As for ideas, I don't really know. Certainly there's no one in the area. But I will call my brother in Geneva. Even though he's been retired from the Richemond for two years, he loves to keep his fingers in the pot, and he stays in close contact with many people. I'll see if he can come up with any suggestions."

Dieter's brother, Frederic, had been the head concierge at the elegant Swiss hotel for decades. Tilla had met him once several years ago when he had come to the Waldhotel to visit his younger brother. He was a world-class hotel man who shared the same high standards of professionalism as Dieter. She would gladly consider any names he might recommend.

"What a good thought. Could you please call him today? Johannes is very firm about getting this resolved."

"Right away, Frau Meier," he said. As with all things placed in Dieter's capable, conscientious hands, Tilla knew the call would most likely be placed before noon.

"Does this mean we'll get to see more of you, Papa?" asked Kati that night at dinner after Johannes told the girls of his decision to leave his firm and come to help Tilla run the hotel.

"Yes, of course, sweetheart, it does," Tilla answered protectively. She hadn't been aware until this very moment that Kati had felt a little neglected over the last several months. Johannes had made a habit of staying late at the office. Most likely he had been so unhappy that Tilla was working all the time that it was easier just to stay there or go out for a drink with one of his partners. Well, Tilla thought, it was just another reason to be pleased that he had made what she was sure for him was a very difficult decision.

Johannes reinforced Tilla's reply. "Kati, I will be here all the time, starting next week."

"Next week?" Tilla exclaimed, unable to stop herself from interrupting him.

"Yes, I spoke with Heinrich today and he thinks that the sooner I get over here, the better. Charles is in Munich until Thursday, but I'm certain he'll agree with Heinrich. It's done. So you see, Kati, we'll have lots more time together, although you know how hard your mother and I will have to work to get the hotel back on track."

"I know, Papa, and I'm glad you're going to be here. Maybe next summer I can work in the hotel too. I'd like to work at the reception desk, right beside Dieter. It would be such fun!"

Johannes wasn't sure that he wanted both his wife and daughter involved in the hotel, but he managed to conceal his uncertainty. "Well, we'll see about that. You'll be getting ready for university next year, and you may feel differently by then. Let's wait and see."

"All right, but in the meantime, if there is ever anything I can do . . . "

"I'll keep it in mind now that I know you're interested," Tilla said.

"Interested?" Kati cried. "I love this hotel, and I'd better start learning now. I want to learn everything, every detail of how it works. After all, who will take over when you're ready to retire?" she asked.

Tilla was shocked and very surprised by Kati's comments. She was not aware how strongly the young girl felt about her family's legacy. She thought back to her own childhood, the wasted time, the lost opportunities. How she wished now that she had spent more time in the company of her father. Things would be so much easier now, so much clearer. . . . At that very moment she vowed to give as much time to Kati as the young girl wanted, allowing her the chance to learn, to absorb, to prepare her to run the hotel if that was truly what she desired.

．　．　．

Word spread quickly about the opportunity at the Waldhotel. Tilla received more than forty letters, each requesting an interview for the general-manager position. The candidates came from all over Europe. There were even two from America. Some she eliminated at once; either their formal schooling or their work experience was not up to the standards of the Waldhotel. Others she replied to and asked to meet with her in Baden-Baden. She found it awkward interviewing the men. Some treated her as if she were a secretary, not the owner of the hotel. Others were completely put off by the idea of having to work so closely with a woman. Several of the candidates were either unwilling or unable to move to Baden-Baden. Her frustration was compounded by Johannes's growing impatience with the situation.

"Tilla, you have got to stop procrastinating!" he finally snapped at her one afternoon. "It's soon going to be holiday time. We must have someone in here to organize the staff, to make sure the functions are scheduled to a maximum, and generally to manage the operation. We cannot go on like this. Did you see last month's figures?" he demanded, slamming a stack of papers down on her desk. "The restaurant overhead is way up, the laundry bills have skyrocketed, and the occupancy rate is down five percent from last year. If we keep this up, we'll have a huge loss by the end of the year. And also, look at this." He continued his tirade as he began to rip through the sheaf of paper.

"What would you like me to do?" Tilla asked in a calm voice. Almost too calm in fact.

"Hire someone . . . hire someone soon," he insisted. "You've seen so many people. Isn't there someone who could do the job?"

"Not so far, no, there hasn't been," she countered.

"Well, I suggest you find someone fast. We're quickly reaching a breaking point here."

After Johannes had stormed out of the room, Tilla sat quietly in the chair facing the fireplace and the portrait of her grandfather. Ever since Johannes had sold out his share of the accounting firm and come to the hotel, things had not been as ideal as she had imagined they would be. They seemed to have differing viewpoints on everything. Rarely did they agree on the simplest way to solve even the most minor problem, so arguments sprang up at the slightest provocation. Their personal life had also been affected. The frequency of their lovemaking had dwindled down to almost nothing. Tilla was startled to realize that she couldn't remember the last time Johannes had touched her. It was just after they had returned from Paris, she thought.

She stared up at the portrait of Ludwig Becker, but tonight his eyes offered her nothing, no encouragement, no reassurance . . . nothing. She returned to her desk, exhausted from the trials of the day, but with an even greater determination to overcome the challenges facing the hotel.

"It's a long shot, but it's certainly worth a try, Frau Meier," Dieter's ever-optimistic voice came over the phone.

"I'll try anything at this point," she said. "What is it?"

"Frederic just called. The last time we spoke, he came up blank. No suggestions, not even a lead. But he called today to say he had been thinking about it and he remembered a young man who was with them for a brief period at the Richemond. He was the assistant manager. This was about five or six years ago. Frederic remembers him as a likable fellow, not trained in the formal way like most of the young kids, but very good at the business. He said he seemed to have an innate feel for the hotel. He had apprenticed somewhere in London for a few years. Then he came to Geneva. He worked there for a short time, apparently was well regarded, and then he had to leave for France. Something about a family situation that required his immediate attention. Anyway, he gave Frederic his address when he left. Frederic found it this morning. He says he liked the young man, didn't really know too much about him, but thought that it might be worth some investigation."

"It certainly is!" Tilla's voice rose with excitement. As improbable as it was, it was the best lead she had so far. "Give me the address and I'll get a note off to him at once."

Dieter proceeded to give her a street number in Paris's very chic, very expensive sixteenth arrondissement.

"Thank you, Dieter."

"Just a moment, Frau Meier, haven't you forgotten something?"

Immediately Tilla thought she had once again missed another important detail—like the Sultan's arrival. She panicked.

"What is it? Please don't tell me I've failed to follow up on something again," she pleaded.

"No, not at all," he assured her, "I just thought perhaps if you're going to write to this young man, you should have his name."

Her nervous laughter filled the line. In her excitement she had neglected to ask this small bit of information. "Yes, I suppose that would be helpful."

"His name is Peter von Hassler—small vee, two esses—like the hotel in Rome."

"Okay, I've got it. Peter von Hassler," she repeated. "Now I'm all set. Thanks again." She put the receiver down gently. She knew she would never forget the first name, it was the same as her dear brother's. Now it would also be easy to recall his last name.

In fact, it was a name she would remember for the rest of her life.

CHAPTER

5

PETER VON HASSLER stretched out lazily in his oversized bed, but his eyes remained closed. He struggled to make some sense of the bedcovers. They were twisted and tangled, a fitting testament to the frenzied activity that had taken place last night. Yes, this new client had been delightful. So many of the women he was hired to be with just wanted to be near a man, to have him hold her, sometimes pleasure her. But not this one. She was so eager and willing to please. She was anxious to do whatever he gave the slightest hint would make *him* happy.

He extended his long, muscular arm to its full reach and patted his hand around the empty space next to him. For a second he thought that she might have gotten up earlier and left. His eyes snapped open. She was lying on her side all the way over at the very edge of the bed, just a hand's distance out of Peter's reach. Her back was facing him, the covers draped softly around her, falling slightly above the inviting cleft of her well-rounded buttocks. Strands of long, silky blond hair, the hue of spun gold, lay gracefully about her shoulders and down her back. Its texture was so fine, untouched by bleach or permanents, that it refused to tangle despite all of the tossing and turning it had endured. He slid over to her slowly, not wanting to disturb her with his movements. Just as he reached out to touch her, he heard the soft knock on his bedroom door. He ignored it. Seconds later the knock came again. Damn! What timing! He'd have Carmela's hide if it wasn't something very, very important. His friends were right; just last week at a dinner party given by one of the grand ladies of Paris there had been a lengthy discussion on how difficult it was to find good help, especially in a city like Paris, where the demands could be overwhelming. But he hadn't really demanded anything of Carmela except to keep the house in immaculate order and never disturb him in his bedroom. He really didn't think that was too much to ask; after all she was employed as a housekeeper. Tap, tap-tap. Oh well, it was late, almost noon now, and he had allowed this woman to stay longer than most of them anyway. It was always a problem getting them out of the house if they stayed for breakfast. They always wanted to talk, to make plans. Peter rarely had any plan in mind except how to get rid of them. He had done his job, and that was that. But this one had been delicious. He reached over and lightly stroked her lovely breasts one last time. She began to purr. The knocking continued. He threw back the covers and stomped out of bed.

"*Oui, d'accord,* okay, I'm coming," he yelled. He heard the woman sigh sweetly and turn over in the bed, but he didn't stop to look back at her. He grabbed his silk dressing gown from the wardrobe and wrapped it tightly around him. He pulled open the door so forcefully that Carmela jumped back for an instant. She was terrified when she saw the anger in her employer's face. She was being well paid in France, saving every penny she earned to send back to her family in Portugal. Her husband and son counted on her. She couldn't afford to lose this job.

"*Je suis desolée,* I'm so sorry, Monsieur von Hassler, but this arrived just now with the postman, and I thought it was too important not to awaken you." Timidly she held out an envelope. The address was barely visible with all of the special delivery stickers pasted on it. Whoever had sent it to him had insisted on getting it there the fastest way possible.

He grabbed the envelope from her shaking hand, not once glancing up at her.

"Monsieur, I'm very sorry," she tried again, this time not being able to contain her fears of being fired. Her sobs caught his attention and he looked at her.

A woman's tears always affected him. They were the one thing he couldn't turn his back on. "It's all right, Carmela. Do not worry, it was the right thing to do. Please, don't cry, it's all right. I was only sleeping." Having spoken the lie, he gently closed the door on the still-frightened woman.

"Darling, is everything okay?" asked the voice from the bed.

One down, now he would have to deal with the beauty. "Yes,

yes, everything is fine, my love. But I've just received some very important correspondence, and I'm afraid I'm going to have to devote myself to it immediately. You'll forgive me, won't you, if I go directly to my study and get started on it? I do apologize. I would have liked nothing more than to continue last night's pleasures on this wonderful morning." Convincingly he nuzzled his lips against her cheek for just a moment and then he headed for his shower. "You'll let yourself out, won't you?"

Peter glanced briefly at the unopened letter before he stepped into the steaming shower. He recognized the German stamps and the return address of the Waldhotel. As the near-scalding water ran down his firm, well-exercised body, he thought about what news the letter might contain. He sincerely hoped it wasn't from his ex-wife, starting anew all that nonsense about how wonderful it would be if they were back together again. He hoped even more that it wasn't something about that nasty tax scandal he had been involved in last year. No, the court had made its decision, and he had paid his dues. That was over. Maybe it was just a letter from one of his old girlfriends. But special delivery? That was the mystery. His curiosity finally overtook him, and he cut his shower short.

Now he was more anxious than ever about the letter's contents, and as he stood with a towel draped around his trim waist, his hair still dripping wet, he ripped open the envelope. Handwritten in a beautiful script on the Waldhotel stationery, it began,

Dear Mr. von Hassler,

Mr. Frederic Rohr, the retired head concierge of the Richemond Hotel and, I believe, a former colleague of yours, has recommended you highly as a man of great capability in the field of hotel management. The Waldhotel Becker in Baden-Baden, with which I hope you are familiar, is in great need of a top-caliber resident general manager. Since my father's death over a year and a half ago, my husband and I, along with the help of several of our more senior staff, including Dieter, the brother of Frederic,

*have been trying to keep the hotel operating at peak condi-
tion. But we all feel it is now time to put the operation into
the hands of someone trained and experienced in the field.
I understand that your position at the Richemond was that
of assistant manager, so this would be an advancement for
you. I am writing in the hopes that you might currently be
in a position to accept this enormous challenge. Frederic
mentioned that you had returned to France to settle a personal problem. If that is taken care of, perhaps it would be
the right time to come and speak with us. We look forward
to meeting with you at your earliest convenience.*

> *Hoping to hear from you soon, I remain,*
> *Sincerely yours,*
> *Tilla Becker-Meier*

Peter dressed and went downstairs to the library, which doubled as
his office. He was still laughing aloud to himself when Carmela entered carrying his morning espresso and croissant. She walked as
silently as she possibly could on the areas of the wooden floors not
covered by the luxuriously thick Oriental carpets. She had already
disturbed Monsieur von Hassler more than she ever cared to, and she
was so grateful to still have her job that she wanted to remain as
invisible as possible. She had gone outside into the garden and picked
a flower to put on his tray as a small token of her thankfulness. As
she was going back into the kitchen, she had seen a tall, pretty blond
lady leaving by the front door. Now she better understood his being
so upset when she had disturbed him. But she was delighted to see
that he was laughing; something had amused him terribly. She assumed it was whatever was in the letter she had delivered to him.

"Ah, Carmela, thank you, that's lovely. Just put it over there,
will you please?"

He seemed fine now, the furor of the morning's incident had
passed. He continued chuckling as she left the room as quietly as she
had entered.

"A personal problem?" he asked himself. Well, that solved it
once and for all. His remaining fears about the last three years all

vanished at that very moment. He had even been able to fool that
sharp old man, Frederic Rohr, one of the wisest and most astute hotel
men he had ever run across. A personal problem indeed. Well, it had
been his problem, and it would be forever. At least he knew that the
real circumstances surrounding his sudden dismissal from the Richemond had been covered up to everyone's satisfaction. Good, he still
had a shot at a hotel career. Of sorts, that is. And at the Waldhotel.
That was really the top. What a reputation, what a clientele. He had
heard that they even studied Ludwig and Karl-Gustav Becker at the
fancy hotel school in Lausanne. Yes, Becker's was supposed to be a
beautiful hotel. Small and elegant. Just like the one he had grown up
in. But the son of a lowly gardener had never even been allowed to
enter the public rooms of that hotel. No, he had been forced to take
the back staircase like a leper, and to remain in his room on the top
floor like a prisoner, observing the activities of the rich and famous
from the small window in the tiny space he shared with his brother.
The one time he had ventured down the main staircase he had been
caught, and the pain and humiliation he had suffered as a result of
his father's beating were as fresh in his mind as if they had been
endured only yesterday. From that day forward he had carried his
need for retribution, his burning hatred of those who had been
blessed with money and position, barely disguised beneath the surface
of his complex personality. He so wanted to be a part of that world
that he would do anything, take any risk, to be close to the privileged.
He had even altered his name, adding the "von" just because it
sounded more important, more prestigious. Now he was being given
another chance to be a real part of a hotel. Everyone he had ever read
about went to the Waldhotel for one reason or another. However, it
was in Germany, he reminded himself. A little quiet, a little sedate
compared with the wild, exotic life he led in Paris now that he had
been able to get some of the money out of Switzerland. The rest of
his income, his "pocket" money, came from his activities as a mod-
ern-day gigolo, one of the highest paid and most in demand in the
entire city. He lived well off the wads of hundred-franc notes stuffed
into his dinner jacket the next morning. His townhouse on the Avenue Foch had been decorated lavishly with expensive favors from
many of the women. The priceless *objets,* the tasteful antiques, even

valuable paintings came from women who feared their husbands would find out if they gave him large amounts of cash. Sometimes these pay-for-pleasure experiences were even enjoyable. Like last night, for example.

Yet with all of this he missed the challenge of a hotel. For Peter was not a lazy man. On the contrary, once he got his teeth into a project, he clung to it with the tenaciousness and viciousness of a dog gone mad. He hadn't done it for years now, but he was certain he could call his skills back into action. The same skills that had gotten him into a world of trouble at the Richemond.

Baden-Baden, didn't they have a casino or something? Yes, he recalled, it was a very grand one, too, with high-stakes betting around the clock. He had heard about the horse racing there, too. Maybe it wouldn't be so bad after all. Maybe he should write back to this Tilla Becker-Meier and set up an interview. Yes, that's exactly what he would do today. Instead of running around, wasting another day going to lunch and then shopping with one of the married ladies who savored his attentions so much, he would answer the letter. He pulled out several sheets of his thickest, most expensive writing paper and began his response in the most charming manner, one capable of convincing Madame Becker-Meier that she had indeed written to exactly the right man.

Riding through town in the backseat of the chauffered car that had picked him up at the Frankfurt airport earlier that morning, Peter was so far unimpressed with the look of Baden-Baden. Its streets appeared quaint and well maintained, and the main shopping area was lined with all the right names—Chanel, Dior, Van Cleef & Arpels, yet he sensed a distinctly provincial atmosphere. It certainly wasn't the Riviera, neither the French nor the Italian. Nor was it Monte Carlo. It lacked the spark, the casualness, and the pizazz of what came into his mind when he thought of a "resort" or a "spa" atmosphere. But he reminded himself that many of the people who came here came for medical reasons, to rest and take the cures, to drink the therapeutic waters. Perhaps the thing that disturbed him most was the absence of attractive women. But, after all, Paris was tough to beat in that department. He was spoiled. The women he knew were always one step ahead of even the latest Parisian fashions. The Germans had never been credited with the spirit, the same joie de vivre as most other Europeans. Still, it might be good for him to be out of the range of constant temptation for a while. He would see. He would give it, and Madame Becker-Meier, a chance. It was the first opportunity he had had for a legitimate job in a long, long time.

"Mr. von Hassler, I hope we've covered everything. Can you think of anything else, any other questions for me?" Tilla asked at the conclusion of their day together.

"Not at this time, but if I do I promise to call you at once from Paris. You can be certain that I won't overlook a thing."

"So it's set, then," she continued, unable to curtail the excitement in her voice, "you'll be here to join us in one month."

"Exactly as we discussed, Madame Meier. I am looking forward to it enormously. We'll have the hotel running as smoothly as your wonderful father would have wanted it. I'll be here, bag and baggage, in just four weeks. Until then, please take care, and give my regards to your lovely family."

True to form, Peter von Hassler charmed Tilla into believing he was the only man on earth who could save the Waldhotel. She had liked him from the moment his handsome six-foot-two frame stepped gracefully out of the car in front of the hotel. His manner, his way of speaking, everything about him was pleasant and pleasing. He dressed elegantly in beautifully tailored clothes, and his hazel eyes and strawberry-colored hair made him even more appealing. Tilla thought he reminded her of another Peter, her dear, sweet brother. Making the comparison only made her like him more.

They had spent the morning together, touring the hotel, meeting key members of the staff, and generally getting to know each other. At lunchtime they were joined by Johannes and Dieter. The two professionals had lots to say to each other. They talked about the hotel's demanding clientele, the changes that needed to be implemented immediately, and of course, about Dieter's brother and the Hotel Richemond. Johannes hardly spoke. Tilla rationalized that he must have been so happy to see that she had finally found a person, a live, skilled individual who spoke all the right languages and said all the right things, that he was content merely to sit and listen. Kati and Eva-Maria stopped by their table just as dessert and coffee were being served. Tilla thought he held Eva-Maria's hand a fraction of a second longer than necessary to display his good manners, but she chose to overlook that small detail, so content was she to have found this gem of a man. Her only thought was to get him to accept the position.

But everything was settled now. They had agreed on salary, living arrangements, and the possibility of a substantial bonus at the end of the year if the hotel performed well. The deal was done. She and Johannes celebrated that night. They toasted to a new beginning for the Waldhotel. She was convinced, without a doubt, that Peter von Hassler was the answer to their every need.

Peter practically skipped to the gate to catch his flight back to Paris. Quite honestly, he couldn't wait to get away from the grayness, the dreariness of the neighboring country. He had to admit that Baden-Baden was beautiful—most charming, with its parks, its trees, and that little river. However, it was hardly the stuff of which a wild life was made. That was why he had agreed to come in a month's time, and not a minute before. He needed to get his fill of Paris before he started his new job. Parties every night, dancing, clubs, costume balls —those were the things he thrived on. But the Waldhotel would be good, once he got his mind set on it. He had been able to assess the situation immediately. Tilla was trying to hold on to the family fortune and at the same time her husband. Johannes was not much interested but probably pretty financially astute. He was there trying to keep everyone together, and Peter would have to watch out for him. If he was smart, he would seduce Johannes into becoming a part of his plan. Not the entire plan, of course. Only the legal part. Everything would be positioned as an effort to help the hotel, to increase the business. Yes, everything for the Waldhotel. That was it. Johannes would become the secret weapon for his success. Brilliant! Poor, unsuspecting Johannes was exactly the pawn he needed to make everything work smoothly. Now he felt much better.

Then there was Dieter. He was pretty smart, maybe even smarter than his older brother. But he would take care of him. He'd go slowly until he gained his trust. Then he'd be just fine.

And finally, he had seen one pretty girl. A very pretty girl indeed. That older daughter, Eva something, yes, she was delicious. Her haircut was a little severe, a little more avant-garde than he was used to, but oh, what a body! She couldn't be more than seventeen or eighteen, but that was all right. He'd had younger women and he'd loved it. He'd have to be satisfied with whatever was available. And she was available. He could tell from the way she shook his hand. She was interested. Well, he'd bide his time. Take it slowly. It would be well worth the wait.

For now, as the plane took off, he looked out the window and saw the borders of the Black Forest in the distance, and Baden-Baden beyond. The next target of his devious mind looked so peaceful, so secure. It would remain that way for at least another month.

CHAPTER

6

PETER'S MONTH flew by. He was out constantly—off to lunches, galleries, and auctions—then he would rush back just in time to change for dinner. Often he would be out all night, returning only after most Parisians had already left their homes for work. Carmela would see him arrive in front of the townhouse from the upstairs window. He would emerge from the limousine, often carrying his cummerbund and bow tie from his evening dress in his hand.

The weekend before he was scheduled to leave for Germany, Peter hosted a party at his townhouse. It was a wild event that went on until well past dawn. He didn't plan on staying in the quiet forest of Germany forever, and he wanted to make certain that none of his friends would forget him while he was away. So he had ordered case upon case of the finest champagne and mounds of jet-black caviar. He had served his one hundred guests a lavish meal of pheasant and lobster. The party was a grand success. He was convinced that no one would forget either him or the devastating hangover they surely suffered the morning after.

Tilla's month dragged on interminably. She counted the hours until Peter was due to arrive. So convinced was she that he was the hotel's savior that she began putting things off she felt would be better handled by him. The file grew daily. Its contents now occupied almost half of the expansive desk. Finally the day of his arrival dawned, and she waited downstairs in the lobby like an expectant bride. When he stepped out of the car, he looked as elegant as she remembered.

"Good morning, Madame Meier," he said. "I can't wait to get started."

They were the exact words Tilla longed to hear. There was no lack of things to be attended to. The correspondence—the letters, the memos, the requests, from the now thick file bulged out from its sides.

Peter acclimated himself well to his new environment. Within a week he had assumed total control of the daily staff meetings. He spent generous amounts of time with each of the key staff members, trying to ascertain what their specific problems were and how he could implement changes to make their jobs, and therefore the hotel, function more smoothly. Tilla was concerned about how some of the senior employees would react to him, but as she watched him interact with everyone, she was certain that she had nothing to worry about. What made her happiest was the relationship he seemed to be developing with Johannes. They were together often, speaking animatedly in the hallways, always rushing off to one meeting or another. Just today Johannes had waved offhandedly to her from the dining room. He and Peter were having lunch together. Tilla thought about joining them, but it looked as if they were in the midst of a serious discussion. She wanted Johannes to operate more independently, to become involved in more areas, so she decided to leave them alone. It was a crucial decision.

"I'm glad Tilla didn't join us today," Peter said to Johannes once he was certain she had left the dining room. "There is something I want to speak to you about."

"I'm all yours," Johannes offered, leaning forward and listening intently. He had taken a liking to Peter from the moment he arrived —mostly because he had freed Tilla from such a heavy work load, but also because he thought he would be able to turn the hotel around.

"Well, Johannes, I've been doing a lot of thinking about how we're going to be able to pull out of this rut we're in. And I've formulated a plan. I'd like to tell you about it and hope that you'll give me the go ahead to put it into action."

"As I said, I'm all yours," Johannes repeated.

"Johannes, not enough people know about Becker's. Yes, those in the know know, those rich enough and lucky enough to travel frequently. But they are such a small group. There are many others, many people of more modest means who maybe only take one or two vacations a year. But when they do travel, they like to go someplace special. I'm not talking about people who are attracted to package trips, or those bus tours where all your meals are planned and paid for in advance. I'm talking about people at a higher level, those with money but not enough to be considered really rich. Those kinds of people, and there are millions of them, have never even heard of the Waldhotel. Many of them don't even know about the Black Forest. Why? Because they've never seen it anywhere or read about it in any magazine. They just don't know. But if they did, I'm convinced we could get them to become our guests."

Johannes appeared to understand what Peter was saying but was confused as to where it was leading. "So what are you suggesting we do about it? How do we find these people?"

Perfect, Peter thought, just as I planned. Johannes has fallen into my trap nicely. "That's exactly it, Johannes. Only we don't find them, we let them find us."

Confusion swept across his future pawn's face.

"How can they find us if they don't know about us?"

He wasn't an accountant by accident, Peter thought. Anything more than moving some numbers around six ways to Sunday on a sheet of ledger paper would be much more than he was equipped to handle. But now was not the time to let on how stupid he felt he was. Now he was nearly in the palm of his hand. "Precisely, Johannes," he encouraged, wanting to convince him that they were reaching a solution together. "They can't find us if we don't communicate with them first."

"Peter, are you recommending that we advertise the Waldhotel?"

Now was no time to hold back. He had mentioned it first. "That's exactly what I'm saying. We must do it, Johannes. It's the one thing that will bring the hotel up to capacity and get it cooking again. We've got to take space in every important magazine, in every country. We've got to get the message out about Becker's. Once people discover it, we're going to be filled to the rafters. We'll have more business than we'll know what to do with." Peter had to contain himself. He was getting carried away, his voice was rising, and people at the next table were staring at him. It was important now to get to the crucial part. If this was to work at all, he needed Johannes's promise of secrecy.

"Peter, grand hotels just don't advertise. It's part of their cachet, their appeal. Even the grandest of the grand, the Ritz, doesn't put ads in magazines telling the world about their services. Why should we?" Johannes countered.

Peter immediately used his comment to his advantage. "You're exactly right," he said, "of course the Ritz doesn't advertise. But Johannes, they are sitting on top of prime real estate. Perhaps the most valuable land in the world. They're smack in the middle of Paris! It's the most beautiful, most romantic city in the universe," he sighed, wishing with all his heart he were sitting at the Ritz at this very moment, having a drink in the back bar. "Not to mention a major financial center. It's a bit different from being out here in the middle of a forest in Germany, in a town of less than forty thousand people." Peter's argument seemed to make sense to him.

"Johannes, I know it will work. There's only one obstacle. A major one, but I'm sure that together we can work around it."

"What's that?" Johannes asked, continuing to show the same innocence as he did on most subjects.

"Tilla," Peter said. "Tilla will never go for this. She sees advertising as a complete waste of money. Her father never did it, and she sees no reason to start it now."

"Have you spoken to her about this?" Johannes asked.

This was the trickiest part. Peter tread gently, yet forcefully. He knew if he got through this, he would be home free. His plan would be neatly in place. "No, I haven't, Johannes. And very frankly I was hoping it was something we would be able to decide on together, just the two of us. So often I've heard you say, and so correctly, I might add, how good Tilla is at organizing the banquets, making certain the meetings run on schedule, and dealing with the guests on a personal basis. She is a superb public relations person for the hotel. No one could represent the Waldhotel better. But she's not a marketing person. She has never been formally trained in hotel management. The idea of spending money on advertising would seem entirely frivolous to her."

Johannes continued listening, but it was obvious to Peter that the idea of doing something without Tilla's knowledge or blessing was foreign to him. His next comment confirmed his thoughts.

"I'm not sure I agree, Peter," he said. But Peter thought he de-tected a slight hesitation in his voice. "I just don't know. Making an expenditure of that kind . . . without her knowing . . . I really think . . . what kind of numbers are we talking about anyway? I'd like to see a budget. I would think that an advertising campaign, the kind you're suggesting, could be very expensive."

"Not necessarily," Peter tried to assuage his fears. He was de-lighted that he had asked for a budget. That was a good sign. "We could start out very slowly, just a few publications, and see what kind of response we get. Then we could make further commitments. You'll see, you're going to love this area of the business. It's actually the most interesting part. The numbers will fall into place if we do this right. We don't need to do everything at once. Of course, we would need to buy enough pages to make an impact, but we could get some professional advice on that aspect."

"Have you thought about approaching Tilla with this idea?"

"Of course, I considered it," Peter said, "but, quite honestly, Johannes, I didn't want to frighten her. She is so conservative, she plays everything so close to the vest, I just didn't want to alarm her. She might think that I'm making too many plans too quickly, and that's the last thing I want to happen. No, Johannes, I came directly to you. I felt sure that you'd be the one who would understand. And I hoped you'd agree with me that it would be so terrific to build this business together. That, I'm sure you'll agree, would make Tilla hap-pier than anything else."

"You're certainly right about that," Johannes said.

Peter remained silent for what seemed like forever. He thought he might just have succeeded in gaining Johannes's support. On the first try. It was too good to be true. Finally he spoke. He had to know.

"Well, what are you thinking?"

"I've got to give it some thought," Johannes replied. He sounded genuinely torn between giving the go-ahead and forbidding Peter to continue to even entertain the notion. "Let me sleep on it and we'll discuss it further tomorrow."

Peter couldn't push any more now. He had to walk a fine line so that Johannes would not think he was being too aggressive, that for some reason it was crucial that he get his support. "Okay, Johannes, that's fine with me. But let's not let it go too much longer without deciding one way or the other. The magazines have long lead times, and the longer we wait, the slower the business may become."

"I understand," Johannes commented. "I'll let you know tomorrow."

Both of the girls were out of school for the summer. Eva-Maria planned to ride and to work part time at a chic, young-clothing boutique in town. The shop carried only the most avant-garde fashions—miniskirts, and the new paper dresses that were all the rage. She felt right at home wearing even the most bizarre new styles. Kati had graduated from school and, true to what she had mentioned months ago, one night over dinner she asked her father if she could spend the summer working in the hotel.

"I'm not sure that's a good idea, Kati," replied Johannes. "Wouldn't you prefer to take the summer off and just relax before you start university?"

"Not really, what would I do anyway? Even if I work full time, I can still ride and play tennis often enough. Please, Papa, I've always wanted to learn more about the hotel. Now seems like the perfect time."

"Personally, I can't think of anything more awful. How boring!" commented Eva-Maria as she pursed her lips toward the hand mirror she extracted from her barrel-shaped leopard-skin purse. Her latest habit was to reapply the newest brilliant shade of crimson lipstick between each food course. It was driving the rest of the family crazy.

"Eva, just be quiet, will you please?" asked her sister. "And why are you wearing that dreadful shade of lipstick? It makes you look like you don't have proper circulation."

"If you knew anything about fashion, or for that matter, were even interested in how you look, you'd know this color. 'Scarlet's Revenge,' it's called. It is the *rage* of Paris right now. Everyone's wearing it. But no, all you want to do is work in the crummy old hotel. Really!"

"And all you want to do is make sure you have the newest bathing suit to wear to the club," Kati countered, her tone of voice more teasing than serious.

"Better than that one-piece number that flattens your chest to nothing! You look just like a little boy!" Eva-Maria retorted, and then winked at her younger sister.

"That's enough, girls, your silly chatter is beginning to spoil my dinner," cautioned Johannes. "Now, please, stop it right now."

Tilla looked at him, surprised by the sharpness in his voice. Johannes rarely raised his voice to anyone, particularly not to the girls. But lately he had been on edge. Something was bothering him. The slightest intrusion irritated him. She would ask him about his irascibility later when they were alone.

"Why don't we try it?" she asked, trying to restore peace and return to the subject at hand. Tilla knew that if she had spent some of her summers behind the reception desk instead of at the tennis club, things would certainly be different now. "If it doesn't work out, or if she doesn't like it, she can quit. It's not that serious, Johannes. What do you think?"

Johannes realized he had spoken a little harshly to his daughters. He was just so confused, so uncertain about the decision he had made in agreeing to go along with Peter and his plans to advertise the hotel. He had decided not to utter a word to Tilla, counting on the strategy to succeed. If it did, he would be a hero in her eyes at last. If it didn't . . . the consequences were too terrible to even contemplate right now. So he returned to the question of Kati's summer plans. After a little more debate about the position and the token salary she would be paid, Johannes was unable to deny his eager young daughter's wishes. She would start the next week as the assistant to the chief receptionist. Dieter would be close by to keep a watch on her, but Tilla was convinced that with her bright, smiling face and enthusiastic attitude she would be a great hit.

Indeed Kati was a big success in her new job. The guests loved being escorted to their rooms by the pretty young girl who was so knowledgeable about the Waldhotel Becker. Often she was one of the first people the new arrivals would meet. She left a lasting, warm impression on everyone she dealt with.

"Why, it's almost as if you were born here," commented one of the couples she had just installed in their luxurious suite facing the Lichtentaler Allee. Opening the tall, narrow doors to their terrace, she had pointed out the proximity of the art museum and the Kunsthalle, where all of Baden-Baden's theater and orchestra performances were held.

"Well, actually you're right," she replied courteously. "My great-grandfather was the founder of the hotel, and both my sister and I were born up on the third floor." She beamed with pride each time she spoke about her family's heritage.

She would then leave the new couple with wishes for a wonderful stay, not wanting to linger a single moment too long. She assured them that if there was anything they might need, it was merely a phone call away. She always believed that people enjoyed knowing that family members were still involved in the hotel. It made them feel more a part of the grand tradition the Waldhotel had always represented.

In addition to the guests, who were charmed by her, the senior members of the staff adored working with the little girl who had become such a delightful young woman. Many of them had been there long enough to remember chasing a diaper-clad Kati up and down the staircase. Now she walked on those very same stairs, in her pretty uniform and flattering high heels, leading the arriving guests to their rooms with authority and grace.

Tilla began to relax a bit, confident that all was in order. She started to enjoy the things she did do, the things, as Johannes had continued to point out, she did best. It was wonderful not to have to worry about every little detail, every tiny element that had to be exactly right or the hotel would run off kilter. Without the weight of that extraordinary responsibility on her shoulders, her spirit was brighter, and the work she did accomplish was much more successful.

But one afternoon a red flag was thrown up. Standing in the kitchen next to head chef Franz Kellner, Tilla was reviewing the menus for that day when Herr Klebe asked to see her.

"Can it wait for just a minute, Heinz?" she asked, puzzled to see him at her side. He was always in his office punching in one set of numbers or another, preparing yet another graph or chart.

"Yes, I suppose so Frau Meier, but it is important, and I'd like to see you soon."

It was unusual for old Klebe to be so forceful. He had been the financial wizard at the hotel for as long as Tilla could remember. He had been with Karl-Gustav for years and years. Always he was a quiet, soft-spoken man who prided himself on being able to report from memory to the nearest pfennig exactly how much money had been spent in any category last year and how much would be required this year. Tilla studied Herr Klebe carefully. His brown tweed pants had seen many seasons, yet they were impeccably clean and pressed. Even in midsummer he wore a lightweight wool vest, and he would never dream of walking through the lobby of the hotel without his jacket. Herr Klebe was a loyal, stable employee, content with his position and never one to complain or cause trouble of any sort. He was a diligent worker concerned only with the welfare of the hotel. Always he had been the most reliable of men. Suddenly she was worried.

"Herr Klebe, is it something about Johannes? Is he all right?" She wasn't aware that they were having any problems working together. Not until now.

"No, Frau Meier, Herr Meier is fine . . . I suppose."

" 'I suppose'?" she repeated his oddly phrased response.

"Yes, I think he is fine. Please, if you'll only give me a few minutes of your time."

Tilla decided that whatever it was he wanted, it was more important at that instant than whether they would offer chocolate or Grand Marnier mousse as that day's special dessert.

Excusing herself hastily, she and Herr Klebe walked upstairs to the privacy of her office.

"Okay, what is it that couldn't wait for even one more minute?" She tried to hide the irritation in her voice but was unsuccessful.

"There are some discrepancies in the figures." He began to remove some documents from the folder she had only now noticed he was carrying.

"Discrepancies? I'm not sure I understand what you mean." She was genuinely confused.

"Please allow me to show you." He started spreading the pages across the desk. "Here you have two sets of numbers, Frau Meier. As you may or may not be aware, shortly after Herr von Hassler arrived, he advised my office, or more specifically me, that from then on he would be compiling the department numbers. When he was finished, he would forward the totals on to me. Of course, as he is the man now in control, I agreed at once, even though it is a change in a procedure that has existed, and has served the hotel well, for the last twenty-five years that I can recall. Anyway, I agreed to his new way of doing things. I certainly wanted to appear cooperative, and for the past few months I have accepted the numbers that were submitted to me. But only last week, when Herr von Hassler went to Frankfurt for the day, I was preparing a report for him and required some data from the month of April. Not wanting to delay the report until his return, I went directly to the person in charge of the department. In this instance it was Herr Moreno, in purchasing. I simply asked him for a breakdown of the figures he had given to Herr von Hassler. With the new system, I only get the totals, you see. So, taking this information back to my office I started to complete my report. To my amazement, nothing matched. Not one of the numbers was the same. I thought perhaps I had made an error, so I went to the restaurant and asked them for numbers from the same time period. Again, there were large differences in the numbers they had reported and the numbers von Hassler submitted to me. I continued checking with some of the other departments, and what you see before you is the result of all the checks. Not one figure is the same. I didn't want to alarm anyone, so I waited until the close of the following month, and then I did the same thing. Of course, by now everyone in the house thinks I'm a dotty old man who can no longer keep track of anything. They all think I've lost my mind because I keep asking them for the same thing they've already given to von Hassler. But I merely wanted to make certain, and now I am certain. Here's the proof—von Hassler is a thief. He changes the numbers before he submits them to me. He's stealing money from the hotel like mad."

Midway through his lengthy explanation, when the reality of what he was saying hit her, Tilla sank down in her chair. The color drained from her face. Her expression was that of a person who wanted desperately not to believe the evidence that was spread out clearly before her.

"To say that I find this difficult to believe is an understatement," she said. "Couldn't there be some mistake, some explanation?" her eyes implored him to tell her yes.

Herr Klebe could see how distraught she was by his accusation, but there was no escaping the truth of his findings. "I'm sorry to be the one to tell you, Frau Meier, but there was no other way. The only thing I knew I must do was to come and tell you directly."

At his words, Tilla's mind clicked with even more alarming questions. Why didn't he go to Johannes with his incriminating information? Why to her? Was there more to this than just Peter's involvement? Did Johannes have something to do with it? The possibilities were too terrible even to contemplate.

"Does Johannes know about this?" she asked, not entirely certain that she wanted to know the answer.

"Yes, he does. Of course, since he is my boss, I went directly to him the moment I felt I had enough information to be sure about this thing."

"And so, what did he say?" she interrupted him, unable to wait any longer.

"Well, he said he was sure that it wasn't true, that von Hassler was to be trusted implicitly, that he came to the hotel highly recommended. I tried to reason with him that recommendation or not, the figures still don't match, but he wouldn't hear of it. Quite honestly, I was astounded at his response. Herr Meier is the most meticulous accountant I've ever worked with. He just couldn't miss this sort of error. I asked him if he would check the numbers, his figures against mine. He said he had no time for that. He was busy preparing the tax statement. He told me to forget it and get on with my own business."

"When was that?"

"Only last week, Frau Meier. But it's been troubling me ever since. I haven't been able to sleep at night thinking about this crook, this devious man living in our midst. So this morning I went to Herr Meier again. But this time he was even more adamant about the issue. He yelled at me to get out of his office and never to mention the subject again. But I can't leave the issue. It's too . . . "

"Terrible, it's terrible," Tilla continued. "The only way to deal with this is to get Peter in here immediately. I'll call him at once."

But it was too late. It was Wednesday, technically Peter's day off if one could reason that a hotel man was able to take a day off during the height of the season. When she called the staff quarters to ask his whereabouts, she was told that he had dressed and gone out for the evening. Where? she wondered. She knew he didn't have many friends in the area. The first time he had ever been in Baden-Baden was when he had come to interview. The confrontation would have to wait for tomorrow. Maybe it was better after all. She would confront Johannes tonight about his peculiar reaction to the whole thing. Going to him now, in the middle of the day, would only be awkward and would further upset their already sinking union. But Herr Klebe's revelations were too troubling. She would force herself to get to the bottom of it. The additional time would also give her a chance to recover from the nausea that had racked her entire body ever since she first heard the incredible news.

Tilla found the strength to bring up the subject with Johannes that night at dinner. He repeated exactly what Herr Klebe had reported. He remained firm in his position. He *had* to support the position he had taken. No amount of discussion could persuade him that something was wrong. He and Peter had made a pact. Nothing short of blatant evidence, which would be very difficult for Tilla to uncover, could ever make him admit that he had authorized Peter to use some of the hotel funds to finance an expenditure of which he knew his wife would never approve.

"Johannes, how can you insist that everything is all right? The numbers are very clear. We are missing money!" Tilla's patience was running thin. She had belabored the issue all evening, to no avail. He was not willing to confront the situation.

"Tilla, for the last time, I am sure there is an explanation, a perfectly legitimate one." He gave her an exasperated sigh, trying his best to convince her. "If we go to him now, with only Klebe's information, he will think we have no confidence in him. I'm sure he won't want to stay. Would you? We hired him to help us turn this operation around, and as far as I can tell, that's exactly what he's doing. Tilla, you know how conservative old Klebe is. He often jumps to conclusions." He silently prayed she wouldn't ask him to cite one, for he would be trapped without a thing to say. "Look, here's what I'm willing to do. I'll take a look at the numbers first thing tomorrow. If I find anything out of place, I'll ask Peter about it at once. I'm willing to spend a few hours checking this out."

Johannes's concession to review the books made her feel a little better, but she still remained unconvinced of Peter's innocence.

"Johannes, for the life of me, I hope you're right about this." She walked slowly out of the dining room, exhausted by the evening's conversation. She climbed into bed, hoping for a night of untroubled sleep.

CHAPTER

7

*T*ILLA MAY HAVE BEEN distraught over Herr Klebe's revelations, but Peter von Hassler approached the evening as if he didn't have a care in the world. Everything in his master plan was proceeding exactly as he had so skillfully projected. Even faster than he had anticipated. There was an abundance of cash, since the hotel didn't accept credit cards. Only hard currency or a guest's signature would do. And there were so many ways to play with the numbers. In fact, it was going so successfully that Peter estimated that by late November he could be back in Paris, with his newly acquired fortune, just in time for the start of the fall social whirl. He had won over everyone in the place, charming and joking his way into their minds, if not their hearts. So far no one was giving him any trouble, and he had been able to set up his operation to his satisfaction. He thought it might be harder to do the second time, but on the contrary he found it easier. He was just more careful and paid more attention to anything that could put a snag in his plans. Oh yes, it was really even much easier than the Richemond had been. He simply called up the advertiser and bought an appropriate amount of ad space. Once he got the invoice, he merely cut a check in the amount requested. Then, right before the closing date, he would cancel the order, endorse the check to his own account, and the matter was finished. He'd been able to get Johannes in his pocket without too much effort at all. He knew that the decision sometimes troubled him, but never enough to admit it to Tilla. In fact, it seemed as if Johannes just wanted to block their "arrangement" from his mind. He never asked Peter for copies of the publications in which the expensive ads were supposed to have appeared. He probably thought it was safer if they never came to him, since he needed to keep the evidence from accidentally falling into Tilla's hands. No, Peter was certain that Johannes would do whatever he could to make sure that Tilla never found out. By the time they started looking for any advertisements telling of the glorious Waldhotel Becker, he would be far, far away.

So as he strode confidently toward the entrance to the casino, dressed beautifully in his finest dinner jacket, he appeared to the rest of the chicly dressed crowd like a man who was looking forward to an evening of gambling in one of the most elegant halls in the whole of Europe. His only regret was that he had been unable to convince Eva-Maria to join him. Something about a fashion show that the store she worked in was giving at one of the clubs. She begged off, saying she just couldn't miss it. It didn't really matter; he knew she had wanted to go with him, and if it wasn't tonight it would be soon. Hopefully, it would be very soon, he thought. It had been so long since he'd been with such a hot young woman. Most of the really beautiful women were guests in the hotel. They usually stayed for only a few days and were almost always accompanied by a husband or lover. As he had predicted, the pickings were pretty slim in the Black Forest.

The casino, the oldest and the largest in Germany, had first opened its graceful doors in 1748, and its sizable revenues were an important part of Baden-Baden's economy. They went directly into the town coffers, enabling the city to maintain its high standards of civic pride. As Peter walked casually from room to room observing the rich crowd, his eyes took in every detail—the beautiful nineteenth-century French furnishings, the hand-painted ceilings and the Baccarat chandeliers. Plush ruby-red velvet draperies hung gracefully the full length of the twelve-foot windows. Fine oil paintings, bordered by thick, ornate gilded frames, made the rooms appear to be elegant salons, rather than gambling halls. Stage designers from the Paris Opera House had been commissioned to furnish the nine gaming rooms in the style of French royal palaces. It was a glorious emporium, and he felt very much at home amid its opulence.

He strolled slowly around each of the tables—roulette and blackjack were always the most crowded. Players often lined up two and three deep, waiting for an open chair. Two hundred and twenty croupiers dealt constantly to over five hundred thousand visitors each year. But Peter was uninspired by these games. The game that made his blood course rapidly through his veins was conducted in a private room all the way at the back of the casino, at the Golden Table. There one played with solid gold and silver chips. Spectators were barred from entering the elite room by red velvet stanchions placed at its entrance, with two imposing men in black tie standing guard to ensure that only qualified, serious players gained entrance. The men positioned around the sacred oval table, bent over in intense concentration, smoking Gauloises and oversized cigars, were the high-stakes players in the house, those who could bet and afford to lose or win thousands and thousands of deutsche marks in the space of one quick deal of the cards. Chemin de fer was the only game in the casino where the gamblers could bet directly against each other, not against the croupiers. There was no limit on the betting and the stakes often rose to ten thousand marks or more per hand. Nine was the magic number, a player could not exceed that with two or three cards. Nowhere was the urge of the "powerful perhaps" in greater supply than around this special table.

The casino was one of the nicest surprises about Baden-Baden. It was much more serious than Peter's usual haunt, Monte Carlo.

As Peter approached the stanchions, he was immediately recognized by the two men guarding the entrance to the most exclusive salon.

"Bonsoir, Monsieur von Hassler," they offered in greeting as they released the thick burgundy velvet tubes to allow him to pass.

"Bonsoir," he responded, a sly smile already crossing his handsome face. The mere proximity to the coveted table made him happy. Peter had been spending so much time in the casino—three or four nights a week over the last several months—that he was recognized by almost every one of the employees.

There was an open chair on the side of the table facing into the room. At once one of the interior guards stepped forward to pull it back for him. He took the seat and joined the other punters.

Peter looked up at the enormous chandelier gracing the table. Its opulence was only a small part of the elaborate decoration of the room. The room's hand-painted ceiling and Empire furniture upholstered in the most luscious burgundy velvet made it the most spectacular in the casino. The heavy smoke curled up sensuously and danced through the chandelier's dangling crystals. He had both won and lost at this table. Most recently he seemed to be on a winning streak. Tonight he felt unusually lucky. It was so much easier to bet if the investment wasn't your own. He had never had any trouble dispensing with, or on the other hand, often increasing, the money of others. On this evening the betting was especially heavy. Around the table sat two wealthy South Americans whom Peter had seen check into the hotel earlier in the week. It was extremely bad form to be playing against them, but he was too involved now to quit. There were also several Germans, and one Frenchman who continued to drive the stakes even higher. The Banker was losing large sums and several times the Banco was drained. Peter stayed in the game for over an hour. He was winning nicely. He was thinking of taking his good luck and quitting, when he felt a light tap on his shoulder.

"You seem to be cleaning up," said the charming voice.

He turned around rapidly. No one was ever allowed to stand behind the players during chemin de fer. He was startled to see Eva-Maria.

"Now my luck will surely hold," he said, trying his hardest not to show how extremely pleased he was to see her. He stood up quickly and motioned for the guards to get a chair for her. She must have known the men at the doorway even to have been allowed to enter the room. So she was not an innocent, just as Peter had predicted. His skills at assessing women had not diminished one iota since his departure from France.

Eva-Maria looked exquisite. She had changed out of the outrageous costume she had been wearing earlier when she left for the fashion show. Then she had been wearing a black leather miniskirt and a brightly colored T-shirt with writing all over the sleeves. Her hair stood out from her head, and she wore no makeup except for a repulsively bright shade of purple lipstick. It was almost enough to make any man change his mind. But now she had made a complete transformation. Her hair was neatly styled, curving softly about her glorious face. Her makeup was light and flattering, with just the right amount of emphasis on her sultry eyes. The dress she wore, a simple, strapless style with a high slit up one side, revealed her long, shapely legs. The tops of her well-developed breasts rose and fell slowly and enticingly as she spoke.

"The party at the club got very boring. I thought it might be more fun over here," was all the explanation she offered. He took it as an invitation.

"I'm certain you're correct. Would you like to play?"

"Yes, of course."

And play she did. She knew all the rules, and after only three hands he could see that she was a reckless gambler. In just short of an hour she had gone through a good portion of Peter's winnings for the evening. But he didn't mind. In the brief time he had been in Baden-Baden, Lady Luck had smiled down generously on him. When he left, he would take a sizable kitty with him. And in reality, it was her money she was playing with.

Her luck changed, and after she had won several hands, she told him that she had had enough of the casino.

"Shall we have a drink somewhere?" Peter knew it wasn't a wise thing to suggest—in the small town anyone could see them—but he couldn't care less. The only thoughts that filled his mind were his overwhelming desire to touch her, to caress her beautiful body, and to cover her lips with his hungry mouth.

They walked slowly, arm in arm, adjusting to the height and pace of one another. Peter smiled contentedly to himself. Soon his conquest of Baden-Baden would be complete.

"Let's go to Pit's, okay?" she suggested. It was the Annabel's of the Black Forest, the most popular of the clubs. It was certain that any of the hotel's guests who had any interest in night life at all would be there. Peter had avoided going often because at a place like Pit's one had to socialize, to talk and dance. The chances of ending up with a guest were great. He preferred the businesslike atmosphere of the casino. But tonight he felt too good even to think of arguing with Eva-Maria.

"Sounds fine to me," he agreed at once, and off they headed in the direction of the club.

For the second time that night the guards at the door immediately recognized the luscious Eva-Maria. They welcomed her warmly.

It was after one, an hour when the majority of Badischers had long been fast asleep. But Pit's was alive with the latest sounds—the Beatles insisted "We Can Work It Out" and the Supremes countered with "You Can't Hurry Love." The Rolling Stones complained that they just couldn't get no "Satisfaction." The fashionably dressed crowd held out their glasses for more champagne. Many of the faces were familiar to Peter. They were registered guests at the Waldhotel.

Eva-Maria led Peter to a small banquette on one side of the dance floor. She pulled on his arm impatiently, urging him to sit down.

"This is my favorite place," she explained. "You can see everything and everyone from here."

And everyone could see them, Peter thought, but didn't say anything. He felt so trapped. How was he going to find a place for them to be alone? This was so different from the unlimited freedom he enjoyed in Paris.

For a few minutes they sat, observing the lively crowd. Everyone seemed to know each other, or if not, everyone appeared friendly and willing to meet new people. Couples moved slowly around the glitzy black-and-silver club, drinks in hand, laughing and smiling. Peter sat with his arm draped around Eva-Maria's shoulder. His fingers made a slow circling motion on her bare skin. He could hardly hear what she was saying over the din. But he couldn't keep his hands or eyes off her. Dancing was the only thing he thought could help. He hated the new unstructured way of dancing—the Mashed Potato, the Hully Gully, the Twist—all those silly names for dances that didn't even require a partner. He waited until the disc jockey selected "Cherish," a very popular slow number, and then he led her onto the crowded floor.

Thankful for the latest craze of "wraparound" dancing, Peter encircled her tiny shoulders with both his arms. She reciprocated, and as the music played, they began to sway back and forth, locked in each other's rhythms. Midway through the Association's romantic crooning, Peter was certain he was going to explode. He was holding Eva-Maria tightly, kissing her softly on her long, graceful neck. But he wanted all of her. The thought of her lying naked in his bed made him even more impatient. But what bed? All he had available was his small single room in the staff quarters opposite the main hotel building. She sensed his desire and responded by pressing her leg firmly between his thighs, making his enormous hardness even more unbearable. They danced until he could stand it no longer. He had to take her somewhere and make love to her, unrestrained and far from the eyes of all of the curious people.

"Come," he said as he led her up the stairs and out into the cool night air. The streets were quiet. Only one car's headlights sparkled in the distance.

They began to kiss in the alleyway leading out onto the Sophien-strasse. His hands explored the inside of the top of her dress. Her young breasts were firm, her nipples hardened at his touch. For the first time in many years, Peter had nowhere to go. He couldn't take her to one of the other hotels in town; everyone knew him. Besides it was two-thirty in the morning, and that sort of thing simply wasn't done in a small, provincial town like Baden-Baden. He didn't have any friends on whom to impose. He didn't even have a car! Out of ideas, and not able to continue kissing her so wildly with no end in sight, he put his arm back around her and began walking toward the hotel.

As they started to pass under the porte cochere, its lights dimmed, the single remaining porter inside, Eva-Maria looked up at him with her lovely eyes. Slowly she turned in the opposite direction, and faced the front door of the staff quarters.

"I'll be very quiet," she assured him.

It took only a second for him to realize the consequences of her suggestion. If he was caught with the Meiers' daughter in his room, he had no doubt he would be dismissed at once. His entire plan would be blown to pieces. On the other hand, it had been so long, and he wanted her so badly. The desires of the flesh overruled. They both took off their shoes before entering the building.

They tiptoed down the darkened hallway to Peter's sparsely fur-nished room. Seconds after he had quietly shut the door they were in each other's arms. Eva-Maria began to giggle as his tongue encircled the inside of her ear.

"Shhhhhhh . . . " he warned her, gently clasping his hand over her mouth. If she made even the most delicate sounds, they would surely be found out. Everyone was sound asleep at this hour. Those on the night shift would be returning to their rooms shortly.

He guided her to the bed. It was only a single mattress, far narrower than what Peter was used to making love on. But tonight it didn't seem to matter as they lay together, their bodies pressed tightly against each other, their lips joined. Eva-Maria was a willing, if unsophisticated, partner. Her innocence only increased Peter's passion. He removed her clothing carefully, slowly unbuttoning her dress and sliding it down along her glorious hips. Gently he rolled down her panties and stockings. Once she was naked, he stood up. Looking down at her heavenly figure, he removed his own clothes. Her eyes focused on his hardness. He held himself and ran his hand the full length of his erection. Eva-Maria moaned in anticipation. She reached out to take him, but he stepped back, knowing full well that if he allowed her to touch him, he would not be able to control himself.

"No," he whispered, "not yet, I want to go slowly. I want it to last forever. Turn over," he said, cupping his hands under the small of her back.

He laid down next to her. With his fingertips he applied the lightest possible pressure, stroking the full length of her back, beginning at the hairline at the base of her neck. Each time he reached the bottom of her spine, he allowed his fingertips to travel just an inch further down her glorious backside. She remained facing the wall in the tiny room. His only confirmation that she was responding to his efforts came from her slight stirring each time he reached the top of her buttocks. Feeling her press softly against his hand excited him even more. Twice again . . . his fingers began gliding faster . . . communicating his urgency to her. Her breath quickened and she could stand it no longer. Moans came from deep within her. She reached around and placed her hand over his. Eagerly she guided it between her slightly parted legs. His fingers had no trouble finding her splendid opening, for it was surrounded with the wetness of her desire. Her lips were swollen and Peter could visualize the inviting pinkness rimmed with the soft blond fur. She pushed herself onto him, yearning for the full length of his pleasing touch. He was determined to give her all the pleasure she wanted. She moaned with greater urgency as her movements quickened. Peter had to reach up and hold her shoulder with his other hand so that she could continue to writhe against his fingers.

"Peter," she cried out, almost too loudly, "I love it."

"I know, my darling," he answered, his voice as calm as hers was frenzied.

His tone, his air of complete authority and calmness, even though he was as hard and distended as he could ever remember, took her to even greater passion. Now her movements came spontaneously and he knew instinctively that she had reached the point of no return. During the next few seconds she would have no control at all over her body. She had given it over to him. Her final gasps came and at the same moment she covered Peter's hand with her own, silently begging him to stop. She was tender now, his fingertips were like needles invading her most intimate parts. Each additional thrust made her entire body quiver.

Again he began to stroke her back. This time it had the opposite effect. It calmed her trembling body. The moment he knew she was coming down, he turned her over gently onto her back. Her legs fell open and he knew that he would have to take her completely now.

Peter mounted her slowly, aware that her lips still burned. When she felt the tip of him at her swollen entrance, her desire was reignited and she thrust her hips up to meet him. Once inside, his rhythm quickened. No longer feeling the need to wait for her climax, he worked himself furiously against her. He exploded fiercely, a combination of basic human need and a true attraction to this wild creature. Knowing the thinness of the walls, he stifled his normal screams of pleasure.

Eva-Maria possessed the tightness of a virgin, but Peter was certain that he was not the first man to enjoy her favors. He would be, however, the first man to awaken in her sexual feelings and desires she had never before thought possible. Their first evening together had created a bond between them—one that would transcend boundaries either of them had previously known.

It was morning. Peter looked about the room—clothing lay in piles, wrinkled beyond recognition. Eva-Maria's stockings hung from the rungs of a high-backed chair. He looked at her sleepy face, her eyes rimmed with the remains of last night's makeup.

"How are you ever going to get to your room?" he asked her in a soft voice, still deathly afraid they would be caught at any moment.

"A legitimate question, considering that, except for the employee entrance, there is only one way in, and that's through the front door," she agreed. "You know where my room is, don't you?"

Peter nodded, wondering how he could get in and find an outfit for Eva-Maria without being detected.

"Do your best," she encouraged him as he slid out through a narrow opening in his door, just in case anyone should be passing in the hall. "Just make sure Suzanne doesn't spot you. She's a real busybody."

"Yes, ma'am," he replied, surveying her nakedness, already thinking of the next time he could be with the luscious young girl. She was apparently thinking the same thing, for her arms reached out to him and she pulled him back to her. Seconds later their desire had risen again, and the need to satisfy each other overruled Peter's need to be at his desk on time.

CHAPTER

8

ERR KLEBE resigned the following month. He said he was sorry, he hated to leave the place that had become like home to him after twenty-seven years, but he just couldn't tolerate the situation any longer. It was fine if Johannes and Tilla wanted to turn their backs and pretend that what was most surely happening wasn't, but he simply couldn't. So he left.

Tilla was distraught about his departure, but she kept her emotions to herself. She didn't want to widen the gap between herself and Johannes, a gap that had already spread too far. She tried not to dwell on it.

For the next few weeks she concerned herself with getting Kati ready to leave for the university. They shopped for new clothes—shoes and sweaters, skirts, and blouses—plus a warm new winter coat that she needed desperately. They spent hours selecting exactly the right things, and for a little while Tilla was able to forget the problems of the Waldhotel.

Peter also kept his feelings to himself. But Peter's emotions were of delight, so pleased was he that Herr Klebe was gone. Even though he was unaware of Klebe's discoveries and subsequent accusations, Klebe was the one person who had the potential to cause him a lot of trouble. The day before he left, Klebe had spotted Peter and Eva-Maria having a drink in one of the small cafés in town. He had given Peter a cold stare and then had turned and left the restaurant without ordering anything. Their one-night stand had continued, developing into a relationship that made them both very happy. He didn't want to admit it, but Peter had fallen in love with Eva-Maria. No one was more shocked at the depth of his feelings than Peter himself. Eva-Maria was rich, and spoiled. She had grown up enjoying all the privileges he had longed for from his tiny upstairs window. But he had no doubts that when he was ready to leave, Eva-Maria would go with him. He stole moments, hours, whatever he could get away with, so that they could be together. They made love as often as possible, often two or three times a day. Their passion for each other became an obsession. So enslaved was she with him that she would sneak into his office and beg him to pleasure her right there. As time went on, they became less and less discreet about being seen together. The incident with Klebe in the café reminded him that despite his overwhelming desire for her, he would have to be a bit more careful.

The day Kati was scheduled to leave for school was among the saddest Tilla had endured in a very long time. The train left for Frankfurt at three o'clock. When Kati came downstairs for lunch, she still hadn't finished packing.

"I'll come back and get whatever I've forgotten," she said, trying to cheer her mother up, to convince her that she wasn't leaving forever.

"You can't be running back and forth all the time," Tilla responded, feebly attempting to assure her daughter that she could always come home but secretly wishing that she wasn't leaving to begin with.

"And don't forget that I'll be working the front desk over the Christmas break. Don't hire anyone to take my place," she added.

Tilla could only smile. Christmas seemed light-years away. The days were still long, the nights were just beginning to feel a little cooler. Nothing could take the place of having her sweet, delightful, younger daughter at home. Secretly she wished it were Eva-Maria who was going away, not the daughter she cherished so. Eva-Maria had refused to return to school, claiming that she was learning a useful skill and enjoying her life in the boutique more than she ever had in college. Despite the protestations of both her parents, she had adamantly refused, and there was really nothing they could do about it. But Tilla sensed there was another, more powerful reason for her decision. She wasn't certain, but she thought Eva-Maria was deeply involved with someone. And that someone was keeping her in Baden-Baden. She was rarely around, only stopping at the hotel to change her clothes and dash out again in yet another weird outfit. When Tilla asked her about it, she merely brushed the thought off casually with an "Of course not, Mother, don't be silly. I like to see a lot of guys." Pushing her on the issue would only drive her farther away. As much and as hard as she tried, Tilla could not gain the confidence or trust of her rebellious daughter.

Kati loved the university. Nothing in her earlier experiences had prepared her for life in a dormitory with so many girls, so much activity, and such fun. She adored Frankfurt—there was always something interesting to do, films to see, museums to visit, concerts, lectures, and of course, plenty to study. It was so luxurious to have a choice of several movies, she could see two or three in one weekend if she wanted to, instead of having to wait two weeks for a new film to come to the single theater in Baden-Baden. She was working hard, studying every night for at least a little while. She was confident that her first marks would be well above average.

Heidi was still her best friend. They had both decided upon the von Goethe University in Frankfurt because of its proximity to home. For a time Kati had considered going to the hotel school in Lausanne, but had decided against it. She felt it was important to get a good general education first. Neither of the girls wanted to be too far away from their families, and the school had a fine reputation for offering a solid curriculum. During the 1968 student riots, the University had been the scene of much activity. The activists had sprayed over the Johann Wolfgang von Goethe name, preferring it to be called Karl Marx University. Now that the days of unrest had passed, the spray paint had been cleaned away, and the University had reclaimed its former appellation. The University of Frankfurt wasn't the most academically demanding school in the country, but it was perfect for the two of them.

Kati had just turned seventeen, making her among the youngest students. Even though they had come to school because of each other, Kati and Heidi were not roommates. The Fichtls and the Meiers had insisted that it would be better for the girls to widen their circle of friends. Heidi and Kati both hated the idea at first, but they soon got used to it. Kati had been paired with a girl named Deirdre. Deirdre was from Munich. She had made it perfectly clear from the very first day that her main reason for being at school was to find a husband.

She devoted herself to this cause. She was out all the time, coming in very early in the morning, sleeping a good portion of the day, and skipping many more classes than she attended. She reminded Kati of her sister. The two of them really had very little in common. Kati ended up spending most of her spare time with Heidi. It was a perfect match, the two beautiful girls from the heart of the Black Forest, discovering and exploring university life and the big city together.

As much as Kati loved being in Frankfurt, she also missed her life in Baden-Baden. The past summer had been the best of her life. She adored working in the hotel; she loved seeing the guests and making their stays enjoyable and unforgettable. She had learned so many things. She couldn't wait until the holiday break, when she would be back in her uniform, behind the desk, anxiously awaiting the new arrivals, the next gala. The hotel was just a series of events, most of them wonderful, many of them challenging. The magic of it was that you never knew what was going to happen next.

Convincing her father to allow her to work there again next summer, instead of going to summer school, became her most important goal.

"There's a new James Bond movie at the main theater. It's called *Goldfinger*. Supposed to be great. Want to go tonight?" Heidi was always anxious to go exploring, and as soon as classes were out, she started to formulate the evening's plan. But as the two girls walked back toward the dorm to drop off their books and papers, Heidi sensed there was something wrong with her friend. She wasn't her normal, receptive, responsive self. Usually she jumped at the idea of almost anything, as long as it sounded like fun.

"What's the matter, Kati? You don't look very happy," she paused for just a second. Concern clouded her face. "Don't tell me, it's not something to do with a *boy*, is it?" So many of their friends had fallen head over heels for some young man during the first few weeks of school, especially those who before had only attended all-girl schools. If one called and took them out, they were either chatty or silly; if one didn't, then they were mopey and sulky. Exactly the way Kati was acting right now. "Well, what is it?" Heidi insisted. Her friend was stone-faced. "Come on, Kati, you can tell me. We'll solve it together." Heidi always loved to hear everything that was going on in Kati's life. She was genuinely interested, and she prided herself on knowing every detail. That's what being best friends was all about.

Kati looked at Heidi and smiled. She was such a good friend. Every day she was reminded how glad she was that they had come to Frankfurt together. Life on campus would have been much different without her there.

"No, don't worry, it's nothing like a boy. You know me better than that," Kati assured her, placing the same amount of emphasis on the word as Heidi had, as if it were some dreadful disease.

"Well, what is it, then? I'm just relieved it wasn't my original diagnosis. C'mon Kati, tell me." She couldn't stand not knowing.

"I'm worried about the hotel," Kati said.

"The hotel?" Heidi repeated, her voice reflecting her amazement. "What do you mean? I know, you're worried that they can't go on without you, greeting the guests and everything, like they've done for umpteen number of years before you were there, before you were even born. Well, it's a real concern, I must say . . ." she teased. "Anyway, you'll be home soon enough to check up on them. Didn't you say you were going down during the two-day break next week?"

"That's just it. I did plan on going home. I already bought my train ticket. Then I called this morning to make sure that someone would be there to meet me. But my mother got on the phone and said that maybe it wasn't such a good time to come. Now, you know, that doesn't exactly sound like my mother. If it were up to her, I'd never have left to begin with. So for her to suggest that I not come is really strange. She acted so funny, but I could tell she was trying not to sound upset. She said everything was all right, it was just a busy time. But I know there's something wrong, something terribly wrong. I could tell from her voice. At the end I think she was starting to cry. Oh, Heidi, I don't know what to do now. I'm really worried about her, and the hotel."

"What about Eva-Maria? Have you spoken to her? Maybe she knows something."

"She wouldn't tell me, and anyway, you can never reach her. She's always out sneaking around with Peter. Besides, she's probably part of the problem. I thought about calling Dieter—I'm sure he knows everything—but he's almost as protective of me as my parents. So he wouldn't tell me anything either."

"Why don't you just go down anyway? Sort of surprise them. There's nothing they can do once you get there. Then you could see for yourself what's going on."

"I thought of that," Kati admitted, "but from the sound of my mother's voice, it would upset her more if I just showed up. No," she said resignedly, "I suppose I'll just have to wait for the holidays."

"In that case, try to stop worrying. I'm sure it's nothing anyway. Maybe you're a little homesick. But we have a cure for that! Can you change fast enough to make a seven-o'clock movie?" Heidi's enthusiastic spirit was contagious, and Kati couldn't help but agree with her friend. But as they sat together that night in the darkened theater, not even the handsome Sean Connery and the weird-looking Odd Job, performing their latest James Bond antics, could tear Kati's thoughts away from the Waldhotel.

Staying on campus over the short break wasn't as bad as Kati had thought it would be. There was plenty to do every minute. Those students who lived too far away to go home for such a short time planned continuous activities—dinners, parties, trips to exhibitions, visits to museums. Kati also used some of the time to study for her upcoming finals.

The Christmas holidays came before they knew it. The saga of finals was over, and the two girls couldn't wait to board the train south.

"The nicest thing about being home will be sleeping in my own bed, with my own nice cotton sheets," Heidi announced as they settled into two facing window seats. They always tried to sit opposite each other so that they could talk and laugh nonstop during the trip without enduring the stares of other passengers who wished to travel in silence. "The ones they have in the dorm are awful, so stiff. It must have really been an adjustment for you, being used to having yours changed every single day!" She was always teasing Kati about her luxurious life at the hotel.

When Kati finally reached the hotel late that night, she sensed that many things had changed during the short time she had been away. The plants outside the entryway looked as if they needed a little attention, the furniture in the lobby didn't shine quite as brightly as it always had, the bouquets of flowers on the tables in the dining room didn't look as fresh as she remembered, and the rug on the grand staircase appeared to be in need of a good vacuuming. Of course everyone was so glad to see their favorite young woman and there were so many things they all wanted to know about her life at school that for the first few days she didn't have time to think about those things, or to investigate why they looked as they did. She had hardly seen Eva-Maria at all. Every time she tried to find her, she was dressing to go out, or just coming in and wanting to be alone.

On the third night after her arrival, Margarethe was in Kati's room turning down the bedclothes for the night. Now that Kati was gone and Eva-Maria was a very mature nineteen, there was really nothing left for Margarethe to do. Mostly she helped Tilla, but she knew she would soon have to decide what she wanted to do next. It was hard, the Meiers were so much like family to her, she hated even to think of leaving. But there was talk that she might go to another family soon, even though she loved being at the Waldhotel so much. So when Kati came home to visit, she wanted to do everything she could for the lovely girl she adored.

Kati noticed that the linens had not been changed that morning.

"Margarethe, what's going on around here?" she asked.

"What do you mean?"

Kati flopped down on the bed and crossed her legs. "Surely you've noticed, Nana. Things aren't right. I felt it the minute I walked through the door, but I didn't say anything then because I didn't want to upset Mother. Everyone has been so busy around here, getting ready for Christmas, that I still didn't say anything today. But now it's just too much. Nothing looks crisp and clean. I've been in some of the rooms and the housekeeping clearly isn't up to standards. Now I see that the sheets aren't even being changed every day. What is going on? Please tell me."

There was such concern in Kati's eyes, such distress over what she had correctly observed, that Margarethe was torn between telling her everything she knew or had heard from the staff and merely trying

to assure her that her worries were unfounded. She ended up somewhere in between the two.

"Well, Kati, you're right. Things have changed quite a bit since
you left. But I don't think there's anything to worry about. I'm sure
that your mother and father have everything under control. It's just
that Herr von Hassler is a bit different than what we've been used to
all these years."

"Different?" Kati cried. "It's pretty obvious to me that he
doesn't know what he's doing. What *has* he done, anyway, cut the
staff to nothing? Tonight there weren't even enough busboys to clear
the dishes before the next course arrived. And now the sheets aren't
even changed daily," she pointed to her wrinkled turned-down covers. "I think maybe he's been spending too much time with my sister
and not enough time on the business."

Margarethe was surprised that Kati knew about the relationship
between Peter and Eva-Maria. But she supposed that anyone with
half an eye could see what was happening. Tilla and Johannes had
both refused to recognize the seriousness of Eva-Maria's involvement
with Peter. Tilla still clung to the hope that it would pass any day.

"You could be right about that, but as I said, I'm sure there's
nothing for you to worry about. Now get some sleep. Tomorrow's
Christmas Eve, and you know what a big day that is around here."
She kissed Kati gently on the cheek as she had every night since the
child was a day old. But tonight was the first night in seventeen years
that she felt she had not been able to put the young girl's fears to rest.

Kati was awakened the next morning by the sound of a loud voice. It
was the most frightening sound she had ever heard. At first she was
certain that it was the noise from a nightmare and that now that she
was awake it would go away. But it didn't stop. She lay in her bed
paralyzed, unable to move. It took her a few seconds to recognize the
voice as belonging to her mother. She was screaming and crying all
at the same time. Kati had never heard sounds like that before. Tilla
was a softspoken woman who never gave in to emotional outbursts.
Her every action was ladylike. Composure was ultimately important
to her. Even when Karl-Gustav died, she had only cried in the privacy
of her room.

The sounds continued. Kati had to find out what was causing this horrible scene. She grabbed her robe from the foot of the bed, hurriedly put on her slippers, and ran down the hall to her parents' bedroom. She stopped short outside the door as the tirade continued.

"I warned you, don't say that I didn't warn you, Johannes," her mother yelled. "How could things have gone so far? Right before our eyes. I just simply don't understand. I'll never understand. He's stolen all of our money, everything we had in life, everything that was left to us, that my father worked so hard for . . . and now," she sobbed, "if that's not enough, he's stolen our daughter too. Oh, Johannes, what are we going to do?"

Kati's father mumbled something she could not understand, and she pressed her ear closer to the outer door.

Tilla's next words explained what she had missed.

"What do you mean, it will be all right? How can you possibly say that? It will never be all right. Everything is gone—every penny, everything—we'll never be able to rebuild the hotel now. You were the one who was supposed to be watching the money. Oh, Johannes, how could this all have happened right before our eyes?" Again her mother burst into uncontrollable sobs.

Kati was petrified. She couldn't face the idea of knocking on the door, for then they would be even more upset to know that she had been outside listening. Her mind raced with the thoughts of the terrible thing that had happened. She had no doubt that Peter was the one they were talking about, the one who had run off with the hotel's remaining money. But Eva-Maria too? Could her only sister really be that stupid, that driven to escape the hotel that she would help to steal their family's money? She pressed her ear so tightly against the wall that it began to ache.

Inside her parents' room, the terrible news continued to unfold.

"Tilla," Johannes began, but stopped suddenly, aware of the impact his next words would bring. "Tilla," he began again, "I knew about the money."

Upon hearing his words, Tilla ceased crying at once. "What can you possibly mean, Johannes? You knew, you knew he was stealing, and yet you continued to allow it? Whatever can you be saying?"

Johannes sat down wearily in one of the bedside chairs.

He revealed everything. The plans for advertising, the attempts to improve the business, his agreement not to mention a word of it to Tilla. As he repeated his version of the story, it became more and more unbelievable, even to him, that he had fallen for Peter's narrowly disguised plan. But Peter had obviously been more clever than he. Johannes had bought his story lock, stock, and barrel. In the process he had deceived his wife, perhaps damaged his marriage beyond repair, and lost a daughter.

"Tilla, I did it all for you . . . for you, and the girls," he cried, his voice echoing the pain in his heart. "Please, you must believe me," he begged.

The lobby was empty. Hans, the late-night receptionist, sat in his chair, preparing to start making the requested morning wake-up calls. Everything else was perfectly still. It was only then that Kati realized how early it was. A glance at the enormous antique clock over the revolving door confirmed that it was a quarter to six on the morning of December 24th. The revolving door remained locked from the night before, so she went immediately to the side door that was always open. Clutching her robe even tighter, she dashed across the alleyway to the entrance of the staff quarters. A light dusting of snow made the pavement slippery beneath her lightly clad feet.

Glancing up to the windows on the third floor, she could see that only two lights were burning in the early morning. Without even counting, she knew whose they were. She tore open the front door of the staff quarters and sprinted up the stairs. She was at the top of the third level before the *minuterie* on the first level had clicked off. She tried to walk quietly down the corridor, not wanting to wake anyone who was still sleeping. Her breath was made audible by the combination of running, fear, and the overwhelming need to find out exactly what had happened. Her heart pounded, a result of fear and anger.

The door of the second-to-last room on the right was open. She peeked in, timidly at first, and then when she was certain that there was no one there, she entered. The room was in total disarray. Every drawer in the tall English chests had been pulled out and left there, revealing the empty spaces. The doors of the closets that lined the walls were also open, the floor inside littered with tissues and plastic from dry-cleaning wrappings. A single black sock lay in the bottom of the closet. The sheets on the bed were bunched together in a twisted pile. The pillows were stacked up against the headboard. Luggage destination tags from previous flights had been torn from the bags and left on the crumpled sheets. In a silver bucket perched on the windowsill sat a half-empty bottle of champagne. Next to it were two glasses. Kati thought she recognized the traces of Scarlet's Revenge lipstick on one of them. How fitting, she thought. They had celebrated their coup, the theft of the hotel's money, and then packed up and left. Left in a pretty big hurry, it appeared. And where did they go? Why did they leave in such a rush? Only one person might have the answers for her.

She walked out of the room and continued down to the last room, the room where the second light she had seen from below was burning. That door was open as well. Dieter sat at his tiny desk in front of the window. He was dressed in a pair of blue-striped pajamas and a navy woolen robe. His feet were covered in heavy sheepskin slippers. He remained unaware of Kati's presence. He merely sat at the desk and stared out the window.

"Dieter," Kati finally said in a quiet, gentle tone.

Her voice startled him. He turned to look at her. She saw the face of a very old man. Gone were the sparkling eyes, the wide smile that were his trademarks. Never had she seen him look so serious, so troubled. Only at that instant did she begin to realize what had actually happened. But still so many questions remained unanswered.

"Oh, Dieter," she cried as she ran to him, her arms thrown open, "I've just heard the most terrible argument, and the awful news. Dieter, what has gone on here? Tell me everything, please, now."

Dieter in turn opened his arms to hug his favorite young woman with whom he would now have to share the events of the tragedy that was certain to have a great effect on her entire life. He held her close to him for a minute, feeling her tremble with fear and cold.

"Look at you!" he scolded. "You should never have run out of the building without proper clothing on. It snowed last night and it's freezing outside. It must be below zero now. You'll be sick for sure."

"I know," she agreed, "but I didn't think. All I wanted to do was find out more about what is happening around here."

Her enormous eyes searched his, and he knew he would have to tell her the entire story. Even though he felt it should probably come from a member of the family, he was aware that neither Tilla nor Johannes was in any condition to explain the situation to their daughter.

"All right, Kati, I'll share with you everything I know, which I'm sure isn't all there is. But first you're going to have some tea, and bundle up in a warm blanket." Dieter went to his own set of closets, a duplicate of the empty ones Kati had just seen down the hall. He handed her a handknit throw that he kept in his room to use when he was reading. She took it thankfully and wrapped herself tightly in the soft cover. She sat in the only other chair in the small room and waited for Dieter to return from the staff kitchen down the hall with their tea.

The steaming liquid warmed her. As Dieter continued to talk, Kati sipped her second and third cups slowly, mesmerized by the wicked, evil tale he told, unbelieving and unable to accept that it was her family, her mother, her father, and her sister about whom he spoke, to whom all this was happening. It seemed so foreign to her, so incredible that anyone was capable of such deceit, such dishonesty. The consequences of what he was saying only began to sink in.

"Did you speak to Eva-Maria this morning?" she said.

"No, Kati, I didn't have a chance. By the time I heard all the ruckus, it was too late. I looked out my window just in time to see Peter coming out the front door with the bags, the money, and the jewelry, and to see your sister get into his car. Then they drove off right away. That's when I went over to wake your mother and father and to tell them what I suspected had happened. He really took the hotel for a ride. I'm sure we won't know the whole of it for a long time."

"What I can't understand is why no one suspected him before now," Kati logically asked. "Someone can't just be stealing all the time, for all the time he's been here, and not be noticed by someone, somehow. Could he have been that clever?"

Of course Dieter knew all about Herr Klebe's suspicions, and Johannes's refusal to recognize them, but he wasn't about to go into all of that with her.

"It's a mystery, Kati. I think that when people are normally trusting and honest, like most or all of the people at the hotel, it never occurs to anyone that there might be a thief in their midst." He knew it sounded exactly like the weak excuse it was, but Kati seemed to accept it.

"Particularly when he and Eva-Maria were so involved. I'm sure no one wanted to disturb that boat. Then it becomes doubly hard to investigate, I suppose."

Dieter looked at Kati, unable to respond. She was so right in her perceptions of what had happened. Peter was regarded as "hands-off" by all members of the staff. For whatever reason, Johannes felt he could do no wrong. He had protected him to the end.

"Well, I guess there's nothing more to do right now. I'm going back to see if I can help my mother." Kati hugged Dieter and left the room.

As she passed Peter's room, she heard a noise coming from inside. Slowly she entered. "Eva-Maria," she cried when she saw her sister down on all fours, searching for something.

"Kati," she gasped, shocked at her presence. "What on earth are you doing here?"

"I could ask you the same thing, but I think I've heard it all already. Eva-Maria, what is going on?"

"Isn't it obvious I'm looking for something?" she answered.

"That's not what I meant, and you know it. What I want to know is how you could possibly do this to Mother and Father? I was awakened this morning by the sound of Mother's crying."

Kati's pleas had very little effect on Eva-Maria. She continued to scrounge around on the floor, looking frantically under the bed and dresser for something she had evidently forgotten. She stopped for one moment when she realized what her sister had said. She looked up at her. Kati could see that she, too, had been crying. "I'm sorry for that, Kati, really I am. I never meant to hurt anyone. I only know that what I'm doing is right for me. For Peter and me. I love him. I have to go with him." She got up, apparently giving up on her search.

"I've got to go now. Peter's waiting for me."

"Where are you going? You'll never be able to escape," Kati said.

"I can't tell you. Don't worry, no one will press charges against

Peter. He hasn't done anything wrong. It's all Father's fault. But I'll have to explain that later. Take care, Kati, I'll call you later from wherever we are. Please remember what I told you. Don't get stuck here like I almost did." She kissed her sister on the cheek.

Eva-Maria rushed out the door before Kati could say another word. By the time she had run down the stairs, Eva-Maria had disappeared. Kati felt even more confused and helpless than she had earlier.

CHAPTER

9

CHRISTMAS DAY was among the longest and saddest in memory. Not even Karl-Gustav's death had cast such a pall over the entire staff. At least then they had been united in grief. Now everyone was just waiting and watching and wondering. No one really knew what would happen next. Kati sat with her mother and father in the dining room, decorated for the holidays with glorious swags of thick pine. Shiny gold ornaments peeked out from the lush boughs every few inches. The thousands of tiny white lights that decorated the trees trailing down to the Lichtentaler Allee didn't seem to sparkle as brightly as they had in years past.

Looking at the joyous diners only seemed to depress the family more. It heightened their realization that this year they had very little to be thankful for.

Kati tried desperately to brighten her parents' spirits.

"Let's look at it this way," she insisted, "we still have each other, and that should be enough to start the ball rolling again." She tried her hardest not to make the remark sound flippant or sarcastic, she really meant it, but it didn't come out that way. Her mother was touched by her sentiments, but she was too despondent even to speak. She merely took Kati's hand in hers and gave her a pained smile. Johannes stared blankly into the room. He was still shocked by the stupidity of his mistake.

Kati was persistent. She felt an overwhelming need to try to pull them together as a family.

"I know what," she announced, "I'll stay here next semester and help everyone get back on track. I'll work the front desk with Dieter, and you, Mutti, can get back to doing all of those things you were doing so well before he arrived." She couldn't bear to say his name, not yet anyway. "That's exactly what we'll do," she continued, her enthusiasm growing, "I'll notify the university first thing tomorrow that I won't be returning next semester. I can go back next fall, and nothing will be lost."

"You'll do nothing of the sort," Tilla spoke at last. The thought of her younger daughter abandoning her education, no matter what the reason, was out of the question. "You'll go back to school next week as planned. Isn't that correct, Johannes?" She turned to her husband only to be met with his vacant stare.

Even though she didn't like the response, Kati was glad that she had forced her mother to say something.

"That's right, Kati, there is no reason even to consider staying out of school. Your mother and I will be able to handle the situation. We still have to assess just how much damage this man has done, how much he has actually stolen. Hopefully it won't be as bad as we originally thought and we'll be able to carry on. In any case, there is absolutely no reason to think of staying here. Your education is crucial for your future." Johannes's tone of voice was hollow and unconvincing.

"But my future is here," she implored, looking around at the guest-filled room. "Don't you understand? The hotel is my future. I've told you so many times. All I want to do is be a part of the hotel. It's ours, it belongs to us, and we have got to do anything and everything to save it, to improve it. Don't you understand, I love this place, and I don't ever want to work anywhere but here." Kati tried to tone down her emotions, but felt that maybe she had already gone too far. But perhaps they understood better now how passionate she was about the Waldhotel.

As it turned out, she returned to school a day earlier than she had planned. Heidi's father had to drive up to Frankfurt for a business meeting. It was much easier, and a lot more fun, for all of them to ride together instead of having to struggle with all of her luggage on the train.

They packed up the roomy Mercedes sedan, taking with them all the things the girls had wanted to have at school but had been unable to carry on the train. Heidi took her stereo, and Kati was delighted that there was room for her small television set.

Despite her happiness at sharing the trip back, Kati's mood remained somber. Her mind relived over and over again the terrible events of the past few days. She stared gloomily out the window as they sped through the small villages on their way north. But Heidi and her father were determined to make her smile. They had started out early in the morning, and by lunchtime they were near the famous university town of Heidelberg. Herr Fichtl insisted on stopping. Heidi's father was handsome and fun; he could have been her older brother rather than her father. He treated them to lunch at a student hangout near the old schloss. He even allowed them to each have a frosty stein of the local beer. By the time they had finished their hearty lunch, Kati's spirits had brightened considerably. Back on the autobahn they laughed and sang old songs. Never had she had such a relaxed, happy time with her own father. Johannes was far too reserved, far too conservative to participate in anything like what they had done.

The spring semester was much more demanding than the fall. Kati had chosen to take one more class than the normal load, and she was finding it difficult to keep up with her studies as well as take part in all the social activities Heidi was constantly cooking up. She worried daily about her mother. Every time they spoke, it seemed as if Tilla was carrying the weight of the entire world on her shoulders. She insisted that everything was fine, that they were going to be able to recover from the losses caused by Peter's mismanagement and theft. But each time after she hung up, Kati felt that her mother was holding back the truth, still trying to protect her from the realities they would all have to face eventually. She spoke often to Dieter, who refused to burden her with all the details of the situation. He would assure her that everyone was trying as hard as they could, but he, too, failed to convince her.

The police had been called in to try to find Peter and Eva-Maria, but their efforts had been unsuccessful. So far they hadn't returned to the townhouse in Paris. Their last verified stay had been three days in the Presidential Suite at the Hotel de Paris in Monte Carlo. Her mother didn't seem to be pressing the police too hard in their search, and this was bewildering to her.

· · ·

"Stop worrying!" Heidi would command her friend every time she saw the look on her face that told her Kati had recently had a conversation with either one of her parents or Dieter. "I've told you a thousand times that everything is going to be all right. Now please, Kati, get that sad look off your face and get dressed. We're due at the dance in twenty minutes."

Kati stood in front of the small mirror in her dorm room, surveying a black skirt she had borrowed from Deirdre. Since the crisis at the hotel she had not wanted to ask for any extra money. She was sure that there probably wasn't any, and she didn't want to be a burden to her parents. Particularly since they wouldn't allow her to quit school and work at the hotel. But tonight as she looked in the mirror at the skirt that really didn't fit her properly, and the old white silk blouse she had worn so often, she was momentarily sorry that she hadn't asked for just a small amount, just enough to have bought a new dress. Heidi had dragged her along when she shopped for the pretty new outfit she was wearing, and when Kati refused to buy something also, Heidi had offered to pay for a new dress for her. But Kati wouldn't hear of it. One thing she would never accept was charity. Her Opa had taught her that. It wasn't something a member of her family would ever do.

Well, she would just have to make it through the night. It was only the spring dance anyway, and it would be over soon enough. Even though she didn't have a brand-new dress, her hair shone brightly, her skin was clearer and more translucent than any of the other girls', and her internal beauty showed through brilliantly. Still, for a brief moment, she could not help but feel like an ugly duckling who lacked the fine feathers of her dormmates.

"I can't wait for Easter break," she confided to Heidi as they walked toward the gymnasium where the dance was to be held. "I can't wait to get home and see what's really happening, how bad things are since Peter left."

"I can't believe you're thinking about that now," Heidi complained. "Look, we're on our way to one of the biggest events of the year. It's time to have fun, to dance, to meet some new people . . . maybe even some boys," she admitted. "After all, Sigrid met some guy at the last dance, and they're going to London over spring break." Sigrid, Heidi's roommate, was very similar to Deirdre in her approach to academic life.

"Boys," Kati spat the word from her mouth as if she had just tasted something unpleasant. "Just a few weeks ago you were so concerned that maybe I had already met a boy. Did you change your mind about them over the holiday?" she teased.

"All I'm saying is that some of them might not be so bad. You'll never know if you don't at least try and act like you'd like to meet them. Now, promise me you'll smile and have some fun," Heidi insisted, putting her arm around her best friend.

"Okay, I'll try, I promise I will," Kati said with commitment as they neared the entrance to the big event.

Once inside the dance, neither Kati nor Heidi lacked for attention from their male classmates.

"Hey, he's pretty cute," Heidi commented about one of the boys who had just asked Kati to dance. She had politely refused. "What's wrong with you? You promised you'd try. Saying no to that handsome creature is not what I'd call trying very hard."

Kati forced herself to smile. "Okay, I promise. I'll dance with the next one who asks me."

"That's better," Heidi said.

They didn't have to wait long. The next dance was a slow one, and three strapping undergraduates approached Kati. Of course she was flattered. Recalling her Frau Bauer training, she said yes to the first one who asked. The young man held her gently in his hesitant arms and moved her awkwardly around the floor.

"Thank you," she said as the music stopped, again remembering her impeccable training sessions in the Grand Salon.

"Hey, Kati," the young man said, not wanting her to get away from him so quickly, "a bunch of us are having a party at Erich's after the dance. Would you like to come?" he asked, anxiously hoping for a positive response. Erich's was their local hangout. Everyone went there on the weekends to drink beer. It was noisy and boisterous, and she just wasn't in the mood.

"No, I can't, thank you. I've got to be up early tomorrow. But I'm sure Heidi will want to go. Why don't you ask her?" she suggested.

The boy's face fell in disappointment. Of course he would also invite Heidi, but he wasn't interested in her. He only had eyes for the beautiful Kati. "Well, sure, I'll ask Heidi too. But I really hoped you would come. Come on, Kati, you're always so serious. Are you sure you won't come?"

"Really I can't," she insisted, "maybe next time."

Kati stayed for another hour. She danced several more dances with some of the most popular boys on campus, boys that other girls would have given their eyeteeth just to talk to, let alone dance with. It was evident that all of the young men found her healthy good looks and sweet smile irresistible. None of them seemed to care that she wore a simple skirt and blouse. Maybe she was too serious. But right now she was far too occupied with her family, or what was left of it now that Eva-Maria had denounced them all by running off with Peter, to become involved with anyone.

At ten o'clock she quietly excused herself and snuck out by a side door. She walked back to the dorm alone, lost in her own thoughts, grateful for the silence of the night.

10

*H*ER SPIRITS soared when the last week before break arrived. Finally it was Friday. She and Heidi would leave on the four-o'clock train and would be in Baden-Baden in time for dinner. Kati had packed that morning and her suitcase sat in her room ready to go.

As usual, Heidi was rushing around until the very last minute. There was never enough time to do everything. Disorganization was her specialty. Plus, she always knew she had the safety valve of her good friend if she got into a pinch—like right now.

"Kati, please, you've got to do me a big favor. Oh, will you? Say yes, please!" Heidi pleaded as they rushed from literature class toward chemistry. They were already ten minutes late.

"Tell me what it is first," Kati answered. "You know I never say yes before I know what the favor is. Especially with you," she joked.

"It's not *that* big a deal, it really isn't. But it's important."

"Okay, I'm listening."

"Well, you see, I checked out three books from the library. You know, for that literature project we had to do. Today is the last day they can be returned, and I won't have any time to do it because I have to meet with Professor Wessel after this class. If I keep them until we get back, it will cost a fortune in fines. Oh, Kati, could you please take them back for me?"

It sounded too easy to Kati. There had to be some catch.

"Sure," she agreed. "Here, give them to me." She held her arms toward the heavy stack of books Heidi was carrying.

"Well, that's just it," Heidi admitted. "I don't have them with me now. I brought my stuff for the trip," she said, displaying her overstuffed duffel bag that served as a makeshift suitcase, "but I left the books."

Kati's premonition was coming true before her eyes. "Where are they?"

Heidi put on her sweetest how-could-you-possibly-say-no-to-your-best friend-smile and replied, "They're in my room."

"In your *room?*" Kati cried. "No wonder you said it was a big favor."

The dorm was almost a mile away, in the opposite direction of the library. Going there and then back to return the books was a long trip that would leave Kati very little time to make it to the station before the train left. But she didn't have any more classes after chemistry. And she was packed. If she rushed, she could make it.

"Fine, I'll do it, but you really will owe me one, or two maybe."

Heidi kissed her. "Oh, thank you, thank you, Kati. I'll make it up to you, I promise. They're in a pile on top of my desk. You won't have any trouble finding them."

"I'm sure," Kati said, shaking her head. "It'll be like finding a needle in a haystack. I know how your desk looks!"

They entered the classroom fifteen minutes late and received stares of disdain from the very strict professor.

The timing was very tight. Kati would have to drop the books swiftly and leave directly from the library if she was to make the four-o'clock train. She practically ran across the campus back to her own room, where she grabbed her own suitcase. Then she sped on toward Heidi's dorm, continuing her race against the clock.

Heidi's room matched her personality. It wasn't that she was sloppy, it was just that she had so many things going on at one time that nothing ever seemed to be in its proper place. Clothes were everywhere—parts of various outfits adorned the chairs, bed, and windowsills. Party invitations and pictures from a recent ski trip cluttered the bulletin board that hung on the closet door. Just as Kati had predicted, the desk had not been spared her unorthodox way of housekeeping. Mounds of papers covered the work space. A hat topped one pile, a scarf another, and a handbag, its contents spewing out, lay on top of yet another stack. Kati sighed. The books must be there somewhere. Heidi had said they would be easy to find. Easy for her maybe. She threw down her coat and suitcase, and approached the mess. She lifted one pile . . . not there. Another, not there. One more . . . no luck. Perhaps the best method would be to sit down and move everything around until she uncovered them. At last she felt a hard edge, something that could pass for a hardbound book. Yes, that was one. Now, only two more to go. The other one was close by. One more and she could begin her mad dash to the library. Just as she was moving the last possible stack to see what was underneath, her eye was caught by a piece of stationery. It was typed on Herr Fichtl's office letterhead. In bold print the subject of the letter was entitled: Katharina Meier Tuition. She grabbed the letter off the top of the stack and could not help but read it.

Dear Heidi,
Enclosed you will find a check to cover Kati's tuition for the spring semester. As we discussed on the phone last week, after the terrible incident at the hotel her parents are in dire financial trouble, and I've offered to pay her school-ing for as long as it is necessary. There have been several bids from outside sources to purchase the hotel, but so far the Meiers have continued to resist considering a sale. However, this may become the only way to help them re-cover from the damage that has been done. In any case, your mother and I are doing this because of your friend-ship with Kati. Of course her parents are most concerned that she never finds out about this arrangement, so you must be careful never to mention anything about it. Please forward the check to the bursar's office as soon as you receive it. They are anxious for payment to be made.

I hope you are having fun, but in addition, that you are studying hard. Don't ignore your science courses just because you find them difficult and time-consuming. Your education will not be well-rounded if you only concentrate on literature and parties.

Your mother and I miss you very much and can't wait to see you over the Easter break.

With love,
Father

Kati sat motionless for several minutes. She was shocked at what she had just read. Shocked and terrified and troubled all at the same time. How could her parents not have told her? How could they turn to Heidi's parents and ask them for such a thing? And why didn't Heidi tell her? They talked about the hotel constantly. Heidi knew it was the only thing on Kati's mind, that she thought about it every minute of the day, and that she was always worried about what would happen to it. How could she have kept her silence when the best thing would have been to tell her the truth? Then Kati could have left school and gone to help at the Waldhotel. The reality of what she had accidentally come across now started to sink in. Tears spilled down her cheeks as she stared at the paper in her hand. The check had been removed, probably deposited last week. Even though she knew she should be appreciative and thankful that Heidi's father was so generous, instead she merely felt betrayed—betrayed by her best friend, and by her parents.

It was good that she was on her way home. She could confront the situation face-to-face and come to some conclusion about the best thing to do. Staying in school while she could be helping at the hotel was not the answer. That much she knew. Beyond that, the issues became cloudy. There was still so much she didn't know. Quickly she stuffed the letter in her duffel, grabbed the library books, and headed back across campus.

Somehow Kati managed to hide her emotions from Heidi. The only clue signaling that something was wrong was when Kati refused Heidi's offer of some chocolates.

"Are you kidding? I've never, ever seen you say no to chocolates," Heidi said. They were Kati's weakness. She could eat them at any hour.

"I'm just not hungry, that's all," she insisted. Even looking at the treats that usually appealed to her so much made her sick to her stomach.

"You've never had to be hungry before to eat five or six of them," Heidi countered. "I know, you're just saving yourself for the incredible dinner they've probably been working on for days, anticipating your arrival tonight. I bet Chef Kellner will have prepared all your favorite things. Wienerschnitzel, bündnerfleisch, spätzle, and that sinful plum cake. Mmmmm . . . I wish I were going home with you."

Chef Kellner. Kati wondered if he was still even there. He was a very good chef, one of the best in Germany. If there was no money left at the hotel, she was certain that his salary was no longer affordable.

Heidi's mention of all that food made her even more nauseous. She smiled weakly. "No, I'm just a little tired, I guess. I think I'll try to get some sleep before we arrive."

This seemed to satisfy her friend. Heidi closed her eyes and appeared to be trying to get a little rest also. The train sped on as the two girls neared their home.

The thought of Herr Kellner and all the others at the hotel was too much for Kati to bear. She turned her face even more toward the window so that should Heidi wake up, she would not see her. But it was too late. Heidi had already seen the tears streaming down the sides of her face.

"Kati," Heidi cried out, "I knew something was wrong. Now what is it?"

Heidi's discovery only made things worse. Kati began to sob loudly. No longer could she hide what she had so painfully found out.

Her crying continued. "I know," was all she could get out before the sobs began again.

"You know?" Heidi repeated, puzzled and concerned at the same time. "You know what?" Kati's shoulders shook uncontrollably. "Kati, how can I help you if you don't tell me what it is? Now, you're obviously very upset. Please try to calm down and tell me what it is." She reached forward and took Kati's hands in hers. The train raced on at full speed.

Kati began taking in big gulps of air, trying to arrest her emotions. "I know," she began again, "about the money."

"The money?" Heidi was genuinely puzzled. She couldn't begin to imagine what she was talking about. "Kati, you're not making any sense at all. What money?"

"The money," she repeated, this time her tone steadier. "The money for my tuition. The money your father sent."

Only at the mention of her father did it register in Heidi's mind what Kati could possibly be so upset about. She was stunned. At first she couldn't figure out how she could ever have found out, but then it dawned on her. Her desk. She had left the letter somewhere on her desk. Of course that was it. Her desk was such a mess. She was so careless. This time her disorganization had cost her. Trying to do her a big favor, her friend had probably had to look everywhere for those stupid books, and while doing so had discovered her father's letter. Of course that was it. Oh, how could she have been so thoughtless? So foolish. She should have destroyed the letter immediately after she had deposited the check. Now the damage was done, and as she looked at her friend's tear-stained face, with its swollen eyes and red nose, she shared the pain she had caused her.

Heidi reached across the narrow space that separated them and squeezed Kati's hand gently, but her fingers remained limp, unresponsive to her efforts.

"Oh, Kati, I'm so sorry. You were never supposed to have found out, to have seen that letter. Certainly you should never have found out like this. We're only trying to help, you have to believe that. It was the least we could do. I'm sure your parents are going to be able to solve the hotel's problems, no matter how big they are. I'm sure of it." But Kati was unbelieving. She just continued to stare at her friend, a combination of anger and pain stretched across her face.

"Why didn't you tell me, Heidi? You knew that I would want to go home, to try to help my parents in any way I could. The hotel is our heritage, don't you understand? It's been in our family for generations. It's the only history we have. You know how I feel about it, and yet you allowed this to happen. . . . I just don't understand." And again she began to cry. She was so terribly frustrated. First her parents didn't understand how she felt, and now her supposed best friend had participated in this secret arrangement. It was all very confusing.

"Please believe me," Heidi begged. "I only did it so that you could finish school and then go back to the hotel."

"By then it will be too late," Kati cried. "At this rate, if there isn't even any money for me to continue school, things must be really awful. It may be too late to save it already. In any case, the only thing I know for sure right now is that I won't be taking this train back with you next week. Now that I know I was a charity case, I'm never going back."

"You were never a charity case, so forget that argument," Heidi replied forcefully, offended that her friend regarded her family's efforts to help as charity. "We were only trying to help. It was never charity." But she knew how strongly Kati felt about her family, her pride ran very deep, and she was really not surprised by her reaction.

Kati's temper softened when she looked up and saw the hurt on Heidi's face. "I'm sorry," she offered, "I know you were only trying to help. But I've got to stay in Baden-Baden and do whatever I can to help the hotel, for all our sakes."

"I understand," Heidi said. "I wish you all the success in the world. I know how important it is to you, and to your mother and father. I'm going to miss you, though, and you know that if there is anything we can do to help, not only with money, you'll let me know."

"I will," Kati agreed.

"I'm going to miss you," Heidi repeated as she kissed her dear friend good-bye and they walked toward the two cars that had been dispatched to take them to their separate destinations. They hugged each other tightly, for a minute longer than usual, knowing in their young hearts that with Kati's discovery the nature of their friendship had changed forever. Of course they would always share the bond of friendship that growing up together had created, but suddenly their innocence and lightness was gone, for one of them was now off to confront the first major challenge of her life.

CHAPTER

11

"Y OU LOOK WONDERFUL," Kati complimented her mother. Tilla was sitting at her dressing table, putting the finishing touches on her makeup. Her face looked tired; the strain of the last few months was beginning to take its toll on her skin. Its texture was no longer as radiant, its color not as healthy. Quickly she ran the tip of her makeup brush over her cheeks one more time in an effort to brighten her appearance. She wore a simple, teal-blue silk dress. The skirt was pleated and the belt at the waistline accentuated her still-trim figure. In fact she was even thinner than usual, having lost several pounds from worrying so much about the situation at the Waldhotel. That was probably the one positive effect the entire situation had wrought.

"It's sweet of you to say, darling," she said, turning to look at Kati as she entered her room. They both knew she didn't look nearly as well as she used to, the dress was from several seasons ago, and her shoes were not the latest fashion, but hearing the praise from her daughter lifted her spirits considerably.

They had all agreed that tonight they would cast their worries aside, if only temporarily, for it was the evening of Margarethe's farewell dinner. Last month she had decided to leave the Meier family to take a position with a couple in her hometown. They were in their twenties, only beginning to start a family. They had just had their second child and felt they could no longer handle everything by themselves. So after almost twenty years from the day she had arrived, Margarethe was leaving the family she had come to love so very much. She would pack her few belongings and depart in the morning. So tonight Johannes and Tilla and Kati had agreed not to let anything spoil their evening. They simply wanted to laugh, to talk about old times, and to wish Margarethe every happiness in her new venture. They would all miss her terribly, but they fully understood her need to move on. It had been a long time since there had really been anything for her to do at the hotel.

"No, I mean it," Kati insisted. "You look great." She crossed the elegant dressing room and adjusted the collar on her mother's dress. "There, that's better. Now, if you just put your brooch on, you'll really be sensational. Here, give it to me and I'll do it for you."

A shocked look crossed Tilla's face. She turned away from her daughter. Trying desperately to regain her composure, to stall for a few precious seconds, she walked toward the mirror. "I don't really think it needs anything, do you? I think it looks just fine as it is. The pin would only look too fussy, too dressy."

Kati had never heard anything like this before. "Too dressy, are you kidding, Mother? Of course it needs it, it's the plainest dress you own. It won't look complete without it." Tilla tried to look unconvinced. "Okay, let's just try it, then; we'll see what you think. If you don't like it, we'll take it off right away. Let's just try it. Now, where is it?"

The moment of truth was near. Tilla knew she had only seconds in which to think of something to tell her insistent daughter. Her mind sped in an effort to come up with some excuse, but it was useless.

"Mutti, come on, we'll be late."

"Kati, the pin isn't here," Tilla said with finality. Just as the words left her mouth, she thought about telling her that it was out being cleaned or repaired, or that it had been stolen, but it was too late. She would never believe it if she lied to her and told her she had lost it. No, it was her most precious possession, the diamond brooch that Johannes had given her so many years ago. She would never be so careless as to lose it. No, she would be forced to tell her the truth. The awful, painful truth. That she had pawned the pin last month in order to make the payroll at the hotel. It wasn't a very valuable item, certainly its sentimental value far outweighed the value of its stones. But she had persuaded the owner of the shop to give her enough money to enable her to pay the employees. She had begged him to put the pin away, not to display it in the case, for it was one of the prettiest items they had, and she was certain that it would sell immediately. He said he couldn't promise her that. After all, he had paid her more than he had planned to and he couldn't afford to let such a beautiful item stay in a drawer on the off chance that she would be able to come back and claim it. So the next day when she walked along the Sophienstrasse she had tried not to look in the shop's window, but she couldn't help it. There it was. The man had cleaned and shined the only piece of jewelry she loved so much. It had been given to her by her husband with such affection, with such adoration, at a time when their love had been new, not tarnished as it was now. He had made a little handwritten sign telling of the origin of the piece and the price. In the past it would have seemed such a small amount to Tilla. She would have been able to go into the store and buy it without thinking twice about it, but now every cent was so valuable to them, just to keep their heads above water. Every day after that she would either cross the street to avoid seeing the brooch or walk hurriedly past the window. But only the day before yesterday as she was passing, her eye traveled to the space where the pin had been. It was almost as if a magnet had reached out and drawn her eye into the vitrine. She stared at the empty space, wanting so not to believe what she knew must be true. The rest of the window had remained exactly as it had been, no other piece of jewelry had been touched. It must have been sold. She continued to stare into the vitrine for a few minutes longer. Tears filled her eyes and she did not even try to stop them as she wept. She wept more for the past and what had been rather than for the diamond pin. She had worn it so proudly for so many years, a visible, continuing sign of her husband's love for her. It represented a part of her life that was over, and she was uncertain whether the emotions she had felt for the lovely man who had given her the pin could ever be recaptured again.

"Well, where it is?" Kati's voice broke her thoughts. "What has happened to it?"

Tilla knew from the innocent look on her face that the news that she had pawned the brooch would come as a complete shock.

"Kati, I had to," she started out warily, "I had to in order to make the payroll. But I'll get it back," she lied, unable to tell her that it was gone forever. "I'll get it back just as soon as the money starts to come in again."

"You pawned it?" Kati cried. "Your brooch? The one piece of jewelry besides your wedding ring that Father gave you? I can't believe it." She sighed and sat down in the chair opposite the mahogany dressing table. Kati recalled the day so long ago when she and her mother had gone into the vault. "Isn't it beautiful?" Tilla had asked the little girl, draping the elegant piece around her fingers. "It's my most precious possession. Your father gave it to me, and it's more special than the grandest piece of jewelry in the world." And now it was gone, hocked in a pawn shop.

"Kati," Tilla's voice cut through her remembrances, "please try not to be upset. It was a very difficult thing for me to do, but I had to. I just couldn't bear the thought of asking some of the staff to wait again for their money. I just couldn't face it. They've all been working too hard; the extra hours they've been putting in are incredible. I just couldn't face it. It was easier to take the brooch and get some money. Besides, in the end, it's only a piece of jewelry," she insisted, knowing that that wasn't the point at all. The brooch had so many wonderful memories associated with it, so many beautiful thoughts.

"Does Father know?"

"Of course not. It would only upset him more than he is now. He's having a hard enough time already. He blames himself for Peter's wrongdoings and for Eva-Maria's leaving. Each morning he wakes up with the saddest look on his face, staring out at nothing. He seems to be taking it harder and harder. So I couldn't tell him. I'm just hoping to be able to get it back before he finds out it's gone," she fueled the lie even further. "But at the rate he's going, he's so preoccupied with a million other things, I'm sure it will be a long time before he even notices it's missing." Johannes had become more and more troubled by his fateful error in judgment. But as hard as Tilla tried, she was unable to forgive her husband.

"Oh, Mother, it's so terrible. I feel so badly. But things are going to change now, I promise. Now we're all going to be together again. That's what's most important. Everything we do will be aimed at putting the hotel back on its feet. I know we can do it. I'm certain of it."

Tilla looked at her daughter's radiant face and for a short moment she was convinced that what she said was true, that they really could make things work again. But her optimism was short-lived, for she knew how deeply in trouble they were. She was so exhausted from trying to turn the tide that she didn't even have the strength to fight Kati after she had shared her knowledge about the tuition money. She had agreed to let her stay at the hotel, but only after she had promised that she would return to school in the fall.

"You're right, sweetheart, I know we can do it, too. Now please, let's keep the brooch issue a secret, our secret. We can't allow it to spoil Margarethe's evening. Remember, we promised ourselves a wonderful night. Not even one mention of our problems. We owe her our most shining, exuberant faces. We'll talk about the theater, the ballet, and the opera—all of the good things in life. Just like we did when your grandfather was alive." Tilla's voice regained some of its former sparkle when she spoke of those happy times.

"She has given you two girls so much. It's only a pity that Eva-Maria isn't here with us to share our good-byes."

"I know, Mother, but there's nothing any of us can do about that right now. Come on, let's go down and have a nice evening." Kati and Tilla walked down the wide hallway together, their arms about each other's waist.

"I've never been so sad and so excited all at the same time in my entire life," Margarethe said. She looked very pretty in a new suit she had bought in a small boutique on the Langestrasse especially for her farewell dinner. It was most becoming to her, very tailored and conservative. The blouse had a little ruffle around the neck and cuffs at the sleeves. It looked so feminine, so much nicer than the uniform they were all so used to seeing her wear. Kati noticed she had even applied a small amount of blush and lipstick. She held up the beautiful picture frame that was a going-away present from all of them. It was a simple wooden frame with a picture of Tilla and Johannes, Kati, Eva-Maria, and Dieter, taken last December, only a day before Peter and Eva-Maria had left. Kati couldn't help but think that in better, more prosperous times the frame would have been made of silver, and maybe even adorned with a stone or two. But she couldn't dwell on that now. She only wanted the evening to be a success.

"I'm awfully sad to be leaving all of you," Margarethe continued as she looked from face to face, first at Tilla, then Kati, then Dieter, and finally to Johannes, who had been so silent all night, "but I have to admit I'm excited at the prospect of having two babies to attend to. The older one is only two, and the new baby is just four weeks old. Imagine," she said proudly. "It's been such a long, long time since I've had to stay up all night with a colicky child." She winked at Kati.

"I'm sure I never had that!" Kati declared, teasing her.

"Well, as a matter of fact, you're right," Margarethe agreed. "But your sister, she was a devil. She had it all the time." Everyone accepted the remark as it was intended, in good humor. But they all recognized the grain of truth in her comment. Eva-Maria's early behavior had only been an inkling of things to come.

"You won't be too far away, anyway," Kati said. "And I bet you'll be coming up here more often than ever to take the waters and visit the spa. You're going to need some relaxation after taking care of those children. They're going to tire you out. Just wait and see. As you said, it's been a long time."

"I'm sure you're right about that, plus I can always use that as an excuse to come and see all of you, and this beautiful hotel." Her eyes scanned the glorious room, stopping momentarily on the antique tapestries that lined the walls, the ornate, intricately carved ceiling, the Savonnerie carpets under the elegant, faultlessly set tables and out to the enormous windows that opened onto the wide esplanade of expertly manicured green lawn stretching down to the Oos.

"You'll never need an excuse. We'll always be here to welcome you," Kati said, not an ounce of hesitation in her voice.

"That's absolutely right," Dieter agreed, seconding Kati's comment and raising his glass in agreement. "But this time you'll come back as a guest, and we'll have the best room in the house reserved just for you. Probably Number 315," he added, mentioning one of the most elegant suites in the hotel.

Kati's enthusiasm and buoyant spirit carried the dinner through to the last clink of their champagne glasses toasting Margarethe's happiness. Tilla couldn't help but think what a different event it would have been without her wonderful daughter. As much as she hated to admit it, she was glad that Kati would be staying at the hotel. She needed her support now more than ever before.

Kati approached the challenges at the hotel with the fierceness of a wild animal. She soon realized how little she really did know about the operation, and this realization only made her more determined to learn everything she could. The one thing she knew for sure was that she was in a race against time, for the hotel had very little cash reserve.

She spent hours with Dieter. He was her key source of information, and whenever he didn't know the answer to something, he was certain to know where to go to find out. Johannes provided very little help. Each time she asked her father for something, he seemed to be in another world entirely.

But Tilla began to consult more and more with her daughter. Kati seemed to have so many things under control, she had such a feel for what needed to be done, what the priorities should be—no detail escaped her discerning eye. She reminded Tilla very much of Karl-Gustav. They discussed everything, every expenditure, every commitment, every way they could think of to get new business and, most importantly, how to keep the business they had left.

Kati derived genuine pleasure from knowing the guests had a good time. She enjoyed suggesting things for them to do and welcomed their comments afterward. She was especially helpful one afternoon to a handsome young American.

"I understand there's great fishing around here," he asked her. She was manning the desk for Dieter while he was off running an important errand. "Do you know if it's nearby?"

He had light blond hair and sparkling green eyes. His face had a winter glow that ended just below the collar of his sweater, a telltale sign of a tan procured on the ski slopes. He stood there, all six feet of him towering over the desk, smiling down in the most friendly manner at the ever-efficient Kati.

"Yes, I do know about the fishing," she answered, always ready and thankful for a chance to use her flawless English. "It's very close. In fact some of the best streams are within six or eight kilometers. I'm sorry," she corrected herself, "just four or five miles from the hotel. If you will have a seat I'll get a map and show you how to get to them from here."

He sat down at once. They explored the map together, Kati's delicate, graceful fingers tracing the route of the streams where she and Dieter always had the best luck.

"Once I caught the biggest fish I've ever seen in my life, right about here," she tapped her pen on the spot. "I brought it back to the hotel and my whole family had it for dinner that night. It was the best fish I've ever eaten!" she exclaimed.

The young man was obviously taken with her charm. He stared into her lovely eyes, thinking desperately how he could continue the conversation now that he had the information he had asked for. "You sound like a real professional angler."

A confused look came over her. "Angler?" she asked. "I'm sorry, I'm not familiar with that word."

"It's just a fancy word for fisherman," he said.

"Oh yes, I love to fish. In fact, I like anything to do with the outdoors. Except for hunting, that is. Especially in the Black Forest. We have almost every sport known to man within a few miles of here." Suddenly she realized how long it had been since she had gone hiking or played a game of tennis. The hotel had taken over her entire life. It also dawned on her that she was very much enjoying this conversation with this special guest.

"Would you like to go with me?" he asked, and then, realizing that he may have been too forward, he quickly tried to explain. "You see, I'm in the hotel just for a few days with my parents. My father is here on business, and I'm on a break from school back in Boston, so I don't know anyone in this area. I'd really like it if you'd come with me." Again he offered her his irresistible smile.

Of course her first reaction was to say no immediately. But he was so sweet, so sincere that she found herself trying to figure out a way to say yes and still get all of her work finished. Tomorrow was Sunday. If she stayed up late tonight and completed the reports for the week, she didn't see what harm it would do to go fishing for a few hours. Yes, she decided she would treat herself, for a change.

"I'd be happy to go with you," she answered. His smile widened. "But I'll have to be back at the hotel early in the afternoon." She saw the disappointment in his face. "The best fishing is first thing in the morning, anyway. I'll have the kitchen pack a picnic for us. Hopefully you'll have your dinner in your bag when you return." He seemed pleased with this idea.

"Well, I'll see you in the morning, then—about seven o'clock?"

"That sounds perfect. Shall I have the operator give you a wake-up call?"

"Yes, I'll need one," he agreed.

"Okay, if you'll tell me your name, I'll be glad to have her call you." She had never before accepted a date with a man whose name she did not know. He had the advantage of knowing hers simply by reading the name tag she wore on her lapel.

"That information would be helpful, I suppose." That wonderful smile again. "Rick, Rick Adams," he said, offering an outstretched hand.

What a perfect American name, Kati thought. She repeated it over and over in her head, and once again out loud in the privacy of her office later that night.

Kati had to practically empty her entire closet before she was able to find her dark green thigh-high fishing boots. They were buried behind the dozens of hotel uniforms that had become like a second skin to her. The boots were dusty from years of disuse, and she was up late cleaning them. But the following morning she was down in the lobby, picnic basket by her side, when the elevator door opened and the adorable Rick Adams stepped out. He was even more handsome than she remembered, and he wore a smile that was a combination of lingering sleepiness and genuine pleasure at seeing her. He was dressed in a typically casual American style—faded blue jeans worn through at one knee and a plaid shirt. She grinned with pleasure when she saw that his boots were larger-size duplicates of hers.

"Good morning," she offered in greeting.

"Good morning, Kati," he said. "I can't tell you how much I've been thinking about this since we made our plan yesterday. I can't wait."

"Then there is really no point in hanging around here. Let's get going!" The night before, she had arranged for one of the porters to pack all of the equipment—the rods, the lines, the bait, and the buckets in which to carry their expected bounty home. All they had to do now was get in the car and drive into the forest.

The stream was high and the fish were plentiful. Kati knew exactly where to park the car, how much bait to put out, and where to cast the line. She had done this so many times with Dieter that she had the routine down pat. She enjoyed sharing her knowledge with Rick.

By lunchtime they had caught seven good-sized fish. Rick was grinning from ear to ear, so pleased was he with the morning's take.

"How about a reward for all of our hard work?" Kati offered.

"If you mean lunch, I'd love it," he answered. "I'm really starving now."

"Me too," she concurred.

Chef Kellner had prepared a feast for them. Three kinds of sandwiches, fried chicken, and a selection of cold cuts. There were several varieties of cheese, and for dessert he had given them brownies and chocolate chip cookies. It was far too much for any two people to eat, and Kati watched in amazement as Rick sampled everything.

"It's pretty American fare, isn't it? Fried chicken and everything," she commented.

"It's delicious," he agreed between bites. "I was really lucky to have met you yesterday," he added. "You seem to have an in with the kitchen staff."

"Sometimes there are wonderful advantages to being the owner's daughter," she responded. She looked at him, and their mutual smiles signaled the beginning of a new friendship.

"Let me take the fish and I'll have the kitchen clean them and prepare them for you," Kati offered as they stood in the lobby, still wet and muddy from their adventure.

"Only if you agree to share them with me tonight at dinner," Rick said. "Catching them is only half the fun."

Kati wanted nothing more than to see him again. She had already missed several precious hours of work, but . . . she had to eat. "Okay, I'd like that. How shall I tell them we want them prepared?"

"Tell them we'll be in the kitchen around eight," he suggested. "We'll do it ourselves. You've shown me how to get them, now let me return the favor. I'm a great fryer of fish," he boasted.

Never had she enjoyed a dinner more. Rick had donned an apron and skillfully sautéed their meal. "Meet you upstairs," he said to the waiter, handing him the two plates and returning the apron to the rack on the wall.

"Excellent!" Kati exclaimed. They shared an icy-cold bottle of the locally produced white wine. Their plates were clean when the waiter returned only a few minutes into their meal.

They spent the remainder of a lovely evening finding out about each other. Rick was in his senior year at Harvard. He planned to go to law school the following year. He was serious about his studies and his future. She had met his parents briefly; his father was a scientist who had come to Baden-Baden to attend a conference. They were pleasant and interesting. He seemed to come from a solid family. Kati listened intently, fascinated with this charming boy who was so different from any of the boys she had met at the university.

Rick was equally impressed with her. He was moved by her commitment to the hotel and thought her dedication admirable but lacking in the offensive aggressiveness he found in some of the American girls he knew. Kati may not have shared his academic background, but her instincts and common sense were far greater than most of his classmates'.

Except for the time Kati adamantly insisted she must spend in the office, they were rarely apart during the next three days. They sampled every activity Baden-Baden had to offer. They swam, played tennis, visited the art museum, and took a ride on the cable car to the top of the area's highest peak.

"Tomorrow's my last day," Rick said as they stood side by side taking in the spectacular view.

Kati already knew. She had made a point of checking the list that morning and it confirmed that Mr. and Mrs. Adams and their son, Rick, would be leaving first thing the next day. They had called yesterday afternoon to confirm that a car had been ordered to take them to the Frankfurt airport. But now, hearing him say it, she was unable to stop the sharp pain that filled her heart. In such a short time he had become a very good friend. She loved being with him, sharing her thoughts and dreams. Now he would go out of her life as quickly as he had entered it.

"I know," was all she could say.

He took her in his arms. It was the first time he had held her. Their only other physical contact had been when he offered his arm to her as they were crossing the street or navigating a steep climb in the forest.

"I'm going to miss you, Kati. I've had such a good time being with you." Slowly he lowered his mouth to meet hers. Taking her face in his hands, he kissed her gently. Kati responded timidly. It was the first time she had felt the roughness of a man's beard against her soft skin. It was a pleasant sensation. She kissed him back quickly. Then once again. After the third or fourth time she allowed her mouth to remain on his for a moment longer. His tongue tenderly parted her lips. Slowly he explored the inside of her warm mouth. Her shyness disappeared as she allowed herself to enjoy this wonderful new sensation. Soon they were pressed close to one another, their mouths locked. They were oblivious of those around them until Rick heard the sounds of children's laughter nearby.

"Come," he said, holding her hand tightly. He led her away from the lookout point to the privacy of a nearby bench. She could feel the last traces of blush draining from her cheeks. She followed him eagerly, not wanting the feelings he had aroused in her to subside. He sat down next to her and took her in his arms. She relished the closeness of him, the lemon-scented fragrance of his skin. She nuzzled her face against his, wanting to feel the harshness of his beard again. Soon a voice interrupted their growing desire. The conductor announced that the last car of the day was descending the mountain in ten minutes.

They shared a pizza that night in one of the small bistros in town and then went to the movies. Kati would have preferred merely to sit and talk with Rick, to stare longingly into his kind eyes, but she knew that doing so would only make tomorrow more painful. So they had sat in the movie theater, holding hands and kissing throughout the entire film. Had her life depended on it, Kati would have been unable to tell anyone the name of the picture, so engrossed was she in her sweet thoughts of Rick Adams.

They walked slowly along the Oos on their way back to the hotel. "I meant what I said earlier," Rick repeated. "I really am going to miss you. I don't know when I'll be back here, but maybe you could come and visit me in Boston sometime." They stopped and kissed again.

"I'd like that very much," Kati said. She couldn't help but think that that was a remote possibility at best. They sat on a bench facing the silently flowing river. "It's time for me to go inside," she finally said, breaking away from his embrace and pulling him toward the hotel entrance. "I'll be down in time to say good-bye to you in the morning." With one last, quick kiss, she turned and walked past the reception desk to the private elevator.

She barely slept. In the morning she tried not to appear bleary-eyed as she waved good-bye to the Adamses from outside the revolving door. She looked pert and pretty and professional in her hotel dress, much different than she had in her tall green boots or her sparkling white tennis outfit. She smiled broadly and waved her hand fiercely until the car turned out of the hotel's driveway. Rick yelled out from the backseat, "I'll write soon." No one saw the tears well up in her eyes, for the second the car was out of sight, she ran at breakneck speed to the privacy of her office. She was greeted by a desk piled high with papers, the price she had to pay for taking a few days off to experience her first taste of love.

Kati celebrated her nineteenth birthday in the hotel with a small dinner party for some of her friends. Heidi came down from Frankfurt for the evening, and the two girls spent part of the day together. She had just become engaged to be married the following spring to Mark, a medical student from Munich.

"Things sure have changed since this time last year," she remarked as the two of them dressed for dinner in Kati's room.

"That's for certain. Look at you, getting married already. And you were always watching me so closely, so afraid that I'd be the one who would be carried away in the night."

"Well, it just proves that you never know. Who would have ever thought that you'd be here, doing so well? I hear that you've helped everyone make a lot of progress. It seems like you were bred for this business."

"I wish it were true," Kati sighed. "Things have improved, but not enough. We were so wiped out by Peter that it's surprising we're still able to open the doors. Sometimes I don't know if we're ever going to be all right again, but I just can't stop hoping."

Heidi admired her friend's drive, her determination to do anything she could to make the hotel a success. By comparison, it made her life seem so easy, so blessed. Everything in her future appeared to be so certain. After they were married, she and Mark would go to live in Munich, where he would establish his medical practice. The home that Heidi's parents had bought for them as a wedding present was very near the hospital. It was a charming old traditional house with three bedrooms, just the right size if they wanted to start a family. She was so happy now that she had found someone special, someone with whom she hoped to spend the rest of her life. She only prayed that her friend would not allow the hotel to stand in the way of meeting a husband of her own.

"Are you seeing anyone?" she asked.

"Are you kidding?" Kati replied, slipping a dress that Heidi remembered from college over her head. Either she hadn't had the money or the interest to keep up with the changing fashions. "Who has time? Do you realize how many hours I spend working every day? It's nonstop, this business. Just when you think everything's under control, something else pops up," she stated, combing her glorious hair back and securing it with a barrette. But a smile crept across her lovely face. She hesitated for a brief moment, debating whether or not to mention Rick. She tried her hardest not to think about him too much. It had been over three months since he had left, and she hadn't heard a word from him. Talking about him would only rekindle the memories, so she decided to skip telling Heidi. "It's worth it, though, I really love it, Heidi."

Heidi looked at her friend in her somewhat shabby, dated dress —her eyes sparkled, her luminous skin touched with just the lightest amount of makeup—she would be so beautiful even if she were dressed in a sack. "Well, just don't eliminate all possibilities," she encouraged, "keep your eyes open, you never know when the perfect guy for you may be lurking in the corridors around here." She worried about Kati. She was so serious, so involved in the hotel. She missed the spontaneous laughter and those carefree days and nights at the university.

"Of course, I will," Kati agreed.

But Heidi was certain that her advice had fallen on deaf ears.

· · ·

"How many dinners did we serve last night, Kati?" Dieter inquired when he bumped into the two girls in the hallway.

"Eighty-seven, but only fifty-six were from the hotel. The others were from outside, which means we're getting some of our other business back," she said with pride. "But I've got an idea about how to increase the number of guests who eat here too. I'll talk to you about it tomorrow. Anyway, Chef Kellner is really putting out some terrific new dishes. The kitchen's reputation is being restored. Once again people are starting to consider the Waldhotel when they want to go out to eat." When the scandal had first broken, their business had declined rapidly, but now people were starting to forget that and only think of the delicious sauces and desserts that were not offered anywhere but in their dining room.

"Right you are," Dieter agreed. He was continually amazed at the young girl's remarkable acumen for the business. Not a single detail missed her traplike mind, and she was always on top of the figures. Her enthusiasm was infectious. She had the entire staff convinced that nothing could stand in the way of their comeback.

"Don't be late for my birthday cake. Herr Kellner has definitely outdone himself this time," she warned. "I peeked into the kitchen earlier. You won't believe what he's created! See you later."

The official beginning of summer in the Black Forest was always heralded by the harvesting of the white asparagus. In middle to late May the fields were stripped bare of their precious crop. Gourmands everywhere looked forward to entire meals based solely on the delicate, tender spears. The annual Asparagus Festival drew people from everywhere to Baden-Baden. The hotel was operating at capacity. Often the lobby was crowded with people Kati knew weren't staying at the Waldhotel, but she didn't care. She was only happy that they were interested in seeing the Grand Salon and taking a late-afternoon tea or drink at the hotel. But one afternoon her attention was drawn to two well-dressed gentlemen standing just opposite the reception desk. She would never have noticed them, for they certainly could have been hotel guests, except for the fact that each of them was holding a writing pad. They were busy talking to each other and madly scribbling notes. She watched for a few moments while they continued their intense discussion. Finding an excuse to cross the lobby, she walked closer to where they were standing. They were speaking English, and what she was able to hear shocked her to the core.

"Well, the size of the desk could certainly be increased, by about three times, I would imagine," said one of the gentlemen, pointing with his pen to where the newly constructed desk would end.

"Yes, that would do it," the other agreed. "Then we'd have room for all of the computers and several reception clerks. This setup is way too small. I don't know how they've managed all these years."

"Very well," Kati wanted to scream, but she held her temper in check. But she couldn't allow them to continue their discussion. Taking a deep breath and trying to appear as calm as possible, she walked up to the two men.

"Excuse me, gentlemen, I'm Kati Meier. May I be of some help to you?"

"Oh, hello, Kati," replied the older of the two. "I'm Mr. Linder and this is Mr. Seidelman," he indicated, pointing to the other man. "We're here to meet with Mr. and Mrs. Meier." He volunteered no other information. It was evident to Kati exactly the purpose of their visit. "You're their . . ."

"Daughter," she replied curtly. Now Kati was doubly annoyed. She hated that they were there in the first place. Now she was astounded by their arrogance. They called her by her first name. "At what time is your appointment?"

"Just about now," he continued, undisturbed by the look on Kati's face. "Could you possibly direct us to their office?"

"I'll have someone call them for you at once," she said, and walked back to the reception desk, trying with all of her newfound maturity to hold back her anger.

"Kristina, please call my mother and tell her I told you to call her and say that Mr. Linder and Mr. Seidelman are here to see her. Don't forget to tell her that I asked you to call." She wanted to make certain that her mother knew that she had seen the two men, the two American strangers who were standing in the Waldhotel's lobby redesigning the reception desk.

Kati grabbed her sweater from the back of the chair where she had been working, reviewing the receipts for the week. "I'll be back in about an hour," she yelled out to the front desk clerk.

She couldn't make the revolving doors turn fast enough. She pushed her way through, not waiting for Clarence, the daytime doorman, to help her. As soon as she had passed the high iron gates that marked the official entrance to the hotel property, she broke into a run. Faster and faster she ran. The strong wind pushed away her tears. They streamed back toward her ears like rain on the windows of a speeding train. By the time she reached her destination, she was winded and her heart pounded fiercely in her chest.

The garden was in full bloom. The many varieties of summer blossoms—zinnias, marigolds, ox-eye daisies, and delphiniums—exploded in colorful profusion for all the visitors to enjoy. The parklike setting that her grandparents had created as a gift to the city they had loved so much was always a very special place for Kati. She had a wealth of memories from the beautiful garden. On lovely days in the fall and spring Margarethe would take the two girls there in their strollers to see the flowers and listen to the birds. Later, when she was older, Kati would come to the park with her Opa—he would be busy seemingly for hours with his precious flowers, handling each of them as if they were priceless jewels. Kati would sit patiently and listen, pretending that there was nothing more interesting in the world, nothing else she would rather be doing than being there in that magical place. "Your grandmother and I planted these peonies right after you were born," he would say, holding the vivid pink blossoms delicately between his fingers.

"Come over here, Kati, and look at these superb snapdragons," he would boast. "They'll be in bloom by next week," he would predict, caressing the unopened stalks.

The day of Karl-Gustav's funeral she had walked to the gardens with Dieter and the hotel's gardeners to pick the dahlias for his casket. They had worked all morning gathering the blossoms, practically stripping the bushes bare.

Her tears began anew now that she was back in her special place. This time she allowed them to run down her cheeks, not caring who might see her. The garden looked so beautiful, so perfect. How could everything be so wrong, so confusing in her life? How could they possibly be considering selling the hotel? She thought they had reached an agreement, an agreement that meant they would keep the hotel in the family at whatever cost. They would work and strive and achieve—they would succeed—and the hotel would again prosper. Now it was painfully evident that her parents had other ideas. She knew there had been other offers, other offers that they had rejected out of hand. They were not interested in selling the Waldhotel—no, not at any price. But now apparently things had changed, and no one had even bothered to tell Kati. She clutched her arms tightly around her shoulders as she thought of those awful men, standing with their pads and redesigning the reception desk to out-of-scale proportions so that it could contain all the computers. Computers at the Waldhotel. The hotel had been founded on the basis of personal attention, personal care for every detail, that was what the guests were willing to pay top dollar for. Now the thought of a bank of computers lined up like soldiers ready to check them in made her ill. But her next thought sent panic throughout her entire being. Why would they be in the hotel with pads and pencils, making sketches and drawings, if they were just there to talk with her parents? Just to discuss the possibilities of buying the Waldhotel? What if, oh no, it just couldn't be, the hotel couldn't already be sold. They wouldn't, they couldn't possibly do that to her, could they? After all her hard work, after everything she was trying to do, after all she had learned. They knew how she felt. She had made it crystal clear. No, it just wasn't possible. But her doubts still remained. There was only one way to find out for certain.

Kati sprang up from the wooden bench and ran back toward the enormous iron gates at a faster pace than she had raced through them only an hour earlier.

"Kati, whatever's the matter?" Kati's appearance had shocked her mother, who was sitting behind the desk in Karl-Gustav's office. She stopped writing immediately and gave her complete attention to her daughter. "What has happened to you? You look awful."

"Tell me it's not true, Mother," she demanded, a little more forcefully than she had intended.

"What are you talking about?"

"Those men, those men who came to see you and Father this afternoon, Mr. Linder, and that other one, I've forgotten his name. . . ."

"What about them, Kati?"

"I know what they were here for, to buy the hotel, right? I can't believe you are dealing with all these people and I don't know a thing about it." Her voice rose, as she was no longer able to control her anger. It reminded her of the time when she had made the painful discovery about Heidi's parents and her tuition. She wanted to scream out, to tell her mother exactly what she was feeling. But even in her rage she knew the hurt it would cause, a wound too deep to heal after the emotions had subsided.

"Kati, try to control yourself," warned her mother. "There is nothing to be upset about. First of all, it's not all those people, it's only Mr. Linder and his company. Anyway, as it turns out they're not willing to meet our price, or for that matter, come anywhere close to it."

"Then it's true! I knew it was when I saw them standing there drawing up new plans for the reception desk. So don't tell me there's nothing to be upset about. I thought we had all decided to stick this out, not to discuss the sale of the hotel with anyone, no matter how interested they were. I thought we had an agreement to try to keep the Waldhotel in the family where it belongs, not in the hands of some foreigners."

Kati's shoulders shook with uncontrollable sobs. She could no longer contain her mixed emotions of anger, confusion, and helplessness. Tilla rose from the desk and walked around the big green leather club chair to her daughter.

"Sweetheart, please, please, don't be so upset," she hugged Kati and tried to calm her. But she knew she was far from successful. Her own fears were so powerful, so all-consuming that even she wasn't certain any longer which was the right course to follow. But she had to try. "Kati, everything's going to be all right, you know that. But we can't afford to ignore any reasonable bid for the hotel. We're not being as profitable as we need to be to continue to keep the doors open. Despite our efforts, we're just not doing well enough. You know the figures better than all of us. The occupancy rate is down, and everything else slides down from that all-important number. Oh, Kati, sometimes I don't know myself what to do next." She tightened her arms around her daughter and tried to stifle her own tears.

"I know, Mother, I know how hard it has been for you and Father, but I still think we can do it. We can pull it out. We can't just turn our backs on the past. This is our hotel, left to us by Grandfather. We'll never be able to achieve anything if we keep being sidetracked by all these offers. We should just say that the hotel is not for sale, period."

"You may be right, Kati, but we've still got bills to pay. The payroll comes due every week, whether or not the hotel is full. We've cut the staff just about as far as we can and still be able to call the hotel a luxury resort."

"Everyone will just have to push a little bit harder," was the determined girl's response.

"You're right," Tilla agreed, "but everyone has their limits. Your Father has never been the same since the morning when he learned about Peter and your sister." It was still too painful even to mention Eva-Maria's name with his. "Sometimes I think he's had all that he can bear."

Kati and her mother sat in the big club chairs discussing at greater length the subject closest to their hearts. They came to no firm conclusions. Suddenly Kati remembered that she had left the receipts in a pile on the desk.

"I've got to go, Mother," she said as she kissed her lightly on the cheek. "I left the receipts in such a hurry, and if I don't get back to finish them, everyone will have to wait for me."

Kati paused at the mahogany door. She turned back to Tilla, who remained by the fireplace. Her eyes were turned up to her grandfather's portrait. She was searching for guidance, for inspiration from him, but today found none. "Don't worry, Mother, it's going to be just fine."

Her words were said with such authority, but as she rushed down the hall, she was haunted by her mother's uncertainty, and most of all her concern for Johannes.

CHAPTER

12

*A*T FOUR FORTY-FIVE the sun was already streaming in through the panes in the long French doors that opened out onto the terrace from Johannes and Tilla's bedroom. Tilla stirred slightly. She opened her sleep-filled eyes halfway, then finally all the way when she realized Johannes was staring at her. He was wide awake, lying on his side, elbow bent, supporting his head on a tightly clenched fist. His vacant stare was uninterrupted by her movements. Even after Tilla was awake, returning his gaze, he continued to look at her in this way. It was as if he was lost in his own thoughts, unaware that his wife was in the bed right next to him. He didn't reach out to hold her, to caress her, as he had every morning during the first few years of their marriage. Never would he leave their bed without a morning hug and gentle kiss. Now he just continued to look straight at her, almost through her. Husband and wife stared at each other for what seemed like a very long time. Finally Tilla could stand the silence no longer.

"Good morning, Johannes," she offered sweetly.

He blinked rapidly several times. Still she was not certain if he had heard her, if she had broken his trance.

"Did you sleep well?"

"Yes," he replied, his tone matching his empty stare. "But I think it's time to get up now."

"Johannes, the sun is only beginning to rise," she insisted, turning her head and reconfirming the early hour on her bedside clock.

"Yes, I know, but I have lots of things to do today. You go ahead and get some more rest," he encouraged her. His lips gently brushed against hers before he climbed out of bed and padded slowly off in the direction of his shower.

Tilla couldn't imagine what it was he had to do that was so important. Lately he hadn't been doing much of anything. He was rarely in his office. Every time she tried to reach him, he was out on an errand or some other excuse was offered by his secretary. Even the staff was starting to complain that they were never able to get an answer from him. She couldn't understand what he did with his time, how he filled his days. Tilla never found enough hours in the day to complete all the things she wanted to do. She worked like a woman possessed and still never finished everything. She squeezed each second out of every minute. How she wanted the hotel to succeed, to regain its rightful position! Nevertheless she was thankful for the luxury of a little time alone before the start of another challenging day, so she pulled up the linen sheets and drifted back into a deep slumber.

Johannes took longer than usual to get dressed. He stood with the palms of his hands pressed up against the cold white tiles of the shower wall, the hot water aimed forcefully at his back. His silhouette was shrouded in a steamy haze. He shaved slowly; for some reason it seemed important to him that the shave be especially close today. He even changed blades midway through and began the process all over again. When he was convinced that he had done a good job, he patted his face dry and stood in front of his open closet, staring at the huge selection of ties. He removed several and held them up next to his face in the mirror before he made his final choice, a muted paisley design that Kati had given him on his last birthday.

The large revolving door was still locked when he was ready to leave the lobby, so he exited into the fresh, crisp air through the always-open side door. The hotel, as well as the town, slept soundly. The only vehicles Johannes saw were delivery trucks. He waved to the driver pulling up to the service entrance bearing the hotel's daily allocation of fresh bread and rolls. Baked goods were one of the few commodities not produced in the hotel's kitchen. An antiquated German law, passed in an effort to protect the proprietors of bakeries, forbid hotels to begin baking before four in the morning. Starting at that late hour would never allow enough time to have fresh breads ready for their early risers, so Becker's had contracts with no less than six different shops, whose trucks arrived at dawn bearing the still-warm breads.

The van arriving from the Frankfurt airport carrying the foreign newspapers rounded the corner at a fast clip. The driver had to swerve to avoid hitting him.

"So sorry," the man yelled out in apology, "didn't expect anyone to be out so early."

Johannes waved his hand in reply and continued walking toward the center of town. The Norman spires of the old parish church reached up into the light blue of a new day. Its doors were open, and when he glanced inside, he saw the priest who had officiated at so many of his family's services, the last being Karl-Gustav's funeral over two years ago.

The town square was beautiful in the soft morning light. Devoid of people, both tourists and locals, it looked elegant and peaceful. Johannes was able to carefully examine the diverse architecture of the buildings he had taken for granted for so many years. Most of the town buildings were constructed in what had become known as the Wilhelminian style, a tribute to Emperor William I, King of Prussia, who, with his wife, Augusta, had spent forty summers vacationing in Baden-Baden. The town hall, the magnificent Kurhaus where concerts and exhibitions were held, the post office—they were all substantial, serious buildings with not a hint of frivolity, constructed of granite or limestone. He studied the classic simplicity of the imposing Doric columns flanking the entrance to the bank on the corner. Their graceful lines were in such stark contrast to the clean, angular facade of the nearby Modernist building that was the House of Congress. The sunlight reflected off the mirrored-glass surface of the sleek, tailored structure.

He stood quietly at the point considered to be the center of Baden-Baden, the place that everyone used as a meeting spot. Under his feet was the enormous color clock that had been a commission by one of Germany's most famous sculptors. The clock, its diameter over twenty feet, divided the day into red, yellow, green, and blue hours. Around the edge of the clock one could determine how many kilometers it was to Munich, Hong Kong, Los Angeles, Sydney, and other faraway places. Thoughtfully he studied the exotic destinations—six thousand kilometers to Nairobi, ninety-three hundred to Rio de Janeiro, fifty-seven hundred to Montreal, seventy-nine hundred to

Miami. So many places he had always wanted to see. But time had passed so quickly. When they were barely more than toddlers, Johannes had often stood at this very same spot with Eva-Maria and Kati. Each child would stand on a city. They would talk about the foreign places. They would make a game of it—describing them, the way the people would look, the food they would eat, and the hotels they would stay in. Then they would raise their sweet, shining eyes, full of hope and enthusiasm, and ask, "Will we go there someday, Father? Will you take us, please?" "Of course," he had assured them. "Someday soon."

Johannes couldn't remember if he had ever stood on the clock alone. He looked down and saw that his feet were firmly planted in the deep blue hours. The clock couldn't have been more accurate.

The intersection was called the Leopoldsplatz, and from there he could see the long stretch of the Sophienstrasse laid out before him. He crossed the wide boulevard, showing no regard for the red light. A single car traveled slowly toward him, but still remained a good distance away. The shop windows neatly displayed their goods, unencumbered by the heavy iron bars that were now a necessity in most major cities. Window-shopping late at night on the way home from a restaurant or movie was still a viable pastime in Baden-Baden. Couples lingered in front of windows in the early-morning hours without fear of being bothered.

He continued slowly by the women's shops filled with new fall merchandise, past the linen and bath boutique displaying the finest selection of goods from Switzerland, past the antique store that specialized in English period furniture.

Johannes stopped in front of the small vitrine at the next shop. All the pieces of jewelry had been removed the night before; in the empty spaces the owner had placed color photographs of some of the things he had available for sale. He stood staring absently into the window, not seeing the photos or the dusty velvet display trays. His mind could only focus on what he had seen there one day, not too long ago. Did Tilla really think he wouldn't find out? Did she think he wouldn't notice that her plain silk dresses were never adorned with the one piece of jewelry she had always claimed meant more to her than anything she had ever owned? Did she really believe that he had stopped caring about her, paying no attention to how she looked?

He recalled exactly how he had felt on the afternoon when he had first seen the brooch in the window. He was walking on the Sophienstrasse, toward his old office, the same route he was taking now. His eye was caught by something, he couldn't say exactly what, for it was midday, and usually his major concern was just getting by all the shoppers and reaching the office. But that day he had been compelled to stop, to look in the window. There it was. He knew the minute he saw it that it was Tilla's brooch. Its design was unique, different from any other he had ever seen. Yes, it was hers, there for everyone to see in the window of the shop, not at the hotel in the safety of her silk-lined jewel case.

He knew immediately what she had done, and why. It explained so many things. How Tilla had mysteriously been able to "juggle the funds," or so she had claimed, and was able to meet the payroll for several weeks. At the time, he had been completely baffled, for it was he who was supposedly controlling the hotel's cash. Her actions had remained a mystery until the day he saw the brooch in the window.

He toyed with the idea of confronting her with the evidence, of dragging her downtown to the window and making her stand next to him and look at the object that had meant so much to both of them. In his heart, he knew it was pointless, and so he had said nothing. Each time she dressed for dinner, wearing an outfit that was usually adorned with the pin, he would stare at the empty space and feel the same pain he felt now as he stood in front of the barren window. He knew that it must have been terribly difficult for her to have sold the pin, but she had done it for her family. They meant more to her than anything in the world. She was determined to save the hotel for her daughters. It was the only thing she would be able to pass on to them. That thought kept him from ever even hinting that he knew what she had done.

His pace quickened after he passed the shop. Everything was a blur now. He turned into the alleyway off the main street and entered the vestibule of his former office. The ancient but sturdy elevator took him to the fourth floor as it had for so many years, until a few months ago when he had dissolved his partnership and had stopped coming every day. His partners had been so understanding, so sympathetic to his need to give the hotel a try. But they hated to see him go. "Of course, Johannes, we see what you must do," Heinrich had said over dinner the night Johannes had announced his intention to leave the firm, "but you know how we'll miss you, and we're going to keep your desk and your office set up exactly the way it is now. You'll be welcome, in fact, you'll be expected to come back and spend some time with us. After all, you can't just leave us after twenty years and never return."

"That's right," Charles had agreed, "we'll be looking for you to stop in at least once a week, regardless of how busy that big white palace is keeping you, and I'm certain it will be keeping you busy. We wish you the best." They had toasted Johannes's decision, and reminisced about the good old days until late into the night.

He thought of that night now as he opened the front door with his keys. The office was spooky in its calmness. When they had first founded the firm, and for several years afterward, he had spent many late nights there alone, laboring over the problems of his growing list of clients. Actually he had only returned to the office a few times since his departure; going there made him even sadder and more disconsolate than ever. He missed being part of the small, but efficient team. He missed being involved in a business that from the outside seemed so mundane, so boring, but to him had always provided a good deal of satisfaction, a business in which he had taken such pride. The hotel was such a different animal. You had to live with the hotel every minute of the day, every day of the year. There was no escaping it. Its demands and its challenges were never-ending. It was like a child who never grew up. Taking your eye off it for one minute was inviting disaster, was tantamount to failure. An inspiration to some, he was sure, but certainly not to him. Accounting was so cut-and-dried, so black or white, so exact—either it was right or it was wrong. At the end of the day you could walk away from it with a clear head and not have to carry the problems home with you. But not the hotel; it was with you constantly. He had watched Tilla over the last two years as she struggled and fought to continue the grand tradition of Becker's. He had seen what her fight had done to their marriage and to their family. He had tried to support her. He had given up his life's profession to help her succeed, but it was futile.

The situation with Peter was the last straw. He had been so

stupid. His deception had crippled him. It preyed on his mind constantly. Peter was brilliantly clever, astutely trained. He possessed a criminal's mind. By the time they had discovered what he had done, he and Eva-Maria were far away in France, untouchable for a long time. Tilla had refused to send the police after them, fearing that it would only bring to light Johannes's mistakes too. For under the terms of the estate, he had no authority to authorize such enormous expenditures of money without first getting Tilla's approval. He wished so that he had listened to Herr Klebe's warnings, that he had taken heed from the honest, sincere man who was only trying to help. He had turned away, unable to cope, unable to believe, and for that dismissal he had paid dearly.

A ray of bright sunlight tore in through the side window. Its beam landed on a spot of carpet next to his foot. Momentarily it shocked Johannes, and he sat bolt upright in his comfortable swivel chair. His nervousness, the anxiety he had felt since awakening this morning had not left him. He knew it wouldn't until the very end.

The single desk drawer was locked. It had always been Johannes's private drawer, and it remained so today. He used the smallest key on his ring to open the narrow compartment. Even though both Heinrich and Charles had keys, he knew the contents would be undisturbed. Everything was in order. All of the insurance papers, the car registrations, the children's funds, and the bank statements were exactly as he had left them. Pushed safely to the back of the wooden drawer was the small pistol. He reached gingerly to the very back and then to the side. For a second he could not feel the hard metal surface. Then his fingers made contact and as they wrapped around the handle of the gun, the cold steel sent a shiver throughout his entire body.

After a few moments of caressing the pistol it felt warm and comfortable in his hand. When he had purchased it several years earlier, the salesman had stressed its merits, pointing out what a "comfortable" model it was, easy to hold and to control. He had told him that it would protect him from any intruder who should dare to venture in. But as it turned out, Johannes had only himself to fear. He was the bad guy. It was strange that their conversation was what came into his mind now. He didn't think about his life or about Tilla and the girls. He had come to terms with those issues a long while ago. Now he only thought about the power of the tiny gun he held gingerly in his hand. As he raised it to his temple, steady as a skilled surgeon, he thought only about how right the salesman had been.

The sound of the explosion was trapped between the thick plaster walls of the old and well-constructed building. It was hours later when Charles arrived to prepare for an early-morning client meeting that he discovered the body of his former partner on the floor of the office where he had worked so happily for so long.

CHAPTER

13

THE FUNERAL was a simple affair. Its somberness was intensified by the cold, wet weather that hung over the peaceful valley like a huge shroud. A heavy fog obscured the entire forest. Only a small gathering of mourners came to pay their respects to a man who, for the most part, had remained a stranger, a mystery to them. Johannes Meier had been regarded as a kind, competent individual. He was always pleasant and amiable when he saw people, whether in town or at one of the social events in the hotel. He was accepted and respected for the simple reason that he was married to the daughter of one of the town's founding fathers. With the exception of his former partners, Charles and Heinrich, he had few close friends, as evidenced by the light turnout. In the opinion of most of the towns-people, suicide was not an approved way to end a life. First, in the eyes of the Catholic church, it was a sin. Second, for those less concerned with religious doctrine, it was regarded as selfish and cowardly. Leaving behind a wife and two children made the entire act even more disgraceful.

Charles had broken the news to Tilla in the gentlest manner possible. But in the end the message he had to deliver was still devastating. "I'm so sorry, Tilla," he offered, going toward her with outstretched arms.

She refused his arms, hitting them down with her fists. "I want to see him. Where is he?"

Charles knew that seeing her husband was simply out of the question at that moment. His body had been removed from the office and taken to the morgue. It would be awhile before they would allow her in to make a final identification. "Not right now, Tilla. You'll be able to go a little later."

For some reason she accepted his words. She collapsed into one of the enormous wing chairs. After a few moments of silence, her screams of raw terror and shock brought two floor maids running into the office without even a thought of knocking. Dr. Rossner was summoned from next door; Suzanne and Dieter helped him to restrain her while he gave her an injection. As the medication took effect, she rested quietly in the same bed that only a few hours earlier she had shared with a distant, troubled Johannes. She remained sedated for three days, getting up for the first time to attend the funeral.

Kati was downstairs in the kitchen working with the pastry chef while all of this was happening. She was deeply involved in a discussion with Wilhelm, their superb maker of all things sweet and calorie-laden, when Dieter found her.

"That's fabulous, Wilhelm," she had said encouragingly after devouring a spoonful of his newest sauce made of currants and raspberries. "It's so light. Will you use it with all of the ice creams?"

"Both the ice creams and the mousses, I think," he agreed enthusiastically.

"It's such a beautiful color. Looks great on the plate, doesn't it?"

She was just finishing arranging an assortment of the hotel's hand-made ice creams and decorating them with the new concoction when she heard Dieter's familiar voice call out to her.

He was shaken to his very soul, doubly upset because the awful task of breaking the news of her father's death fell to him. It was going to be one of the hardest things he had ever had to do.

Kati accepted the news stoically, internalizing her emotions much more than her mother had. Once she had fully realized what Dieter had said, she stood with her head bowed, her hands covering her forehead. "No, no," she said softly, almost in a whisper, "how could he have done something like this?" she asked repeatedly to no one in particular. When she finally raised her face to Dieter, he saw she had bitten her bottom lip until it bled. Tears rimmed her lovely eyes, eyes that were feeling the greatest amount of pain she had ever known. She had gone directly upstairs to be with Tilla, who was now resting quietly. Assured that Suzanne would remain by her mother's bedside in case she should awaken, she then went to find solace in a place that had become so familiar, so comforting to her in time of need—the dahlia garden.

Dieter knew instinctively where she was going when he saw her leave the hotel. He went in search of her later in the afternoon.

"Well, I guess it's up to us now, isn't it?" she asked him once he sat down next to her on the bench in the lovely white gazebo.

"Yes, it looks that way," he agreed sadly. "Oh, Kati, so many terrible things have happened to us during the last few years," he shook his head, recounting their tragedies silently in his mind.

They both stared absently at the beautiful flowers.

"I'm worried about your mother," he continued. "She was horribly shocked. I think she immediately blamed herself for everything that's happened. If she hadn't insisted on keeping the hotel, and having your father join her, maybe none of this would have occurred."

"That may be true, Dieter," Kati agreed, "but for her there was no other choice. Fighting to keep the hotel open, hiring a manager, those were all things she had to do. Maybe my father should have been more aware, more concerned about what was going on between Peter and Eva-Maria, but he shouldn't have done something like this. It wasn't his fault entirely. No, for my mother there was no choice. Just as there's no choice now as to what we must do."

Dieter put his arm around the brave young woman and held her close to him. He could feel the slight movement of her shoulders and he knew as she turned her head close against his chest that her tears had finally come. He tightened his hold on her and stroked her hair gently.

"You agree, don't you, Dieter?" she asked between sobs. "We've got to keep going, to keep trying. If we give up now, everything will be lost, and it will all have been for nothing."

"Yes, Kati, you're right. I just hope your mother will be able to recover quickly and pull herself together. She needs to get back to work."

"Yes, it will be the only thing that will help her. We must be patient with her, though. We'll just have to wait and see how strong she can be. In the meantime it's going to be up to us." She looked at him with her wet, tear-stained face. What he saw, through the grief and sorrow, was the face of a committed, iron-willed young woman. Now more than ever before, the granddaughter of his oldest friend was determined to restore whatever remained of her family's legacy.

. . .

Tilla made a concerted effort during the next months to focus on the job that needed to be done at the hotel. She would awaken early, grateful for the dawn. Morning after morning she was exhausted by another sleepless, seemingly endless night of tossing and turning. Her thoughts tormented her relentlessly. She replayed the events of the previous months—Eva-Maria's elopement, the hotel's problems, Johannes's conspiracy with Peter, and now his tragic death. She reviewed each event over and over again in her mind, striving for an explanation that didn't exist. But despite her efforts, her heart was no longer in the hotel. She was like a precious porcelain vase that had been dropped and had shattered into a thousand pieces. The finest, most skilled craftsman had been called in to repair the damage, but like the vase, tiny fragments of her were still missing. She feared she would never be the same again. Her level of concentration was at an all-time low. She forgot many more things than she remembered, making it difficult for those around her to do their jobs properly and effectively. She would tell one department about something and then neglect to mention it to another. If she wasn't double-checked on every detail, her efforts would predictably result in confusion and oftentimes disaster. On several occasions Kati came very close to losing her temper with her, only managing to hold herself back at the last minute. She was as patient and as understanding with her as a parent with a child. Dieter watched and admired the young woman as he too attempted to keep a thousand balls in the air all at once.

Kati's determination grew, fueled by each small success, challenged by each failure. Over the next year she learned a little about all of the departments, and a great deal about those she felt were crucial to the ultimate success of the Waldhotel. The kitchen became her prime target. She would get up an hour earlier than usual each morning and head down the steep stairs to the basement. There she would find the morning staff already busy at work preparing the breakfast trays. To save precious time, the silver and linen had been set out the night before. Karl-Gustav used to refer to it as "setting up the chariots." Once complete, the trays were then sent by dumbwaiter to the appropriate floors. There they would be met by the floor waiters and dispatched to the designated rooms. Becker's had a policy of trying to deliver a breakfast order within twelve minutes of the time a guest telephoned. The staff was so programmed, so determined to meet this schedule that it became a game, an early-morning challenge that everyone enjoyed. Kati was right in there with all of them, the sleeves on her uniform turned up, an apron tied snugly around her tiny waist. She would toast the muffins, run the orange juicer, grind the coffee beans. Whatever needed to be done.

"You did it again! Bravo!" Kati would announce proudly over the kitchen's megaphone. "Except, that is, for Room 402, whose order didn't arrive until twenty-two minutes after it was placed," she added, with extra emphasis on the twenty-two, just to make certain they didn't become overconfident.

"That's only because they changed their mind two times, Fräulein Meier," one of the waiters yelled from the back room. "First they asked for orange juice, then they called back and asked for grapefruit, then two minutes later they wanted another order of toast."

Kati smiled. Many of the apprentices, who were always assigned the morning shift, were about her same age. They liked her spirit and willingness to get down in the trenches with them, and they learned right away that no job was too menial for her.

"You're right," she agreed. "Okay, let's scratch that one and make it a perfect morning." Her decision brought cheers and clapping from the entire crew and started the day off on the right foot. From there, in a good mood, and certain that her forces were all in place, she would go back upstairs and hold the daily staff meeting. Tilla still attended, but it was clear that Kati had taken charge. The department heads admired the young woman. Over the past year, by dint of hard work, patience, and unrelenting tenacity, she had earned their respect as well. The older members of the staff saw the image of her grandfather in everything she did. Her business sensibilities bore an uncanny resemblance to the master hotelier.

The morning meeting over, she would go to the small office next to Karl-Gustav's. Her mother continued to occupy the large desk, but she was rarely there. More and more correspondence was forwarded directly to Kati, where the sender was assured of prompt attention and action. She would spend the majority of the day in the small room, sorting through the mail, telephoning suppliers, and trying to solicit new business. She counted on Dieter and his staff to service and nurture the business they still had.

"I know our payment is long overdue, Herr Liebmann. I'll try to have a check sent at the beginning of next week. Please bear with us just a little longer. Things are improving," she would plead with the owners of companies from whom they purchased their supplies. She was becoming fatigued from constantly asking favors, from begging them to have just a little more patience with them. Most of the people were friends of her grandfather's, but after such a lengthy time, many of them were no longer willing or able to continue to grant her credit.

Dieter would come into the office during his short breaks from his desk. They would continually strategize how they could save the hotel.

"I've spent all morning trying to carve out some dollars to use for renovation, but they just aren't there," she sighed, not knowing where else to look for funds.

"I know, Kati, it's been hard enough to keep up with the bills and the payroll, let alone spend money fixing up some of the rooms," Dieter unhappily agreed.

"But we've got to do it," she insisted, "even if we only find money for some of the suites. We have to be in a position to compete. Otherwise we're going to lose it all! They're spending a fortune at the Europäischer Hof. Have you seen it? They've replaced all the marble in the lobby and in the bathrooms, redone the entire dining area, even the breakfast room, which was perfect to start with. I also heard they've torn out the old swimming pool and are replacing that too. They seem to have an unlimited supply of money, unlike us. We're not even able to meet our debts every thirty days."

The Europäischer Hof was just two blocks away and the same age as the Waldhotel; its original owner had been a friend of Karl-Gustav's. He, too, had died several years ago, and the hotel had recently been purchased by one of Germany's leading industrialists, who had a passion for grand resorts. Many times the man had been a guest at Becker's. He had closed the Europäischer a year ago and had begun extensive renovations. Now the newly refurbished hotel was due to open next month. Kati had gone over to see what had been done. She was astounded at the work, the remarkable changes, and the beauty of the new hotel. The Europäischer Hof had always been the second hotel in town. It had accommodated the overflow from Becker's when they were completely booked. Those who wanted a degree of luxury and could not afford to stay at the Waldhotel reserved at the Europäischer Hof. Now this egocentric mogul had created a splendid hotel, as beautiful as the Waldhotel, if not more so. It frightened Kati to death. This could be the last straw for her hotel. When people saw the lovely new rooms, the elegant antique furnishings, and the inviting dining areas, why would they continue to come back to Becker's, where everything was beginning to look a bit shabby and worn?

"Oh, Dieter, I'm so frustrated. I only wish we had been able to prepare for this in some way. If only we could get some extra funds so that we could freshen up a bit and be competitive. We've stretched ourselves to the limit. We've used up the equity loan on the hotel. Now no one will even speak to me with our recent payment history," she said.

"Kati, the one thing you're forgetting, the most important thing, is that no matter how beautiful the new hotel may be, we still have the top staff. We have the best, most professional, most committed group in the region. We have a team. No one can take that away from us. People will forget the glamour and sparkle of the new place when the service is less than perfect. You'll see, we'll continue to survive," Dieter said in his most confident tone.

With all her heart Kati wanted to believe that what he said was true. "I hope you're right, Dieter, but I'm still certain that in the beginning, in the near term, let's say for the first six months after the opening, we're going to be hurt. Our business is going to suffer. Everyone will want to try it at least once. That's always how it is when something is new. People can't wait to stay there. Especially in Baden-Baden, where things have been the same for so long. Excitement is created here when a new restaurant opens. Imagine an entire hotel! That's really news! I only hope we were convincing at the meeting yesterday. I got the feeling that not all of them were sure about the future of the hotel. I can't really say that I blame them."

"You were terrific, Kati. Everyone has the greatest faith in you. Several of the staff told me so after the meeting broke. I don't think we'll have any trouble with them leaving."

She certainly hoped not. That was why yesterday morning she had called a gathering of all the employees. She wanted to assure them of security in their job, to plead with them in the subtlest way possible not to accept or even consider going to work for the competition. She knew that the Europäischer Hof's personnel people were starting to contact some of her key employees. She just couldn't afford to let it happen. The loss of staff would be a blow from which they might not be able to recover.

"I do so hope you're right," she admitted. "Anyway, now is no time to stop believing everything you tell me." Kati smiled. Without Dieter they never would have lasted this long. "The staff is the only resource we have left. We certainly don't have any money. I have to be able to count on every single one of them to weather this new storm." When the storm would hit and how severe the damage would be was, at this point, anyone's guess.

CHAPTER

14

I T WAS WELL AFTER two o'clock when Kati was finally able to sit down behind her desk and go to work. November was the busiest month of the year, since preparations had to be made for the many holiday events. Now it seemed there was more than ever to do.

She had been even further delayed today because she had stopped in the middle of the morning to keep an appointment with Dr. Hoeffer at the clinic next door. Tilla had been having several sessions a week with him. He had summoned Kati last week, saying he must have an opportunity to speak with her.

"The good news is that she's willing to accept the fact that she needs help," the doctor had begun. "As you are aware, she's been coming regularly. But the problem doesn't appear to be improving. In fact," he hesitated before continuing, "I think she's getting worse."

Kati sighed. She had been terrified that this was what she was going to hear.

"The holidays are very difficult for her," Kati said. "With each passing month she becomes more withdrawn and introspective. Now she's even more distant, more removed. She spends the better part of her day in the apartment. Hardly ever does she get out of her bed before noon. We've tried to work around her at the hotel because I didn't want her to feel those pressures, too."

"I know," said Dr. Hoeffer, "she's told me as much. She feels guilty about it, but there's really nothing she can do to remedy the situation right now. Kati, I'm afraid your mother's very ill. She's suffering from what we call serious depressive melancholia. The symptoms are exactly as you've described them. She's removed from daily life, shows very little interest in anything, and has an extremely low energy level. Even the smallest task becomes a major effort. I think we're going to have to try a more effective series of treatments."

"What are you suggesting?"

"Electroshock treatments."

"Electroshock?" Kati repeated. How horrible. Of course she had heard about them. But they were only for crazy people. People who could no longer live a normal life. There were a last effort to bring a person back to normalcy. Visions of her mother strapped to a table enduring the intolerable pain of the treatments filled her mind. They were so drastic, seemingly inhuman. Her mother had never been ill a day that she could remember. Her father's suicide had broken her; perhaps she would never recover. Suddenly and uncontrollably Kati began to shiver. She tried to control herself, but her efforts were in vain.

"I'm sorry, sorry," she whispered. "But I'm so afraid."

"Don't be silly, Kati. It's a perfectly normal reaction. Electroshock is a very severe measure. I'm just sorry all of this is falling on your shoulders. It is unfair. But I'm afraid you're the only one who can help me reach your mother. You're the only one who can help me to convince her that she needs the treatments."

Dr. Hoeffer was a very well-respected physician. She valued his opinion. She had no choice but to agree with him. Slowly she pulled herself together.

"The mind is a very powerful tool, Kati. It can inflict equally strong positive and negative control over an individual's entire body. Unfortunately in the case of your mother, it has run her down both mentally and physically. I've consulted with two of my colleagues in Frankfurt about this. They agree with my diagnosis and suggested treatment. Now, with your consent, we'll need to confront your mother."

"Would you like me to speak with her first?" Kati offered, feeling it was her duty to do so if he felt it would help, but dreading the confrontation.

"Yes, I think you should, Kati. I know it will be a difficult thing to do, but it might make it easier for her to accept."

"I'll find the right time soon," she said. "After we've talked, I'll let you know her reactions. Don't worry, Doctor," Kati assured him, "we'll make her well again. I'd do anything to have my mother back. She's really the only family I have left."

"How well I know, Kati," the kind gentleman agreed. "When I

first came to Baden-Baden and started my practice here, I watched your grandfather build the Waldhotel to greatness. Once a year he would hold a beautiful dinner for all the interns and residents and their wives. We looked forward to it all year, since we were not making the kind of salary that allowed us such a treat. Karl-Gustav was a much-admired man. I hear, in fact, that you're just like him. Everyone is rooting for your success."

"Thank you, Doctor, thank you for everything. We're trying our best. I only hope it's good enough." Kati gathered her coat and muffler, put them on, and started toward the door. "I'll be speaking with you soon."

As Kati relived the conversation with Dr. Hoeffer and tried to formulate in her mind exactly how she would approach her mother on this most delicate of subjects, she realized she had failed to thank him for not pressing her to pay their sizable bill. He had been caring for Tilla for well over a year, and their indebtedness was considerable. Not once had he sent a reminder asking for the money. Grateful that the fond memory of Karl-Gustav still lived on in the minds of so many Badischers, she jotted a note to herself to at least make a token payment to the tolerant, generous man.

The telex machine at the side of the room began spewing out its daily messages—requests for room reservations, confirmations of supply orders, guest messages. Its clicking noise interrupted her thoughts. She dove headfirst into the business of the day. It was only when she reached for the fountain pen nested in its marble holder that she noticed the manila envelope propped up against the edge of the desk. It was marked, CONFIDENTIAL—EYES ONLY—FRAULEIN KATI MEIER. There was no return address in the corner, no canceled stamps. There was no indication it had been posted at all. That's odd, she thought. Usually the secretary placed all of the incoming mail in the box on the right-hand side of the desk. It had been full today when she arrived. No, the envelope had to have been delivered by someone already in the hotel, someone who knew intimately the location of the offices, for hers was difficult to reach from the main corridor.

Her interest piqued, she reached for the silver letter opener and with one smooth motion sliced open the sealed end of the mysterious correspondence. The single sheet of elegant Waldhotel stationery had been filled with a handwriting as familiar to her as her own. Recognizing the penmanship was simple compared with grasping the meaning of the letter. She read it through once quickly. The second time her eyes fixed on every word, trying desperately to understand fully the impact of its message. As soon as she was certain she had recovered sufficiently to speak, she grabbed her phone and dialed the three digits that had become like a lifeline to her.

"How could you not have told me?" she screamed into the phone once she was certain of his voice. "I can't understand why you, you of all people would let me find out this way," she continued.

"Kati, wait a minute, slow down. What on earth are you talking about?"

"This letter on my desk, that's what. Are you saying you don't know anything about it?"

"That's exactly what I'm saying," he replied.

She thought for a moment. Maybe he was telling the truth, but she found it difficult to believe. Dieter knew everything; he was on the main floor all the time; he knew who went where and when. She just couldn't imagine that he was unaware of this terrible news. Maybe he wasn't hiding the truth, maybe he didn't know anything. Kati sometimes jumped to conclusions too quickly. She often accused people unjustly of keeping things or information from her. Like the time she had met the two men in the lobby who were interested in buying the hotel. She had wrongly thought her mother had already sold the hotel out from under them. Perhaps it was immaturity, after all she had only just turned twenty-one, yet she had taken on the responsibilities of a much older, more experienced person.

She forced herself to calm down and continue her conversation.

"Well, if you really don't know, then I guess I owe you an apology," she admitted.

"I repeat, Kati, I am in the dark about what has you so upset and I assure you I haven't kept anything from you. If you want to tell me now what it is that has made you so outraged, I'll be pleased to try to help."

Dieter was so sincere and so honest that she immediately felt pangs of guilt for even thinking that he was capable of deceiving her.

"I am sorry, Dieter, really I am. Please accept my apology. This thing has just hit me like a rock. I think you'd better come up here right away so that we can put our heads together."

Dieter found her sitting in her desk chair, still clutching the letter in her hand. Her face told the entire story. She looked unbelieving and confused all at the same time.

"I don't know how they could do this to us," she said. "Especially at a time like this. Especially right now when we need them more than ever. On the other hand I can't blame them. It's an offer they cannot refuse. No one in their right mind would. But it's also an offer we can't afford to meet. In fact, we can't even come close. Whatever we could come up with would be just a token amount. It wouldn't even be worth presenting to them."

Dieter listened patiently. Still he couldn't imagine exactly what she was speaking about. Finally Kati realized he didn't have a clue.

"Here, read it for yourself."

She handed the paper to him. He had to straighten out the crumpled edges in order to read it. She had clutched the paper so tightly that it was torn in several places.

"Kellner?" Dieter cried. "I can't believe it!"

"Read on," she urged. "Unfortunately, that's only the beginning."

She allowed him to finish the entire page before continuing.

"So you see, they're all going. All seven of them. We're pretty well wiped out, wouldn't you agree?"

For a moment Dieter, the man whose main function was to provide an answer to every question, had absolutely nothing to say.

"The Europäischer Hof will have some top-flight kitchen staff, won't they? I figure between all of them they're getting about eighty years of experience." Not only had Head Chef Kellner decided to accept the Europäischer Hof's generous offer, but he was taking six members of the staff with him. The sous-chef, the saucier, and four apprentices were also leaving. Soon. Very soon. The resignation letter gave her only three weeks to find replacements, and in no time the busy Christmas season would be upon them.

"Oh, Kati, I'm so sorry. Believe me, I had no idea. Most of them wouldn't confide in me at this point anyway. They know we're too close. Besides, I couldn't have kept a secret like this. I would have been up here with the news the minute I heard anything. This is far too devastating a situation to ignore. I'm really surprised that you thought I would keep something like this from you."

"I said I was sorry and I truly am," she repeated. "It's just one thing after another these days, and I guess I thought you might be trying to protect me. I'm so anxious for some good news I could scream. I just came from Dr. Hoeffer's office. Mother's diagnosis isn't good either. It's just been too much for one day. I am sorry."

"Apology accepted," he said. "Anyway, we've no time now to dwell on that. We'd better get on the phone right away and start recruiting some new people. The timing couldn't be worse, right before the holidays and all. I'll get busy immediately."

"In the meantime, how are your cooking skills?" Kati asked.

"I make delicious sandwiches," he offered, "and my blueberry pancakes are known throughout the forest."

"Exactly the menu I had in mind for New Year's lunch," she joked. The sparkling eyes became deadly serious. "We may have lost the battle, Dieter, but the war is still on," she proclaimed.

"That's the spirit, Kati," he said encouragingly. "We'll get through this one too. But we don't have a moment to waste."

She was already dialing the number of the cooking school in nearby Strasbourg before he was out of the room.

By the end of the day she had exhausted most of their possibilites. Even the few leads she was able to get all said exactly the same thing —yes, they would in fact have some apprentices available, but certainly not until after the first of the year. Not one person she spoke with gave her any hope of hiring anyone before then. After the first of the year they would be coming to an empty hotel, she wanted to scream. Becker's was ninety-two percent booked from the eighteenth of December through the middle of January. Considering the hotel's situation, and what they had gone through this year, she couldn't ask for much more than that. In fact, she was delighted. But she stood to lose all of that business if the kitchen was not up to speed. Right now she couldn't think how they could possibly get enough help to remedy the situation.

She had spoken with Kellner, expressed her shock and disappointment, and begged him to stay through the end of the year. But it was futile; he had already committed to the other hotel. His decision was firm. In the end all she could do was wish him the very best and plan to spend as much time with him as possible before he left.

The crisis had taken up so much of the day that she was forced to remain in her office late into the night. She began to nod off while reading through the latest purchasing reports. She gathered the stack of papers and went next door to her grandfather's old office to curl up on the comfortable leather sofa. Her intention was to finish the ledgers there, but she dozed off almost immediately. It seemed only a few minutes, but in fact it had been over two hours, when the piercing ring of the telephone jolted her out of a profound sleep. She jumped up, scattering the papers that had fallen against her chest when she had no longer been able to keep her eyes open.

She cleared her throat before picking up the receiver. Still she was uncertain what time it was. How long had she been on the couch? Had she slept through the night, or only for a few minutes?

"Hello," she said in a scratchy tone, unable to conceal her sleepiness.

"I awakened you, didn't I? I'm sorry," said the caller.

The sound of her sister's voice roused her, and suddenly all traces of drowsiness vanished. She hadn't spoken to her since that never-to-be forgotten Christmas Eve almost four years ago, but there was no mistaking a voice she had grown up with, a voice so distinctive it could only belong to Eva-Maria.

"Hello, Eva-Maria, how are you?"

"Fine, Kati. I was calling to see about you. I heard that you've been having some problems at the hotel."

"Problems"—that was the understatement of the decade. Problems, that was for certain. But which ones, and how Eva-Maria could have found out about them remained a mystery.

"Yes, that's true," Kati agreed, but offered nothing more. She knew if she said what she was feeling—that Eva-Maria was the cause of most of the real difficulties, the important ones—such as their father's suicide and their mother's abysmal depression, the conversation would end before she was able even to determine the reason for her call.

"Well, I just wanted to know how you were doing, that's all." She sounded as if she was prepared to end the conversation at that point.

"Under the circumstances, which, I must say, you have been instrumental in creating," Kati stopped herself before it was too late, "things are okay. Mutti is very ill, however, and I'm not sure if she'll ever be the same again." Suddenly it occurred to Kati that her sister might not even know about their father. They had not been in contact with her since she and Peter had left the hotel on that cold night in December. Surely, she must know, Kati reasoned. It was evident she was in touch with someone in the hotel.

"That's too bad," she replied, as if she had heard that the weather report was not good or that some other small, inconsequential disappointment had been mentioned. "I was really only concerned about you, though."

It was among the strangest comments Kati had ever heard, but she had decided long ago that her sister was indeed a very different person than anyone else she had ever encountered. Eva-Maria lived in another world altogether—her thoughts and actions were explainable only to herself.

"Well, Eva-Maria, I'm fine. If you've still got a friend at the hotel, you know that I've been trying to run the place, to maintain it, and hopefully someday to restore its business. Since Father's death Mutti hasn't been able to help too much. She's very depressed. I'm not certain if she'll ever be the same again."

Eva-Maria exploded into the phone. "Well, it's no one's fault but her own. She pushed Father into doing what he did. She gave him no choice, insisting that he become a hotelier. He never wanted to leave his practice. He was never interested in the hotel. But she drove him into it. Once he was in, there was no turning back. She insisted that he make the hotel a success. Peter gave him the idea how to do it. But then he became greedy, taking the money for himself. Why do you think he killed himself, Kati? It's only because he couldn't face the consequences of what he had done."

Kati was shocked. Eva-Maria had to be lying. But she had to admit that it did answer so many unanswered questions. Like why her mother never pushed to have the police go after Peter. Why she had been so reluctant even to discuss what had happened with Kati. Still she refused to believe that her father could have been involved in anything so terrible. Even if she wanted to, how would she find out if there was any truth to what Eva-Maria was saying? Her mother was in no condition to even be approached on the subject. A confrontation of any sort would put her over the edge at this point. "Are you crazy, Eva-Maria? Are you really trying to tell me that Father had something to do with Peter's stealing money from the hotel? You're out of your mind. He's brainwashed you against your entire family."

"Kati, don't be a fool. Of course Father was in on it. He knew everything. It was only when Mother was about to find out about it that Peter realized it was he who would have to take the blame. So of course we were forced to leave. I love him, so I went with him."

"I really have nothing to say to your outrageous accusations," said the confused, bewildered Kati. "They are too unbelievable to even deserve a response."

"All right, Kati, continue to think as you wish. Someday you'll see. All I can say to you, the only advice I can give you, is to get out of the hotel as soon as you can. You're just wasting your time. You have nothing there. Why don't you move to Munich or Frankfurt and start a life of your own?"

"No, Eva-Maria, I could never do that. Despite all the problems, I'm happy here in Baden-Baden. I'm happy in the hotel. You are the only member of the family who has been able to turn your back on history and on your entire family." She had had enough. She placed the receiver gently in its cradle and returned to the sofa. She stared into the remains of the fire she had started earlier. Now only its reddened embers remained, smoldering and hissing softly. Could the distant, uncaring woman on the phone really be her sister, the one she had grown up with—shared a room, laughter, and tears with—throughout her entire childhood? Could the accusation she had made possibly be true? It was too painful even to consider. And if it was true, Eva-Maria wasn't the only member of the family to desert the rest.

Her wise old Opa had once told her that life would never fail to fascinate her. He said it would offer her a wider range of emotions than she ever thought possible. Only now did she begin to understand what he had meant.

She walked slowly through the darkened hallways and down the staircase to leave a note on the reception desk. There was not a rustle. Everything was still. The guests were sleeping soundly, hopefully in comfort and appreciation of all the Waldhotel worked so hard to provide. She glanced around slowly—she saw the beauty of the rooms—the fabrics, the paintings, the special color of the paint— each element had been selected with such care and concern. All of a sudden she understood completely what her grandfather had felt about his hotel—the affection, the pride, the almost physical attach- ment he had had for it—and she experienced the very same emotions. It wasn't true what Eva-Maria had said. Not about her father. And not about the hotel. Absolutely not true. On the contrary, this was her life, the only life she had. She loved it passionately. There was no place else in the world she would rather be than right here. Yes, this was her home. Suddenly she was again fortified to do whatever was necessary to protect that which meant everything to her.

CHAPTER

15

*H*E RAN AS FAST and as furiously as his long, lean legs would carry him, but by the time Christophe Robillard reached the end of the platform, the train was a good ten yards in the distance, puffing mightily on its way eastward. For one brief moment he considered making a gallant leap and attempting to grab onto the last car. But his sense of distance was acute, and he knew he'd never make it. He would only end up as a grim statistic. No, he couldn't even chance it. He was far too excited to be headed where he was going to put himself in the slightest danger. He ran his elegant, thin fingers through his wavy black hair in despair. *"Merde!"* he shouted to no one in particular, as there was no one else on the platform. "Damn it! If only I hadn't answered the phone." No amount of swearing could change things. It was too late. The train was gone.

Sunday afternoon was a slow time at the Lausanne station. The trains ran much less frequently than on the weekdays. He returned to the station house to check the schedule.

He was in luck. There was another train, not an express, mind you, but a local, an excruciatingly slow local, which would take hours longer than the one he had just missed. But at least it would get him on his way. However, his problems were not over. He would miss his connection in Zurich and would be held over there until Monday morning. Then he could board an express for the short ride north to Baden-Baden. He would still arrive later than they expected him, so he headed for the international telephones to make the call to inform them of his delay. He had promised them he would arrive late on Sunday and be ready to start work first thing Monday morning. Now he would lose half the day. Also, he felt rather stupid calling to tell them he had missed the train. What a way to start a new job! Particularly one as wonderful as he knew this one was going to be.

His father had an uncanny way of telephoning at the most inopportune moments. Christophe had finished packing, had closed his valises, and was in the process of taking one last look around his simple room in the dorm when the phone rang. He contemplated letting it ring, but at the last moment he grabbed the receiver.

"You sound as if you're in a rush," his father said.

"Indeed I am, Father. You know I'm leaving today. My train's in less than an hour. I've got to run."

"I only called to see if you're still going to go through with it," he asked.

"I wouldn't miss the opportunity for the world. I told you that last week. I've made my decision. I'm not about to change my plans at this late date. Now, please, I've got to go. I'll call you from Germany when I get settled."

"All right," his father said resignedly. "You know very well what I think of your decision. It's a huge mistake to leave school at this point, particularly for a hotel in Germany. And one in the middle of the Black Forest to boot. You only have one semester left. A degree from the hotel school in Lausanne, the finest in the world, is worth far more to your future than this position. You'll find out as much about fine food there as you would in London, perhaps even less, if that's possible," he complained, with the typical disdain most Frenchmen have for any food not produced or cooked in their sacred homeland.

"I know exactly how you feel, Father," Christophe replied. "I'm sure you'll change your mind if I'm successful. Look, I think it's the opportunity of a lifetime. Where else could I be offered a head chef's position at my age? And at such a prestigious resort? You've often said yourself that if there was an equivalent of our hotel in another country, it would be the Waldhotel. We even share some of the same guests. Many people who come to us in the summer also spend a week or two out of the year in Baden-Baden. Now, please, I've got to hang up. I'm going to miss the train."

And so he had. Now he was standing in the station with two hours to spare until the next one left.

Kati received the message about Christophe's delayed arrival while she was having Sunday lunch in the dining room with her mother and Dieter.

"Oh no," she sighed when the operator handed her the message.

She turned to Dieter, her face pained. "I hope we haven't made yet another mistake. It certainly isn't starting out very well."

"He sounded very upset and was most apologetic about it, Fräulein Meier," commented the operator. "He made me promise that I would deliver the message to you in person as soon as I went on my break," she added. "I really do think it was something beyond his control."

"Thank you for telling me, Kristina," Kati said kindly.

"Well, maybe I'm just jumping to conclusions," she said to her mother.

"Yes, I'm sure that's it," Tilla responded. It was less and less often that she was able to participate in a conversation. Her mind was clearly not on the hotel and its problems. After many long and painful discussions, Kati had finally been able to convince her to begin the new treatments, but they weren't scheduled to start until the following week.

Kati couldn't help but be extremely cautious. After all that had happened, she had lost her trust in nearly everyone, particularly someone she had never met. But after two weeks had passed and there were no prospects in sight, she had become desperate. When the call came in from a man named Christophe Robillard, a student at the famous hotel school in Lausanne, she was more than happy to speak with him.

He had heard about the job from one of his professors, who at one point was considering applying for the position but had then decided against it. Christophe was aggressive enough to go after the job on his own. He felt confident that he had learned enough to pull off the job. It was a long shot, but he wanted to try it anyway.

"How much experience do you have?" Kati had asked.

"Certainly not as much as you need," he replied honestly. "But I've got more energy and ambition than you can find anywhere else." He couldn't tell her that he had grown up in a hotel, one of the finest hotels in the world, the Villa Soleil, only a few kilometers outside of Cannes. He couldn't tell her that as early as his mind could recall, he was tugging at his father's apron strings, asking him what he could do to help with the preparation of the elegant food. Christophe's grandfather, Amaurey de Beaumont had founded the Villa Soleil the same year Ludwig Becker had started the Waldhotel. They had been keenly interested in each other's progress, but they had never met. Henri-Etienne de Beaumont, Amaurey's only son and Christophe's father, took the reins after Amaurey's death. Like Karl-Gustav, he had become a world-class hotelier. Christophe couldn't tell her that when he had enrolled in the school in Lausanne, he had chosen to use his mother's maiden name, Robillard, instead of his given name, so that he would never be recognized as being the son of the great hotelier. He didn't want to tell her any of these things. It was so important, indeed it was crucial to him, that he become a success on his own, without the burden of being associated with his father. He needed to add his own distinctive imprint to the hotel world. His idea of what constituted good management differed greatly from that of his father. He aspired to run the Villa Soleil one day, and it looked as if he would have the opportunity to do just that. Even though his older brother, Phillippe, had a financial stake in the property, he had no interest whatsoever in running the place. He was off in New York living his own life, dealing with his problems in a different way.

So he mentioned none of these things. Nevertheless, he succeeded in convincing Kati to let him come and take over the kitchen. He realized how great her needs were. It was less than four weeks until Christmas Day. Twenty-four years old and head chef at one of the finest hotels in Europe. He was ecstatic! He still couldn't believe his good fortune.

Kati sensed that his enthusiasm was genuine, and since the day they had spoken, she felt herself anxiously awaiting his arrival. She had been totally honest with him, explaining the hotel's tenuous financial situation. He understood and agreed to accept a token salary. If things worked out, they would review it in the spring. She had also been able to round up two apprentices whose plans had suddenly changed. They, too, were willing to work for the experience and asked for little money.

Now she would have to wait one day longer than she had planned to meet this stranger in whom she had such high hopes.

Kati was walking across the lobby late Monday afternoon when, out of the corner of her eye, she saw the revolving door's heavy glass panels swing around with far more force than usual. Stepping out was a man she knew instantly had arrived on the train from Zurich. He was tall, much taller than she had expected. However, she realized, she hadn't really expected anything in particular. Of course, she knew that Christophe would be a few years older than she. But she had been far too busy to think about what he might look like. It was a pleasant surprise indeed. He was very handsome, with dark, almost black hair, and vivid blue eyes. He was conservatively and professionally dressed in a white shirt and striped tie. The deep blue gabardine of his double-breasted suit only served to highlight the color of his eyes, eyes that sparkled in anticipation. She paused for a second and then walked straight toward him.

"You must be Christophe Robillard," she said, never stopping to think for an instant what she would do if it wasn't he.

His kind blue eyes, the color of the Black Forest sky on a clear day, smiled at her. "Yes, I am," he replied, his accent leaving no doubt that French was his native tongue. "I'm terribly sorry to be late."

"It's not a problem. We were only disappointed because we were anxious to meet you," Kati said, accepting his outstretched hand. Immediately she noticed his hands. They were wonderful, with long, elegant fingers. His touch was soft, yet masculine. Suddenly her reverie was interrupted.

"You are Kati, then?" he asked.

She began to laugh. In her determination to prove that her instincts were correct, she had failed to introduce herself. "Yes, I'm sorry, I am." She dropped his hand, fearing that she had already held it too long. "Did you have a good trip?"

"Yes, thank you, I did. Only it was a little longer than I had planned. I was forced to spend the night in Zurich, which is why I am late in arriving."

"Yes, I know. Kristina, our telephone operator, the one who took your message, explained to me that you had been delayed. She said it sounded as if something beyond your control had happened."

"Yes, it was completely out of my control," Christophe agreed. "The train pulled out of the station, leaving me behind on the platform."

Kati looked at him, confused at such an odd explanation.

"I missed the train," he admitted. "I was late getting to the station." Something in Kati's nature made him want to be honest with her from the very beginning. She was a beautiful young woman, but in addition to her physical beauty, her face held a special warmth. Despite her businesslike attitude, she appeared to be very vulnerable. He did not want to deceive her, even in the smallest matter.

Suddenly they both laughed together. At his words Kati understood him completely. She liked him for being so truthful. Her doubts began to disappear and she forgave him for being delayed. Once again her hopes rose that she had made the right decision in letting him come to the Waldhotel.

"Would you like to go to your room and spend some time getting settled?" she offered.

"No, I'd really prefer to get started right away, if that fits in with your schedule," he countered.

Once again, a smile crossed Kati's face. It was exactly what she wanted to hear. "Fine," she agreed, "I'll just have one of the porters take your things across the street. Then we can get started. But first, let me introduce you to Dieter, our head concierge. I've a feeling that he is going to become your new best friend."

Christophe nodded his head. No doubt Dieter was a top-notch concierge. A hotel simply did not earn the reputation of being a grand hotel without having a terrific concierge. He would probably be able to help him a great deal. His instincts told him that the charming Kati would also become his good friend.

They worked with a vengeance to prepare for the holiday onslaught, and together they came through it remarkably well. Christophe knew his way around the kitchen with his eyes closed. Everyone appeared to enjoy working with him. He seemed so well informed about hotel operations, and even Dieter commented that he was extremely knowledgeable in many areas.

Kati thought nothing of it—she merely chalked it up to a fine education, for which the school in Lausanne was recognized. Knowing the kitchen was under control gave her much-needed extra time to concentrate on building up their business again. She was grateful for the gift of Christophe Robillard.

. . .

Tilla's news was good as well. The shock treatments had been effective in snapping her out of her deep depression. As unpleasant as they were, she had gone religiously. To her credit she never missed a session. With Kati's love and support, she had endured them. Slowly she began to reawaken—her spirits lifted, her appetite returned, she laughed again.

One afternoon in late April she returned to the office she had abandoned so many months before. Kati was startled to find her there as she ran in to get something out of one of the files.

"Mutti, you surprised me," she said. "I'm so glad to see you here. You must be feeling very well."

"Yes, I feel good," Tilla answered. "It's about time I got back into the swing of things, don't you think?"

"I sure do," Kati said, her voice overflowing with joy. She went over to the desk and hugged her mother tightly.

"I may need a lot of help, though. You'll have to bring me up-to-date where I left off," Tilla said.

"No problem. Get your questions together. I'm only next door. Whenever you need me, buzz on the intercom and I'll come running," Kati cheerfully offered. She didn't want to let on that she was less than enthusiastic about Tilla's return. She would be watching her every move, monitoring her every step. Things were just beginning to run smoothly. Kati had organized the systems and personnel, and she wasn't willing to let anyone disturb them. As pleased as she was with her mother's progress, they had all spent too much time undoing many of Tilla's mistakes. Kati would have to make certain that everything she did was checked and then double-checked.

Tilla's heart filled with love for her young daughter, who had matured so much during the last year. She was so proud of her, but so worried as well. Kati looked tired all the time. Mostly from carrying the weight of this place on her shoulders, Tilla reasoned. What she had just uttered was so true. . . . Kati had always been there whenever she had needed her. Now that she was well, it was her turn to try to make up for all the pain and heartache she had caused her most precious little girl.

. . .

By the time the first spring flowers dared to poke their heads through the hardened earth, things looked better for the future of the Waldhotel Becker than they had in several years. The staff was in place; their morale was high. The cuisine was well received, and the occupancy rate was climbing. Kati was delighted, as well as exhausted, from the almost nonstop pace that had become normal over the past two years. She felt confident enough about how things were going to take a well-deserved break. It was just for three days. She decided to go to Munich for a brief visit with Heidi and her husband, Mark. She had only had the opportunity to meet Mark at their wedding, and they hadn't had the chance to talk very much at all. The reception was so crowded, and every time she started to speak with him, he would be whisked away to pose for yet another photograph or for the cutting of the cake. She was really looking forward to being away. She yearned to relax with her best friend and not have the constant worries from which she could never escape when she was in the hotel. So, after many last-minute instructions and extractions of promises to call if anything went wrong, Kati finally departed for Munich.

She adored the cozy, cheery house that Heidi had so lovingly decorated. When she first arrived, Mark carried her luggage upstairs to her room, as Heidi grabbed her hand and insisted on taking her on a tour of the rest of their tiny home. The room next to Kati's was completely outfitted as a nursery. The walls were covered with a dainty floral-patterned paper, a mixture of the lightest hues of pink and blue. In another corner was a huge collection of stuffed animals. There must have been thirty toys—she spotted a giraffe, a lion, a bear, an elephant, a monkey, and even a tiny mouse complete with whiskers and a devious look on his face. Kati recognized Heidi's own teddy bear, which had graced her bed both at her home in Baden-Baden and later at the university. An antique crib covered with delicate white lace sat regally in another corner awaiting the arrival of a brand-new life.

"Are you trying to tell me something?" Kati asked.

One look at her friend's beaming smile and her question was answered.

"Oh yes, Kati, isn't it exciting?" Heidi practically screamed. She wrapped her arms around her oldest, dearest pal, with whom she had

shared so many important moments. But perhaps none more memo-
rable than this one. "I didn't want to tell you on the telephone. I
thought it would be so much more fun to celebrate after you arrived.
I'm glad you finally got here. I couldn't have kept the secret much
longer," she said, pointing to her tummy and gently rubbing the small
mound that showed her progress at four months.

"I'm so happy for you both," Kati exclaimed.

That night, after enjoying a lovely dinner with Mark and Heidi, Kati
lay awake in the guest room, thinking about the life she had chosen.
As pleased as she was for her best friend, she felt saddened that her
friendship with Heidi had changed. No longer would they have the
same carefree relationship they had shared in the past. No longer
would they share the same concerns or have the same needs. Heidi
had moved on to a totally new stage in her life. Soon she would be a
mother, while Kati seemed to be light-years away from starting a
family of her own. Her short friendship with Rick had been the
closest she had ever been to being involved with someone. When
would Kati ever meet a man with whom to share a home? When she
finally fell asleep, the joyous voices of small children playing with
their stuffed toys filled her dreams.

During the trip home Kati continued to reflect about many thing
that she had pushed aside in her mind for a very long time. Heidi's
pregnancy jolted her into thinking about just what she was doing.
Was it really worth it to devote so much of herself—all she had to
give, in fact, to the hotel? Years later, would she regret not having
chosen a different course, perhaps an easier road? One where her
success was more easily guaranteed? She knew there were no guar-
antees in life. That much she had learned in a hard and painful
manner. What would she change if she could, she asked herself?
Would she live somewhere else? That was out of the question. Work
at something else? That was unthinkable. Besides, she wasn't qualified to do anything else, and even if she were, it would most certainly
mean working for someone. That wasn't what she wanted at all.

By the time the train pulled in to the charming station in Baden-
Baden, Kati had decided once and for all that indeed this was her
home. This was where she had to be. All the other important things

in life would come in time: a husband, a baby, a life of her own. That much faith she still possessed.

She walked briskly past the freshly painted dark green flower boxes overflowing with a profusion of daffodils, irises, and daisies. The beauty of the town never ceased to astonish her. She practically ran the entire distance to the hotel.

16

"**A**RE YOU SURE you can handle everything, Mutti?" Kati asked one last time. She was on her way to Strasbourg for a two-day hotel-management seminar. She had read about it in one of the industry publications and it sounded like exactly the type of information she needed to learn in order to perform more efficiently at the hotel. There were lectures, films, and discussions by prominent members of the hotel community. She decided to go. Now her only hesitation was leaving her mother in charge for the weekend. Dieter was off on a well-deserved and much-needed short vacation.

Tilla had been so good of late, her spirits so high, and everything had gone smoothly during Kati's recent trip to Munich. Surely she could keep things under control for the next forty-eight hours.

"Kati, sweetheart, please don't worry about a thing. Everything will be fine here. Go and enjoy yourself, and learn all you need to know to make this place even better."

"Okay," she said, at last convinced that not much could happen between now and Sunday night. The hotel was only half full, so the demands were not overwhelming. "You have Dieter's phone number at his brother's in case you need him."

"Yes, I do, Kati. Now please, go, or you'll be late."

With lingering reluctance she kissed her mother good-bye and headed for France.

Henri-Etienne de Beaumont's limousine pulled up in front of the Waldhotel just minutes after Kati left. It was merely a stroke of fate that she was not there when he made his very first visit to a hotel he had heard so much about from his father, and more recently from his son.

"Father, you are welcome to come and see the hotel, see where I'm working, but I insist that you not let anyone know that I'm your son or that I'm related to you in any way. I've built up a great deal of respect here from everyone I work with, and knowing who I really am will only spoil it and make my success here that much more difficult," Christophe had pleaded with Henri-Etienne last week when he had called to suggest that he come to Baden-Baden for a few days.

"All right, Christophe. I'll be like a phantom in the night. If I see you in the hallway, I'll walk right by you," he said sarcastically.

"Father, please, this is really important to me. I'd appreciate it if you could take my request seriously."

"Okay, okay," he had at last agreed. "I'll be on perfect behavior. It would be nice if we could have a dinner together, at least. After all you've told me about this charming town, I'd like to see some of its attractions."

"Father, you must be kidding. I couldn't possibly go out for dinner. Especially on a weekend. Who would run the kitchen? It's not as if I have three sous-chefs under me," Christophe retorted, a little more sarcastically than he had intended. "I'm sorry, Father, but dinner is really out of the question. But we can have a drink or an early breakfast. We'll go out to someplace in town."

"Fine, that will be just fine. I'll see you on Friday, then. Call me in my room when the coast is clear."

"You're right, son," Henri-Etienne said that night when they met for dinner in town. "The hotel is quite wonderful. Needs a lot of work, though. Especially with the Europäischer Hof looking so sharp. I went over there this afternoon. They've got Becker's beat hands down —everything is tip top, the rooms are larger, the dining room is among the loveliest I've seen. It is really first-class."

"Yes, they've managed to steal many of the staff also. They took Becker's chef and several of his assistants. He's a good man. That's what gave me this opportunity. I just love it, Father. People seem to like my cooking."

"It doesn't surprise me a bit, Christophe. After all, it's in your blood."

Tilla felt the man's eyes on her as they followed her every motion— up and back, up and back, up and back—staying glued to her until she had completed her daily routine of swimming fifty laps in the hotel pool. Now that her mind was healthy again, she wanted to get her body back into shape also. She wanted to take care of herself, to take pride in her appearance. Walking past the boutiques on the Sophienstrasse, she yearned to start wearing pretty clothes again. Under the strict supervision of the hotel's physical therapist, she had begun working out regularly. So far she was pleased with the results. Apparently this gentleman thought she looked pretty good too. When she felt it was safe to look, she glanced in his direction, trying her best to be as inconspicuous as possible. It was difficult, as they were the only two people at the pool. The man was lying on one of the comfortable chaises. He pretended to be looking out through the large plate-glass window, which offered a beautiful view of the river and the Lichtentaler Allee. He wore the hotel's lush white terry robe. As soon as she looked away, she felt his eyes back on her. She looked at him again, and for one brief second their eyes met. She smiled tentatively and then turned her head away at once, pretending to be occupied with the newspaper she had brought to read while she rested after her swim. She'd only had a half second's glance, but what she did see was very interesting. He was handsome in a rugged way. His features were not refined. His wavy black hair had been left long at the sides and back, giving him a distinctly sporty and youthful appearance. She judged him to be in his mid-fifties, but he possessed the carriage and attitude of a much younger man—very self-assured and a little on the arrogant side. She found him terribly intense, and very attractive.

It had to be her, Henri-Etienne thought. She fit Christophe's description perfectly—about five feet six, with auburn hair worn to her shoulders. Her face looked somehow sad, drained of life. He remembered his son telling how Madame Meier had been ill for some time following her husband's suicide. He could sympathize with the devastation that such an event could bring. Yes, he was certain the woman he had been watching was Tilla Becker-Meier. She was not bad-looking, a little older perhaps than he was accustomed to. Her daughter would have been a more logical candidate. Henri-Etienne usually made it a point not to date anyone older than half his age. Therefore, any female over twenty-nine, unless, of course, she was an extraordinary beauty, didn't have a shot at romance with the great hotelier. His current mistress had just celebrated her twenty-first birthday. He considered her just about the perfect age to fulfill his wildest fantasies and participate in his casual escapades. He thought of her now as he approached Tilla.

"You're Tilla Becker-Meier, are you not?" he asked.

"Yes, I am," she replied, noting the man's charming French accent.

"Please forgive me for intruding. I'm Henri-Etienne de Beaumont, and I'd like to compliment you on your wonderful hotel. It's my first visit here and I find it delightful." That was stretching the truth a bit, for he found it quite staid and much too quiet to satisfy his taste. He yearned for a wilder environment. Yes, the Black Forest was beautiful, but what good did a lot of trees do one, anyway? Where were the sea, the yachts, and all of the activity associated with the water? Well, it didn't matter right now. His son loved the place, and he was determined that he should have it.

"Why, thank you, Monsieur de Beaumont. I'm very pleased that you're enjoying yourself. Nothing makes us happier than to have satisfied guests. You're a hotelier yourself, are you not?"

So she had heard of the de Beaumont family. That was a good omen. It might make his work a bit easier.

"Yes, I am, indeed. My father founded a hotel in the south of France, which I now run. Perhaps you've visited it?"

"Unfortunately never," Tilla answered, "but I would love to someday. I understand it is a very special property. Many of our guests speak very highly of it."

"Perhaps I could tell you all about it over dinner tonight. If you're free, that is. I know *personne* in the area, and I'd be pleased if you'd join me."

Tilla was a bit taken aback by his forwardness. But what harm could it do? Both Kati and Dieter were gone. She had planned to have a quiet dinner in the apartment. Yes, she would agree to dine with him, but only on her conditions.

"I'd be pleased to have dinner with you, Monsieur de Beaumont. But only if you agree to be my guest. We can eat in our dining room. We have a wonderful new chef whose cuisine I'm certain you will find to be excellent."

He could not contain the smile that crept across his face. He found the irony of the situation very amusing. "Very well, I accept your kind invitation. Shall we say about eighty-thirty?"

"You were right, Madame Meier. The food in your dining room is superb," commented Henri-Etienne as he finished the last of his sweetbreads. They were one of the most difficult items on the menu to prepare; just a moment too long in the pan and they became leatherlike and impossible to eat. Although he personally did not care for their distinct taste, he had ordered them especially to test his son's culinary skills. Christophe had passed with flying colors. "Please send my compliments to your chef. I believe he is even better than you say."

"With pleasure," Tilla had said.

They spent an enjoyable evening together, talking mostly about the hotel business. Tilla found herself opening up a bit about the Waldhotel, about the difficulties they had had since the death of Karl-Gustav. Henri-Etienne was a good listener and he seemed genuinely interested in their problems. It was also the first time since Johannes's death that Tilla had been alone in the company of a man. Of course, for a long time she had been too ill, too unconcerned about the world. A man's company hadn't mattered at all. But tonight she felt feminine again. She practiced smiling, tilting her head just so, and laughing with this stranger from her father's homeland.

In bed that night, the covers pulled up snugly, she closed her eyes and relived the gentle kiss Henri-Etienne had given her when he had said good night.

Henri-Etienne left early the next morning to return to the Villa Soleil. He had made a good start. On his way home he finalized his game plan for the Waldhotel.

CHAPTER

17

*T*HEY WERE the most beautiful flowers Tilla had ever seen. When the porter first entered her room, hidden behind the mass of brilliant color, she couldn't imagine who could possibly have sent such a gorgeous offering.

"Hans, you must have made a mistake," she said to the rosy-cheeked young man who had recently joined the hotel as a trainee.

"Not at all, Frau Meier. The card is addressed to you. Here it is," he said. Immediately Tilla recognized the elegant, oversized card Sonja Fichtl used in her shop.

"My many thanks for a lovely evening" was all it said.

Henri-Etienne de Beaumont. What a thoughtful man, Tilla decided. Certainly nothing more than that. Although Tilla couldn't deny that during the past week, in the secrecy of her most private thoughts, she had thought often about him. They were sensual, sexy thoughts. His powerful arms around her, his strong hands caressing her body, his lips on hers. She was shocked by the vividness of her dreams. But surely he couldn't share her feelings. As much as she wanted to believe otherwise, she was certain that the flowers were only a gentlemanly gesture, the purpose of which was exactly what the card said. No more, no less.

When the third bouquet arrived the following week, she allowed her thoughts to change. Even Sonja had called her. Sonja had remained a good friend during her illness, visiting and calling whenever she found time in her busy schedule.

"Someone is crazy about you," she said to Tilla. "I hope you're enjoying them. Monsieur de Beaumont insists on the freshest and finest roses available. The last bunch had to be flown in from France. He wanted you to have the exquisite Tropicana color. I told him how difficult they were to find, that it would be extremely expensive to get them, but he didn't seem to care. He just wanted them."

"I'm not certain what it all means," Tilla responded, "but I'm loving every minute of it."

"The weather is at its most beautiful now, Tilla," he had told her on the phone the night before last. "Please come for a visit. I want very much to show you my hotel. And there is something I want to speak with you about. It's not the Waldhotel," he had added, not explaining exactly what he meant, "but I'm sure you will enjoy it."

Tilla debated and debated. At last she decided to make the trip. She was forty-eight years old. She felt good. She was still attractive. When was she going to start living her life again, if not now?

"I'm really looking forward to going away," Tilla admitted to Kati as they finished packing her small suitcase. "I love all the nice things we bought, too. It's been so long since I've had any new clothes!" she said as she removed the tags from each of the new, carefully chosen purchases they had carried home with them after their shopping excursion along the Langestrasse earlier that day.

"They're terrific," Kati agreed. "You're going to look smashing wandering around the Riviera in them. I especially like the yellow bathing suit you found at that new shop. The color is wonderful. It reminds me of the umbrellas we had on the lawn one summer. I loved those umbrellas. Do you remember them?"

Tilla nodded.

"I wonder what happened to those. I must make a note to see if they're still around somewhere. It would be fun to dig them out and put them back again this year. Anyway, the suit looks great on you."

Tilla's figure was still thinner than normal. Her swimming routine had worked wonders, and she had worked herself into a trim, attractive shape. She had also cut her hair. It hung loosely and gracefully around her shoulders, softening her entire face. She looked at the yellow suit once again before adding it to the pile. It was nice. It was cut much lower than any suit she had ever worn before. When she tried it on in the shop, she had thought about Henri-Etienne seeing her in it. She wanted very much for him to find her attractive.

They reviewed the final selection of clothes and then Suzanne entered to complete the packing.

Kati looked at her mother and smiled gently. "I'm just so happy you're well enough to travel. It will be very good for you. As short as it was, my weekend visit with Heidi and Mark really gave me a nice rest. You'll be a new person when you return, you'll see. Just don't get into any trouble on La Croisette," she cautioned, referring to the elegant promenade along La Napoule bay in Cannes. "You know how charming those French men can be," she teased, convinced that the possibility of her mother meeting someone and falling in love was probably very remote. Of course she hadn't seen the flowers that had been arriving almost daily, nor did she have any idea Tilla was off to visit Henri-Etienne. She just so wanted her to have a good time. More than anyone, Tilla deserved to relax and enjoy herself.

Kati had been so pleased last week to hear her mother talking about going away. When she broached the subject, it was almost as if she was asking Kati's permission to go, for they had reversed their roles long ago.

Tilla had assured her she was well enough to travel and was more than ready for a few days away from Baden-Baden. She hadn't been further than the outskirts of town since she and Johannes had gone to Paris. That seemed like another lifetime. Kati confirmed with Dr. Hoeffer that her mother was stable enough to be out on her own. He encouraged her to let her go, saying it might be just the last dose of medicine she would need to bring her completely back to normal. So Kati had agreed wholeheartedly. She had boosted Tilla's spirits even more by taking her shopping for some spring clothes. There really hadn't been any extra money for the new outfits, but Kati had managed to scrape together enough to purchase a few nice things. For the first time in a very long time she had asked the new accountant to issue her a check for her personal use. At first she had felt guilty, but after seeing the smile on her mother's face, she didn't regret it for one second.

Kati never questioned why Tilla had chosen to go to Cannes instead of some other place. Her mother had always had a special fondness for the French Riviera. It was an easy flight. The weather at this time of year was guaranteed to be delightful, so she thought it was perfectly appropriate for her to spend a few days there.

. . .

"*Ma chérie,* I want you to have a wonderful time. I know you will. Shopping is one of your specialties. Now buy some very pretty things. Not too much fabric, mind you. I don't want too much of your delicious body hidden under some fag designer's creation," he said, rubbing his hands over Morgan's firm breasts. He felt himself hardening, but he had no more time to spend with her. She had to get out of the hotel and on her way to Paris before Tilla's plane landed. It would be impossible to execute his plan if his young mistress were still at the Villa Soleil when she arrived. It was bad enough that on Tilla's first night here he had promised to escort another of his acquaintances to a party. Well, she would just have to understand. He'd make it up to her tomorrow night.

"Now off, my love. Raymond is waiting for you. I'll see you Monday night," he said, slipping a wad of five-hundred-franc notes into her waiting palm.

The air was the first thing Tilla noticed when the door was opened and she exited the plane at the busy airport in Nice. The air on the Riviera was a presence. Countless poets and writers—from Petrarch to Pagnol—had extolled its virtues, and they had been correct in doing so. Lovers spoke of the air's sensuality. It was almost supernatural, as if a divine spirit hovered nearby. The French spoke of *la douceur de l'air*—referring to the softness, the gentleness, the mildness of the environment. It possessed an indescribable quality that existed nowhere else on earth. Certainly Tilla had never felt it anyplace else.

Her last visit to the south of France had been right after Eva-Maria was born. She thought of that trip now. It evoked pleasant memories of a time she knew she could never bring back. She paused for a moment midway down the ramp and inhaled deeply. Ahh—now there was no doubt in her mind that she was doing the right thing by making the trip here.

"Madame Meier?" a voice called out as she took her first step on French soil.

"Yes," she answered with hesitation in her voice. The man had startled her. Suddenly she realized how long it had been since she had had any contact with the outside world. Kati and her doctors had created a womblike environment for her in the hotel while she slowly recovered from her illness. She had been protected and sheltered. Except for her one evening with Henri-Etienne.

"This way, please," the man said. Her nervousness showed. "Are you feeling all right, Madame Meier? Was your flight bumpy? Sometimes with the warm summer air . . ."

"No, no, I'm fine, thank you," she managed to say.

The enormous Rolls was parked on the tarmac not more than twenty yards in front of them. The man took her luggage and she followed him toward the car.

"But what about customs?" she started to ask.

"Do not worry, Madame Meier. Monsieur de Beaumont has taken care of everything for you."

Henri-Etienne leaned casually against the side of the car. He wore white slacks and an impeccably tailored blue blazer. His light blue shirt was open at the top. His sockless feet were clad in expensive loafers. She was a bit put off by the large gold medallion he wore around his neck. Tilla wasn't used to seeing men wear jewelry.

When he saw her, he smiled broadly. She looked just as she had at the Waldhotel. Conservative and a bit matronly. She looked even plainer in contrast to the other fashionably dressed women who were arriving for a visit to the Riviera. He reminded himself it was only for a weekend, just long enough to get what he wanted from Tilla Becker-Meier.

"Welcome to the French Riviera," he said in greeting. Nothing in his demeanor showed that he was less than delighted to see her. He pulled her forward to him and kissed her on both cheeks. "Please, get in," he offered as the driver held the door open for them. "We've only a short drive, twenty minutes or so, to the hotel."

It had been ages since Tilla had felt so special. Henri-Etienne pressed the electronic button that opened the smoked-glass windows in the backseat. She leaned back, her neck enveloped by the softness of the lush upholstery. She shut her eyes for a moment and enjoyed the smoothness of the ride, all the while breathing in great quantities of the extraordinary air.

They exchanged the usual pleasantries as Tilla tried to hide her mounting anxiety about coming for a weekend to visit a gentleman whom she hardly knew.

Henri-Etienne pointed out things of interest as they rode along the seaside. She looked around, amazed at the amount of building that had taken place since she was last there.

Suddenly a pleasant scent filled the air, a scent that brought back memories of her childhood—a clean, clear, sweet odor reminiscent of freshly laundered clothes. It was overwhelming in its intensity. She had been listening so intently to Henri-Etienne, gazing into his steely-black eyes as he spoke, that she had failed to notice the change of scenery as they climbed into the mountains. She sat straight up and looked out the window. For as far as she could see, the land was a brilliant purple hue. Thin shafts of the potent herb shot up out of the ground and swayed gracefully in the breeze. Lavender! The rich terrain of Provence had become a sea of vivid color, unbroken for miles. The gravel path they were traveling on was lined on either side by magnificent umbrella pines, so typical of the Mediterranean area. They were far above the sea now, high above the frenzy and traffic of the overcrowded coastline. It was several degrees cooler than it had been at the airport. Thankfully she had taken Kati's advice and carried a sweater.

"Where are we?" she demanded of Henri-Etienne.

"Welcome to the Villa Soleil, Madame Meier. We've just entered the property through the main entrance back there." He pointed backward in the direction of two imposing gates, their ironwork forged into the complex scrolled design that was the de Beaumont family crest. "It will take us just a minute longer to arrive at the reception area."

The car floated on. The driver slowed to a crawl so that he could negotiate the narrow entryway under the large canopy outside the main building.

Tilla was certain she had never been to a more beautiful spot. The stucco facade was draped in ivy and bougainvillea. She took Henri-Etienne's hand and stepped out of the car. As they approached the large open archway, she stopped abruptly. Through the door she looked down a long, wide hallway. At its end was an expanse of glass across the entire width of the building. Beyond were the glittering waters of the Mediterranean, the distinctive azure blue that gave its name to the entire coastline. Drawn toward the view, Tilla walked slowly down the corridor, oblivious to the splendid surroundings.

Without so much as a cursory glance she passed the elegant Renaissance and Louis XV furniture and museum-quality Flanders carpets. She stepped out onto the terrace. It was edged with a low stone wall. Before her lay the most breathtaking view. The hotel was built into the side of a hill at the base of the Esterel Massif, the range of volcanic mountains bordering one of the most beautiful sections of Provence. Small buildings, miniatures of the main house, dotted the side of the property. Their wide windows opened out off private terraces to the same view she was looking at now. Its twenty acres of serene privacy were accessible only via the curvy, often treacherous road on which they had just been driven. In the valley below she could see a typical sleepy Provençal village. It was clear enough to spot the old men enjoying an afternoon drinking *pastis* and playing *pétanque* on the obligatory court always placed near the town center. Overfed cats lounged lazily on the walls marking the boundary of the dusty clay court. Children and their dogs dashed in and out of the narrow cobbled streets playing kickball. Farther on, the sparkling Mediterranean stretched out to infinity. Off to her distant right the Bay of Angels was perfectly defined, each of the countless coves and inlets discernible. Directly below her the active harbor of Cannes, which she had seen from the plane, welcomed some of the largest and most luxurious yachts in the world. To the left of the expansive terrace was the hotel's swimming pool. Spectacular was the only word that came to mind. It seemed to have been carved directly out of the basalt-rock formations on the hill. The bluish tint of the stone coupled with the reflection of the water gave the whole setting a haunting, fairy-tale quality. It was so inviting she could almost feel the temperate water on her body.

"We drain it completely at dawn every morning and refill it with fresh water," he said.

She turned to Henri-Etienne. "How rude of me!" she exclaimed. She realized she had been so drawn toward the view that she had just continued walking after she had left the car.

"Don't be ridiculous, Tilla. I hope it pleases you. Many times my guests come out onto the terrace and become completely mesmerized by the view."

"In fact, I am mesmerized," she replied. "This is the most spectacular setting I've ever seen. I truly didn't expect anything so remark-able. It's paradise."

"Yes, yes, it is," he agreed fully. "In all the years I've lived here, almost fifty-nine to be exact, I have never tired of the view. Of course when my father bought the property, that little village down there was much more charming and authentic than it is now. I'm afraid the developers in the area have brought us the worst the world of new construction has to offer. The coastline has always been overbuilt, with its high rises and chock-a-block apartment buildings. Everyone feels this insatiable need to be close to the sea. I much prefer to be up here, where it is cooler and much more tranquil. The panorama is spectacular. It has so many different faces. On an especially clear night, like tonight might be, you can count up to twenty-three light-houses stretching out into the Mediterranean. It is quite an extraor-dinary sight."

"I'm sure it is. It's so peaceful being here. What a delight! I can't wait to take a swim."

"You're invited to do all of that and more. We have two tennis courts on the other side of the property, sheltered from the wind and far enough away so as not to disturb the guests. Should you wish to play, please let the concierge know. He'll be glad to arrange a game. Your bastide is ready. I've reserved the one I consider to be the most comfortable, and since you appreciate the view so much, it also has the advantage of having one of the best vistas. It's right up there."

Henri-Etienne pointed to one of the small stucco structures that Tilla had noticed earlier.

"It's the one farthest east," he continued. "Its water view isn't blocked by that peninsula," he said, pointing in the distance.

"I'm certain it will be quite wonderful. It doesn't seem as if you have a bad room in the entire complex."

"Not really bad," he agreed, "it's just that some of them are better than others. I wanted you to have the very best."

He was certainly making an effort to be charming. But somehow it was unnerving to Tilla. Perhaps, she reasoned, it was only because it had been so long since she had had a conversation alone with a man.

"Please, you must be tired from the trip. Even going a short distance these days is draining. The airports are so busy."

Tilla all of a sudden realized how delinquent she had been in thanking Monsieur de Beaumont for picking her up at the airport. She had become so involved in the beauty of the Villa Soleil, she had forgotten all her manners.

"You certainly made it easy for me, however. I apologize. I should have thanked you immediately for your kindness. It was wonderful having you there right as I got off the plane. As you may know, I haven't traveled recently."

"Think nothing of it, Madame Meier. It was my pleasure. And yes, I know. We didn't speak much about it at dinner, but you mentioned that you hadn't been feeling quite up to par. That is why I'm going to suggest that I get one of the porters to take you to your room right now so that you may relax and enjoy. Unfortunately, I have a long-standing engagement this evening, so I'll be unable to ask you for dinner. My next suggestion is that we arrange for a lovely dinner in your room, or in the dining room, whichever you prefer. Of course, if you have friends in the region you would like to see, my car is at your disposal."

"No, it's been so long since I've been here, I no longer know anyone. I'd be delighted to take something light in my room." Tilla was greatly relieved not to be dining with him that night. She needed some time alone. She'd had quite enough activity for her first day out. A quiet night would give her the chance to rest. She wanted to be ready to hear exactly what she had traveled so many miles for, whatever it was this mysterious man had in mind.

"Wonderful, then I'll get you on your way. Please follow me to the desk and I'll arrange for everything."

They walked side by side back through the wide hallway. This time Tilla became aware of the beauty of the interior rooms as well. They were startling in their superb quality. Each piece of furniture had been carefully selected and perfectly placed. The total look was one of understated elegance and old-world charm. The crispness, the perfection, the loving, constant attention to every minute detail was evident. It reminded her of the way the Waldhotel had looked and had been maintained when she was a young girl. Before her father's unexpected death, before all of the tragedies they had been forced to endure.

"Excuse me for just one moment, please," said Henri-Etienne. He stepped behind the reception desk and disappeared into the back office.

Tilla was left standing nearby. Two employees greeted her warmly, with just the correct amount of friendliness. Monsieur de Beaumont's staff had obviously been put through some rigorous training. Tilla noticed a large leather-bound book on a nearby table. Assuming it was a guest registry not unlike the one they had used for so many years at the Waldhotel, she opened the first page and began to leaf through it. Every page was filled with familiar names—celebrities, dignitaries, heads of government, writers and artists. There was no end to the list. Albert I of Belgium with Queen Elizabeth and her children, the Crown Prince of Japan, Bernard Shaw, Picasso, Chagall, Marlene Dietrich, Rita Hayworth. The list went on and on, filling every line in the thick volume. She recognized many of the guests as also having stayed at Becker's over the years.

"We're all set, Madame Meier," Henri-Etienne announced. "This is Martin," he continued, pointing to a well-groomed, smiling young man. "He will take you to Les Fleurs, which is the name of your bastide, and make certain that you are comfortable. Call at once if you should desire anything at all. Please relax tomorrow, do whatever you feel like. Should you wish to brave the coastline, my car will be waiting. Let's plan to have dinner around nine tomorrow night. I'll call for you then."

"Thank you, Monsieur de Beaumont. I'll look forward to it."

"*Moi aussi,*" he added. He took her hand and raised it to his lips. He kissed it lightly and gallantly. "I wish you a very pleasant stay."

It was a villa fit for a king, a queen, a famous writer, a movie star, or any of the others who had been lucky enough to have visited at the Villa Soleil. The furnishings continued in the same style as in the main building. Everything was chosen with the comfort and pleasure of the guests in mind. Nothing detracted from the beauty of the countryside.

Tilla threw open the doors leading out onto the terrace. After spending so much time in the confines of her room at the Waldhotel, she couldn't get enough of the outdoors. Carefully she unpacked her new things, placing them neatly in the lovely wooden armoire. She left the yellow bathing suit out. She changed into it at once. She was out of the room and headed toward the pool in no time. On her way she walked by several of the other small buildings. They had each been given a name which was written on the hand-painted Provençal tiles surrounding the entrance. Les Oiseaux (the birds), Ma Joie (my happiness), Ponant (for the gentle wind that came out of the west each year), and La Fou (for the small river that ran north of the property). They were all charming, but she agreed that the location of hers, Les Fleurs, was the nicest.

The pool lived up to her expectations. The temperature of the water was perfect, not bracingly cold, just brisk enough to still be enjoyable. It was so liberating to swim under the cloudless sky. The pool at the Waldhotel, although beautiful, was enclosed. One could see out to the Lichtentaler Allee, but the sensation was very different in the fresh, open air. She relished the feel of the water as she worked it against her body. It was the first reawakening of sensuality, of response, that Tilla had felt in over two years. She felt like a woman again, and she found it very pleasurable. The sun soon dropped behind the mountains and the temperature fell as well. She bundled up in the lush terry robe and marched briskly back to her luxurious suite, invigorated by the exercise. Just as she was crossing the narrow pathway outside her room, she looked down to the road below just in time to see Henri-Etienne de Beaumont pulling out from under the canopy in a lipstick-red convertible. Its brilliant, vibrant color was in stark contrast to the peaceful, comforting hues of the landscape. Somehow it looked out of place, as if it belonged only to the fast-paced, glamorous Corniche, which ran along the water. Maybe that was where he was headed, she reasoned.

Henri-Etienne was an enigma to her. She had so many unanswered questions, beginning with what she was doing here at all. But she was enjoying it too much to dwell on any of them at the moment. Right now she planned to take a luxuriously long soak in the elegant bathtub that shared the view from her terrace. She would worry about everything later. Tomorrow. Or the day after. At this point she wanted to prolong the dream for as long as possible.

She was still outside on the terrace, mesmerized by the changing artistry of the light as night fell, when she heard a soft knock on her door.

"Madame Meier, your dinner as ordered by Monsieur de Beaumont," the waiter announced as he wheeled the cart into the living room. "I hope I am not too early," he said.

"Not at all," Tilla assured him, realizing she hadn't eaten all day and was suddenly starving.

"Monsieur de Beaumont thought you might enjoy one of our local fish. He asked the chef to prepare one of the most delicious varieties found in the region, the dorade."

"I know it well," Tilla said. In fact it was her favorite fish, delicate, light, and possessing a specific, delightful taste. She looked at the perfectly cooked fillets on the tasteful china. They had been lightly sautéed and presented elegantly, surrounded by small vegetables indigenous to the area. She was certain it was going to be wonderful. The wine he had selected, a dry white, complemented the entire meal. The fish was outstanding; the *haricots verts*—the dainty green beans grown throughout the south of France—were remarkably crisp. The simple green salad was brushed with the lightest Provençal olive oil. She relished everything, and the plates were empty of food when the waiter returned for the cart some time later.

After finishing her dinner, Tilla had telephoned Kati, who seemed delighted that the trip had gone smoothly and that she was having such a good time. Tilla had been pleased that Kati was dashing off to tend to some guest crisis and was unable to talk for very long. She knew she had not been completely honest about her plans, and she had wanted to avoid furthering the lie until she understood herself exactly why she was at the Villa Soleil.

Now tucked warmly under the feather-light down comforter, Tilla began to read a book that had been placed by her bedside. It told of the history of the area, the founding of nearby Antibes by the Greeks of Massilia in the fifth century B.C., and the subsequent invasion by the Romans. She got as far as 1794, when Napoleon and his family lived in Antibes and he was charged with defending the coastline, when she drifted off into the most peaceful sleep she had experienced in months.

CHAPTER

18

*I*T WAS A PERFECT DAY in paradise. Tilla had left the heavy draperies open, not wanting to miss a moment of the early-morning sun as it rose over the Mediterranean.

She was up early and was again attracted to the luscious waters of the swimming pool. Two other guests had the same notion. A waiter was at her side the moment she emerged from her swim, offering to bring her breakfast out to one of the small tables if she so desired. She thought yes, and so her morning began delightfully with fresh coffee and juice. She was reminded of the true meaning of "croissant" from the first taste of the freshly made, light-as-air pastry she found on her plate. Only the French could produce such a masterpiece.

She decided to sport one of her new outfits and venture into Cannes. The car arrived at her doorstep precisely as she was finishing dressing.

She wandered aimlessly in and out of the shops. Each was more chic and expensive than the next. She was amazed and fascinated with the beautiful French clothing. Too often German women traded style for comfort or warmth. In this temperate climate none of those concerns existed. Everything was made to tempt, to taunt, and to amuse. Kati would love the fun dress she found for her. They would never be able to get anything as stylish in conservative Baden-Baden. She hoped there would be a special occasion soon so she could wear it. Maybe it would be on a date. She worried so about Kati's lack of social life. She hadn't been out with anyone that Tilla knew about since returning to the hotel from university. The flattering dress she now clutched in the elegant shopping bag would be sure to capture any boy's heart.

As she strolled along, the shadow of the Rolls was never far behind. She was thankful later when she looked at her watch. She had been walking for hours. It was time to return to the hotel and get ready for her dinner with Henri-Etienne.

"I understand you enjoyed your meal last evening," Henri-Etienne said to her as he walked forward in greeting.

"Absolutely, thank you. The dorade was superb. It tasted as if it had been in the sea only hours before."

"That's not far from the truth," he agreed. "I insist on everything coming in as fresh as humanly possible. Most of the time we're fairly successful. We're blessed with this extremely fertile soil. We can grow almost anything."

Tilla's thoughts returned to the Waldhotel. Karl-Gustav had always insisted on the very same thing. But recently she knew they had had to make some concessions due to prices they could no longer afford and the loss of some of their key suppliers to the Europäischer Hof. Since his arrival, she had watched Christophe try to reestablish some of their previous standards, but it was going to be a struggle.

"Well, I'm glad you are a fan of things from the sea. I've taken the liberty of reserving at a restaurant known for its fish. I hope you'll enjoy it."

"So far the trip has been perfect. I'm certain I will."

The Rolls was waiting under the canopy when they exited the lobby. Tilla assumed Henri-Etienne did not find her sporty enough in her conservative linen dress to ride in the racy convertible.

"We're going to Bacon, Raymond," he advised the driver, mentioning the name of one of the most famous eateries on the entire Côte d'Azur. "Please take the coastal route so that Madame Meier can enjoy the view."

"Yes, sir," he replied as they wound their way down the private road.

It was almost dark. The shadow of night became increasingly black as they sped in a southwesterly direction toward Antibes. Henri-Etienne took her hand in his and held it gently. Occasionally he would brush the top of her hand with his fingertips. His touch sent shivers throughout her body. Tilla responded on a purely physical level. It was what she wanted. Even though she remained confused about Henri-Etienne's intentions, for the time being she was content merely to enjoy herself.

"I was reading about Antibes last night in that informative book you have placed in the rooms. It was quite engaging. Until I fell asleep, that is."

"Yes, it is interesting, but it can have that effect on people sometimes. Enough history can be too much," he laughed.

They rode through the pine-forested peninsula and Tilla could see the entrances to many of the most spectacular estates on the coast marked discreetly with columns or small, tastefully lettered signs.

They had just passed the famous beach called La Garoupe when the driver swung the car into the restaurant's crowded parking lot. The spectacular setting offered a sweeping view of the Bay of Angels. Throngs of people were waiting, but when the maître d' spotted Henri-Etienne, he snapped his fingers and they were ushered at once to a table next to the window facing the water. It was obviously the best table in the house.

"How charming," Tilla exclaimed. "I must say, Monsieur de Beaumont, you do live in such style here on the Riviera."

"We try to make the best of it," he joked, surveying the roomful of attractive people. "This restaurant is known for its bouillabaisse. I hope your love of seafood goes that far. If it does, you're in for a treat."

"Have no fear. It certainly does," Tilla assured him.

"There are two theories about the origin of the dish," he commented as the waiter presented them with their large bowls of steaming fish stew. "Are you familiar with them?"

"No, I can't say I am."

"The Marseillais claim that bouillabaisse originated in their fair, but dreary city. According to the story they have propagated, any fish chowder that uses saffron as a main ingredient is guaranteed to cause sleepiness or drowsiness. Of course, we know this is not the case. It may be that any food eaten in such enormous quantity is certain to make the diner heavy-lidded. Anyway, the story continues that bouillabaisse was invented by Venus. She would feed her husband, Vulcan, great quantities of the dish so that she would be assured that he would be sound asleep when she had scheduled a rendezvous with her lover Mars. Since the Greeks occupied Marseilles for a period, perhaps the tale has some merit. The second, more unimaginative story also credits the dish with a Greek origin, since fish soups are commonly found in Greek cuisine. History has recorded that the Greeks were responsible for bringing the olive tree into Provence, so at the very least they must be credited with contributing at least one important ingredient. However, most people believe that it was inevitable that a recipe of this sort would be a natural product for the seaside city."

"That's fascinating," Tilla commented. "It's fun to eat a meal with such a history! And such a treat to have so many varieties of fresh fish available. In the heart of the Black Forest it is often not possible to procure everything one wants in that department. I remember my father's frustration when he was not able to get a special ingredient for a dish he was so anxious to offer his guests. It was sometimes very hard for him since he was trained in France with Escoffier. He was spoiled."

"Ah, I do sympathize, but you have different things to choose from there. The wild game, the venison, the beef. It is hard to match."

"It's true. I suppose every place has its own selling points."

Tilla found Henri-Etienne's charm irresistible, and as he continued to hold her hand under the table, her dreams returned and she imagined his hands exploring her hungry body. She suspected, however, that there was much more to him than that. He seemed somehow troubled, and perhaps not as pleasant a man as he appeared. She was nearing the end of her second day as a guest in his hotel, and she was still uncertain why he had asked her there in the first place.

"Of course, I knew of your father, Tilla. He was a superlative hotel man. There probably exists no other like him in the world today."

"Thank you. I must admit that I agree with you completely. He is very much missed."

"I can only imagine," Henri-Etienne replied. He shifted in the banquette and turned to face Tilla straight on. Never did his hand lose contact with hers. "Tilla, I've thought a lot about you, and about the hotel, since I left. I had a wonderful time being with you, and I loved the Waldhotel."

Tilla sensed that he was coming to the point of this entire escapade, so she merely nodded her agreement.

"Tilla, I want to buy your hotel."

The mystery was over. The secret was out. So that was it. The only reason he had brought her here was to get her to sell him the hotel. He didn't find her attractive for one minute. He only wanted the Waldhotel. She felt ill. She wanted to run from the table, to flee the restaurant. But she was torn between the true meaning of what he had just said and her dreams of what their relationship could become.

"I'm sorry, but the hotel is not for sale, Henri-Etienne," she managed to say.

"Come now, Tilla, don't you see what a great marriage it would be? Two of the most prominent families in the hotel world combining forces to create the most luxurious resort to be found in all the world. Surely that idea excites you. You must admit you need someone who has the financial resources to restore Becker's to its former condition. Your business has been hurt terribly by the Europäischer Hof, which is at best a second-class hotel."

"I can't disagree," Tilla said, "but my daughter informs me that things are looking much better, and that we may be able to reverse that trend very soon."

"Tilla, I understand your daughter is a beautiful, intelligent young woman. I'm sorry I was not able to meet her when I was there. She has enough of her grandfather in her to have been able to learn quite a bit on her own. I hear she runs herself crazy, works like a dog, and is dedicated to Becker's. But with all due respect to the talented young woman, she will never be able to recapture the spirit of the resort. That must be done by someone with far greater experience. I have that experience, Tilla. I'm certainly not a male chauvinist, I believe that in many instances a woman can do just as good a job as a man, sometimes better, in fact. But this is just not one of them. The hotel needs to be run by someone with many years of knowledge about the business. Between the three of us I know we can get the hotel back where it belongs. In addition, you must admit, it is no life for a pretty young woman. The future is very grim. She will remain chained to her desk while she becomes an old maid."

Everything he said was true, but all Tilla could envision was Kati's reaction the last time she had found out they were contemplating a sale. But what Henri-Etienne was suggesting was a marriage, a merger if you could call it that, of the two families. She had to admit it did sound interesting. Did he really mean that they would all work together? Maybe she had jumped to the conclusion that all he wanted from her was the hotel. Even so, she just wasn't ready to let go.

"Henri-Etienne, I am very flattered that you would like to buy the hotel, but it is simply not for sale. And quite frankly, I don't understand why you are so interested in it. It is such a different operation from yours, at least from what I've been able to see of it. It's in an entirely different country, with a culture far different from what you are used to here."

Henri-Etienne could never admit the real reason for his interest in the hotel. He wanted it for his son. He needed it to win back the love he had lost so long ago. Years before, he had been divorced by Christophe and Phillippe's mother after she found him in bed in one of the bastides with a young French film star. So shaken was his ex-wife that one night she dove off the side of the pool into the craggy mountain below. The children were twelve and fourteen at the time and were understandably devastated. After years of therapy Christophe had managed to come to terms with the situation and was able to communicate with his father. However, their relationship remained very unstable and not without a great deal of pain on both sides. Following the doctor's advice, the elder boy, Phillippe, had been sent away to study in Boston. After finishing school, he had moved to New York, where he dabbled in drugs and alcohol. He rarely returned to his homeland.

Purchasing the Waldhotel was Henri-Etienne's last-ditch attempt to make amends to the only son with whom he still maintained some kind of connection. He had convinced himself that by buying the property for Christophe, and allowing him to run it, he could win back the love of his younger boy. He was determined to get it.

Henri-Etienne was savvy enough to table the conversation about the hotel while they enjoyed the delicious food at Bacon. He wanted to give Tilla a chance to think about his offer. She had appeared genuinely shocked when he finally mentioned it. What could she possibly have been thinking he wanted to speak to her about? It didn't matter now. Now she knew exactly what he had in mind. It was only a matter of time before he would convince her to sell the Waldhotel to him. He would start talking about it again over dessert.

He got no further on his second attempt. She was firm—the Waldhotel Becker was not for sale.

The ride home was quiet, each of them lost in their own thoughts, Henri-Etienne stymied as to why she was so resistant to his offer and Tilla trying to convince herself that holding on to her family's legacy was the correct thing to do.

"Let's have a drink, shall we?" Henri-Etienne suggested.

Tilla readily agreed and hand-in-hand they walked down the long hallway and out onto the terrace. It was even more breathtaking at night, and as Henri-Etienne had predicted the afternoon before, they were able to count lighthouses far out into the sea.

"Eight . . . nine . . ." Tilla pointed, enthusiastic as a small child playing a new game. She was enjoying herself more than she had in a very long time. The subject of the Waldhotel was temporarily forgotten. She felt alive, stimulated by this intriguing man. "Ten," she continued. Before she could locate the eleventh glistening jewel, Henri-Etienne turned her around slowly and covered her mouth with his. It was the sensation she had been dreaming of since the night he had kissed her at the hotel. She responded hungrily, her lips opening to his, their tongues slowly exploring each other's mouths.

"Come with me," he asked, his voice offering an urgency that excited her even more. She knew full well what going to his bastide meant. And she wanted it very much. The evening had confused her terribly. She couldn't distinguish Henri-Etienne's emotions for her versus his interest in the hotel. She wanted so much to believe that he truly liked her, that he truly wanted her, as he was now suggesting.

Still she continued to question his motives. She had been so taken aback, so shocked to hear that Henri-Etienne wanted to buy her hotel, that she knew she had to force herself to take some time alone to think over everything they had talked about. Was he using her, pretending to like her, when all he really wanted was the hotel? Or were his feelings for her genuine?

"No, no, thank you, I can't go with you," she said with more hesitation in her voice than she wanted.

He looked shocked and disappointed all at the same time. Instinctively he knew that if he was ever to get the hotel, he would have to accept her answer. "All right, Tilla. I am disappointed, I must admit. I want to be with you so very much. But I understand, and I'll wait. Shall I walk you to your room?"

She nodded.

He kissed her lightly at the entrance to Les Fleurs, a kiss of much less urgency than those they had shared on the terrace only minutes before.

"Thank you for a lovely evening" was all she said before closing the door.

Tilla changed her reservation and departed early the next morning for Germany. She left a note for Henri-Etienne at the front desk telling him how much she had enjoyed her stay.

CHAPTER

19

"WELL, IT'S CERTAINLY not the food that's keeping them away," Christophe joked. "We haven't had any complaints on that end."

Kati sat on the floor of her office, surrounded by a mountain of paper. They had agreed to work late that night to clean up some issues they just never seemed to find the time for during the day. After dinner Kati had changed into her jeans and denim work shirt. She had scrubbed every trace of makeup off her face and had pulled her hair back into a thick ponytail. She looked fresh and young, and very beautiful. Christophe sat on the floor next to her. He couldn't keep his eyes off her. He loved the way she looked in her casual clothes, even more attractive and approachable. It was a pleasant change from the severe navy-blue suit he saw her in all day.

"I know, I know," Kati agreed. He may have said it in a joking manner, not wanting to appear as if he was bragging, but he was telling the absolute truth. Under his direction, the food at the Waldhotel had never been better. Because of his enthusiastic spirit and formidable talent, he got the most out of the staff. They were really a team now. But the numbers just weren't reflecting the improvements they had made. Guests were still venturing into town or to the other restaurants in the surrounding area for dinner. Even those who stayed a week or more, those who certainly could have taken a dinner or two with them, had continued to go elsewhere to eat. She stared into the blazing fire trying to think of a remedy. Suddenly her eyes lit up. She sat up straight. "I've got it," she announced.

Christophe looked up from his papers and smiled at her. He loved working with Kati. She was more serious than any of the girls he had known before, yet she was fun-loving and spirited at the same time. She was constantly on the move, propelled by her intelligence and energy.

"Well, are you going to tell me, or is it a secret?" he teased.

Her delicate lips curled into a mischievous smile. "No, I'm not going to tell you. But I'll bet you that I can increase your dinner business next month by twenty percent."

"That's a pretty aggressive figure. It must be some great idea."

"Yes, I think it is. Actually, it's one I've had for a while. I just never found the time to work it out. I mentioned it to Dieter months ago, but then I didn't follow up on it. I guess now's the time," she added, looking very pleased with herself. She seemed confident that her idea would work.

"Okay, I'll accept your wager. What exactly are we betting?"

She laughed. "Oh, I haven't thought about that. I was just so sure my idea would work, I didn't bother to think of that."

"Well, what would you like to bet?"

Christophe moved closer to her. He rearranged some of her papers to make room for him to sit next to her. He waited for her to look up at him. His blue eyes captured her attention. "I'd like to bet a kiss," he said.

Her smile widened. "A kiss," she repeated. "Are you sure you can afford one?"

"Yes," he agreed, sounding very businesslike. "I also think it is appropriate to the nature of the wager."

They laughed together.

"There's just one more thing," he added. "In case I win, I'd like to start practicing"—he paused, taking her face between his hands—"now," he whispered as he covered her mouth with his.

Kati responded to his touch, timidly at first, and then with all the yearning she had stored up during the time they had worked together. Until this very moment she had blocked out her attraction to Christophe, fearing that it would ruin their wonderful business relationship. The hotel had become so important to her that she had refused to allow her own emotions to unfold. Now she let them flow as he held her in his strong arms.

"Oh, Kati, I've wanted to do this since the morning I met you."

"I've wanted it too," she confessed.

He smiled at her, delighted to hear her admission. "We've got a lot of lost time to make up for, then."

Christophe got up and walked to the door. He closed it and turned the key. Kati became worried and for a moment considered getting up. Never before had she been alone behind closed doors with a man. But instantly he was beside her, and the warmth of his arms dissolved her fears. She could no longer hide her feelings for him.

The days following their first "test kiss" were fraught with anxiety and uncertainty for Kati. She longed to be with Christophe again, but at the same time she wanted to protect their working relationship. It was crucial that no one in the hotel become aware of their personal situation. If they continued to be with each other, as she prayed they would, it was going to be a difficult balancing act. In the meantime, she still had a hotel to run. Plus she wanted to earn her next kiss fair and square.

"Yes, that's exactly what I wanted," she said to Dieter. She held the small card in her hand and proofread the copy one final time. She had selected a heavy, cream-colored stock and had chosen to print in dark blue ink. Each card had a simple gold border. Once more she read the message aloud:

> *The Waldhotel Becker is a symbol of tradition in the world of grand hotels. Its unique location and architecture, history and legends give it its heartbeat. One of our primary goals is to maintain great restaurant service. We feel that our chef, Monsieur Christophe Robillard, is providing exactly that service. Of course, the challenge of maintaining this kitchen is pointless unless it is constantly tested. Considering the above, we would be honored to have you dine with us at some opportunity during your stay and hope you will let us know what you think.*
>
> *Sincerely,*
> *The Becker-Meier Family*

She smiled, pleased with the final product. "Can you give them to the floor maids so that they can all be in the rooms by this afternoon?"

"I don't see why not," he replied cheerfully. "I hope they work, Kati. It's a wonderful idea. I think it will achieve what you want it to both tactfully and tastefully."

"Yes, I thought so too. It wasn't really my idea, you know. A while ago I found some notes of Opa's. He must have been preparing to give a speech to one of the hotel associations. His notes went on and on about the intimate relationship between the hotel guests and management. He said that in order to be really successful, you had to make the guest feel a part of the hotel, and therefore a part of its success. He claimed that you have to make the guests think that they are in the game with you. If you can do that, he said, your success is guaranteed. So I'm counting on these little cards to do just that. I'm sure they're going to help. I have a lot riding on them," she added, but not revealing her secret.

Since Tilla's return two weeks earlier Kati found that her spirits vacillated from semidepressed to ecstatic. She would enter Kati's office in the morning looking tired and lethargic. When asked what was the matter, she would deny that anything was wrong, insisting that she had merely slept badly. Several times she had been called away from the dining table or from a meeting for a phone call. Often she would return looking much happier and less frantic than she had when she left.

"Mutti, did you meet someone during your trip?" Kati asked after the third time she noticed this dramatic change.

Tilla smiled. "No, Kati, of course not. No . . . you mean the phone call? Don't be silly, darling. That was only one of the staff calling to ask a question."

Kati didn't believe her mother for one minute, but she pretended to accept her thinly veiled excuses. She didn't want to pry. She was sure that if Tilla had met someone, it was going to be difficult enough for her to adjust, to accept a new relationship. She certainly didn't need a nosy daughter asking so many questions.

In fact, Kati's suspicions were right on target. Much to Tilla's surprise Henri-Etienne had called her the day she returned from her stay at the Villa Soleil. He apologized profusely for missing her that morning, but of course he could never have known that she would change her plans and leave so early. She had accepted his sentiments. Again she thought it would be the last time she would hear from him. But he had called again the next day. And the next. Now they talked sometimes as many as three times a day. They spoke about all kinds of things, most of them having to do with the running of the hotel. She often asked his advice, and on more than one occasion he gave her valuable help. Slowly she started to appreciate his many years of experience. Tilla found him to be a good listener. He seemed to be interested in the hotel's problems because they were Tilla's problems, not because he wanted to purchase the hotel. In fact, not once in their many conversations did he again mention his desire to buy the Waldhotel. At first this surprised her, but after a time she began to think that maybe his concern really was for her and not solely for the Waldhotel. She began to look forward to his calls. He rarely disappointed her.

"Why don't you come back for another visit?" he asked one night.

Tilla was hesitant. She enjoyed their long-distance communications. Talking on the telephone was easy and pleasurable for her. There were no strings attached. When they were ready to say goodbye or good night, it was so simple. There were no awkward moments as there had been on the last night of her first visit. Now he had asked her to come again. She wasn't certain.

"Can I let you know tomorrow?"

"Of course, Tilla," he had answered sweetly. "You have a standing invitation. You are welcome to come whenever you would like. The weather is beautiful now. Of course it's almost the height of the season, and the coastline is packed, impossible, but up here it is still peaceful and quiet."

Visions of the beautiful Villa Soleil property filled her thoughts. The invigorating waters of the swimming pool. The delicious fresh fish and new vegetables. She called him back the next day and told him she would come.

"Kati, I'm treating myself to another few days in the south of France," Tilla announced at dinner that night. "That is, of course, if you don't need me here."

Kati smiled up at her mother. Tilla had just confirmed what she had suspected all along. "Great," she said. "Have a good time. I'm sure we can manage without you for a few days around here. But it seems that someone in France can't do the same." Tilla looked as if she hadn't any idea what her daughter was suggesting. So Kati gave up. "When will you be going?"

"In the morning."

So soon. Maybe it was more serious than Kati had imagined. She couldn't stop to think about it right now. She and Christophe were going to a concert, and she was already late. She had looked forward to being with him all day. More and more often they were spending the evenings together. Each time they met, she couldn't wait until the next time they would be alone together. She glanced at the clock. She'd have to rush. She'd get more information on her mother's secret later.

"That's wonderful, Mother," she said. She leaned over and kissed Tilla's cheek. "I'll see you in the morning before you leave, then."

She dashed from the table, anxious to be in the arms of Christophe once again.

CHAPTER 20

HE CÔTE D'AZUR was teeming with people. Her flight had been full of travelers anxious to arrive for their day in the sun. She felt like a schoolgirl as the plane touched down. She allowed herself to be excited at the prospect of spending a few more days getting to know the interesting man who was pursuing her with such fervor. She had to admit that she loved the attention. It made her feel like a woman again.

This time Henri-Etienne came alone to meet her at the airport. He pulled up to the curb in his red convertible.

"Welcome," he hailed, "I'm so glad to see you." He gave her a warm welcome hug. She fastened a colorful scarf around her hair, and they sped away from the crowded Nice airport. The trip to the hotel, which had taken only half an hour last time, now took almost two.

"Now you know why I cherish this location so much," Henri-Etienne said as he pulled the car up under the canopy. "I wouldn't have made that drive for anyone but you," he added. He said it with such conviction that she believed him. She wanted so much to know that it was true. "Come," he said, offering his hand, "I've had the chef prepare a special lunch for us on the terrace."

The beauty of the area increased as the weather warmed. As she stood now overlooking the frenetic coastline, she could distinguish all the new flowers that had come to life since her last visit. Lavender was still the predominant color of the surrounding hills, but now the marguerites, carnations, and jasmine had added their blossoms to the landscape. She breathed deeply, wanting to experience every delightful scent the region possessed.

After lunch, relaxed by the sunshine and wine, they took a leisurely swim. Tilla fell sound asleep on one of the comfortable lounges. Henri-Etienne's voice awakened her gently. "Perhaps you'd like to take a nap?" he asked.

Immediately she panicked. She had just arrived. Would she have to go with him so soon? She wasn't ready, and for that reason his next words pleased her immensely.

"I've got to go to a meeting now. I shouldn't be gone more than a few hours. I've made reservations for us for dinner at eight-thirty. How does that sound?"

"Perfect," she replied. He kissed her gently on the forehead and was gone.

Le Moulin de Mougins was considered by many to be the best restaurant in Provence. By all, it was considered the most fashionable. Henri-Etienne held Tilla's elbow gently as they were escorted to a cozy table in the charming sixteenth-century olive oil mill that had been converted into a restaurant by one of France's most revered chefs, Roger Vergé.

Their rich, artfully presented dinner of the best ingredients the region had to offer was sumptuous. Even more enjoyable was their conversation. Henri-Etienne was attentive and amusing. He seemed to really be enjoying himself. They laughed and talked and not once did he mention his desire to purchase the Waldhotel. By the time Monsieur Vergé made his usual tour of the tables at the end of the evening, they were completely engaged in each other.

"Did you enjoy your meal, Henri-Etienne?" the handsome, silver-haired culinary genius asked.

Henri-Etienne looked up, startled by the master's sudden appearance at the table. "*Mais oui,* yes, of course, it was superb, as always," he replied. He introduced Tilla, who offered her congratulations as well.

The air was filled with the scent of jasmine when they left the restaurant. Slowly they walked arm in arm through the town of Mougins. Once a sleepy, two-café town, it was now extremely popular with tourists from around the world. They watched the locals and some summer visitors who were engaged in a late-night game of *boules.*

"Are you ready to go home?" he asked.

Home. The Villa Soleil. It sounded so right. Tilla liked the idea of it. She was also beginning to like its owner. She looked up at him, still trying to read the expression of the complex man. All she saw was his tanned face and his attractive, compelling eyes that begged her to come with him.

This time she didn't even bother putting on her scarf. She let the wind whip freely through her hair. She felt young, and alive, and reckless.

Henri-Etienne drove the car through the hotel entrance and up the road to the bastides. Instead of turning in the direction of Les Fleurs, he continued on to the top of the hill. Tilla remained silent, knowing and wanting to go where he was taking her.

"You are beautiful," Henri-Etienne said as he looked at her body in the half-light that filtered through the curtains in his villa. She smiled cautiously at him, suddenly overcome with shyness. It had been so long since she had been in an intimate situation with a man. She had been a young girl when Johannes entered her life, and she had been faithful to him throughout their marriage. Henri-Etienne sensed her hesitancy and played the role of a gentle, caring lover. He held her tenderly. When he felt she was more relaxed, he stroked her face, her neck, and her throat. The tips of his fingers reached her breasts. Her nipples hardened, and she shuddered slightly, but her eyes begged him to continue. Henri-Etienne fondled every inch of her. He was a patient lover. Tilla was a much more inhibited, much less experienced partner than he was used to, so it was easy for him to contain himself and take her to climax before having his own pleasure. There was no doubt in his mind that he was the first man she had been with since the death of her husband. Finally he made her so crazy that she begged him to enter her, to extinguish the fire he had created.

"Henri-Etienne, I can't stand it any longer," she begged. "Please, take me." They were the first words she had uttered since they had been in bed, so unused was she to expressing her own desires. He felt how difficult it was for her to speak while making love. Gladly he entered her, bringing her immediately to another frenzied orgasm. He held her tightly as he erupted in her. Soon thereafter he was fast asleep in her arms.

Tilla lay motionless in the bed, exhausted from their lovemaking. She had never been so satisfied. Even during her earliest days with Johannes, the depth of physical response had not been as great. She watched as Henri-Etienne's powerful chest rose and fell in a pattern of contented breathing.

She was unable to join him in a peaceful slumber. That night's sleep was as restless and disruptive as the night's before had been peaceful and comforting. Tilla was up and down several times. Each time she feared disturbing Henri-Etienne, but he never moved from his position on the soft pillows. She wrestled with one of the toughest dilemmas of her life. Even though a word hadn't been spoken, she knew Henri-Etienne's offer still stood. Was it something she shouldn't pass up, knowing full well that the prospects of finding another buyer for the hotel in its current situation were extremely slim at best? Did he really wish to merge the two families, to create a great hotel again? Were his feelings for her genuine, or simply a pleasant way for this charming bachelor to spend a weekend? Was she, as he had rightly pointed out, dooming Kati to an unfulfilling life in the hotel? They were all questions to which the answers were not forthcoming. She tossed and turned during the remainder of the night, but as the morning light filtered into her room, she awoke feeling positive about the decision she had made.

CHAPTER

21

SHE SOLD the hotel to Henri-Etienne that morning.

"Don't worry, Tilla, you've done exactly the right thing," he assured her yet again when he detected a hint of indecision sneaking into her expression. They sat on the terrace, finishing an exquisite lunch of lobster salad and the last drops of a bottle of perfectly chilled champagne Henri-Etienne had ordered to celebrate his purchase of the Waldhotel. He looked at her now, the sweet, fragile woman whose mind he had changed using one of the oldest tricks known to man. He had played on the most basic of human needs—her sensuality and sexual desires. Desires that had been repressed for so long it was as if she had been reborn once they were rekindled by his magic touch. He had also taken advantage of her none-too-stable mind. Now it was crucial that she leave the hotel without a second thought, confident that she had made the right decision. She mustn't have one iota of doubt in her mind, or his plan wouldn't go through, and he would never gain control of the hotel he coveted so fiercely.

She sighed and looked up at him. It was clear that she had come to trust him a great deal in a very short period of time, a feeling he had worked hard to elicit from her. All the phone calls, all of his pretended interest in the silly, inconsequential problems of the Waldhotel. Yet he remained just the slightest bit uncomfortable knowing what would have to happen in the end. Not enough, however, to change his mind. No, definitely not enough to change his mind.

"I certainly hope so," she said. "It's really Kati's future I'm worried about, you know. The hotel is the only thing we had left."

He looked at her careworn face, unable to turn back now on the lie he had so masterfully persuaded her to believe. "I told you, there's absolutely nothing to worry about. Kati's future is now in my hands." Truer words had never been spoken.

"Oh, my," she said, having glanced at her watch, "I lost all track of time. I've got to get packed and headed for the airport. The plane leaves in little more than an hour."

Thank heavens she had finally noticed, Henri-Etienne thought. He couldn't bring himself to mention how late it was getting; it would have seemed so cold, so uncaring. Tilla had to leave the Villa Soleil feeling that Henri-Etienne was sorry to see her go. But missing her flight would cause an unmitigated disaster. Morgan would be returning from a short trip to London only minutes after Tilla's plane was scheduled to take off. When Tilla had accepted his invitation, he had sent her off on yet another shopping spree. Her tolerance for those little sprees was insatiable. Just like his desire for her, he thought. Of course, he really didn't have anything to worry about. Raymond was a pillar of discretion. Henri-Etienne had hired him only after having been assured by his former employer that he possessed that very quality. But Henri-Etienne couldn't risk even the remote chance of any foul-up occurring now. No, not now, just when his dreams were within days of coming true. All he wanted to do now was get Tilla packed, out of the hotel, and sent safely on her way back to Germany.

Then he could humor Morgan by watching her model all her new purchases for him. Oh, yes, he could imagine her firm, ample breasts bouncing up and down lightly as she shimmied her lovely little body in and out of yet another curve-revealing outfit. He felt his excitement growing at the prospect of looking at her. After he had sat patiently while she tried on all her new clothes, she would be compelled to thank him properly for his generosity. Yes, she would have to show proper gratitude for her little weekend shopping excursion—by teasing him, caressing him, stroking him, and finally pleasing him—as only she could.

"Here's everything you asked for, Monsieur de Beaumont," chirped the secretary as she placed a folder full of papers in front of Henri-Etienne. "Will there be anything else?"

"No, Françoise, I think that's all, *merci*," he answered.

The girl twirled around and headed back inside to her office. Tilla watched the outline of her derrière, molded by the skin-tight jeans and accentuated even further by the super-high heels she wore. She disappeared down the corridor. Tilla thought how wonderful it must be to be young, to have one's entire future ahead. Ever since last night she had become so terribly self-conscious about her body. She looked at every woman on the premises with a critical eye, examining in minute detail every part of their anatomy. Henri-Etienne was only the third man to have ever seen her naked. Once, before she married, she had had a brief fling with a beau, but after she became Johannes's wife, she had remained steadfastly loyal to him. Last night had been one of the most difficult yet fantastic nights in her memory. She had felt so wanted, so desired, so womanly. After they had made love for a while, to her great surprise she had even begun to relax and respond to his touch without shame or embarrassment. Henri-Etienne had complimented her, saying her body was beautiful and sensuous. He had spoken soft words of praise when he took her breasts in his mouth. She couldn't help but think he must have compared her to the other lovers in his life. Didn't every man? She honestly didn't know, but she assumed they must. How did she compare? Was she a good lover for him? Or was she too old, already in her late forties, compared to those he was used to? These were questions that would have to remain unanswered, at least for the time being. That didn't stop them from continuing to prey on her mind as the man whose bed she had shared now placed before her the papers authorizing the sale of the only asset she had left in the world.

"Tilla, if I can just ask you to sign here, and here, and once more here," he indicated, shuffling the papers in front of her. "I think that's all. I'll have my lawyers take care of the rest of the details and send copies back to you right away."

She looked down at the documents spread out before her.

"I can't sign these yet," she said. "I have to take them back to Germany with me and let my lawyers have a look at them."

"Tilla," Henri-Etienne said gently, not wanting her to detect his impatience. He had to get her to sign the papers now, before she left the hotel, before she showed them to anyone. Before she had a chance to change her mind. He took her hand in his and held it to his lips. He kissed her fingertips lightly.

Tilla responded at once, unable to conceal the effect his touching her had on her entire body. Suddenly she felt wanted—sensual, a woman again. All of the memories of last night flooded her mind.

Once more she allowed herself to be swept up in the illusion that he really cared for her.

"Tilla, if we're going to be partners, if we're going to succeed in bringing our two families together, in reestablishing the greatness of the Waldhotel, you simply must put your trust in me. Now, if it will make you feel better, after you sign, I'll have copies of all these papers made and you can take them with you. Françoise will make duplicates of everything. But there won't be any point in doing that until you've signed. Now, please, Tilla, let's finish up here so you can get packed and on your way. I don't want you to have to rush. Besides, aren't you anxious to get home to tell Kati all the news?"

Being reminded of Kati brought on a whole new set of concerns. She had labored over her decision to sell, but not nearly as much as she had thought about how she would tell her daughter. Her breath quickened and she felt her head start to spin. Anxiety overtook her. Her mind told her she had made the right decision, the one that would ensure Kati's future, but her heart beat frantically against her chest and dizziness clouded her vision. She wanted nothing more right now than to get all this over with, sign the papers, pack her things, and go to the airport. She would be able to find solace and quiet on the airplane. During the flight home she would sort out her feelings, her attraction to Henri-Etienne, the events of the last two days, and, most important, just how she would tell Kati that she had sold the hotel. By the time they touched down in Frankfurt, she would have her thoughts organized. She would be in control again, and everything would be fine. Yes, she was certain of it. Of course it was going to be all right. With these calming thoughts her heartbeat slowed, her breathing steadied, and she was able to regain her composure.

"Okay, show me where to put my mark," she asked Henri-Etienne. Her confident steady voice immediately brought a smile of relief to his face. Quickly he grabbed the stack of papers and began presenting them to her one by one.

"Here, I'll make this as simple as possible." He offered her his beautiful gold fountain pen. "Sign once here." She looked up at him and was met with a smile. Then she complied, her hand shaking so violently that at first she was unable to hold the pen steady.

"Once more down here," he indicated. Deep in her heart she

knew that she should have taken the papers unsigned back to Germany with her for her lawyers to review. Karl-Gustav, and even Johannes, had always warned her about signing things without first seeking legal advice. Once again she hesitated. She looked up to face Henri-Etienne. He met her indecision with a comforting smile, one that left her feeling better. His eyes gleamed, and the only thing she read in them was a genuine affection and desire to better her life. She grasped the pen firmly between her fingers and continued to sign as he pointed to the blank lines. By the time they reached the final agreement, she was writing at a brisk pace, dotting the *i*'s and crossing the *t*'s in her name with a fierce determination.

The second the ink had dried on her last stroke, Henri-Etienne picked up the papers in both hands and tapped them on the table to organize them. Her anxiety returned. He reached out and took her hand in his again. His dark eyes met hers, and silently they pleaded with her to trust him.

"Thank you, Tilla. Everything is going to be just fine. I'll take these to Françoise now so she can make the copies and have them ready for you before Raymond takes you to the airport. Okay?" he questioned, all the while gently stroking the back of her hand.

"Yes, Henri-Etienne. I'll go to my room now and prepare my luggage. Will you send someone up in about ten minutes?"

"Of course, *ma chérie*," he assured her, taking both of her hands and helping her up from her chair. They left the enchanting patio for the last time and walked slowly toward the entrance. She felt his hand slide down and caress the top of her buttocks as she walked. She gave him a shocked look and pulled away from his grasp. Oh, it was all so different, such a change from the strict rules to which she was accustomed. She was so unused to being touched in public. In a way, however, she was delighted. It only confirmed that he did care for her and that selling him the hotel was the right thing to do. She had shared his bed last night. He had gazed at her naked body in the half-light that filtered into his room. She had lain with him and allowed him to touch her and pleasure her in ways totally foreign to her. So she supposed she really shouldn't be too surprised when he called her by such a name and reached out to touch her as they walked.

• • •

"I'll be seeing you in a couple of weeks," he assured her as he held her face between his hands and kissed her on both cheeks. "Good-bye, *ma chérie*. Call me if you have any questions, or any other thoughts about our agreement. Everything is in the folder if you need it. Don't worry about a thing," he added, shutting the door firmly on the Rolls.

"Thank you for three of the loveliest days I've had in a long time," Tilla replied, unwilling to take her eyes from his face. "You have a beautiful hotel in the Villa Soleil."

"Thank you, my sweet lady. Have a good trip home." With that Henri-Etienne tapped twice softly on the side of the highly polished automobile. The sound was a signal to Raymond that it was time to leave. He pulled the car slowly out from under the canopy and headed down the winding road. When Tilla turned back to wave one last time, the new owner of her family's legacy had already disappeared.

CHAPTER ·

22

"**W**ELL, I HOPE she's better very soon," Kati said a bit brusquely, unable to conceal the irritation in her voice. Immediately she regretted it. It was just that she had come to depend so much on him. They discussed every single detail together. Neither of them made a move without the other.

"I'm sorry, Christophe, I know you can't pick the times when your relatives get sick. I'm just upset that you have to leave right now, just when the convention is due to check in. We'll make do, that's all. But you'll call me and let me know when you'll be back, won't you?"

"Of course, sweet, I promise. Kati, again, I'm so sorry. But I just got off the phone with my father, and from the way he described it, she could be near the end. She may not last much longer," he answered, his voice cracking. He looked helpless and deeply concerned. "I really don't understand it, though; Grandmère is such a healthy, sturdy type. She's hardly ever been ill. I saw her only two months ago. She seemed to be just fine. I guess things can change pretty fast when you're in your seventies."

Indeed Christophe did find it very peculiar that his grandmother should all of a sudden be so desperately ill. But his father had insisted. He had begged him to come home, to return at once to the Villa Soleil. "You will regret it for the rest of your life if you do not get here in time," he had warned. So he had approached Kati in the most honest way he knew, telling her exactly what the situation was. He knew that his absence from the hotel at such a critical time would greatly disturb her. Nor did he want to leave her. She had become so important to him. He adored her. He hated the thought of upsetting her in any way.

Kati's thoughts traveled back in time to her own grandparents. Her father's father had been killed in the war. She had never really known her grandmothers—Johannes's mother was already long dead when she was born, and her mother's mother had died when Kati was only four years old. But she had had her Opa. He, too, had been in good health up until the moment he died. That terrible afternoon when her mother had stood at the entrance to the Grand Salon, waving frantically to Margarethe. That day had been such a turning point in her life. It was one none of them would ever forget. Karl-Gustav's death had created a void so great, so massive, that they still struggled every minute of every day to fill the space left by his departure. She thought of him now—his kind, loving face; his huge, imposing presence—and she longed so to have him back again. Her heart went out to Christophe, who was now facing the same kind of immense loss she knew so intimately. It was very hard to lose someone you loved so much, as he apparently did his grandmother. Now she lay dying in a hospital in France. So he had to go, whether or not the hotel was going to be full starting tomorrow. Whether or not the sous-chef and the others would be able to maintain some semblance of order and efficiency in the kitchen. Whether or not she would miss their late-night walks she had grown to love. Silently she admonished herself for being so selfish. She was appalled at her behavior, her lack of caring. What had happened to her principles, her sense of priority? Of course he must go, and she shouldn't complain for one second about him doing so. Christophe had been such a blessing from the very minute of his delayed arrival, not only to the hotel but to her. Through his enthusiasm and commitment he had managed to turn the entire food operation around. He had worked diligently and patiently and the results were astounding. Food costs were down, productivity was up, the menu was first-rate, and the guests seemed to enjoy the meals he was responsible for producing. Compliments came rolling in, and business was booming. Her little cards had worked. Not only had their business from the hotel increased, but she had earned her kiss as well.

She examined him now, his handsome face with its finely chiseled features, the caring blue eyes that she had never seen flare with anger or impatience as he painstakingly taught the other members of the staff how to prepare or present one of the meals. The muscles of his well-developed and well-cared-for body rippled beneath the white shirt and apron he wore as he stood in her office, explaining what needed to be done while he was away. In spite of all the time they had spent together, the long hours they had pored laboriously over the minutest details, and the more enjoyable hours they had spent in each others arms, she still felt she hardly knew this handsome young man who, by joining the staff at the Waldhotel, and by becoming her first real love, had made such an extraordinary change in her life. Still he remained an enigma to her. Somehow she felt that he carried within him a deep, dark secret, his own burden to bear, and he was unable or merely unwilling to reveal that secret to anyone.

"So, you won't forget to remind Danielle to pick up the menus from the printer on Friday? They close at four, and if she doesn't pick them up before then, the weekend is shot."

"No, I won't forget," she said, but as she spoke, she jotted down a note to herself on the growing list of things to be done that afternoon.

"Okay, I think that's it. I'm going to go and pack." He moved toward her. Kati stood up and came out from behind the desk. Christophe put his hands on her shoulders. Just as he was bending down to kiss her, they both heard a noise in the doorway.

"Oh, excuse me," Tilla said when she realized that Kati had someone with her. She had entered the office with such determination, so intent on speaking to her daughter at that very minute while she still possessed the strength she knew she would need to make her announcement, that she was oblivious of her surroundings. She halted abruptly and stared at Kati and Christophe. Now some of the wind had been knocked out of her sails. She hoped desperately that she could regain it.

"It's okay, Mother, come on in. I think we've about finished. Christophe has to leave for a few days. We were just reviewing the things that need to be attended to while he's gone. Stay . . . sit down, I'll only be a minute more."

"Oh, yes, all right, fine . . ." Tilla responded, her mind a million miles away, terrified that if she wasn't able to speak to Kati alone right now, she would lose her firm resolve to tell her what she had done. As she sat in the small chair facing her daughter's cluttered, paper-strewn desk, she could feel her willpower slowly slipping away. She had gone over this scenario countless times, rehearsing in her mind the best approach to take. Always she would begin the conversation by saying that selling the hotel was clearly in their best interest. The sale would only strengthen the image of the hotel because Henri-Etienne had the money to put into renovations and changes—he would make it beautiful again, he would restore it in a manner they couldn't even dream of. It would free Kati from the incredible burden she had been carrying, and she could have a life of her own. She reminded herself of all these things and more, but still she had reservations about how Kati would react to this astounding news. News that would affect their lives almost immediately. Monday morning, in fact. Of course, she could never tell Kati about the relationship that had developed between her and Henri-Etienne. It would only upset her more, for she would think that Tilla had certainly been tricked into selling. She couldn't bear for Kati to think that, for in her own heart she tried to believe that her feelings for him had nothing to do with her decision.

This morning she had awakened realizing full well she could postpone their talk no longer. Henri-Etienne had been calling several times a day, insisting that in order to get moving he needed to start sending some of his people down to begin examining the hotel's books and affairs. She had been able to hold him off for the last week, making as many excuses as she could, but now he was insistent. He had called earlier today to say that two members of his organization would be arriving on Monday morning to start their work. So her time was up. She absolutely must, she absolutely had to tell Kati today. Right now. Now, while she was so certain about what she had done and why. While her courage held out. So fiercely was she concentrating, so set was she on announcing the changes that would be taking place at the hotel that she was startled when Kati's voice finally penetrated her thoughts.

"Mother, are you listening? Is something wrong?"

Tilla jerked her head around and faced her daughter. Lines of worry and concern were etched upon her face. Ever since her illness Kati had treated her with kid gloves. Any sign that might signal a recurrence of Tilla's depressed state of mind frightened her to death.

"Are you all right?" she repeated.

"Yes, darling, I'm fine." She tried to sound as positive, as upbeat as she could, but she was unable to fool her perceptive child.

"You don't look fine, Mother. In fact, you look a little pale. Are you sure you're feeling okay?" Kati asked again gently, coming around the desk and sitting down in the other guest chair next to Tilla.

"I promise you, sweetheart, I'm fine. In fact, I feel better today than I have in a long while," Tilla assured her, peppering her words with a small lie. "Now, what's going on with Christophe?"

Kati breathed a sigh of exasperation. "Oh, Mother, it's really one thing after another, isn't it? Just when you think everything's under control, something goes haywire. Christophe has done such a good job in getting the kitchen staff organized and running on track. They're all geared up for the arrival of the convention tonight. Now he's received word from his father that his grandmother is dying. So he has to leave today. I hope he'll only be away for a short time. I don't know how long they can keep it together without him. At least he's only going a short distance."

"Oh, Kati, I'm so sorry. He's such a wonderful young man. Where is his family?" Tilla asked, taking advantage of a much-needed chance to delay her announcement a few seconds more. Her courage was renewed by hearing Kati's complaint about the enormous, never-ending problems of running the hotel. She had opened the door for Tilla's news, and in order to soften the blow, she needed to capitalize on Kati's feelings right now.

"They live somewhere in the south of France, not too far, in fact, from where you went last month. Somewhere about forty-five minutes from Antibes, up in the hills," Kati replied.

"Oh, well, I hope he's back soon. In the meantime I'm sure the other staff can handle the work. They're a good group. You don't give them enough credit."

What could she possibly be talking about? Kati wondered. Her mother was totally unfamiliar with the staff. They could be monkeys, for all she knew. Tilla had not ventured down into the kitchen area since well before Christophe's arrival. Maybe she's just trying her best to be encouraging, she reasoned. Anyway, it was still a problem, and she wished that Tilla would say whatever it was she needed to speak to her about so that she could make a game plan to see them through yet another rough time. But it wasn't in her nature to be impatient or short with her mother, no matter how trying the situation.

"Yes, you're right," she agreed, the conviction in her voice overpowering the always-present temptation to give in to the enormous pressures. "This is mild compared with what we've been through, isn't it?" She reached out for her mother and hugged her close to her. Memories flooded through both of them—Eva-Maria's scandal, Johannes's suicide, Tilla's illness. Yes, they had handled those crises. Indeed this one seemed minute, almost inconsequential, by comparison.

Tilla pulled back and looked solemnly at her daughter. Now was the time. She began slowly, trying with all her might to remain the master of her voice. She couldn't make her announcement with even the slightest tinge of hesitation. "Kati, I've got something to tell you. Something wonderful," she began again. "I . . . I . . . ," and suddenly the words left her throat.

A look of fear returned to Kati's eyes. "What, Mother? What is it?" she asked, concern streaking her entire face.

"Oh, Kati," she continued, taking her daughter's hand in hers. "It is wonderful news! It is going to change our lives so much, so much for the better, you'll see. Kati, I've . . . I've sold the hotel."

The expression on Kati's face turned at once from concern to abject horror. "You've *what?*" she cried, a little louder than she had expected. It was almost a scream. Tilla was frightened by her reaction. It was even more explosive than she had imagined it would be. Hearing the tone of Kati's voice made it difficult for her to remain strong.

"Now, please, Kati, calm down and let me explain everything to you. I don't want you jumping to conclusions. I can only start out by telling you that it is in our best interest—that everything is going to be much better for us, especially for you. The new owners will take this terrible burden off your shoulders. You'll be able to return to school, just as we'd always planned, before your father—"

"Mother, I'd hoped you'd realized by now that the last thing I want to do at this time is to go back to school. I love it here at the hotel. Now, just when things are starting to improve, you tell me that you've sold it, without even mentioning it to me. I can't believe it, I just can't . . . ," she said, clenching her hands together until the knuckles turned white.

"Kati, please, I'm going to explain, if you'll just give me a chance," Tilla implored her precious daughter.

Tilla's sureness held while she tried her best to explain carefully and patiently to Kati what had happened. She told her all about Henri-Etienne, the Villa Soleil, and his plans for the Waldhotel. While she talked, she avoided looking directly at her, for when she did, her train of thought was disrupted by the puzzled, confused expression on Kati's face. By the time she had finished telling her everything about the sale, she hoped she had made some progress in reaching Kati. Her hopes were destroyed the moment Kati spoke.

"Mother, as far as I'm concerned, you have just sold the only thing we had left in the world. The only thing of value, the single opportunity we had to make a future for ourselves. Right out from under us, without even talking to me, or to Dieter, or to anyone who might have been able to help you make the right decision. Or maybe even to have stopped you. We were just starting to make progress. We've restaffed; we've turned the restaurant around. The occupancy rate is the highest it has been in three years. Now you're suggesting that we work for someone else. They now own the hotel. They will make all the decisions. Well, I'm not interested in working for any-one, particularly in my own hotel. Oh, Mother," she sighed, "there are so many unanswered questions, so many open ends that, by the sound of it, are not covered in your arrangement. In the way you've described it to me, anyway. I suppose you've signed all the papers and contracts already?"

"Yes, yes, I have," Tilla admitted weakly, pained to the depths of her very soul by the realization that what her daughter was saying was absolutely true.

"Oh . . . ," Kati cried out, as if in physical pain. Suddenly she got up from the chair she had collapsed into as Tilla had slowly explained what she had done. "I'm sorry, Mother, I've got to get some fresh air. It's stifling in here, and I'm afraid if I stay one minute longer, I may say something I will live to regret. For the moment all I can say is that I'm sorry—very, very sorry." She could stand it no longer, and a wave of nausea swept over her. She turned and ran from the room.

Tilla was too stunned to respond. By the time she had gathered her senses and run out into the hallway, Kati was nowhere in sight. She ran to the top of the staircase and peered down into the empty space.

"Kati, please don't leave me, Kati, I need you. Come back and let's talk some more. Please . . ." Her pleas went unheard, for Kati was already out the front door of the hotel and headed toward the only place where she had ever found help or guidance before—her grandfather's garden.

Tilla leaned over the railing and held her head in her hands. She longed to have her old life back—carefree days filled with laughter and happiness—days shared with her father, her husband, and her daughters. Those she had loved were all gone. Now she feared she might also have lost the last person on earth whom she loved so dearly. She prayed that Kati's reaction was only temporary. The news had hit her suddenly, but Tilla was certain she would adjust to the idea of a new owner and that they would both, in time, benefit from her decision.

Finally, realizing that Kati was gone, she walked slowly back to the privacy of her apartment. She felt old, and tired, and hopelessly confused.

She threw herself on her bed and wept until there were no more tears.

C H A P T E R

23

"SURELY YOU don't think Henri-Etienne is going to put up with this nonsense much longer, do you?" one man asked the other. "He can't afford to lose his shirt on this property. He bought it for Christophe, you know. He's always trying to make up to him for what happened to Dominique. My guess is that he'll take his son out of the kitchen and put him in charge upstairs with the concierge. Dieter seems like a pretty sharp fellow, been here a long time. He could really help the boy get his feet wet. Dealing with the clientele here is a little different than in the south, you know. The people who come here seem to have a different attitude than at the Villa Soleil. A little more refined, I think. They don't seem to like too much action." He sighed, dreaming of the wild, sensual, devil-may-care attitude of the sexy women on the Riviera. "But the nutty mother and the daughter, they'll have to go, and soon, I would imagine."

"Yes, I suppose you're right. He needs to get some strong management in here right away. The place is a mess. If it keeps going like this, he won't have anything left but the property."

Kati stood outside the closed door listening, paralyzed. She hadn't meant to eavesdrop. She had only returned to the office to pick up some papers she needed so that she could finish her report for Monsieur Licard, the new operations man who had been sent by Henri-Etienne. But when she heard his two assistants talking in the office, she couldn't help listening. She hadn't liked or trusted any of them since the moment of their arrival, but she had worked with them, provided them with answers to their seemingly endless questions. She had worked late into the night to prepare lengthy reports that they wanted on their desks first thing the next morning. She had done all of that and more, mostly because right at the moment she didn't have any choice. Tilla had sold the hotel lock, stock, and barrel to a man Kati had yet to meet. Now they had nothing they could claim as their own. So, for the time being, she had had little choice but to cooperate and give them the material they requested. Besides, it had kept her close to Dieter—and to Christophe, who was becoming more and more important to her every day. In many ways. But now, quite by accident, she had overheard two incredible things, and she was reeling—unwilling and unable to take it all in. She felt her dislike for the mysterious, faceless Henri-Etienne de Beaumont slowly turning to hatred. She also despised these two men who would serve as the agents to take away the only home she had ever known, to destroy the only future she had ever dreamed of. With Eva-Maria gone, her father dead, and her mother vacillating between reality and illusion, the Waldhotel represented the only stability, the only strength in her life. It had been there for her from the beginning of memory, and through these past horrible days. She forced herself to believe it always would be.

She leaned back against the wall, too stunned to move or speak. If anyone had passed her in the hall, seen her or spoken to her, she would have been unable to respond, so shocked was she by their conversation. Of course, deep in her heart she had realized early on there might be no place for her and her mother once Henri-Etienne had extracted from them all the information that would be useful to him. She had willingly given his men all they asked for simply because she had no other choice, nowhere else to turn, and the feeble hope that maybe, just maybe, if she made herself invaluable. . . . Being difficult would only have made everyone more miserable, especially Kati. She was in no mood to make things worse than they already were, and despite her mother's foolishness, she could not find it in her heart to punish her even further by creating problems. Ever since the arrival of Monsieur Licard and the others, Tilla had seemed to fall back into her depression. Once again she was spending most of her day in bed. When Kati had asked her last week when Henri-Etienne was expected, she merely looked at her, her face drawn, her eyes like two dark holes, and shrugged her thin shoulders.

Somehow it was easy for Kati to accept her mother's deception, for she felt that deep down, regardless of how misguided her efforts were, they were still made on Kati's behalf. But what she was hearing now she found impossible to accept. That Christophe had deceived her, had deliberately not told her the truth, was more than she could stand. It was impossible for her to imagine his hiding something like this from her. They had been spending more and more time together, and even though she felt he had been a little distant since his return from France a couple of weeks ago, she merely assumed it was because he had so much on his mind with the arrival of the new owners. But the new owners were his family! It was more than she could bear. Only last night after the final lingering diner had been ushered from the dining room and the kitchen closed for the night, she and Christophe had taken a walk along the Oos. Hand in hand, they had sat on one of the green benches lining the river.

"The Waldhotel is on its way to being wonderful again," Christophe had assured her.

"Thanks to you," she replied. "We couldn't ever have gotten through these last few months without you. Would you like to have your own hotel someday too?"

Nothing in his eyes, not one flicker or sideways look revealed the lies he was feeding to Kati. "Yes, I'd like that," he had said. "I've still got a lot to learn, though. I'm sure it will be quite a while before I'll have a place of my own."

"You know what I'd like?" Kati asked, her expression glowing at the prospect of what she was about to say. "I'd like to have a whole brood of children. All ages, all sizes. Do you know how much fun it was growing up in the hotel? Especially when my grandfather was alive. My sister and I were treated like princesses. We used to invite our friends over and call up room service. We'd have big slumber parties in the best suites when they weren't booked. Oh, it was wonderful. I hope my children will be able to have as much fun as I did." She smiled at the thought of her delightful childhood memories in the hotel.

Once again, nothing in Christophe's demeanor gave his deepest secret away. "Yes, it must have been terrific," he agreed, not for a second admitting that he shared some of the very same memories from his life at the Villa Soleil.

Christophe turned to her and kissed her gently. Soon their light kisses had turned to longer, more passionate ones. Kati enjoyed his mouth on hers and she gave no indication that she wanted to stop.

Only when she felt the tips of his strong fingers lightly stroking her nipples did she insist that they return to the hotel. Christophe agreed. He had never given her any argument when she had stopped him before. He was patient and kind with her. And honest, she had believed. Until this very moment. Her thoughts became scattered, and her rage grew. Her mind was filled with so many things, she felt she had to talk to someone at once, or she would scream out in frustration.

Dieter was finishing up some paperwork at his desk when he happened to glance up and see Kati running down the staircase. Her face was a vision of confusion and anger. It was midday and the lobby was quiet. Not a single guest was in sight. The clip of her heels on the marble steps echoed throughout the main floor as she came bounding down. One look told him she had somehow found out what he had only recently been able to piece together.

"Can you have a cup of tea with me?" she asked, her voice on the verge of cracking, her eyes brimming with tears.

"Of course, Kati," he replied. "Is it about Christophe?" he asked gently, and when she nodded, he got up and followed her into the Grand Salon. It was rare that Christophe ventured upstairs at this hour, so busy was he with the staff preparing for the evening meal. She silently prayed this would not be one of those unusual occasions.

They sat at a small table in the far corner of the room. A waiter attended to them at once and brought them their tea.

"Nothing to eat, Fräulein Meier?" the waiter suggested in a pleasant tone.

"No, nothing at all," she replied, motioning him away with her hand. She wasn't even certain the tea would stay down in her current state. Her stomach was doing somersaults.

"Oh, Kati," Dieter sighed, "what more can possibly happen here?"

"I don't know," she answered, her beautiful eyes filled with the hurt and sorrow of this latest painful experience. She pulled herself together and sat up straight in her chair. "How did *you* know about him, anyway?"

"I only found out yesterday afternoon. I'll tell you how later, so don't go jumping to the conclusion that I've been keeping anything from you."

"Okay," she said shakily, certain that her beloved Dieter would never willingly keep such desperately important information from her. He was the one friend she had left in the world at this very moment. "But please tell me everything."

"All right, I will," he began. "The day before yesterday was so hectic with the arrival of the ambassador and his crew that I didn't even have a chance to get a bite of lunch. By the time things finally settled down, it was well past four o'clock. I decided to make things easy and go to the kitchen myself and look around for anything I could find. I was scrounging in the pastry area trying to come up with something to tide me over until dinner when I heard someone shouting from the main kitchen. Whoever it was, he was extremely agitated and angry. I listened more closely and recognized the voice as Christophe's. He was speaking on the telephone. He was yelling, talking about Licard and the other man who came here with him, what's his name . . . ?"

"You mean the fat one, Monsieur Archambaud?" Kati offered.

"Yes, that's right, Archambaud. Anyway, he was talking about them. Then his voice became quieter, more controlled, and I heard him say, 'Father, you promised me this would never happen.' I thought I couldn't possibly have heard him correctly, but only a few sentences later he said it again. Then he said something even more disturbing. He said, 'Ever since Mother died, you've been doing things like this.' That must have angered his father because that was the end of the conversation. Apparently he hung up. It must have been his father on the phone."

"That still doesn't explain how you knew—" Kati interjected.

"Please don't interrupt, Kati," Dieter continued. "I know that conversation doesn't tell the whole story. That night when I finally had time to think about things, I remembered that several years ago there was a huge scandal involving a hotelier in the south of France. I couldn't recall all the details, but I did remember that the owner's wife found him in bed with his mistress. The wife was quite beautiful, and very famous. A singer, or an actress, I think. Anyway, they soon divorced, but she remained so troubled and distraught over her discovery that one night she dressed in her finest clothes and jewels and went out to the hotel swimming pool. She dove off the side of the pool, but not into the pool. This was a very special pool, built into the side of a mountain. It occurred to me that it was just like the one your mother had described to me when she returned from her visit last month. Anyway, the wife plunged to her death into the mountains below. Of course, it was in all the papers. Pictures of this woman and her family. It was so tragic. She had two sons, two beautiful boys who were left to be raised by their father, the hotel's owner."

Kati shifted in her chair. So far she couldn't imagine what all this had to do with the Waldhotel.

Dieter sensed her impatience. "Just a minute, Kati, I'm coming to the point," he said.

"I'm sorry," she offered, reaching out to take his hand. "I just don't see what this story has to do with anything."

"I understand," he agreed. "Neither did I until I called Frederic in the middle of the night and woke him up to ask him if he knew the name of the woman and the hotel. Sure enough, I can always count on his sharp memory. He remembered even more about the story than I did. The woman's name was Dominique Robillard. She was a very famous French chanteuse. The man's name was Henri-Etienne de Beaumont. He was the owner of the Villa Soleil. And now the owner of the Waldhotel. Kati . . . Henri-Etienne is Christophe's father and the woman was his mother."

The look of pain that swept across Kati's face seared Dieter's heart. It was a helpless look that bespoke her innocence, an innocence that during the last few hours of this horrible discovery had been erased forever. Never again would she be so free to trust, to believe. From now on she would always be burdened with second thoughts, questions, and inquiries. Gone were the days of blind faith. Oh . . . why was he the one who was always having to confirm the tragedies of this beautiful young woman's life? Why was he always faced with the task of trying to explain sometimes inexplicable human actions? Yes . . . Eva-Maria had run off in the middle of the night with the scurrilous Peter. No . . . he didn't understand why Eva-Maria would do such a thing. Yes . . . her father had put a bullet through his head.

No . . . he couldn't imagine why anyone would take his own life. And yes . . . Tilla had sold the hotel out from under them. The Waldhotel seemed to be gone from them forever. Yes . . . in a way he could understand her mother's actions, for she was hopelessly misguided and confused, but in her heart she was trying to do the best for her daughter. And finally no . . . he could not explain why Christophe, a man she felt so much for, with whom she had shared her secrets and confidences, with whom she had felt the first blush of love, had deceived her so completely and so cruelly.

"What do you think they'll do with us?" she asked.

As difficult as it was going to be, Dieter knew it was no time to sugarcoat his reply. "I think they'll ask you to leave the hotel."

"Leave the hotel . . ." she repeated slowly in the same voice she would have used if a death sentence had been levied against her. "Yes, I suppose you're right, Dieter, we will have to leave. They have no use for us any longer. We've shared with them everything we know. After all, it's their hotel now, and we'd just be extra baggage."

In happier times the weak pun would have been cause for laughter, but at the moment, nothing seemed sadder, or more truthful.

"I'm afraid that's right, Kati. On the other hand, I think there will be many changes around here, from what I've seen so far anyway. Maybe it would be just as well if you and your mother are not here."

"What about you?" Kati asked, for even in her most difficult moments she was still concerned about others, especially about the man upon whom she had come to rely so very much. She couldn't imagine her life without him in it on a constant, daily basis.

"Me . . . ?" Again Dieter decided that truth was the best response. "Me . . . I'll probably stay right here. You know, Kati, I'm not young anymore. I'll be sixty-eight next year, and it's really no time to start looking around for another job. Besides, the Waldhotel is the only job I've ever had. Your grandfather gave it to me, started me out shining shoes. But if they don't want me, that's fine too. I've saved enough over the years to do all right for the rest of my days. Though, to tell you the truth, I don't think I'll have that kind of luck. They need me more than I need them. So I imagine they'll keep me around for a while, at least."

Kati managed a smile, but held her words. The full impact of what they were speaking about in such real terms was just beginning to register in her confused mind. Dieter's heart ached to see her in such pain.

"So where do you think you and your mother might consider going? Will you stay in Baden-Baden? I'm sure you could find a lovely house somewhere, maybe out by the riding trails, or up on the hill."

His words, his talk of living elsewhere, dragged her back to the present. Her face regained its tenacious, determined composure, and her piercing eyes looked up to meet his.

"No, Dieter, we will never stay in Baden-Baden. The hotel has been the only address my mother and I have ever known. If we are forced to leave it, then we'll have to make a brand-new start in another town, maybe even another country. . . ." Even as she spoke and the wheels of her memory spun over the geography she had studied so diligently, she knew there couldn't be any substitute for her beautiful homeland. But for the time being, her mind was set. "No, we'll have to go away. Away somewhere where no one knows us and knows of our disgrace. Of how we lost the one thing that meant everything to us."

Dieter listened with sadness in his heart. He believed every word she was saying, for she spoke the truth.

"Kati, don't you have any idea at all where you might like to live? A different place, with a different climate? A different culture? You could meet so many new people, learn a new skill, find a husband and have a real family life. You could get out of this demanding, consuming business once and for all."

He was embarrassed to hear himself speaking such empty, dishonest words. Kati belonged in the hotel. He looked at her now as she sat, poised and elegant, and perfectly capable of becoming a fine hotelier. She was the very image of her grandfather. The hotel world was as much a part of her as her winning smile and warm personality. It was in her blood, and no amount of distance or change would ever alter her fundamental makeup. No, she was born for this world, and he was heartbroken to see her being separated from it. He hoped it wouldn't be for too long.

A thoughtful look came over her sweet face. "No, Dieter, I've not an idea in the world where we'll go. Not an idea. But I had better start thinking, hadn't I? I don't imagine we're going to have too much time to decide."

He had already said too many things of which he was not proud. He had tried, at the expense of absolute honesty, to say the right words that would make her feel better, would assure her that everything was going to be fine. This time he didn't disagree with her.

C H A P T E R

24

THINGS MOVED faster than anyone, certainly more quickly than Kati, Tilla, or Dieter, could have thought possible. Two more of Henri-Etienne's men arrived the following week, but still there was no sign of the great man himself, the man who had been given the status of a monster in Kati's mind. A man who was the source of so much pain and heartache for Tilla.

Kati had managed to avoid spending any time with Christophe, claiming too much work, tiredness, or a variety of other excuses so she would not have to face him alone. He had made plans to attend a food show in Milan for two days beginning the next day, so she only had a few more hours before he would be gone. She knew she wasn't ready for a confrontation, yet she didn't completely understand why she was hesitating to tell him that she was fully aware of his deception, his lying, and his real motives for trying to become so special to her. The only reason she could find, the reason she dared to share with herself only in her most private moments, was that somehow, in some way, he was not responsible for this horrible situation. She only allowed herself to entertain that hopeful thought for the briefest time, for her rational mind told her nothing could be further from the truth. Often, before she went to sleep at night, she would say a prayer that all that had happened was merely a bad dream and that when she awakened, everything would be all right again. It would be the same as it had been in the past, during the wonderful, carefree days when her Opa was alive and the hotel prospered. But just a few hours later she would awaken with a start, only to find the same empty, desperate feeling in the pit of her stomach. Only then did she begin to realize that nothing that had occurred was a product of her imagination—all of it was real. Very, very real.

Four days after Kati had coincidentally heard the truth uttered through closed doors, Tilla stood in the doorway of her daughter's office, her head lowered, her shoulders bent from the sobs that she could not stop. Kati looked up from her desk and sighed. So numb was she to the reality of what was going to happen, so many times had she replayed it over and over again in her mind during the last torturous days, that when it finally did, it took her a few moments to adjust. It was like a death that was long expected, but the finality of it produced a new level of shock, of horror, of fear. Of course, she knew what had happened, the only details missing were what exactly had been said and by whom, and how much time was left before they had to go. At this point everything else was fairly easy to predict.

"Oh, Kati, I'm so terribly, terribly sorry," Tilla managed to get out between sobs.

Kati merely looked at her mother. She was torn between an outpouring of sympathy from seeing her in such pain, and speaking her mind in the clearest of terms. She chose instead to deal only with the facts rather than continue to allow the situation to be such an emotional trauma. The damage was already done. Saying what she really felt would serve no purpose, except to upset Tilla even more.

"How long can we stay here?" Kati asked.

"That's the most awful part," she cried. "They want us out by the end of the week."

Kati was past the point of being surprised. With all that had happened, she was amazed they didn't have to leave by the end of the day.

"Mother, please come in from the doorway and sit down. We'd better start discussing our plans right away."

Tilla sat in the large wing chair and stared straight ahead. Her sobs would not subside. Tears rolled freely down her thin, sunken cheeks. Her hair hadn't seen the coiffeur for days, and her skin was pale and without a trace of makeup. She looked as tired and as terrible as she had during the worst days of her illness. "I never thought he would do this to me," she said. "He was such a nice man, seemingly so concerned about the hotel, so interested in turning it around. Never, not for one minute, did I think that we wouldn't be a part of it."

"Well, it's too late to worry about that now. I've had our lawyers review all the contracts, and they are watertight. We've no recourse at all against Monsieur de Beaumont. We can no longer make any claim at all to the Waldhotel or its property." This fact had only been confirmed to her yesterday. Hearing herself say it out loud for the very first time Kati thought it sounded so cut-and-dried, so final. In fact, that was exactly what three of the region's best legal minds had told her after a painstaking review of all the paperwork. Somehow it didn't make things any easier. Even worse was the way they were supposed to receive the money from the sale. It was scheduled to be paid out in small increments over a long period of time. The chances of their seeing it on a timely basis without an enormous amount of legal battling were very slim. For now they would just have to take their first payment and decide where and how they would live.

"Oh, Kati, I just never thought anything like this could possibly happen," she reiterated, drying her eyes with her handkerchief. "He said he was doing it so that our two families could merge, could create a grand hotel once again."

"What he meant was *his* family, Mother, not ours. He only bought the hotel for his son; it had nothing to do with us or our family at all."

"His son?" Tilla suddenly showed a sign of interest. "Henri-Etienne doesn't have a son. Surely he would have mentioned it if he did. He never said anything about having any children."

Kati's temper, even where her mother was concerned, could not hold out a moment longer. She erupted, screaming at the top of her lungs. "What is wrong with you, Mother? Don't you ever understand anything? Monsieur de Beaumont bought this hotel for Christophe, Christophe Robillard, his son. Yes, the very same Christophe who has been working in the kitchen these past months. The same Christophe who . . ." She couldn't go any farther. It was pointless to talk about a relationship that never really existed, other than in her mind, and only in his long enough to get what he wanted. She could hardly believe her mother was claiming to know nothing about any of this.

"Kati, I had no idea, really I didn't. Henri-Etienne never once spoke of his son, and never, ever did he tell me that any relative, anyone he even knew, worked here. Oh, Kati . . ."

"How did you think he knew so much about the hotel? All the numbers, all the details he needed to draw up such a favorable contract? How could anyone without inside information have known those details? Didn't you ever question that?"

Kati threw herself down in the other chair, exhausted by this pointless exchange. Feelings of guilt overcame her. She knew that the damage had already been done, and no amount of screaming or crying or being cruel to her mother could change any of that. In the end, her outburst had only served to make both of them feel much worse.

Tilla seemed to have aged an entire decade during the last few minutes. One look and Kati realized that of course she was telling the truth. She had had no idea that Christophe was involved.

"Oh, Mother, there are so many things that I don't understand either," she sighed. "Maybe someday it will all make sense. Right now it's very confusing. All we can do is decide what our next move will be."

"Yes, yes, you're right," Tilla agreed.

"Will you give it some thought? Think about where we might go," Kati asked. "I don't think we should stay in Baden-Baden, at least for the time being. We should go somewhere else for a while. Don't you agree?"

It was clear that Tilla wasn't listening. She had risen from the chair and was starting toward the door. She moved slowly and precisely, each step an obvious effort—the movements of an elderly person. Kati watched, unable to believe that the delicate, fragile person she saw totter slowly across the room was her mother. Tilla Becker-Meier, who had provided her family with guidance and strength and had raised her two daughters with such fortitude and care, had become a weakened, broken woman.

"Mother, promise me you'll think about it?"

Tilla turned and steadied herself against the door frame. "I will, sweetheart, I promise," she said. Then she turned and walked toward her apartment, once more seeking the solace and protection of her bed.

CHAPTER

25

"PARIS? Mother, you can't be serious!"

Tilla couldn't have been more serious. One look at her face and Kati knew her mind was made up.

"Yes, I am, Kati, I think it's exactly where we should go. A long time has passed now, and your sister can't possibly turn us away in a time of need. We'll go straight to Eva-Maria's and stay with her until we decide what we want to do next. Besides," she added, "I have such wonderful memories of Paris. It's so beautiful there. It's where your father and I spent many special times. In fact," she continued, her voice becoming unsteady, "in fact," she repeated, "it is where . . ." She couldn't continue. Pain clouded her eyes. After all the time that had passed, the memories of Johannes were still impossible to speak about.

"Okay, Mutti," Kati calmed her at once. "Don't cry, please. Of course we'll go to Paris if that's what you think is best." She held her mother like the fragile child she was.

Kati recalled her last conversation with her sister—Eva-Maria telling her that she should get out of the hotel and start a life of her own and intimating that Johannes was involved with Peter in the theft, and Kati's refusal to believe. The horrible end to their conversation and the silence ever since. Kati was certain that Eva-Maria would have no desire at all to take them in, maybe not even to see them. But she hadn't been able to come up with a better suggestion. Besides, looking at her mother now, she knew she could not refuse her. Perhaps she had talked with her older daughter.

"Mother, have you spoken with Eva-Maria? Have you actually discussed any of this with her?"

"Well, no, I haven't," she admitted. "I thought it would be better if we went to Paris and then called her from there. I think it would be the right thing to do. Once we're there, she'll have to help us."

Kati knew that going there first wasn't the proper way to handle the situation, but she was too tired to argue with Tilla. At least it was a decision, something her mother seemed incapable of making these last few days. France would be a dramatic change for them, the excitement and pace of Paris couldn't be more different than the quiet, peaceful Black Forest.

"Okay, Mother, I'll tell Dieter to arrange for train reservations for tomorrow morning. Shall we leave around ten?"

"That would be perfect, sweetheart," her mother said enthusiastically. "Oh, Kati, you'll see. It will be wonderful. We'll all be together again, just like before. Everything will be fine."

An exhausted Kati merely smiled. She hoped her mother's words held some measure of truth, for there was certainly nothing left for them at the Waldhotel. Nothing except for packing their scant belongings and waiting for tomorrow.

Kati was down on her hands and knees bent over the already bulging suitcase. She was trying to fit the last of the silver-framed pictures into the unrelenting bag when she felt a pair of eyes at her back. She turned her head slowly to meet the intruder.

He stood staring at her from the doorway. It appeared he had just returned from his trip to Italy, for he was dressed casually in a smart jacket and khaki pants. He looked sporty, and handsome and energetic—all the qualities that had attracted Kati to him the very first time she had seen him step through the hotel's revolving door. The qualities she had grown to love during their romance. Now, seeing him alone for the first time since she had discovered his treachery, she no longer saw the kind, sweet man with whom she had shared some of her deepest thoughts, told many of her secret wishes. She had allowed his mouth and his hands to join with hers. She had rejoiced in spending some time with him at the end of each long day. They both worked so hard, so diligently, and she had always thought their motivations for success were the same. He had entered her mind as well as her heart. Now she knew all of it was a lie. She cursed the day she had first heard his name.

"Kati, may I come in?"

"Please leave me alone. Isn't it obvious I'm busy?" She returned her attention to the suitcase, more frustrated than ever by its refusal to close.

"Here, let me help you with that," he offered, entering the room and approaching her from behind. She could hear the soft sound of his footsteps as he neared. Her throat tightened and she began to shake. She took one deep breath as he continued to move across the room toward her. She wouldn't, couldn't allow him to see her fall apart. That she cared about the hotel was one thing, that she hated him and his family for what they had done and the manner in which they had done it was another. But to admit that she truly cared for him, that she had allowed her thoughts to be possessed by him, that late at night she dreamed of his kissing her, his gentle mouth slowly caressing hers, their arms intertwined—no, that she would not permit.

"I told you, I'm busy. Can't you see that? I don't need your help! Now, please, go away," she hissed, a little louder and with less control in her voice than she would have liked. Her back still faced him. She tried to keep her shoulders from moving, but the trembling had increased. Her body had a mind of its own. She was unable to remain still.

"Kati, please, if you'll only listen to me for one minute. Please, I can explain everything. . . ."

"Are you crazy? Explain everything? No, I've learned all that I need to know, all that I really want to know, can bear to know, at this point. What you have done to me is the worst thing that has ever happened to me in my life. In fact, in both my mother's and my life. And it seems that the insults, the injuries know no bounds. Do you want to know what just happened? Only a few minutes ago?" She didn't stop for him to answer. "I called down to the desk to ask for some help. I wanted a porter to come up and help me pack up that portrait of my grandfather," Kati said, pointing to the oil painting above the fireplace. After Kati had taken over Karl-Gustav's office, she had asked for his portrait to be moved upstairs from its home on the first floor, where it now hung beside the image of Ludwig Becker. "I waited and waited for someone to come. Finally I called down to the desk to see what had happened. One of your father's henchmen got on the phone and told me that the portrait was part of the sale and that we could not take it with us. That I was not to touch it or try to remove it or there would be trouble. Can you imagine anything so cruel, so heartless? That painting was a gift, a gift to my family. It doesn't belong to you, or to your horrible father, or to anyone other than to my mother and me. Now I'm told that we can't take it with us, that we're not to touch it. What kind of animals are you? With a father like yours, I'm surprised you even have the capacity to fake kindness, to parade around making people think that you're a warm, caring human being!"

Her last words were like a kick in the teeth to Christophe. He would have welcomed a hard slap across the face or to have been the target of some object hurled across the room at him, anything other than hearing such words from Kati. He cared deeply for the beautiful girl. Ever since his father had called him home on the false pretense of his grandmother's illness to tell him his supposedly wonderful news, he had been heartsick. No amount of persuasion would change his father's mind about Kati and her mother, although he had repeatedly tried to convince him that it wasn't necessary to remove them from the hotel. Surely there was a place for them. He had even threatened to walk out on his father and his tainted gift, until Henri-Etienne promised that Kati's fate would remain the same, no matter whether Christophe stayed or left. He had returned to the hotel desperate to tell Kati what had happened, and what was going to happen. That it was none of his doing. That it was completely out of his control. He had been a coward because, uncertain of how to tell her, he had waited too long, and inevitably she had found out on her own. Now it looked as if it would be impossible even to get her to listen to his side of the story, let alone reverse her feelings of hatred for him.

"But Kati . . . ," he began again.

"Christophe," Kati said as calmly as she could manage, "you will never be able to explain everything to me. I'll never, ever understand how you could have done this to me, and to my family."

"Kati, you must listen to me," he pleaded. "I knew nothing about my father buying the hotel. I had nothing to do with it, please believe me. The first I heard of it was after it was a done deal, when he called me to come home, claiming that my grandmother was ill."

This last comment got Kati's attention, and she turned around and faced him for the first time. That he would continue the lie, continue to deceive her was more than she could stand.

"What do you mean, you didn't know? How can you expect me to believe that? Well," she paused, "maybe it's not so silly after all to think I'd believe you, after what has happened. I fell for all your other lies."

"Kati, it's the absolute truth. My father took it upon himself to contact your mother. He has never been known to be shy in his business dealings. He was the one who convinced her to sell the hotel to him. I knew nothing, nothing whatsoever about it until I went home to France. Please, you must try to understand. Since you've never met my father, I can imagine how hard it is, but he is certainly capable of doing something like this. You see, ever since my mother died, or rather, killed herself, he has been trying to make up for it to both my brother and me. However, Phillippe would have no part of it. He moved to the States to get as far away from my father as possible. I'm his only hope. Buying the hotel for me, even though it's the last thing I'd ever have wanted him to do, was his way of trying to make things right again. He's just never been able to understand that the only thing that would make it right would be to have my mother back again. Someday I hope he'll see that it's the one thing he'll never be able to do."

Kati had listened to every word he said. In all the time they had spent together he had never mentioned any of these things. In fact, he had done his best to conceal his past, his family, everything about him that was important. For that she could not forgive him.

"Christophe, why didn't you ever tell me any of these things before? Why didn't you admit to me who you are, who your family is, that you have been in the hotel business, just like my family, for generations? I still don't understand, I'll *never* understand how you could carry this secret around with you and not even divulge it to a friend. I was your friend, you know. But it doesn't really matter anymore. Tomorrow we'll be leaving. The hotel will be all yours to do with as you please." As Christophe reached out his arms to her, she felt her composure beginning to crumble. She ran past him and out of the room before her tears came.

. . .

She took the back elevator and left the building through a seldom-used side door. Never before had she felt unable to meet the eyes of the employees and guests. Most of the staff knew that they would be departing in the morning, but she had no desire to see any of them now.

The wrought-iron entrance gate to the garden was open, which usually meant the gardeners were working. She marched swiftly through. Sure enough, at the far end of the colorful display she spotted two of them trimming some of the bushes.

"Let me borrow your clippers for a minute," she asked one of the two men.

"Of course, Fräulein Kati," he said, reaching into his satchel and pulling out a pair. "Do you need anything else?"

"You don't by any chance have an extra trug, do you?"

"Why yes, I just happen to. It's over there by the gate," he pointed. "Let me get it for you."

"Don't bother, I'll take it myself. I'll put everything back in the storeroom later tonight."

"No problem, Fräulein Kati, I won't be needing them. You know where they belong."

"Thanks," she said.

She walked in the direction of the still-blossoming late-spring flowers. Her task was made easy by the sturdy and recently sharpened clippers, and in no time at all the basket was overflowing with a myriad of colorful flowers. She closed the gate firmly behind her when she left, listening intently to the heavy metal clanking together. It was one of the sounds, familiar since childhood, that she wanted to hear before leaving.

The cemetery was at least a kilometer away. Her steps were quick-paced and determined, and it took her no time at all to reach the gravesites she had come to visit. The Becker-Meier plots were well tended and held a very prominent place on the grounds at the top of the gently sloping incline. Slowly she approached the gray granite headstones. Marianne Becker's was the first one she came to. Marianne, her Opa's wife, the love of his life for over fifty years, her mother's mother. Kati hadn't really been able to have the full benefit of knowing this beautiful, charming woman. She had died when Kati was still so little. But of course she had flowers for her. She laid the loose blossoms at the base of the stone. Two plots away was a smaller, less elaborate headstone. "Oh, Father, what a terrible end to your life," she whispered to herself. "You left us nothing, not even a note to tell us of your last thoughts. Some days I almost understand why you did it, but most of the time I find it a cowardly, disdainful act. I'm sorry for that. Someday I hope I'll find it in my heart to understand and forgive you, if that's what you want." Kati stood looking down at the headstone for a moment longer. She took one flower from the wooden trug and placed it gently on Johannes's grave.

Next lay her beloved Opa. It was hard for her to believe that it had been almost seven years since her grandfather had died. Sometimes it seemed as if it had only been a short time, other times she felt he had been lost to her for many years. Not a day passed when she did not think of him, when she tried to draw from her memory those few things she remembered him telling her about the hotel.

She knelt at the monument and spoke. "I'm so sorry, Opa. In a way I'm glad you're dead, that you aren't here to see what has happened. Of course, if you had been here, you would never have allowed it to happen. But I'll be back. I don't know when, but someday. This I promise you." She placed all the remaining flowers at his grave and stood tall, allowing the gentle breeze to wash over her.

She took the long route back to the hotel, walking slowly along the river. She looked hard and long at the magnificent trees, their springtime branches quickly developing their fullest summer foliage. In only three or four more weeks they would be at their most beautiful, heavily laden with leaves. As she passed the Fichtls' house, she slowed her pace. She hadn't spoken with Heidi since the hotel had been sold, and she made a mental note to call her in Munich as soon as they were settled. It would be shocking and unfair for her to find out they were gone when she brought the baby home again for a visit with her parents.

Heidi and her baby. What a wonderful thrill it had been for them to be together. She had brought the baby home a month ago, and Kati and Christophe had gone to visit. They had spent a glorious afternoon with the little child. Christophe had bounced the sweet infant on his knee. The baby, a little girl, was plump and red-cheeked and blessed with the same luscious scarlet hair as her mother. Heidi was at the height of happiness. Mark's practice was growing daily, and they seemed still to be very much in love. Perhaps, just perhaps, Kati had thought, someday she, too, would know the joys of motherhood. She had dreamed again and again about holding the baby in her arms. It had been an incredible feeling. After they left, she and Christophe had even talked about how wonderful it would be to have a family. Now all those dreams had turned into a terrible nightmare, and it seemed she was light-years away from realizing her own happiness.

By the time the hotel was in sight, the sky had darkened. A late-spring downpour was surely on the way, and her beautiful river looked swollen and heavy. Thunder clashed overhead, and she ran for cover from the angry skies. It was the hotel's last chance to protect her.

It was still raining lightly the following morning. They had so few bags, the porter managed to get them all into the trunk of the car that would take them to the station.

"I'll be there in the morning to drive you," Dieter had said the night before when they returned to the hotel. Tilla, Kati, and Dieter had gone into town for dinner. Both Kati and her mother had agreed that they would prefer eating out to the trauma of taking their last meal in the hotel dining room. Dining out also reduced Kati's chances of running into Christophe again. She had ignored the several messages waiting for her when she had come in that afternoon.

For the first day in such a long time, Kati had not stepped into her hotel uniform that morning. Instead, she chose the cheeriest outfit she could find—a bright red sweater over a nice cotton shirt, and a perfectly tailored pair of gray slacks. Anyone seeing them would think that they were just another mother and daughter off for a weekend of shopping and sightseeing.

She said her good-byes to those staff members she had missed during the week, and with her head held high and her eyes dry and clear, she walked down the staircase and out through the revolving door. Tilla was already in the backseat, her eyes focused straight ahead. Dieter slammed the trunk shut and headed for the driver's seat.

"There you are," was all he said as he stopped and held the door open for her.

He turned the engine on and was pulling out of the driveway when Christophe came running toward them. She thought of telling Dieter to floor the accelerator and continue on, but it was too late. He had braked, and Christophe pushed his head in through the half-open window.

"Kati, I've been calling and calling you. Where have you been?"

"I have a train to catch. What do you want?"

"I want your forwarding address," he said.

Never would she admit to him that they didn't have one. He was the last person she wanted to know just how uncertain they were of their future.

"Why on earth would you want that?" she asked.

"I want to send your grandfather's portrait to you. I spoke with my father last night and insisted that you have it. He agreed."

"How kind of him. His generosity is astounding," Kati answered. Even the mention of the portrait, left hanging in Opa's former upstairs office, brought renewed pain to her heart. "I'll believe it when it is finally delivered to us."

"Kati, it will be, I promise," he insisted, straightening to his full height. "Just tell me where you're going to be."

Kati refused to tell him the truth. "You can get our address from Dieter," she said curtly. "Dieter will always know where to get in touch with us."

"All right," he agreed. "I'll speak with you when you return," he said to their loyal friend.

Kati started to roll the window up the rest of the way; her sleeve was becoming damp from the rain. As far as she was concerned, the conversation was over. Christophe apparently had more to say, for he held his hand out to stop the glass from rising.

"Kati," he began. "Kati, I'm sorry for everything. Someday, when I'm in the position to, I'll make it up to you, I promise."

Kati turned and looked at him, at his eyes staring straight into hers. She saw the same look he had given her just before he had kissed her for the very first time. She reached up and pried his fingers away from the glass. He tried to grab her hand, but she pushed him away.

"Dieter, please," she said, her voice as urgent as he had ever heard. "Drive this car out of here right now."

She didn't dare turn back. Her hand was still clutched tightly to the top of the glass when they reached the station.

26

PARIS was horrible. It was gray and wet and cold, a cold that penetrated right through Kati's bones and made her shiver as she walked the long platform toward the telephone station. April in Paris. The wind circled up and whipped around her in heavy gusts, making it nearly impossible to walk in a straight line. She balanced herself by grasping the largest suitcase with one hand, slinging the unwieldy shoulder bag over one shoulder, and grabbing the remaining case with her free hand. Tilla struggled with the other two pieces. What had seemed earlier like a light load was now hopelessly cumbersome, and there were no porters in sight. They climbed the high stairs cautiously, stopping every few steps to rest and shift their loads. People pushed their way past them, impatient and irritated that the two women had created an obstacle, a momentary delay in their frenetic schedule. Everyone seemed to be in a rush. Men dashed past with briefcases flying, and women took the stairs in their high heels at a fast pace. Certainly no one stopped to ask if they could be of any help with the heavy bags, as they would have in Baden-Baden.

Kati changed some money and bought a few jetons for the telephone. The lines at this time of the day were two and three deep, so she parked Tilla and their things safely against a wall opposite the phones.

"Just stay here and rest for a minute, Mother. I'll only be a short while," she assured her. Tilla looked tired and old. The last few days at the hotel she had been virtually helpless, unable to cope with their imminent departure. The entire task of organizing their leave had fallen to Kati. She had dealt with the situation as she had dealt with the many other crises over the past few years—she cast aside her own emotions and problems and did what needed to be done.

Once inside the booth it took her a few minutes to acquaint herself with the operation of the foreign phone. She could feel the impatient stares of those next in line. One woman even had the audacity to press her face up against the glass and give her an intimidating look. Kati pretended to ignore her, but she was unused to such rudeness and pressure.

She searched madly through her handbag and at last located the small piece of paper on which she had written the number. The jeton clanged to the bottom and the meter indicated the number of francs she had as credit toward her call. She dialed each digit slowly, leaving her fingertip in the hole and following its circular path until the dial returned to its original position. Her breathing was coordinated with the motion of her finger. Dial . . . inhale . . . release. Dial . . . inhale . . . release. She was startled by the anxiety she felt as she called her own sister.

One ring. Two rings. At the end of the third ring someone picked up the phone. "Hello, the von Hassler residence," said the cheery voice.

"Hello, may I speak with Eva-Maria, please?" Kati asked in flawless French.

"Who is calling?"

"It's . . . it's her sister," she managed.

There was a long pause at the other end. "Her sister?" questioned the voice.

"Yes, my name is Kati. I'm Eva-Maria's sister. May I please speak with her?"

"I'm sorry, Mademoiselle Kati, your sister is not here," the woman said, although it still sounded strange to her. Carmela had been in the von Hassler employ long before Eva-Maria had moved into the townhouse, but in all that time she had never heard her mention a sister. Come to think of it, she never mentioned her family at all. "Your sister," she repeated, "and Monsieur von Hassler are out of town. They are in Italy. I'm sorry."

"In Italy," Kati repeated slowly. "When will they be back?"

"In ten days," the housekeeper said. "They only left yesterday afternoon. I'm sorry you missed them. Is there a message? Or a number where she could telephone you when they return?"

"No . . . no . . . there is no message. Just please tell her I called."

"Is there a number where she can reach you?"

The time on the meter was running out. She would either have to add another jeton or finish the call. There was really nothing more to say.

"No, no, there is no number. I'll call back. Thank you." She hung up the receiver slowly and stood in the booth. They had certainly not counted on this. Of course, Tilla had assured her, Eva-Maria would be at home in Paris. When they called her and explained to her what had happened, she would tell them to come over immediately. Tilla had been so sure and so convincing that Kati had not even bothered to challenge her, or to contemplate what they would do if that didn't come to pass. It was Kati's nature to plan and to worry about every little detail, but this one time she had allowed her mother to convince her that everything would be fine. When they had been advised that they were no longer welcome at their own hotel, Kati had been so anxious to leave and so absorbed in their preparations that she had been willing to believe that her mother was right. Now they were stuck in Paris with no immediate plans.

Bang! Bang! Bang! "What are you doing in there? Your makeup? Your hair? Are you finished? Please, we are all waiting, can't you see?"

Kati turned to see the face of the fat, sloppily dressed woman pressed up against the glass of the booth. It was the same one who had glared at her earlier. Now her hand was raised to shoulder height and she was preparing to hit the door again.

"Sorry, pardon me," Kati said as she edged herself out of the booth and past the fuming creature.

Well, they certainly hadn't come prepared for this set of circumstances. The trip had been a quiet one. Tilla had spent most of the time sleeping or staring out the window, and Kati was thankful for the silence after the events of the last days. They had only spoken about when and what they would have for lunch, and whether or not they should reserve a table in the dining car. They had decided to go to the car, but the conversation over their sandwiches and drinks had been virtually nonexistent. Now they were stuck in the cold, damp Gare de l'Est, surrounded by harsh, impatient people. Everyone else had a destination. Theirs was undetermined. Besides Eva-Maria, there was not a single soul they could call.

Kati walked slowly toward Tilla, whose attention was captivated by all the people rushing about.

"It's quite a scene, isn't it? I was almost attacked in the phone booth," Kati said.

"Yes, it's bustling," her mother agreed. "Oh, but Kati, isn't it exciting? It's so active, so alive. Everyone looks so important, rushing off to one place or another. Don't you think it's going to be fun here? Such a change from the quietude of Baden-Baden!" Her head turned and followed the path of a young, chicly dressed French woman as she ran for a train.

"Yes, I suppose it is exciting," Kati commented, her mind distracted by their dilemma. Right now she was only concerned with where they would sleep that night. Tilla was too caught up in the scene to notice that anything was bothering her daughter. She continued to look around as if people-watching was the sole reason for their being in Paris. Kati stood by her side trying to formulate a plan. Where could they go? They didn't know anyone in Paris well enough to call and ask if they could impose on them for a few days. A hotel, she supposed. Yes, they would have to check into a hotel, at least until Eva-Maria returned. She found it to be the height of irony that they had been banished from their own hotel and now were put in a position of searching for yet another one in which to spend their first night. But which one? There were hundreds of hotels in Paris. Kati wasn't familiar with any of them, except for the very grandest ones, and they certainly couldn't afford any of those now. Not now, in their situation, with the tiny first payment they had received from Henri-Etienne and their future so unclear.

The crowd was starting to thin out, so Tilla finally turned her attention back to Kati. Kati had sat down on top of one of the suitcases. Her head was in her hands, and she was obviously deep in thought.

"Kati, whatever's the matter?" Tilla asked. "What did Eva-Maria say?"

"Eva-Maria's not home."

"Not home?" Tilla cried, never once having considered that possibility when she insisted on coming without even calling. "When will she be back?"

"Ten days from now."

"Ten days!" she cried out. "Where are they? Whom did you speak with? Was Peter there?"

"Just a minute, Mother," Kati insisted. "I'll tell you everything. Eva-Maria and Peter have gone to Italy. They only left yesterday. I spoke with the housekeeper, who told me they wouldn't be back for ten days. So," she continued resignedly, "we're on our own." She looked up to see her mother's shocked expression.

"Oh, Kati, what will we do now?"

"That's just what I've been thinking about," she said, fighting to keep from lashing out at her mother. "I suppose we'll have to find a hotel, for the time being anyway, and wait until they return. Do you have any other suggestions?" Another look at Tilla's face told her she didn't. Once again Kati was left to make the decision on her own.

The Hotel Perle was located in a narrow alleyway just off the Rue du Bac. It was a small hotel with only fourteen rooms, and Tilla and Kati were lucky to get the last room available. It was tiny, with space enough only for two skinny single beds, a narrow table, and one closet, which was adequate for their few things. They placed their empty luggage on a shelf that had been built over the window. Only then could they walk about the room without bumping into each other. The room was clean and cheery, the owners had used fabrics from Provence for the curtains and bedspreads, and the bright colors gave a warm, cozy look to the space. It was the height of the tourist season in Paris, so Kati was thankful that the nice man she had asked at the café nearby had been kind enough to recommend the hotel. It was in the most active part of the Left Bank; they were surrounded by the Sorbonne, the Odéon, and the great concourse that was the Boulevard St. Germain. It was the heart of the student quarter. There were countless restaurants and coffeehouses. Most were suitable for their sparse budget. Kati was determined not to become depressed about the situation, so when Tilla decided to have an afternoon nap, she took a walk and explored the neighborhood.

The narrow streets were packed with young people, many carrying satchels overflowing with books and papers. She stopped every few feet to peer into the shop windows, which were filled with the most fashionable clothing. She found a bookstore and purchased some magazines and a novel. Better brush up on my French, she thought.

Kati had only been in Paris once before, when she was ten years old. Her parents had brought the girls for their first visit. They had gone first-class, staying at the beautiful Hotel Crillon on the Right Bank. They had eaten in the finest restaurants, visited the museums and monuments, and Tilla had bought them each a special party dress from a wonderful shop on the Faubourg St. Honoré. She thought about those dresses now. Hers was a light, cerulean blue, with a full petticoat, and it tied at the waist with a dark blue satin ribbon. It had puffed sleeves that were also edged with the same blue ribbon. It was made of silk, a thin, elegant silk that moved gently across the stiff petticoat when she walked, making a swishing noise she could recall to this day. She remembered how pretty and how grown up she had felt when she first put it on and went downstairs to join her family for her grandfather's birthday dinner. Eva-Maria had chosen a more sophisticated dress, bright red with little bows on the sleeves. Funny, she thought, even then her sister had been more fashionable and daring than Kati.

It had been years since she had thought about those dresses, even longer since she had seen them. They were still there somewhere, packed away in a storage trunk in the basement of the Waldhotel. She hadn't even bothered to go down there before they left. Perhaps later, when they had an address, she would write Dieter and ask him to send the rest of their things. How she would love to see that dress again. She felt tears forming, but refusing to allow them to come, she continued walking at a brisk pace, determined to think brighter thoughts.

The shopkeeper was placing the afternoon batch of pastries in the bakery window just as she was passing, and she couldn't resist the temptation. Armed with an elegantly tied box containing the rich goodies, she headed back to the hotel. One more stop at a flower stand to buy a bouquet of spring blooms and she had everything. Tilla would be pleased to wake up to the sight of the colorful blossoms, accompanied by the smell of freshly baked treats. She would ask them to send some tea up to the room. Yes, that would be fun. They could eat their pastries and drink a cup of hot tea and talk and decide what they would do while they waited for Eva-Maria to return.

The next week passed quickly. Every night after they had eaten a good meal at one of the inexpensive restaurants near the hotel, Kati and Tilla would make a plan for the following day. They would find an exhibition or a movie or a gallery they wanted to visit. Kati would unfold the enormous detailed plan of the city on the narrow bed and then map out the fastest or most interesting route. Of course, since the weather was so unpredictable, she would also chart the Métro route or the bus they could take if it was raining. Taxis were far too costly. Armed with the guidebook, newspaper, and the indispensable map they would start out fresh the next morning on their latest adventure. Her mother seemed in better spirits than she had been in a very long time.

The night before they knew Eva-Maria was scheduled to return, they planned nothing for the next day. Kati was up early, and as soon as Tilla awakened, she urged her to go downstairs and make the call.

"Kati, you're already dressed. Please go and telephone your sister," Tilla asked her before she was even out of her bed.

"Isn't it a little early? It's only eight-thirty."

"No, I'm sure someone will be up. If she's there, we could pack up and be across town before the morning traffic gets too bad."

Kati shrugged and started down the stairs to call. Her mother was so certain that Eva-Maria would welcome them with open arms and would ask them to come over to her house right away. Kati remained unconvinced that her estranged sister would be interested in seeing them at all.

"No, I'm sorry, Mademoiselle Meier, your sister has not returned. Perhaps they will be coming tomorrow. Will you call back then? Or do you have a number now?" asked the same housekeeper with whom she had spoken before.

"Yes, I'll try back. But in case they arrive later today, please tell her that her sister and her mother are very anxious to hear from her. We're staying at the Hotel Perle." Kati gave the housekeeper their number.

"I'll be sure to tell her, Mademoiselle Meier."

Kati walked back upstairs to tell her mother the results of the call. On the one hand, she was sorry that they had not yet returned; on the other, she was almost afraid of what would happen when they were finally back. Tilla and she were having such a good time, they were seeing so many new and interesting things. They were watching their money very carefully. Why shouldn't these carefree, enjoyable days continue for a little while longer?

She called again the next day and was told that yes, Eva-Maria and Monsieur von Hassler had returned but were out again.

"When do you expect them back?" Kati asked of the housekeeper, whose voice was now familiar to her but whose name remained a mystery.

"Sometime later, I'm not certain," she said. Was her voice a little curt, a little less polite than she had been in the past? Or was it only Kati's imagination already preparing for the worst?

"Well, all right. Did you give her my messages and my number at the hotel?"

"Yes, Mademoiselle, I did."

Kati left the phone cabine feeling both frustrated and annoyed. Why wouldn't Eva-Maria return her calls? Could she still be angry with her from their last conversation, which had ended on such a sour note? She supposed so. She had seen her sister harbor grudges for longer periods of time over lesser issues.

They both skipped dessert at dinner that night and returned to the hotel early, expecting to find a message. From the hotel's entryway Kati saw that their box remained empty except for their room key.

"I'm sorry, Mademoiselle Kati, no one called," said the proprietress, who had been alerted to watch for an important call for the beautiful young woman. She placed the key gently in Kati's hand.

"Maybe they had something to do this evening," Tilla offered as they slowly climbed the staircase to their tiny room. But there was no way of camouflaging the fact that their spirits were down, and neither of them was interested in planning anything for the following day. The map remained folded on the small table. Once they were both in bed, Kati shut the light out, but the sounds of Tilla's tossing and turning throughout the long night kept her awake until dawn.

Three more calls went unanswered. On the fourth try she reached the maid again. "Please, Madame—I'm sorry, I don't even know your name."

"Carmela," said the woman.

"Carmela, please, I must speak with my sister. It is terribly important. Can you get her to come to the phone?"

There was a very long pause. So long, in fact, that Kati wondered if the woman had forgotten about her.

"Are you there? Hello? Are you on the line?"

"Yes, Mademoiselle Meier, I'm here. I'm sorry, but your sister will not speak with you."

"Won't speak with me? What did she say?"

"Nothing. . . . I'm sorry, I must hang up now. Please, I'm very sorry."

"Wait!" Kati begged. "Just a minute, please. I have to know what my sister said. Please tell me."

Carmela, separated from her family in Portugal for so long, would do anything to speak with them, to see them again. She was completely baffled by Eva-Maria's actions. Nothing was more important to Carmela than her family. She couldn't understand anyone not wanting to see her very own sister. But she couldn't risk her job trying to figure it out. If she said anything other than what she was instructed to say, she would be fired on the spot. Then all of her plans would be blown sky high. No one else would employ her, and it would be ages before she'd ever be able to save enough money to send for her son.

"I'm sorry, Mademoiselle Meier, I work for your sister. I can only tell you that she is not taking any calls from you. I'm sorry," she repeated. She placed the receiver back on the hook, disconnecting the call before she was compelled to repeat some of the terrible things she had heard Eva-Maria say about her family.

Tilla's expectant face greeted Kati when she entered the small room. "Well, did you finally reach her?" she asked, her voice still filled with hope.

There was no point in hiding the truth from her. Kati's worst fears had been confirmed, and there was no reason left to think that things would change. Eva-Maria wanted nothing to do with them. She had made it painfully clear.

"Mother, Eva-Maria won't take our calls. She told the house-keeper not to put us through. She doesn't want to speak to us, let alone open her house to us. She's just not willing to see us."

"But she has to speak with us, to see us. We're her family!" Tilla insisted.

"Mother, I couldn't agree with you more," Kati responded, trying to comfort Tilla and erase the pain-filled expression from her face. "However, the truth is, Eva-Maria hasn't put much stock in family relations for the past several years. She's apparently not interested in starting now."

"Don't be so flip about it, Katharina," Tilla warned. It had been ages since her mother had called her by her full name. Obviously she was terribly distraught by the news of her elder daughter's continuing rebellion.

"I apologize, Mother, but I was afraid this would happen. From the beginning, when you first suggested we come here, I thought Eva-Maria wouldn't want to see us, wouldn't want to have anything to do with us. After all, when you think about it, she chose Peter over us years ago. I don't think I'll ever be able to understand her reasons for behaving this way, but I do know how strongly she feels about it."

"Oh, Kati," Tilla cried, "I just can't believe that if she saw us, and heard about everything that has happened, she wouldn't want to help us, to be with us and try to see us through this difficult time. Oh, Kati, please, go and speak with her."

Kati found it hard to imagine that Eva-Maria would allow her into her house if she wouldn't even come to the phone to speak with her. But when she looked into her mother's tear-stained face, she knew she would do whatever she could to try to alleviate some of her pain.

"All right, Mother, I'll go to her house. Maybe once I'm there, waiting at the front door, she'll have to see me."

"Shall I go with you?"

"No, I think you should stay here. It's starting to rain now and it sounds to me as though your cold is getting worse. You've been coughing all afternoon. I'll go see if I can convince her to meet with us. I'll be back as soon as I can." Kati put on her raincoat, grabbed an umbrella, kissed her mother on the cheek, and quickly left the room.

Avenue Foch was among the grandest and most beautiful residential boulevards in Paris. Its wide expanse of meticulously manicured trees spread out like a powerful arm from the Arc de Triomphe. Kati walked slowly past the imposing mansions. Each one was more elegant, more opulent than the one before. Finally she came upon number fourteen. The four-storied home was not the largest or fanciest on the street, but its limestone facade was intricately and ornately carved. High wrought-iron gates surrounded the property on all sides. One had to look carefully for the discreet brass plate engraved simply 14, Avenue Foch.

So this is what they bought with the money Peter had stolen from her family, she thought. Kati pressed the small bell. She waited for what seemed like a long time, the rain seeping through her umbrella, before the sound of a man's voice came over the speaker.

"Yes?" he inquired, probably unable to see from within the identity or even the sex of whoever was under the umbrella.

"Hello, I'm here to see Eva-Maria," Kati replied forcefully into the speaker above the bell.

"Who is calling, please?"

"Please tell her it's her sister, Kati."

"Very well."

Silence replaced the crackle of the intercom, and again Kati waited for what seemed a long time. A movement caught her eye and she tilted her umbrella back and looked up into the tall, elegant windows on the second floor. Standing in the window, holding the lace curtain back to one side, was Eva-Maria. At the exact moment Kati started to raise her hand to wave, a buzzer sounded, releasing the lock on the enormous front gate. Quickly she turned to push the gate open before the sound ceased. She walked up the path to the front entrance. The wide door swung open just as she approached it. Greeting her was a large, heavyset man she assumed was the butler.

"Please come in. If you'll give me your things and go into the library, Madame will be down in a moment." He ushered her into a room off the main foyer before Kati was able to absorb fully all the details of the glorious house.

The library was one of the most tastefully appointed rooms she had ever seen, with its ornately carved ceiling. The boiserie was extraordinary, far more exquisite than she had ever seen in a private home. The furnishings were imposing, but even so looked comfortable and inviting. Kati was engaged in reading the titles of some of the many leather-bound books when she heard the door slide open behind her.

"Kati," Eva-Maria said as she swept into the room. Had Kati not been absolutely certain of her whereabouts, it would have been difficult for her to say for sure whether or not the person who stood only a few feet in front of her was her sister. Eva-Maria looked every bit the grande dame. She was dressed in a very expensive, well-tailored spring suit. Its waist was fitted, and, in the mode of the day, its exaggerated collar stood out away from her face, accentuating her upswept hairdo. She wore extremely high-heeled, extremely uncomfortable-looking shoes. On her left hand was a sapphire of considerable size, and each wrist held a thick gold bracelet. More than appearing rich and opulent in an overdone way, Eva-Maria looked very old to Kati. She was only twenty-three, but she surely could have passed for a matron ten years older. Kati felt much, much younger than her twenty-one years, and certainly very dowdy in her conservative skirt and sensible rain shoes. Suddenly it seemed to her that she had been staring at her sister's appearance for a very long time.

"Eva-Maria," she answered and moved toward her. They embraced briefly, but without much emotion on her older sister's part. Kati felt Eva-Maria pull away from her almost immediately.

"Eva-Maria, why wouldn't you take our calls? You must know

by now what has happened," Kati asked at once, going straight to the point, not wanting to be forced to comment on the house, on Eva-Maria's appearance, or on Peter.

"Of course I know," Eva-Maria replied, walking quickly to the far side of the room and picking a cigarette from a silver holder that sat on one of the thin-legged side tables. She sat down and was immediately engulfed by the lushness of the deep sofa. She lit the cigarette and exhaled into the room. "I am fully aware of everything that has happened at the Waldhotel. And I'm sorry, sorry for you, that is. I told you, I warned you years ago to get out of there, to go out and make a life for yourself. Now I can see that you didn't listen, didn't take my advice. Look what's happened to you now. Honestly, the situation you're in is no one's fault but Mother's. I didn't take your calls because I simply cannot bear to see her. I can't forget or ever forgive her for what she did to Father. I don't see how you can either. Now she's gone and sold the hotel to that dreadful de Beaumont man. He'll try to run it just like his hotel in France, and it simply won't work."

"Eva-Maria, stop it. You've got to forget all the terrible things that happened in the past. Forget all the terrible things that have occurred. For whatever reasons, they *did* take place, and they affected our lives terribly, particularly mine and Mother's. I tried my best at the hotel, and we were doing pretty well, or so I thought, and then she went and sold it. She only did it to try to protect whatever we had left. Not for any other reason. She realizes now that she's made a mistake, probably the mistake of a lifetime, but that's no reason to condemn her forever. We've got to go on."

"Yes, you will have to go on, but without me, and without any help from me. I've washed my hands of the entire situation."

Just as Eva-Maria was taking a last deep draw on her cigarette, the door burst open and the sounds of tiny feet echoed across the parts of the wooden floor not covered by priceless Aubusson carpets.

"Maman, Maman," cried a little voice.

Kati, still standing, turned to see a beautiful little girl, dressed in a frilly white pinafore, rush past her toward the sofa where Eva-Maria was sitting. Following close behind her, winded from the chase, was a uniformed nanny.

"I'm so sorry, Madame. She got away from me, the little rascal. Broke out of her room like a firecracker, she did," said the red-cheeked nanny in a heavy Irish brogue. "I suppose she just wanted to see you before she went down for her nap."

"That's all right, Millie. Come here, darling," Eva-Maria said to the adorable young child, who was already struggling to get up on the sofa next to her mother. Her chubby little legs couldn't quite reach. "Here, let me help you. Ooops! Up you go!"

The little girl threw her arms around her mother's neck and hugged her tightly. Eva-Maria shifted the child off her lap, obviously to avoid the possibility of her skirt becoming wrinkled. She looked down with concern on her face and, locating the spot where the child had momentarily landed, stroked the elegant material several times.

Kati, still standing, stood in wide-eyed amazement. She had no idea that Eva-Maria had a child. News of a baby had never reached the gossip hotline at the hotel. At that moment the child became aware that someone else was in the room besides her mother.

"Who is that lady?" the little girl asked, pointing to the dumbfounded Kati.

"Why, Petra, that's, that's your Aunt Kati," she replied, seemingly amazed by her sudden realization that Kati was the child's relative.

"Hi, Aunt Kati," the glorious, golden-haired girl offered. Her innocence brought a smile to Kati's face. Of course she could have no idea, no clue that the two sisters were in the thick of a horrible family problem, a problem so large that until this very second Kati wasn't even aware of the existence of the precious young child.

"Hello," Kati said in return. "What's your name?"

"My name is Petra, and I'm almost three years old."

"Petra's a lovely name. I don't think I know any other Petras."

"Me either," she responded. "Maman, I don't think I want to take a nap today. I'd rather go to the park."

"You can't go to the park today, silly, it's raining," her mother replied.

"Well, then I'd rather play with my new doll," she insisted, seeming to have an answer to everything.

"After your nap. Now go along with Millie. Your aunt and I

have some things to discuss. Now, run along. I'll see you when you wake up." She picked the child up, held her in outstretched arms, out of the range of her suit, and handed her over to the nanny.

"Will you be here when I wake up?" she asked Kati from her position over Millie's hefty shoulder.

"Probably not," Kati answered, "but I hope I'll see you again soon."

The child seemed content with that answer. "Me too," she said, just before the nanny closed the heavy doors behind her.

"I had no idea, Eva-Maria," Kati said, her voice unable to conceal her astonishment.

"No, I don't suppose you would have. I didn't tell anyone at the hotel."

"Anyone at the hotel? How about anyone in your family? Eva-Maria, for the life of me, I will never, ever be able to understand your coldness, your lack of caring, lack of love, for mother and me. Even if we've made some mistakes, done things you may not have thought were right, you certainly shouldn't be the first one to cast a stone. You are in no position to do that. Now I find out you have a beautiful daughter. How can you deprive Mother of seeing her only grandchild? Your hatred surely can't run that deep. Don't you know how much pleasure she would get from seeing that little girl? Getting to know her? Being a grandmother to her?"

"That's enough lecturing, Kati. How could you ever think it would be possible for Mother to be a grandmother to Petra? Peter wouldn't allow her in this house, for one thing."

"So is that what this is all about? What Peter will allow and won't allow? Eva-Maria, I have never known you to be so willing to fall under someone's control. Isn't your freedom one of your most cherished possessions? Have you given all of that up now that you're married to Peter?"

Kati's last comment hit home. She could see that Eva-Maria was visibly shaken when she suggested that her husband was controlling her life, her decisions. Eva-Maria looked at her in stunned silence.

"That's just the point. I'm not married."

"What do you mean, you're not married?" Kati said, hardly able to believe what she had just heard.

"How much clearer can I make it?" Eva-Maria screamed. "I'm not married. When Peter and I left the hotel, I knew I was carrying his child. With all that was going on, I didn't tell him until we were in France. When I finally did tell him, thinking that he would be delighted, he told me I could have the child but he would never marry me. By that time it was too late to do anything about the baby, so I had it. I really don't regret having her. She's what keeps me going. So now you have to understand. Even if I wanted to help you and Mother, I can't. I'm stuck here. I depend on Peter for everything. He's generous with me and he's a good father to Petra, so I have no choice. And very few complaints."

Kati sat in stunned silence in the chair facing Eva-Maria. She watched her sister's face turn from raw vulnerability to its previous hardened look.

"I think we've said all we have to say to one another. I really must get on with my afternoon."

It was clear that her sister was asking her to leave. More than twenty minutes had passed since she had been escorted into the library. Eva-Maria hadn't even offered her a cup of tea.

"All right, I can see that you have nothing more to say to me. But please think about one thing."

"What would that be?"

"Please let Mother see your daughter. Just once. We'll meet somewhere if you don't want us to come to the house. But please, just allow her that pleasure. You don't even have to explain your relationship with Peter if you don't want to. But don't deny her the right to see her grandchild."

Eva-Maria turned her face to Kati. She inhaled deeply on a freshly lit cigarette. "All right, I'll think about it. But I won't promise."

"Thank you," Kati replied. "You know where to reach us."

Eva-Maria put the half-finished cigarette out in the malachite ashtray. She uncrossed her legs and started to get up.

"Don't bother," Kati said. "I can find my own way out."

She closed the door firmly behind her and ran down the walkway and out the forbidding iron gate. She continued running, her tears flowing freely down her cheeks. She had gone two or three blocks before she realized that her whole body was soaking wet, drenched from the continuing downpour. Her umbrella remained in a closet on the Avenue Foch. She ducked into the Métro station and waited for the train to take her back to the other side of the Seine. For her mother's sake she would calm herself before she entered the hotel.

CHAPTER
27

THEY COULD NOT remain tourists in Paris forever. After almost two months of sightseeing, movies, and visiting galleries, Kati swore that if she ever saw another monument, she would scream. Also, in the not-too-distant future, even though they were being as frugal as possible, their funds would start to run out.

"Mother, we've got to think about finding some work if we're to remain in France. For that matter, even if we go somewhere else, we must find jobs," she would insist. Kati didn't dislike being in Paris at all. In fact she was beginning to rather enjoy the faster, more vibrant pace of life. Now that her French had returned to near perfection, she was enjoying it more than ever. So each night at dinner, after they had been served their carafe of wine, Kati would rekindle the subject of what they were going to do. For the last couple of weeks, Kati had been spending more and more time by herself since Tilla's cold had still not completely disappeared. She sometimes coughed violently during the night. Often she preferred to stay in their hotel room, reading and resting, waiting for Kati to reappear and tell her of the day's adventures.

Each night Tilla's response was the same. "Jobs? Kati, what could we possibly do? I've never held a job in my life."

"Neither have I, Mother, but that can't stop us now. We know a lot about the hotel business, about catering to people. I'm sure we'll be able to find something."

Tilla kept insisting that they wait a while longer. Deep inside she was still convinced that Eva-Maria would call them. But with each passing day, her conviction was slowly wearing down.

One humid, sultry night as Kati was returning from a visit to a new exhibition at the Petit Palais, her attention was caught by a sign in the window of a small pension around the corner from the Hotel Perle. It was not a very nice-looking building, certainly not one of the more charming ones in the district. It looked a bit run-down, but not too shabby. She estimated that it had about fifteen or twenty rooms. The sign said they were looking for help in their restaurant; they needed a manager as well as a hostess. Well, she certainly knew how to run a profitable restaurant. Her mother could learn to seat people and monitor the waiters. She studied the simple menu posted outside the entrance to the restaurant and then looked into its windows, which faced out onto the street. The prices were low and the selection appetizing. She quickly estimated that the tiny eatery could seat about sixty people. It was almost full with evening diners.

Despite her mother's assurances that everything would be all right, she realized that Tilla's words were not based on fact. She had called and written to Monsieur de Beaumont asking when their next payment would come but had so far received no response. Her efforts to find employment had met a stone wall. Who would employ them? They didn't have any marketable skills to offer an employer. They didn't have any references at all. Time and again she had been told that without more experience there was no chance of being hired. Getting a job to support themselves was going to be close to impossible.

She entered the Pension Grifont with great trepidation, but knowing full well that she would be a fool to pass up an opportunity if one existed for them here. The bell attached to the top of the door clanged as she entered. The large man seated behind the reception desk looked up when she approached. The gruff expression on his face left him when he saw the beautiful girl. Mostly they catered to professors and parents of students, people on a tight budget. Rarely did a young woman of such style and obvious good breeding enter his hotel. He smiled at her and stood up. His enormous girth, stretched his dirty shirt to its limits. An expanse of belly was evident where the buttons had spread apart.

"My, my, Mademoiselle, how may I help you?" he said, moving out from behind the desk to have a better look at her.

Kati was immediately repulsed by both the man's appearance and his attitude. But her feet remained firmly planted on the worn rug on the lobby floor. She couldn't run—he didn't seem like the type of man who would be very concerned with references—this might be their one chance to get a start.

"Good evening, Monsieur. I see from the sign you have in the window that you have openings in your restaurant. I would like to apply . . . for both my mother and myself."

He seemed displeased that her mother was involved, but he was too mesmerized by the girl's startling good looks to put an end to the conversation.

"What experience do you have?" he asked, still wondering what such a well-dressed young woman was doing applying for a job in his humble pension.

"I've worked in a restaurant before," she said, almost too quickly.

"Oh, yes, I see. Where might that have been?"

"In Strasbourg, where my family is from." It was not a total lie. Her ancestors had come from the Alsace. Kati had never even been to Strasbourg, but it was nearby, and it was in France. Happily, the answer seemed to pacify his concerns.

"What did you do in this restaurant?"

"Well, I was involved in the hiring of the waiters and the rest of the staff, as well as some of the purchasing. Let's see, you can serve about sixty people in your place, can't you?"

"Sixty-five if I crowd the tables a little," he agreed. He sat down in a chair opposite the desk and motioned for Kati to do the same. This was becoming more and more interesting. The girl was beautiful, she would certainly add a touch of class to the place. Maybe they could start to attract a more upscale clientele. If people saw a beautiful girl through the window, instead of his fat wife, they might be more inclined to come in and have a meal. She seemed to know what she was talking about. From their conversation he learned that she knew how many times they should turn their tables, both at lunch and at dinner, and she talked intelligently about supplies and staff. He couldn't believe his good luck.

Kati sensed the man was feeling positive about her. "I can oversee the restaurant, and my mother can work as a hostess, and as an extra waitress if need be," she offered. Wait until Tilla heard this. She would be so ashamed at what they had come to. Waiting tables at someone else's restaurant? She would be shocked. And in a small, unattractive bistro at that. Kati was only being a realist about the situation. Better to be here than on the streets, which is exactly where they would be in a few weeks if their check didn't come through. Yes, that was the other thing she needed to tell him. "Oh, and also, we'll be needing rooms. We have no place to live right now."

The man wasn't sure about this. He drew himself up, exposing even more of his robust stomach. Then a smile crossed his face. Maybe it was better to have them here, under his roof. He could work them harder. He could demand even more of them if they were dependent on him not only for their salary but for their living conditions as well. Also, it wouldn't be so terrible to see her pretty face around the place every morning. Yes, she would brighten things up for sure.

"Okay," he agreed, "but only one room. Bath in the hall. And it's at the top of the stairs, five flights. I can never rent out that room anyway."

"Oh, thank you, Monsieur . . . " Kati realized she didn't even know his name.

"Grifont, Monsieur Grifont. Welcome to the Pension Grifont." He offered his hand. She ignored it, pretending to cough at that moment. "When can you and your mother start to work?"

Kati thought quickly. She would need a few days to get Tilla used to the idea. A weekend would do. "We'll be here next Monday morning," she said.

"Fine, that's just fine. I'll be expecting you."

Kati picked up the things she had bought for them to eat in the room that night and started to leave. She felt his eyes traveling up and down her back as she shut the rickety door behind her.

It took Tilla quite a while to adjust to the idea of the Pension Grifont. The living conditions were far from perfect. Their room was even smaller and less nicely furnished than the one they had shared at the Hotel Perle. The customers who came into the restaurant were rough, and they could be crude and demanding. But slowly she reconciled herself to their situation. Late one night after they had been there for about four months, Kati came out from the kitchen and saw her mother sitting at a table with a man who had come in alone to have a simple, quiet dinner. Tilla looked animated; she was smiling a smile that Kati had not seen since long before they had left Baden-Baden.

"Nice-looking man," Kati teased later as they were finishing cleaning the tables.

"Yes, he was," Tilla agreed, then looked at Kati's gloating face. "Oh, don't be silly, Kati, we were just having a conversation."

"That's how it all starts," Kati cautioned, still teasing.

Tilla laughed with her darling daughter. To this day, Tilla was certain, and very thankful, that Kati had never found out about her brief liaison with Henri-Etienne. She prayed she never would. It would only make her decision look even more stupid and foolish than it had been.

"You're the one who should be going out, dating some nice young Frenchman."

Kati nodded her head and turned to the next table. No, she was not ready for any involvement right now. It still pained her to think of another young Frenchman, to reminisce about the feelings she had had for him, about his gentle touch. And of course about the lies he had fed her. Someday, she hoped, the pain would subside and the wounds would heal. She thought often about Eva-Maria and her precious daughter. Heidi and her baby. Someday . . .

Madelaine Grifont and Tilla became friends. Monsieur Grifont's wife was far more charming and pleasant than he. Though far from sophisticated, she and Tilla managed to find a common bond, out of either loneliness or the unspoken knowledge that they were both stuck in situations not of their choosing but because of circumstances they could do nothing about, at least for the time being. Madame Grifont was not well educated, but she seemed to enjoy going to cultural events, about which Tilla was often knowledgeable. Tilla, in turn, was happy to impart her knowledge of art, opera, or dance merely in exchange for the woman's company. They made plans to go out at least once a week. Kati was pleased with their relationship and encouraged her mother to go. She knew she hadn't been feeling well lately. The cough that had started several months earlier persisted, and she didn't look particularly healthy. All efforts to get her to see a doctor had failed. "It's just the change in climate and atmosphere," Tilla insisted. "I'll be fine, don't worry so much." But that didn't stop her incessant coughing from keeping Kati awake more and more nights. So Kati was delighted when her mother told her that she and Madelaine were thinking of going away to a spa for a few days. "To take the waters, rest and relax," Tilla had said. "You know, just like at home, only I'm sure it won't be as nice," she sighed. They couldn't really afford it, and it would be difficult running the kitchen as well as the floor of the restaurant without her, but Kati felt it would do her mother good. She assured her that she could handle the extra load. It was only for four days anyway. Maybe her cough would be gone when she returned and she would have some color back in her cheeks.

On the third night after they had left, Kati was alone in the kitchen putting away the last of the perishables. The rest of the staff had long since gone home, and she happily counted the number of patrons they had served. Business had increased steadily since she had arrived. The food was fresh and simply prepared. The prices were good, and word had spread quickly that the Pension Grifont was now a delightful place to dine. They turned their tables at least two, and often three, times each night. Lunch business was also picking up. It was fun making a success of something. It was the only thing that kept her spirits up. Especially on a night like tonight, when she longed for the luxury of her old bed at the Waldhotel. She was exhausted.

"Mademoiselle Kati, we had quite a night, didn't we?"

Oh, please, she prayed, not him. Please make him go away. I'm too tired for this, she thought. "Yes, Monsieur Grifont, we served one hundred and fifteen meals tonight," she answered, her back turned to him while she continued trying to squeeze containers of leftover food into the inadequate refrigerator.

With the growing success of the restaurant, and Kati's willingness and ability to handle the work, Monsieur Grifont had become a grand seigneur overnight. He played the part brilliantly, smoking and drinking with his buddies each evening at a table in the rear of the room. Even when the place was jammed and the staff was running like mad to service all the demanding customers, he would never, ever consider lifting a finger to help. He just sat with a wet, half-chewed cigar dangling from his mouth, a brandy in his hand. At first Kati was angry, but over time she had learned merely to ignore him. He had given her a job, and for that she was thankful. She was able to put some money away for the future, and they wouldn't have to stay here forever. So she paid as little attention to him as possible, speaking to him only when it was unavoidable, and then only about subjects that concerned the restaurant. But she couldn't ignore him now. He had moved across the kitchen and was standing in back of her. She wasn't certain if there was enough room for her to stand up without bumping into him. His overwhelming bulk towered behind her. She could smell the stench of a stale cigar and the heavy odor of liquor. As he spoke to her, she could feel the heat of his stagnant, alcohol-soaked breath on her neck.

"Kati, my little one, get me another bottle. This one is empty," he said, his voice slurred.

She stood up slowly and turned to him. His face was inches from hers, and he brandished an empty cognac bottle in his fist.

"It's in the closet," she said, pointing in the direction of the cabinet where all the liquor was stored.

"I know where it is!" he shouted. "I know goddamn well where it is! I asked you to get it for me. Now do it, and do it right away."

He had spoken to her harshly in the past, but never had his words been laced with such a threatening tone. Momentarily she panicked. The restaurant was completely empty. There were only two couples staying in the hotel. They were young, from America, and they were probably out exploring and enjoying the city right now. She realized that she was alone in the hotel with him. She moved quickly in the direction of the cabinet. If she could only get him the bottle and get out of the kitchen and up to the safety of her room, she could lock herself in and go to bed for the night. She was inches away from the closet when suddenly he turned and lunged at her.

"On second thought," he said, "maybe I've had enough to drink. But what I haven't had is you, my little one." He leered at her in the most disgusting manner. His eyes traveled from her lips to the tips of her breasts and finally rested on the triangle between her legs. Not once did his eyes meet hers.

In the split second after she realized what was happening, Kati bolted for the door. Even intoxicated, he was fast. His enormous hand reached out above her head and blocked her from pulling the door open.

"No," she cried, fear ringing out in her voice, "no, let me out of her. Now . . . please . . . let me go!"

"Just a minute, little one. You don't want to go now. We've some unfinished business to take care of. Just you wait a minute." His face was in hers, and the smell of his breath nauseated her. She felt certain she would be ill any second. But the reality of what he was trying to do kept her from moving at all.

"No . . ." she shouted, but this latest effort was met with a slap across her face. Tears, not of pain but of humiliation and fear, sprang to her eyes.

"Now, don't cry, my darling Kati," he said in the most teasing, taunting manner. "In the end you may just learn to like this. Then you'll be begging me for it."

He disgusted her. She searched around the room frantically to find something she could grab, something with which to harm him. The knives were all put safely away, and she would never be able to pull down one of the heavy copper pots hanging overhead. He would stop her before she ever got it off the hook.

Once again she tried to bolt from the room. He turned swiftly and caught her by the shoulder. His plump, strong fingers pulled forcefully on her apron, tearing both the strap and the blouse beneath. Her left breast, firm and pink with its tiny nipple, was exposed. Seeing her nakedness, he took a deep breath. "Oh, my Kati, you are lovely, aren't you?"

Kati screamed and covered her skin with the torn cloth and her hands. She screamed again, but the noise went unanswered. Now she knew beyond any doubt that they were alone in the house.

"Oh, no, no, leave me alone," she screamed, her voice growing even more frantic as the bile rose in her throat.

"Oh no, my darling. Not just yet." Monsieur Grifont pulled Kati's hands away from her chest. The other side of her blouse dropped away, exposing both of her tender breasts. He held her wrists in one hand and with the other he loosened the buckle of his belt. He unzipped his trousers and pulled them down, along with his grayed, threadbare underware. Kati's eyes grew even wider with fear and disgust when she saw his enormous hardness. She shut her eyes tightly and prayed that the torment would end, that he would come to his senses and leave her alone. But Kati's eyes on him had only excited him more, and with one motion he threw her to the floor. She wrestled with him for endless seconds, but his strength and weight quickly overpowered her. She refrained from moving for fear of being hurt even more. His rough hands pulled her skirt up around her chest, and then his hands quickly returned to her and ripped her panties away. His mouth sought her nipples. He took them between his teeth and sucked and bit them until she screamed in pain. Kati lay horrified as he forced his powerful leg between hers. With all his might he pried her trembling legs apart. She could feel his erection, like the point of a knife, entering her. She lay silent with her eyes shut tight, trying with all her concentration to think of something else besides what was happening to her. The last thing she remembered was the terrifying sound he made as he exploded inside her. It sounded like an animal in pain. Then he collapsed on top of her. She rolled the now-motionless weight off her and ran to the bathroom she shared at the top of the stairs, clutching the remainder of her clothes tightly to her violated, abused body.

The warm washcloth soothed the welts on the inside of her legs and on her chest. She rinsed it frequently, for it became soaked with blood almost at once. Her tears were gone. All that was left was her hurt and anguish, and an experience she would be unable to escape for the rest of her life. The only thing she was grateful for was that her mother was not there to see her. By tomorrow night she should be able to camouflage any remaining evidence of what she had been through. But the mental scars would remain forever. Of that she was certain.

Tilla returned from her brief holiday the following night. She was in such good spirits and had so much to tell Kati about her trip that she failed to notice that her daughter was quieter than usual and had several poorly disguised bruises on her arms and neck. Kati was thankful that Tilla hadn't noticed that anything was out of the ordinary. She tried desperately not to think about it any longer, but it was impossible to block the horrible memory from her mind. Every morning she walked the streets looking for a new job, and each night she awoke, drenched in the sweat of her nightmares.

After the incident Monsieur Grifont acted cool and indifferent toward Kati. They only spoke when absolutely necessary. Kati went out of her way to avoid being alone with him at any time. She feared that she would not be able to control her temper if she had the opportunity to harm him. When they were in the kitchen together, she had a strong urge to plunge the largest knife through his heart. The mere sight of him made her ill, and the smell of his clothing near her made her relive the terrible scene all over again.

Late one Saturday night, after a particularly busy evening, she climbed the stairs to her room. Not only had they been busy, but one of their best waiters had called in sick, leaving them shorthanded. She was exhausted. Tilla and Madelaine had gone out for a short walk. The door to their room, always closed, was ajar. She pushed it open. There stood Monsieur Grifont. She moved back toward the staircase, prepared to run at his first movement.

"What are you doing here?" she asked him, her voice lowered so as not to disturb the other guests.

He was startled. Obviously he had not expected to be caught. "Kati, I'm just leaving a little box of chocolates for you. I thought you might like them." He held the box out to her. She took it from him and hurled it across the room. The veins in her neck throbbed against her skin. Blood rushed to her face.

"Get out," she said. "Get out of this room immediately. Don't you ever come near me again. If I ever catch you in this room, or if you dare to ever come near me again, I'll kill you. I swear I will. But first I'll burn this horrible pension to the ground. You filthy, disgusting animal. Do you understand me?" Her hands were shaking and she steadied herself against the railing. It was clear by the look on his face that she had reached him. He brushed past her quickly and headed down the stairs. She closed the door of the tiny room, thankful that she was alone. Then the tears came, and she relived every second of her horrible experience.

She had saved every penny the two of them had made. In just a few months she could afford to take some time off and look even harder for other, more promising jobs. The plan kept her going until fate dealt the Meiers another stroke of poor luck.

Kati rose every morning around five and, taking the clothes she had selected the night before in her arms, she would tiptoe down the hall to the small bathroom, where she showered and dressed without disturbing her mother or the other guests. Upon her return from the marketplace where she went to purchase vegetables and poultry for the day's meals, she expected to see Tilla in the kitchen as she always was by late morning. When she hadn't appeared one morning, Kati went in search of her.

The lobby was quiet. The front desk, usually manned by Madelaine, was empty. A stack of keys left by guests as they went out were piled up on the counter. Strange, she thought. Where was everyone?

She took the stairs slowly, saving her energy for the long day ahead. As she reached the landing on the top near their room, she heard her mother crying.

"Don't tell Kati, promise me you won't tell her," she pleaded.

Tilla was speaking to Madelaine. Something was dreadfully wrong.

"Don't tell me what . . .?" There was no need for her to finish her question. Her mother lay on the narrow bed, still in her night-gown. Her face was as pale as Kati had ever seen it, and her hands shook as she raised them to cover her mouth when she coughed.

"Oh, Kati, I was just going to dress and come down," she lied, trying to hide her illness and fear. She could barely get the words out before her entire body was wracked again by a fit of coughing.

"Mother, what's the matter? Are you sick again?" she cried, rushing to the side of the bed.

Tilla shook her head slowly from side to side. Kati looked imploringly at Madelaine for some answers. Tilla had obviously shared more about her problem with her than with Kati.

"Kati, I think we'd better get her to a hospital," Madelaine said, rising from the other side of the bed. "I'll call a taxi and we can take her there now."

"Mother, what is it? Why didn't you tell me you weren't feeling well?" She had seemed fine to Kati recently, though Kati knew she'd been so wrapped up in her own dark thoughts she might not have been paying enough attention to Tilla.

Tilla just shook her head and began to sob. "I'm so sorry, Kati. Yes, I think I'd like to go to the hospital now."

Madelaine later revealed to Kati that Tilla had been diagnosed with an infection when she was at the spa. The doctors there had suggested that she stay on for another week or two, but Tilla insisted on returning to the hotel, claiming she felt too guilty about leaving Kati alone with so much work to do.

Tilla remained in the hospital for three weeks. Kati visited her every morning and every evening until visiting hours ended and the nurses forced her to leave. Tubes led in and out of her mother's arms. She continued to lose weight, seemingly by the hour. All the doctors could say was that she had contracted a bronchial infection that had worsened and was now compounded and complicated by pneumonia. Kati's heart broke each time she visited, for Tilla didn't appear to be getting any stronger. Finally, at the end of the third week, she began to come around. After extracting a firm promise that she would stay confined to her bed and rest for several more weeks, the doctors allowed her to be released from the hospital.

They returned to the pension, where Monsieur Grifont carried her up the steep stairs. Kati couldn't bear to watch him as he put his arms around her and lifted her tiny body, but she had no choice in the matter. Tilla was far too weak to manage the climb, and he was the only man around. Even worse, completely against her will, Kati depended on him now more than ever. She had to have her job in order to keep up with the mounting medical bills.

"Now that you're up here, you're going to stay put until you are completely well," Kati cautioned sternly. Madelaine concurred, saying that if there was anything she wanted, all she had to do was to ring the large silver bell she placed on her bedside table.

"Thank you, thank you both," Tilla whispered, her voice still scratchy. "I can't tell you how wonderful you've both been to me."

"All we want is for you to get well," Kati assured her, kissing her on her thin cheek and pulling the covers up snugly around her neck.

Tilla improved slowly. After six more weeks, she was finally able to leave her room. She started slowly, insisting on coming down to help in the restaurant, doing simple chores like folding napkins and polishing some of the silver pieces. Eventually she was able to help set the tables and even seat a few customers at lunch.

She gained weight and appeared to be on the road to recovery, until one night when the coughing recommenced, and she and Kati were up until dawn.

"You've got to see the doctor today," an exhausted Kati said when the attack had at last subsided.

"No, I don't want to. I'll be fine. I don't know what happened. Really, I'm fine now."

But later that week it happened again, and Tilla became so frightened that she agreed at once to return to the clinic.

"I'm afraid we're going to have to put her back in the hospital. I don't like the look of her, or the sound of that cough," the doctor had explained.

Reluctantly, but too sick to do otherwise, Tilla reentered the hospital. Again she was hooked up to various terrifying-looking machines. This time nothing seemed to work against the infection that had invaded her system. On the third night she grew delirious, and nurses were assigned around-the-clock duty. They bathed her constantly with cool cloths, trying in vain to break the fever. She drifted in and out of consciousness, oftentimes not recognizing either Kati or Madelaine. Fearing the worst, Kati had tried to contact Eva-Maria. Finally on the tenth call she left a message with the housekeeper, telling her that she must come to the hospital at once. But she never arrived.

When Tilla fell into a coma the next night, the doctors couldn't give them any idea of how long it would last. Kati visited daily, her heart breaking every time she opened the door hoping to see her mother sitting up in bed. All she saw were Tilla's closed eyes and unresponsive body. Kati found her only distraction in books. She began to reread the classics, choosing from a list in the library. She would stop there on the way to the hospital, turn in the book she had finished the previous night and check out the next one on the list. She would sit by her mother's bedside, holding Tilla's limp hand firmly in hers, and reading aloud to her mother's unhearing ears. She would lose herself in the story, continuing to read well into the night and until she grew so hoarse she could only whisper.

So absorbed did she become in the heroes and heroines of great literature that she was jolted one night by a sound. Suddenly she realized it was coming from her mother. The book on her lap fell to the floor with a thud. Kati sat upright and was greeted by Tilla's open eyes.

"Mutti, it's Kati, can you hear me?" asked the startled young woman.

Tilla's eyes were calm, her look peaceful. "Yes, yes, I can hear you, Kati. Are you all right?"

"Yes, Mother, I'm fine, I've just been sitting here by your side, waiting for you to get better."

"I know you have, my sweetheart. I love you." She smiled gently and Kati surrounded her hand with both of hers. Tilla squeezed it softly, almost imperceptibly.

"Kati . . ." her mother said, her voice becoming weaker.

"Yes, Mother, I'm here."

"Kati, don't forget the Waldhotel. Remember your grandfather. He was a wonderful man."

"Yes, yes, I know, Mother. I'll never forget the hotel. You just get better, and then someday we'll go back there. Someday—" At that very second Kati felt Tilla's gentle grasp loosen and she knew her mother was gone.

CHAPTER
28

HE MONTHS following her mother's death were torture for Kati. She felt more alone than ever before, and once again her future was uncertain. Her financial situation was disastrous. Medical bills and funeral expenses had depleted her meager savings, and she was forced to remain at the Pension Grifont until she had earned enough money to move on.

The days there were very predictable and seemed never to end. She would rise early and walk through the quiet streets on her way to the marketplace. The remaining hours were spent in the kitchen. She willed herself to focus her entire concentration on the creation of new dishes.

After the last customer had gone, she would lock up. Then she'd slowly climb the stairs to her room. Still plagued by the terrifying memories of her experience with Monsieur Grifont, she would drag the now-empty second bed in front of the door. At least she would hear him if he tried to come in. So drained was she from the long day's schedule that sleep usually came quickly. Rarely did she leave the hotel except to do the obligatory shopping. Madelaine tried her very best to comfort her, including her in plans and activities whenever possible, but after a time even she realized it was futile. They had nothing in common except their love for Tilla.

Avoidance of Monsieur Grifont was a priority, and so far she had been able to keep her distance. Occasionally he would try, in some small way, to make her job a little easier. As callous a man as he was, he could see that the young woman was suffering beyond belief.

Eva-Maria had made an effort to see her sister a few times after Tilla died. Despite attempts to feel otherwise, Kati was so overcome with dislike and contempt for her that each visit ended badly. They would sit together in Eva-Maria's grand library, with Petra playing nearby. Peter was always off on one business trip or another, so Kati never saw him.

"I'm sorry," Kati finally said the last time she had seen her. "I just can't forgive you for not seeing Mother, particularly after she became ill. And I'll never be able to understand how you could deprive her of the joy of seeing her only grandchild. That troubled her deeply, especially at the end of her life."

"And I'll never forgive her for what she did to Father," Eva-Maria countered. After those painful confessions had been made, there remained very little to say. Since then they had not seen each other again.

With the coming of spring, Kati seemed to emerge from her gloom. The warmer weather and occasional sunny skies gave her the much-needed impetus she required to begin to pull her life together again. During the last nine years she had lost her grandfather, her father, her mother, and her home. Her only sister was lost to her also, although she still held hope of a reconciliation someday. For now she was alone, and she was wise enough to realize that the only person she could count on was herself.

She began a long and tedious job search. She felt better and stronger, and she could no longer tolerate being at the Pension Grifont. It was time to move on to a better life—time to put her loneliness and fear behind her.

Along with Lasserre, Vivarois, and Pré Catalan, Restaurant Claire was among the oldest and most famous restaurants in Paris. Unlike the others, which had sometimes made their reputation on the customers who frequented them, the Restaurant Claire had built theirs simply by consistently serving excellent French food. Sylvie and Guillaume Lazare were a charming French couple whose robust looks served as a testament to the goodness of their kitchen. They were the third generation of Lazares to operate the renowned eatery.

It was purely serendipitous that they currently needed someone to help them out in their kitchen and that Kati had heard about the opening. Had she not been listening to the conversation between the two men who sat next to her while she was having a coffee one day on the Boulevard St. Michel, she would never have known about it.

Restaurant Claire . . . the name had lingered in Kati's mind since overhearing it that afternoon. That night she looked up the address and telephone number, then later discarded the idea of calling. She would go directly there the next morning. The restaurant was across the river, on the Right Bank, located on a tiny side street just off Avenue Victor Hugo. Once or twice she had heard some of the pension's better customers talk about having a meal there, but never had she had the opportunity to dine there herself.

The first time she walked down the street, she completely missed the restaurant. Searching for the oftentimes partially hidden blue enamel signs indicating the Parisian street numbers, she realized she was already at number 23. The restaurant was number 15. It was so discreet, its existence was marked only by a dark green awning. She had passed right by it. The singular sign confirming that it was in fact the Restaurant Claire was the small plaque indicating that it had been awarded two stars from Michelin, the most prestigious and demanding culinary guide in the world. She turned back and entered the elegant, wood-paneled dining room. It was late morning, and only two people scurried about the room, rearranging the flowers and setting the tables in preparation for the arrival of the lunch crowd.

"I'm sorry, Mademoiselle, we do not open until twelve-thirty," said a man who was perched on top of one of the banquettes. He was pulling out the dead stems from the sumptuous flower arrangement and replacing them with fresh ones.

"I'm not here for lunch," Kati replied. "I would like to see Madame Lazare."

"Oh, I'm sorry," he apologized. "Please wait there for just a minute." He filled in the vase with a few more blossoms. His task complete, he climbed down from the banquette with his now-empty basket and walked toward her. As he got closer, he realized what a beauty the girl was. Her glorious hair was pulled back and tied with a ribbon. She wore very little makeup; it wasn't necessary, for she had flawless skin. She was simply dressed in a cotton skirt and crisp white blouse. She wore no jewelry except for a single strand of large pearls. They were a soft, translucent shade of the palest pink. Without all the fancy clothes and gaudy earrings he was used to seeing on so many of the supposedly "chic" French girls, she looked more elegant than any of them. "I always assume that people are only coming here to eat. It's my nature. I never think to ask first. Sorry."

"It's all right. I don't have an appointment. I was only hoping I could have a word with her," she said hesitatingly, all of a sudden losing some of the confidence she had had earlier in the morning.

"I'm sure she can see you. Come, I'll take you. I can usually find her. She's my mother."

The young man was very kind, and she began to relax. He was not at all good-looking. His ears were rather too big for his head, and his smile was crooked. He carried a few extra pounds, yet another testament to the wonderful food at Restaurant Claire. But he was charming, and she was glad that he was the one who would take her to Madame Lazare.

She followed him down a narrow corridor and through the kitchen to the back of the restaurant. She only had a second's glance into the kitchen, but what she saw looked wonderful. The assortment of pots and pans hanging from the ceiling was extraordinary. They seemed to have everything in every size, every shape. Everything necessary to produce excellent French cuisine. It certainly wasn't the old, rusted, makeshift equipment they had been forced to use at the Pension Grifont. Some of the equipment was new, all of it was shiny and sparkling and in its place, organized and efficient. She hadn't seen such an operation since the Waldhotel. Oh, the Waldhotel. All the staff was probably down in the basement right now, preparing the day's meals. All the people she had loved working with so much. And of course, Christophe. They had spent hour upon hour in a kitchen very similar to this one. Stop it, she urged herself. Now is no time to be reminiscing about the past. With any luck at all, the Restaurant Claire could be her future. Still, she longed to go in and have a quick peek, but the young man continued walking. Of course, she thought, he had no idea she was interested in their kitchen. Well, if everything worked out right, she would have enough time later to explore every nook and cranny in the inviting space.

They reached the end of the hallway. On the right was a closed door with a hand-painted sign, probably a gift from the staff, which said—Madame Sylvie Lazare, Chef de Grande Cuisine.

The young man stopped in front of the door. "She should be

inside. I'll go and check. May I ask, though, what it is you want to see her about? She may want to know," he added, trying to disguise his curiosity. She was the loveliest girl he had ever seen, and he was dying to hear what incredible good fortune had brought her to his parents' restaurant.

Kati's enormous eyes looked up at his. "I've come to see about a job."

"A job? What kind of job would you want here?" The words slipped out before he could stop them. He looked at her incredu-lously. What could a beautiful, obviously well-bred and well-educated girl possibly want with a job in their restaurant? It had to be a mistake. The only job this pretty thing should have was staying at home and raising a herd of children as lovely as she.

"I heard, I heard from a friend, well, not actually a friend," she quickly corrected herself in case she might be questioned about it later, "but I did hear that there was the possibility of an opening in the kitchen here. I have quite a bit of experience and I'd be very interested in applying. I . . . I . . . need a job very badly," she admit-ted, lowering her eyes. She knew that this moment was her only chance at getting behind that closed door.

"Oh," he said, touched by the girl's honesty and sincerity. Her eyes told him that every word she said, particularly the part about really needing the job, was true. She was not at all what she had seemed only minutes before when she had walked through the front door. Her plight made her all the more attractive to him.

His silence was killing her. She looked up at him and with her pleading eyes implored him to help her.

"Well, in fact, you're right," he continued at last. "There is going to be a job open here very soon. The position you would be taking is mine. You see, I'm the oldest son, and for four years now I've also been the second in command around here, working directly for my father, who has been the head chef for more than twenty years. But now I've got a chance to go and spend a year studying in the States. In New York, in fact. I'll be staying with my cousins. So they need someone to replace me while I'm gone. Of course, I plan to come back, but it's the chance of a lifetime, and I've just got to go."

Kati's face dropped as she listened to his story. She felt badly that she couldn't share his obvious excitement about going overseas for a year, but right at the moment she was only concerned with herself. What they needed was someone who had much more experience than she. They really needed a sous-chef. After all, this was one of a handful of Paris's two-star restaurants. They couldn't afford to fool around, to take a chance with their precious rating.

"I see, well, yes, it does sound exciting. I do have several years of training, and I'm very good at basic dishes, but maybe—" Just as she was going to admit that she wasn't the right person for the job, he interrupted her.

"I'm sure you are," he said enthusiastically, "and even if your training isn't complete, I'm not leaving for three months yet. The plan was for us to get someone in here as soon as possible and have them work with me, side by side, until I leave. In three months, almost anyone with a strong foundation in the kitchen should be able to catch on to what our restaurant is all about." His voice rose with enthusiasm as he spoke. The mere thought of working side by side for ten or twelve hours a day with this beautiful girl was almost too much for him to bear. "Wait here," he told her. "I'll go in and talk to my mother right now. Then I'll introduce you to both of my parents and we'll see what can be arranged. Wait, just wait here," he repeated, holding both of his hands out in front of her as if to freeze her in position. Then he disappeared into the small office.

A brilliant smile crossed Kati's face. Maybe there was a chance. It sounded like it. Please, she prayed, let them hire me. Now. Today. And this very night I can move my few things out of the Pension Grifont, and never, ever have to go there again.

Dame Fortune finally smiled on her. After a few culinary tests that seemed much simpler than they really were, she was hired that very afternoon.

Sylvie and Guillaume Lazare had passed their charm down to their oldest son, whose name she finally found out later that afternoon was Jean-Louis. Sylvie Lazare was now a handsome woman in her late sixties who, Kati suspected, must have been a great beauty when she was a young woman. Her smile was friendly and warm. She welcomed Kati into their lives with open arms.

The magic continued when Guillaume telephoned a friend who had a tiny flat for rent not more than two blocks from the restaurant and Sylvie went with her to see it. It was in a small, well-maintained building on a desirable street.

"I hope you like it," commented Madame Bonnet, the robust, heavy-bosomed wife of the building manager, as she pulled shut the iron elevator door. The lift was tiny, and the two heavyset women and Kati barely fit in together. The ancient apparatus pulled them steadily to the fourth floor. How luxurious, Kati thought, not to have always to be faced with five flights of steep stairs. Kati held the gate back while the two large women eased themselves slowly out of the iron cage.

"Hummmph," Sylvie said, straightening out her dress. "Too many of Guillaume's wonderful pastries. You're so lucky not to have to worry about that," she said, admiring Kati's trim figure.

"It's just down the hall here," the woman directed them. "Let me open the door so you can go in. I think it's charming."

The two women stood aside and allowed Kati to enter first. The apartment's living room was not large, but it had high ceilings and two large French windows that looked out to the small garden in the back of the building. Kati gazed around and was pleased with the comfortable, pleasant furnishings. They were not grand by any means, but they were certainly a vast improvement over what she had recently become used to. The bedroom was tiny. The bed had a lovely brass headboard and was made up with fresh white sheets with lace all around the edges of the pillows. There was a small wooden dressing table against one wall, whose oval-shaped mirror reminded her of the one Tilla had had in her room at the Waldhotel. The bathroom contained a full-sized bathtub, a real luxury after the single-stall shower at the Pension Grifont. The most pleasing thing about the apartment was its smell. After the last tenant had moved out, all of the walls had been treated to a fresh coat of bright white paint, and the entire place had been scrubbed until it shone. She took several deep breaths, inhaling the delightful clean scent.

"Oh, you can still smell the paint. I'm sorry. My husband just finished it last week. I really should open the windows during the day."

"No, no, I love the smell. It's all so beautiful," Kati insisted. "I just love the apartment, Madame Bonnet. How much is it?" she asked, anxiously praying that it was not way beyond her limited means.

When she heard the price, her face fell in disappointment. It was far more than she could afford right now. The Lazares had offered her a good salary, and, if everything worked out, in a couple of months she would be able to afford it easily. She had a little money now, but she was afraid to use it all up on rent. What if for some reason the job at the Lazares didn't work out? She really needed to save something just in case. She looked quickly from Madame Lazare to Madame Bonnet, not knowing what to say or how to get out of the situation gracefully.

"You do like the apartment, don't you?" asked the kind woman.

"Yes, yes, I do, it's just . . ."

"Kati, if you like the apartment, you shall have it," Sylvie spoke. "I think it's perfect for a young girl. It's *très mignon*. It couldn't be closer to the restaurant. You can always walk. Don't worry right now about the rent. We'll work something out for the first few months. After you get on your feet, then we'll see about repaying us. Okay, Madame Bonnet, she'll take it. And I think she'll probably be staying here starting tonight. Is that right, Kati?"

Kati was thrilled. She couldn't believe Sylvie's generosity. It was even more astounding compared to the horrible people she had worked for since coming to Paris. Not only was Sylvie generous, but she had instincts that were right on target. Somehow she sensed that Kati was anxious to leave an unpleasant situation. Her gratitude was overwhelming. Tears rimmed her eyes. "Yes, that's right. I'd like to move in tonight. I just don't know what to say, how to thank you. Oh, thank you, Madame Lazare," she said, rushing forward to hug the woman in appreciation.

"My name is Sylvie, and it's all right, Kati. There's nothing to cry about. We're delighted to do it. Now you get settled and we'll see you tomorrow. I can't wait to taste the rest of your cooking."

"I'll try not to disappoint you," Kati said, wiping the wetness from her cheeks. "Thank you so very much again. I'll see you first thing in the morning."

On her way to the Pension Grifont to collect her few things, Kati explored the narrow, well-kept streets surrounding her new apartment. It was quiet. There would be no sound of raucous laughter from drunken students late at night. Except for a small grocery and pharmacy, the neighborhood was mostly residential. She stopped in the pharmacy and treated herself to a bottle of bubble bath in her favorite scent. She still couldn't believe her good fortune. It was the first time she had had a living room, bedroom, and bath all her own since leaving Germany. She couldn't wait to get back to her new home, shut out the outside world, which looked considerably better to her than it had this morning, and take a long, luxurious soak in her new bathtub.

CHAPTER

29

KATI'S FIRST few weeks in the new kitchen were rocky. It was a challenge acclimating to the new equipment and to the established way of doing things. Every kitchen had its own rhythm, each chef his own style. It was taking her awhile to become accustomed to all the idiosyncrasies of the Restaurant Claire, and she couldn't help feeling impatient with herself. She wanted so badly for it to work out. Although cooking came almost naturally to her by now, she still had much to learn. Guillaume was a delightful man. He was patient and instructive and always had a kind word for her. He reminded her very much of Opa.

Jean-Louis was never far from her side. He was anxious to spend as much time as possible with her.

"Kati, do you want to try a new sauce tonight?" he would ask.

"Sure," she'd reply with a smile. Together they'd work out just the right proportions of ingredients. When it was completed to their satisfaction, they would send a sample out to one of their better guests for a review. More often than not they got a positive response.

Jean-Louis also loved practical jokes. One evening he staged a mock surprise birthday party for Kati. As she entered the kitchen ready for an evening's work, the entire staff jumped out from their assigned hiding places.

"Surprise, surprise, Happy Birthday, Kati!" they shouted in unison. She knew at once who the perpetrator had to be. Her birthday wasn't for months, and the whole thing had been done simply in the spirit of fun.

"I just thought I'd liven things up in the kitchen tonight," he told her later after they had cleaned up the remains of the elegant cake he had prepared for her. "It can get to be such a routine in here, night after night. Three fillet of sole for table six, one steak au poivre, au point, on nine. . . ."

She was still giggling from the idea of it all.

"What's so funny, Mademoiselle Meier?" he asked.

Kati was standing at the large double sink, washing her hands for the last time that night. She shook with laughter. "You don't even know when my birthday is!" she insisted.

When she looked over at him, she saw that his face had become serious. "You're right, I don't know when it is. It's just one of the many things I don't know about you." He moved closer to her. "But I want to know everything, Kati. Every detail about you. What you like, what you dislike, your favorite flower, your wildest dreams. I think you're terrific, Kati. I'm so glad you're here."

Kati didn't know what to say. She treasured Jean-Louis's friendship. He was almost solely responsible for helping her to forget the recent past and move on to a bright, new future. But the words he spoke sounded like something more serious than a simple friendship.

"Jean-Louis, you're wonderful. I loved my party. And I'll be glad to let you get to know me. In fact, it will make me very happy." She felt that her response was warm and sincere, but she didn't want to encourage his thinking about becoming a real boyfriend to her. His entire funny face broke into an incredible smile. She was relieved. He seemed to be pleased with her answer. She only hoped he would remain content with her sisterly feelings for him.

"That's terrific, Kati. Bravo!" Guillaume and Jean-Louis exclaimed when she presented her first new addition to the menu. They clapped their hands together in delight. In between the praise, they had both cleaned their plates. She had prepared everything herself, without one bit of help from either of them.

"You're really superb, you know that?" Jean-Louis had said. He meant every word. Kati was extremely competent in the kitchen. If she stuck with it, Guillaume had declared she could one day be a truly fine chef.

Jean-Louis's affection for her continued to grow. In his opinion, the days they spent together were too short. Each night he couldn't wait for the next morning to arrive so he could go back to the restaurant and they could work together again. By the time he left almost three and a half months later, he was madly in love with her. In fact he was so enamored of Kati that he would gladly have given up his year in the States if only he could have gotten to first base with her. But that thick-walled exterior allowed no one, as far as he could tell, to enter. So now he was almost glad to be going, frustrated as he was. They had become friends, good friends, but each time he had tried to take things one step farther, he had been met with such force, such refusal, that it seemed as if another person had taken over Kati's body. Walking home one night after seeing a movie on the Champs Elysées, he had put his arm gently around her shoulder. Just as gently her hand went up and took it away.

"Please, Jean-Louis, don't."

"Why, Kati, why? Don't you know how much I care for you, how much I want to take you in my arms and kiss you?"

"Please, don't even speak of things like that." She smiled up at him, anxious to keep things as they'd been.

He had made the mistake of thinking that her refusal was just her delightful way of being coy. So when they reached the steps of her building, he put his hands on her shoulders and leaned forward to kiss her.

"Stop it," she cried out in a voice that sounded more frightened than angry to him. "I asked you not to do that." She turned and ran into the house, slamming the door behind her, barring him from making the apology he was more than willing to offer.

Kati rushed into her apartment. She was shaking with fear, and tears were streaming down her cheeks. Jean-Louis was her best friend. They had such fun together. He and his family had been so kind, so good to her. But she couldn't bring herself to let him touch her. Any sort of physical contact completely repulsed her after her dreadful experience with Monsieur Grifont. Her tears wouldn't subside, and that night brought back all the old, terrible memories she had tried so hard to shut out. The loss of the hotel, the horrible Pension Grifont, her mother's death.

She met daybreak fully dressed in yesterday's clothes, still sitting on the sofa in her living room. When would she ever be able to trust, and to love again?

"Kati, I'm really going to miss you," Jean-Louis had told her the night before he left. "If I write to you, will you answer my letters?"

"Of course I will. I'll write and tell you everything that's going on. Right down to what vegetable we are serving," she joked. Vegetables, and their selection, was one of Guillaume's pet peeves. He was a real stickler on the subject, and the closest thing they had come to almost arguing during their time together had been about what vegetable was correct with what dish. But even after Jean-Louis's outpouring of emotion, she was still unable to change the nature of their friendship. Not in the way he wished, anyway.

Jean-Louis was sorely missed by everyone. The Lazares' younger son, Robert, just didn't have the same outgoing personality as his older, livelier sibling, and Sylvie and Guillaume spent even more time with Kati than ever before.

Sylvie had a weakness for clothes shopping, practically an obsession. She knew all the places to get beautiful French clothes at reduced prices. "Let's go shopping," she would say to Kati about once a week, and her eyes would light up with thoughts of the bargains they might find. Kati enjoyed going with her, and although she had long since paid off the loan the Lazares had given her for the apartment and had saved most of her earnings, she was reluctant to spend any money frivolously. But she didn't mind humoring Sylvie by trying on some of the fashions.

"Oh, Kati," she would say, "that dress looks wonderful on you. Here, let me get it for you as a present." Kati would always say no and ask where she would wear such a creation, but Sylvie would insist. "When he comes home to visit, you and Jean-Louis can go out to dinner some night and you can wear that dress."

Kati smiled when she mentioned Jean-Louis. Sylvie had often told her that she would love to see Kati and her son together, but she was never pushy about it. Always, she respected Kati's privacy, and Kati loved her for that.

As time went on, she became the daughter the Lazares never had. They did not demand anything of her, nor did they pry by asking painful questions about her past. Kati basked in their unqualified love, and soon she began to bloom. Here was the warmth and security she'd longed for and had almost stopped daring to hope could be hers.

. . .

The knocking sounded as if it came from far away. Then she heard a voice.

"Mademoiselle Meier, I have something for you."

At first she thought she was dreaming, then she sat upright in bed and realized the voice was coming from just outside her door. Oh, who could it possibly be? She was dead tired. It was the one day she had to sleep a little later than usual. She wasn't due at the restaurant until five o'clock.

"Mademoiselle Meier," the voice called out again.

This time she recognized the man's voice. It was the manager of the building. He had used his passkeys to open the front door. Thankfully she had put the chain on the night before. Now she could just see his nose peeking through the narrow opening.

Clutching her robe tightly around her, she went to the door. She couldn't imagine what he wanted at this hour. Well, it wasn't really that early. The clock indicated it was already after ten.

"Coming, Monsieur Bonnet, coming," she said as she released the chain and swung the door open.

The man apologized profusely for waking her. He knew the hours she kept and how hard she worked for the Lazares.

"Really, I'm sorry, Mademoiselle, but you have to sign for this delivery. It's a rather large piece, and I didn't want the boys to take it back and then have to make arrangements to have them come back again another time. You know how they are, we might never see it again. It looks important."

"Yes, yes, you're right," she agreed, not having the faintest idea what he could possibly be talking about. She wasn't expecting anything, let alone something big and bulky.

Minutes later the door opened again and two delivery men carried in a large crate. "Where do you want this, Mademoiselle?" asked one of them from behind the unwieldy package. Looking around the room, there wasn't really much choice. The package took up most of the space.

"Over there would be fine," she pointed. "Just lean it up against the wall. But you'd better let me check and make sure you've got the correct address. I'm not expecting anything."

But sure enough, it was for her. The customs stickers indicated that it had been shipped over a month ago from Germany.

The men left and she was alone with the enormous package. It was well crated, and it took her quite awhile, and much clipping and snipping with her none-too-sharp scissors, to make any headway with it. At last the final wrapping dropped away, and there, in her own tiny living room, many miles and an entire culture away from her homeland, was the portrait of her grandfather. Her wonderful Opa. Her breath quickened. It had been such a long time since she had been close to her past. Sometimes she believed that the Waldhotel, and all the memories that belonged to it, had only been a dream. She ached for the smell of the rose garden. She longed to wake up to the sound of the ducks on the River Oos. The portrait served as a reconfirmation of the existence, the reality of her heritage, a heritage she was still trying to recapture. She had promised her mother, but more important, she had promised herself that she would not let it be forgotten. She stared at the serene oil, studying Karl-Gustav Becker's ruddy good looks for a long time before she noticed an envelope taped to one side of the frame. The crest of the Waldhotel Becker was engraved in one corner, and the letter was simply addressed to Fräulein Katharina Becker-Meier.

Inside the short note read, *"A promise is a promise, regardless of whether or not you think I'm capable of keeping one. I hope this will help to change your mind. With love and wishes for your happiness, Christophe."*

She stared at the handwriting on the note. Christophe. Did he think of her often? Why had it taken so long for him to send the picture? All the memories came flooding back. Their good times together. His handsome face pressed close to hers. The feel of his lips as they touched hers. Her last memory of his hand on hers as she clutched the car window when they pulled out of the Waldhotel for the final time. How she had struggled to believe that what he said was true.

She crumpled up the note and threw it into the trash. She told herself she didn't give a damn about Christophe and his promises. She wanted to erase him from her mind. The only thing about the de Beaumont family that she was concerned about was the money they still owed her.

. . .

Dieter, she thought. Yes, it had to have been Dieter. He was the sole person who knew where Kati was living. Christophe must have asked him for her address. But why? She had told him she never wanted to hear from him again. Ever. Maybe he had decided the portrait would be worth enduring a note from him. He had been right. She treasured the painting. Even though it was far too big to hang on any of her walls, it held a place of honor in the apartment. She leaned it against the far wall. It was the first thing she saw when she came home at night.

Jean-Louis also kept the promise he had made to her. At least one letter a week arrived for her. He told her everything, sharing all the details of his life at school. He loved living in New York, but said that he also missed Paris very much. What he really meant was that he missed Kati very much.

Kati answered almost every letter. Most of her news concerned the restaurant. It had become her entire life. She wrote about the most minute details—the new items on the menu, the different things she and his father had tried, which were met with varying degrees of success. She thought her letters must be quite boring; rereading the last one before she posted it, she found that most of its contents were about the new multiburner gas stove they had installed the previous week. It was superefficient with eight gas jets. The Cadillac of stoves. Once they were used to it, it would certainly make everyone's life much easier. How terribly boring, she thought as she reread it. Only the occasional mention of a new movie or new exhibit. He must be awfully put off by these correspondences! Apparently not, for about ten days later another letter would arrive from Jean-Louis, thanking her and telling her how much he enjoyed hearing from her.

From time to time, among the bills and magazines she received, there would also be a letter from Christophe. She recognized the handwriting immediately. Her hands shook each time she removed one from the mailbox and placed the letters in a drawer, where they remained unopened. When she had collected three or four of them, she would bundle them together and march directly to the post office. She marked them "Undeliverable" and sent them back. As much as it hurt her, she wanted him to have no reason to believe that she had been interested enough to read them.

Despite these occasional painful reminders of her past, Kati was happier than she had been in a long time. She had established a pleasant routine. Work consumed most of her time, but she still made an effort to visit the new shows at the museums and to try new restaurants—always keeping an eye on the competition. Sometimes she would go with Sylvie, but often she was content just to be by herself. She felt a comforting sense of independence. There was money in her savings account. She loved her little apartment. The pain of all that had happened was slowly subsiding. Slowly . . . day by day . . . she was able to distance the tragedies of her life. At last she was beginning to plan her future. For the first time she felt in control.

Word spread through the restaurant community that food critics from around the world would converge on the city the following week to attend a convention. The Restaurant Claire would of course be on their "must" list of places to dine, and preparations were made to assure that service would be impeccable should any of them choose to honor them with a visit. Of course, by the end of the week, they did.

Guillaume entered the kitchen wearing his freshly starched white apron and tall, imposing toque. "They're here, Kati," he announced with unmistakable pride in his voice. "I've taken their order. Come over here and let's get started. They've picked your favorite," he said, a sly look in his eye. Immediately Kati knew what they had selected.

Of course they had chosen the most difficult item on the menu. *Le gratin de huîtres à la coque*—oysters in an eggshell and scrambled eggs in an oyster shell—required an incredible amount of precise coordination on the part of all the chefs involved. To the uninitiated it sounded a bit odd, but to a true gourmet, like their special diners tonight, it was a veritable culinary delight. All the components had to be prepared and added not a second too soon or a millisecond too late or the whole thing would be ruined.

Kati's nerves flared. She reminded herself that she had made the dish successfully a hundred times. She knew how to do it. It was merely a matter of coordination, she told herself. She was excited by the challenge of playing an integral part in the making of the meal. She rushed to the refrigerator and began pulling out the ingredients they would need. Silently they concentrated on measuring exactly the right amount of spices and herbs needed to make the dish absolutely perfect.

"Okay, Kati, I think I'm ready over here," Guillaume advised her.

"Coming, Monsieur Lazare, I'm just about finished here," she added cheerfully, gathering her contribution to the meal and walking steadily toward him.

Just as she was approaching him, she heard the explosion.

Sylvie Lazare's was the first face Kati saw when she awakened in the hospital. Her left leg was held high above the rest of her body by traction, and her hands were bandaged. Slowly she reached up to touch her face, only to discover that it, too, was covered with heavy gauze.

"Kati," the sweet woman cried out when at last she saw the girl's eyes open. "Kati, can you hear me?"

"Yes, yes, I can hear you." She looked around the room quickly. "Sylvie, what's happened? Where am I?" A look of sheer terror swept across her face.

The woman's eyes teared. It was too painful for her to retell the story of the tragedy one more time. The harsh reality of all that had occurred had still not completely been absorbed. Of course Kati had no idea what had happened. She had been horribly burned, and in such tremendous pain that the doctors had kept her heavily sedated until now.

"Oh, Kati, I'm so glad that you're finally awake. How do you feel?"

Kati tried to turn her head, but immediately a wave of pain coursed through her body. She grimaced and lay still.

"Kati, don't try to move. Shall I call the doctor?"

"No, no, I'm okay," she insisted. "Tell me what happened."

"There was a terrible explosion," Sylvie started slowly. She wanted to remain as calm as possible so she would not upset Kati.

"Anyway," she began again, trying desperately to get a hold on her emotions, "there was an explosion, and then a fire broke out. They think it was caused by a leak in the new gas stove. Something wasn't hooked up properly. A problem with one of the lines or something, they said. So it exploded." That was all the information she could get out before she fell completely apart. Whether her eyes were open or closed, all she could see before her was the rubble that had once been her whole life. Oh, she prayed, make the horrible pain subside. Jean-Louis would be home tomorrow. He would make it better, she told herself.

"Oh, Sylvie," Kati said, trying again to lift her head. Once more, excruciating pain shot through her entire being. She cried out and turned her face toward the wall.

"Kati, take it easy, try not to move. You've been sedated for almost two days. Please, be very careful. I'm going to go out now and find the doctor." Sylvie rose from the chair she had pulled up close to the bedside. She was halfway across the room when Kati spoke again.

"Guillaume," she said. "Where is Guillaume?"

Sylvie stopped as if struck by lightning. Kati could see her shoulders rise and fall with her sobs. Slowly she turned back toward the bed, and in that instant Kati knew that once again a very important person in her life, a man she had come to trust and to love, had been taken from her.

CHAPTER

30

"WELL, THIS HAS certainly taken a lot longer than I ever expected," Kati said once the last bandage had been removed. Still she smiled at the doctors and nurses, with whom she had spent more time than anyone since the tedious process of the reconstructive surgery had begun.

"The healing process can be terribly slow, Kati," the doctor commented, all the while running his hands gently across her cheek and down her neck, examining the uneven texture of the still-damaged, vulnerable skin. "You've been a model patient, I must tell you. In all my years of practice, I don't think I've ever had anyone, certainly not anyone with the kind of serious injuries you sustained, be so patient and willing to follow orders. You listened to every word I said and worked with me every step of the way. The results we've been able to get are a direct reflection of that cooperation. You've been terrific. I hope you're as pleased as I am with what we've been able to do."

"I am, Doctor. You know I'll be forever grateful to you."

Kati took the hand mirror he offered and closely examined the right side of her face. It was well over a year since the devastating fire had demolished the Restaurant Claire, claiming the wonderful Guillaume Lazare in the process. The Lazares had refused to give up, refused to move from the location that had meant so much to them. Sylvie insisted that they gut the space and rebuild the restaurant exactly the way it had been on the day of its demise. Besides wanting to preserve a family tradition, she claimed it would make her feel closer to Guillaume. She said she would still be able to sense his spirit hovering in the kitchen every night.

Kati had agreed to stay and help them during the period when the construction was taking place. They had found a small place only three blocks away that would serve as temporary quarters until the original restaurant was rebuilt. It would only have ten tables, but it enabled them to guard some of their income during the renovation. Kati would continue to work in the kitchen alongside Jean-Louis. Besides, she had a year of reconstructive surgery ahead of her. Where else would she rather spend it than with the Lazares, who had been so good to her?

Jean-Louis had come home immediately and assumed his place as head of the family. He was still young and of course did not have the experience of his father, but his ebullient personality, his determination, and his talent in the kitchen captured the hearts of everyone who worked with him and enabled the restaurant to maintain its fine reputation.

He had also been a pillar of strength to Kati. After the most serious and painful operation, when her eyes had to remain bandaged for almost two weeks, he had come to visit her every afternoon before he went to the restaurant.

"What'll it be today, Mademoiselle?" he would call out in his cheerful voice as he entered her room. "A classic, something by Baudelaire, *Le Monde* for the intellectuals, or *Vogue* for the latest fashions?" From under her bandages, Kati would smile and hold out her hand to him. They would select something, and for the next hour he would sit and read to her. Then he'd bring her up-to-date on everything that was happening at the restaurant. Unable to see, she could feel his affection surrounding her like a down comforter. The entire process would have been unendurable without his kindness, but she was saddened that she couldn't return his love in the way he wanted her to. As much as she would have liked, Kati remained scarred by her past. She was unable to let go, to release her feelings. Every time she dared to give her heart to someone, they had been taken from her. After Jean-Louis had been so good to her it was going to be terribly hard to break the news to him that she was leaving.

Kati continued to stare into the mirror at her reflection. Long ago she had become used to the changes caused by the fire. When they had first allowed her to see herself, her screams had echoed throughout the corridors of the hospital, and the nurses had rushed in to subdue her. The left side of her face was scorched in three places, and the entire right side of her face had been charred. A heavy cast-iron skillet had hit her face, breaking her cheekbone and crushing several of the tiny bones around her eye. The skin was a thousand different shades of bruised blue and green. The luminous complexion, the skin that had required only the lightest dusting of blush to make it glorious, were gone. Gone was the glow that made men's heads turn and follow her in the streets, in the Métro, in the restaurant when she happened to go into the dining room. Layer after layer of dead, burned skin continued to drop away, revealing raw, painfully sensitive new layers that were not yet strong enough to endure the dirt and pollution of the modern environment.

The doctors had carefully explained the type of treatments she would have to endure. They had been hopeful, promising her that if she was patient, they would be able to restore her former appearance. They would perform a series of operations. In between each one she would have to allow time for a period of recovery. After the wounds from the burns had healed, they would be able to begin. They would start by rebuilding her cheekbone and the bones surrounding her eye. They could reposition the cheek and orbit bones with minute plates and screws, but in order to do this they would need to do some bone grafting, taking material from her ribs or hip. She had listened quietly and then accepted their advice. From that day forward she was as stoic and as committed to the recovery process as she was to rebuilding her life.

Now the day had come when the final bandages were ready to be removed. She continued to stare, moving the mirror around so she could examine her face from every angle. To say that she was immediately pleased with the results would have been a lie. It would take some time for her to get used to this face. It was no longer ugly or disfigured. It was just different from the face she had known as her own. She knew the doctors had been the finest and had done the best that was possible. Still, she needed time to adjust.

"Thank you again, Doctor," she repeated, handing the mirror back to the nurse. "I know you've all worked extremely hard for me. I appreciate everything you've done." She held out her hands to him and prepared to leave his office for the last time.

"We'd all like to see you again," he added. "If you have any trouble, the least sign of a problem, please don't hesitate to call us immediately, at any time." The doctor and his entire team had come to love and admire Kati. During the past year he had yearned to improve the technology of modern medicine, to find new methods that would enable him to improve the results of Kati's surgeries. He only wished he could have done more for this courageous woman.

"Don't worry, Doctor. I'm going to be leaving Paris, but not without saying good-bye. And when I have a new address, I'll be certain to write you and have my records sent on."

"Fine, Kati, we'll be delighted to forward everything we have. May I ask where you'll be going?"

"Home," she answered. The word sounded so good to her that she repeated it again slowly. "It's time to go home."

"Jean-Louis, please," she implored, "wipe that sad, puppy-dog look off your face right now. I can't stand to see you look that way."

"All right, Kati, I'll try, but you know how hard it is. I just don't understand why you have to leave right now. The restaurant's just getting back on track. We've only been open for two weeks. We need you. It's going to be terribly hard here without you." What he meant of course was that *he* was going to have a very hard time without her. Kati had been an angel since the catastrophe. Not once had she allowed her own pain and suffering to overshadow the loss that all of the Lazares were feeling. She was always there, oftentimes not saying a word, just sitting with Sylvie, or Robert, sharing their sorrow and being available to them if they wanted to talk. Jean-Louis had dealt with his grief by throwing all of his efforts into building the business up again. But his love for Kati continued to grow. It also continued to be unrequited.

"Jean-Louis, please, don't make this any harder than it already is. I told you, I promised all of you that I would stay until the restaurant reopened and all of my surgery was finished. Well, both of those things have happened, and now I have to leave. It's time to go home," she said again for the third time that day. Each time she said it, it sounded better and better. She longed to see the Black Forest again, longed to smell the scent of the trees. More than anything else she longed to walk through the corridors of the Waldhotel, to be close to that which was familiar to her.

She had been in Paris for almost three years, a city that—even with her perfect command of the language and small group of friends—remained extremely foreign to her. So tomorrow morning she would once again pack the same valises that she had carried here from Germany and board the train traveling east.

"But Kati, when will we see you again?" he continued, unable to accept the fact that her decision was final.

"I don't know," she replied honestly. "But someday, I promise. After all, I'm leaving my grandfather's portrait for you to keep for me. You know how much it means to me. I'll have to come back to get it sometime."

"I sure hope it's soon. You know, Kati, how much I care for you. Even more now than when you were—"

"Pretty?" she offered, not at all offended by his words, for his intention was clearly not to hurt her.

"No, that's not what I meant," he insisted. "Oh, I don't know what I meant. Please forgive me. I'm just so upset to think that tomorrow at this time you won't be here."

"Please don't. It only makes me sad too. I'll never forget you, Jean-Louis. You and your whole family. For what you did for me. You are the best friends I have in the world right now. I'll never be able to thank you enough or stop caring about all of you," she assured the young man who was so in love with her but whom she couldn't love back. Still, she wasn't ready to give herself to anyone. Everyone she had ever loved had been taken from her, and the pain had been excruciating. Those she wanted to give her love to only hurt her, like Christophe, and that pain had been far more acute than the worst physical discomfort she had experienced during the past year. She guarded her emotions closely, and so far no one had been able to cross over the wall she had erected around herself. A wall that kept her feelings in and other people's out. She prayed that the day would come when the burden of her past would lessen and she could give herself to someone completely.

· · ·

She was delayed in getting to the station because Sylvie and Jean-Louis had begged her to stay and have one last lunch with them.

"Come on, Kati," Jean-Louis had insisted. "There are plenty of trains. I worked all morning to make your favorite meal. Can't you smell it?"

Indeed the kitchen was filled with the scent of poule en pie, the French version of an American pot pie. It was Kati's favorite, and Jean-Louis prided himself on making a superb example of it, mostly, she knew, because she loved it so much. She walked over to the stove and lifted the lid. Vapors of the rich sauce wafted up as the chicken meat simmered in a thick broth. Soon he would remove it and pour the delicious mixture of chicken, fresh vegetables—carrots, peas, turnips, celery, and onions—into the puff pastry shell. Then he would seal the pastry tightly around the edges. The pie was then placed in the oven until the crust was a yummy golden brown.

Kati replaced the lid. Her mouth watered. How sweet of him to go to all this trouble on her last day. Especially when they had two full sittings that evening. She turned to him, her eyes moist with appreciation for his goodness.

"Of course I'll stay," she said.

Lunch lasted over two hours. They had talked and laughed about all the fun times they had shared. Kati was still overcome with giggles when Jean-Louis mentioned her *faux* birthday party. Attentive waiters had replenished the wine frequently.

By the time she was finally ready to leave, she was light-headed, making it even more difficult for her to hold back her tears.

"Don't cry, Kati, please," Jean-Louis and Sylvie said in unison. But it was too late. Sylvie's eyes were also moist, and she hugged Kati to her ample bosom. "Oh, we're going to be lost without you," she said.

"As I would have been without you two years ago," Kati responded. "But I must go home now. It's been such a long time. I'll be back, though. We'll see each other again, I promise. I love you both very much." Even though she had missed her train, she was happy that she had stayed. During the ride east, the sound of their recent laughter echoed in her ears, making her departure a little easier.

. . .

The delay caused her to arrive in Baden-Baden at eleven that night. She couldn't have cared less what time it was, so happy was she to see the old station. It was empty at that hour, but she had no fear as she walked slowly up the platform. It was a beautiful night. The sky was crystal clear, the constellations easily identifiable. Kati stood with her head held back, inhaling the crisp, clean forest air. The scent of spring was everywhere. It was many degrees cooler than it had been in Paris, and she wrapped her light coat tightly around her. Now she rarely went out without a scarf on her head. The doctors had said it would help avoid possible infection of her still fragile skin, and she touched the scarf to be sure it was in place, with fingers that trembled as she took in every detail. The freshly painted benches, the charming flower boxes. Even the posters announcing events at the symphony and art museum, things she had always taken for granted, were a delight to see. She walked directly toward the hotel as if drawn by a magnet. Had anyone stopped her to ask her a question, she would have been unable to respond. Now that she was finally here, she couldn't wait to see her home. As her footsteps reached the end of the clock at the Leopoldsplatz, the hotel came into view. She dropped her bags and stood staring at the magnificent building. What a glorious sight! All the beauty of Paris, the grand examples of the finest architecture, could not compare to the brilliance of the Waldhotel.

Several people walking past her turned and stared, but she didn't care. She was so happy to be there. Gathering up her things she continued walking toward the entrance. The parking area was crowded—Mercedes, Jaguars, and limousines—cars of every make and size were lined up under the canopy. Of course, there must be a dance tonight. After all, it was Saturday night, and she had read on one of the posters in the station that the Opera House was giving a special performance of *Madame Butterfly*.

It was midnight. She couldn't just march into the hotel and walk up to Dieter's desk. No, that would be too much of a shock for him. Also she didn't want anyone to know she was here. Not yet, anyway. She would just wait outside. His shift ended soon and he would be coming out and heading across the street to his apartment. Yes, she'd wait here for him. The parking attendants must be on a short break, she realized, for no one had approached her and asked her what she was doing standing outside the hotel with all her luggage. She discreetly placed her bags behind a large car and went to stand behind one of the large columns flanking the entrance. She and Eva-Maria had played hide-and-seek around these thick white structures when they were young. Life had been so simple then, and the hotel had been filled with her family. Now no one was left. Opa, her father, her mother. Even her sister seemed to be lost to her now. The only thing that remained the same, she thought sadly, was the columns. More than twenty years later they still served as a good lookout post.

She waited for what seemed like hours, peeking out each time she heard the swishing sound of the revolving door. So far Dieter still hadn't appeared. He rarely followed any sort of schedule, she recalled. He would stay at his desk until all the work that had to be completed was done. If he had had many interruptions during the course of the day, everything else would only stack up and still be there, waiting for him when it finally quieted down at night.

Soon the dance was over and many of the guests began to leave the hotel. Kati recognized some of them; they included many of the local people. She saw Dr. Hoeffer and his wife get into their car and drive away. Kind Dr. Hoeffer. He had been so lovely to Tilla, and to this day he had never been paid for his services. Someday she would make that up to him, she vowed.

As the valets brought up the cars, it became harder and harder for Kati to remain hidden behind the pillar. She ducked around the back side of the column when the headlights of the cars beamed on it. The moment they had passed, she slid back around to the other side.

Now it was getting crowded; lots of people were leaving all at once. They were starting to line up outside the hotel entrance since the valets were backed up with the car orders. She quickly retrieved her bags and resumed her position.

Oh, if he would only come out soon, before anyone noticed her. Suddenly it occurred to her that the chances of being recognized were indeed very remote. Those who hadn't known her intimately would probably not recognize her. She was not the same, beautiful young girl who had left there three years earlier. Not only was she older, but her once-exquisite face was now changed, the agony of her ordeal still evident in every feature. Her long, flowing, girlish tresses were gone, replaced by a short, more sophisticated haircut. She was still attractive, but in some ways her new, tragically gained maturity had made her even more beautiful.

Most of the guests had departed. The door started to move again, and her heart began pounding as a new fear swept through her. In her single-minded desire for home and Dieter, she hadn't allowed herself to think about what she would do if Christophe came out first. Again she peeked out hopefully. It was almost one, and the temperature was dropping steadily. She was shivering from a combination of cold and anticipation when *swoosh, swoosh* came the familiar sound. Dieter pushed his way through the door. As he stepped out, his attention was captured by her waving hand.

"Dieter, over here," she whispered urgently, not wanting to also draw the notice of the valets.

He looked straight at the young woman with a scarf tied around her head. For a moment he stood staring, not recognizing this stranger.

"Dieter, it's me," Kati said. She was shocked that he had not recognized her instantly, but outwardly she smiled and continued to beckon him in her direction. Kati had not seen Dieter since the day he had driven them to the station. He looked older and a little tired to her. His face was drawn, as if he had lost some weight. In his letters he hadn't mentioned anything about being sick, but it wouldn't be like him to complain.

Suddenly he recognized her. Her smile was unmistakable. When he saw her perfect white teeth and sparkling eyes, there was no doubt in his mind who was perched on the edge of the granite pedestal.

"Kati," he cried out, a little too loudly, for she immediately raised her hand to her lips. "Kati," he repeated, stepping over to her and embracing her with a warm, loving hug. Finally he pulled back and looked at her. She was thankful for the dim lights under the entryway. She wouldn't have wanted him to see her for the first time in a bright light. What had taken her so long to almost get used to would still be quite a shock for anyone else. "Kati, when did you get here? Why didn't you come inside? It's really cold out here tonight."

"I didn't want anyone to see me. Anyone but you, that is. Now isn't the right time. Let's wait awhile. Can we go inside?"

"Of course, of course, I'm sorry," he apologized, suddenly realizing that despite his warnings of the cold, he continued to stand and talk with her. "Come, where are your bags?"

"Right here," she indicated.

"Good, let's take them upstairs and get you a nice hot cup of tea. How long have you been out here?"

"About an hour, I suppose."

"Well, on second thought, maybe we'll have to make that tea a brandy. I don't want you getting sick on me. Now that you're finally home." He carried her small bag in one hand and wrapped his free arm securely around her.

Kati smiled again and kissed Dieter on the cheek. "Oh, Dieter, it's so good to be here." At once she felt so comfortable, so relaxed. She had the distinct feeling that if she had returned five or ten or even fifteen years from now, the homecoming would have been the same from her beloved Dieter.

"So tell me everything," Dieter said once they were settled into his familiar room in the staff building across the street from the Waldhotel. It looked exactly the same as she remembered it.

After being with her for a while he had begun to adjust to her new face. The changes were subtle, but she just didn't look the way he was used to seeing her. She had been humorous about it in her letters. "I simply have more pronounced cheekbones than I was born with. If I were a model, it would probably be a blessing." Still it was startling to look at her, for he was constantly searching for the face to which he had grown accustomed. Concentrating on her smile and looking at her unchanged eyes made it a little easier for him.

Kati had written to him often, telling him of Tilla's death and then of her job at the Restaurant Claire. She mentioned her brief encounters with Eva-Maria. She wrote about the Lazares and how wonderful they had been to her. About Jean-Louis and their kitchen escapades. She had shared with him all the important things that had happened during her time in France. Except of course, the rape, which she refused to confide to anyone.

They talked for hours. Dieter recounted everything that had happened at the Waldhotel since the takeover, details he had been unwilling to trouble her with in his letters. Henri-Etienne hadn't spent any money at all renovating or redecorating as he had promised.

What he had done, however, was make his son the general manager of the hotel. Christophe had become greatly dependent on Dieter. The experienced man helped the younger one every step of the way, and he genuinely liked him. He tried not to hold him responsible for his father's dreadful treatment of the Meiers. There had been other changes at the Waldhotel as well. Some seemed to be for the better, but most were merely designed to cut costs.

"I can't believe you really like him," Kati said in astonishment, referring to Dieter's high praise for Christophe. He knew how she felt about him and his betrayal of her. Yet, almost against her will, she was eager to hear more about him.

"Kati, I truly think he wasn't aware of what his father had done until he called him home to France and told him."

"Well, perhaps," she said hesitantly, wanting to believe it with all her heart, but unable to change her mind completely.

"I think what I like best about him is the way he handles the staff," Dieter continued. "Only last month we had a situation here that could have been a real disaster. Had he not reacted the way he did, we could have had some serious problems."

Kati's eyes told him she was anxious to hear the full story.

"You remember old Herr Conrad, don't you?" he began.

"Of course, how could I forget him?" Kati answered. Herr Conrad was probably the oldest member still on the Waldhotel staff. He had served as the hotel's chief electrician for as long as she could remember. He was a kind old man who was now in his late seventies.

"Well, ever since the changeover, Herr Conrad, not unlike many of the older employees, has become very concerned about his job. Of course, he realizes that someday he will have to retire, but he would much prefer to pick his own time, rather than be told by Monsieur de Beaumont that it is time for him to go. Well, he decided that he would make himself more valuable by posting a formidable Keep Out sign on the door to the electrical supply storeroom. He wouldn't allow anyone to come in, and when they insisted, he turned it into such a mess that no one else was able to locate the tools or replacement parts they needed. Finally it got so bad that if something needed to be repaired, it was easier just to go to the local hardware store and buy it. This became expensive and caused even further delays in getting the problem fixed. Christophe got wind of this and requested a meeting with old Herr Conrad. He asked me to join them because he knows I'm one of the old man's best friends in the hotel. We went to Christophe's office, Herr Conrad muttering and complaining all the way that he was certain that his days at the hotel were numbered. Once we were all seated, Christophe began to praise old Conrad, telling him how valuable he is to the operation, how we couldn't do without him, and on and on. Of course there is really a ring of truth to everything he was saying because Herr Conrad is the only one left around here who knows about the archaic electrical system we have. If anything were to really go wrong, he's the only one who could possibly find the solution. Christophe continued with his praise, all the while convincing Herr Conrad that he was still a member of the 'family' and very important to the house. Of course, being in this position, he should certainly want to make sure that the Waldhotel guests were serviced in the fastest, most efficient manner possible. By keeping his stockroom in such disarray, he was not allowing others to make timely repairs, Christophe explained patiently. Guests were beginning to complain. Wouldn't it be a terrible shame if the service level of the hotel were to fall down because only one individual was able to find a needed part? So, as a favor to the hotel, would he not consent to having some of the men help him reorganize the store-room? Herr Conrad agreed at once to Christophe's request, and you should see the workroom now. He takes it personally if anyone puts a light bulb back in the wrong place." Dieter started to chuckle. "You should have seen it, Kati. He was wonderful. I don't think I could have gotten the same results if I had been asked to handle it myself. So, you see, that's the kind of thing that makes me feel that he is a compassionate young man."

At the end of his story Kati was laughing too. Knowing how stubborn and hardheaded old Herr Conrad was, she was forced to admit that Christophe had pulled off quite a coup. Still, it would take more than a few stories to begin to change her mind about him. She would have to see for herself.

"That's some feat," she admitted, but not wanting to dwell on Christophe any longer. "Have there been any other major changes?"

"Well, we take credit cards now," he said.

"We, they," she quickly corrected herself, "accept credit cards now?" she repeated in amazement. Becker's Waldhotel had never accepted anything but cash, or more frequently a guest's personal check, as payment for their stay. Most of their better clients were never even presented with a bill. An invoice would arrive at their home or place of business following their visit.

"That policy certainly must attract a different crowd," she commented.

"It surely does," he agreed. "You won't believe some of the people who come to stay with us now," he sighed, shaking his head in sorrow. "Well, you'll have time to find out everything soon enough. Tomorrow will come very quickly. Let me make up the bed so you can get some sleep. I'll bet you're exhausted."

Kati was tired, but she wasn't yet ready to go to sleep. She had to tell Dieter the rest of her plan and what she wanted to do now that she was back.

"There's just one more thing before we say good night, Dieter."

"Yes, my little one, what is it?"

"Dieter, you've got to help me get a job."

"Of course, of course, Kati," he agreed. "We'll have plenty of time to ask around and see what is available. I don't want you worrying your pretty head about any of that right now. You can stay here with me until you find what you want. Now you need some rest." He stood up and started to walk toward the closet where he kept the extra set of linens he used on those rare occasions when he had someone stay in his room with him.

She smiled up at the gentle man who could recall in an instant the day Kati had been born. He had missed the point of her coming here entirely. How could he possibly have known, though?

"No, Dieter, you don't understand. I don't want a job in town. I want to work at the Waldhotel."

"The Waldhotel?" He stopped dead in his tracks and retraced his steps back to the living room. "Kati, why on earth would you want to do that?"

In a tone that left no doubt about how serious she was, she answered him. "Because despite all that has happened, the Waldhotel is still my home. Someday I hope I'll be able to reclaim it, but until then I just want to work here. I'll do anything. I've earned my stripes in a kitchen, and I'd be a good addition to any team. I'll do whatever job is available, but it must be at Becker's. Oh, Dieter, please, say you'll help me. Please . . ."

He could not deny the young woman he cared for so deeply. "Of course I'll help you, Kati. If you're sure it's really what you want, I'll go first thing in the morning to Christophe's office and tell him that you're back. He won't deny you a job, I'm sure."

"No, no, never," she responded vehemently. "No, Dieter, you don't see what I mean. You see, I want to work at the Waldhotel, I must work there, but it is imperative that no one knows who I really am. I don't want anyone there, particularly Christophe, to have any idea. I just want to do whatever job they give me, work hard all day, and then leave at night. No, no one can know my identity."

"Kati, you must be kidding. Why, there's no way that you can go across the street and begin working in a hotel in which you grew up and expect that no one will recognize you. You're only fooling yourself. You would only remain unknown for a matter of hours before word would spread like wildfire that you were back. There are many, well, maybe not many, but certainly enough people still there who have known you since you were a child. There's simply no way you could get away with it. Even if you could, I don't understand quite why you would want to."

"Dieter, Dieter, please, I've thought about all of those things. First of all, you've got to be the first one to admit that I've changed drastically since I left. After what happened outside the hotel tonight, there is simply no denying it. *You* didn't even know who I was. Also, I've been in France for three years. My French is nearly accentless. I can present myself as a French girl. I'm going to call myself Catherine from tomorrow on. It will work, I know it will. Only you and I will know who I am. It will be our secret. Just as we had all of those secrets in the past when I was little. Please, Dieter, being back at the hotel is the only thing that can make me happy again. I know it. Please say you'll help me. And that you'll guard our secret forever."

He couldn't deny her. "Okay, Kati . . . Catherine, you've convinced me. I'd do anything for you, even the craziest thing, which I still think this is. But if you're sure it's what you want, I'll do whatever I can. But right now I'm exhausted. These last few minutes have completely drained me. Let's get some sleep and we'll finish cooking up this wild scheme in the morning. Which is not too far off," he added, checking the clock and finding it was already four A.M.

"Oh, Dieter, I knew you'd understand. Thank you. Thank you." She kissed him on both cheeks before he padded off to his small bedroom. She crawled between the covers and was asleep on the sofa before he turned out his light.

CHAPTER

31

$\mathcal{K}$ATI REMAINED in Dieter's room most of the day. She took a long walk in the late afternoon, exploring and revisiting the city she loved. By the time evening came, she was so anxious for him to return home with news of her possible employment that when he finally did arrive, she barely allowed him to get through the door before she was up from the sofa, a thousand questions spilling from her lips.

"You're as impatient now as you were when you were a small child," he chided her. "Now sit down, let's have a drink, and I'll tell you everything."

"Okay, okay, what can I fix you to drink?" she asked without really caring what he wanted. She just needed to get him something so they could sit down and talk.

"So you see it's not a very big job," he said after he finished explaining the outcome of his efforts. "I'm sure you'll be bored working in the *garde-manger* all day after what you've been doing." The *garde-manger* was the area in the kitchen where food was stored until it was needed by the other side of the kitchen. As the orders came down, those working in the *entremetier,* or "hot" kitchen, would announce over the megaphone what they required. It was the job of the workers stationed in the *garde-manger* to pull the ingredients out and transfer them over to those waiting on the other side. It was strictly a support function for the main kitchen, where all of the real cooking took place. No, it certainly wasn't what she was used to, but it was a job.

"That's all right. At least I can look across the hallway and watch the excitement." The kitchens were separated by a small hallway and glass partitions. Everyone could see what everyone else was doing all the time.

"So I talked the new chef into taking you on, sight unseen. I did have to tell him that you were a friend of a friend."

A shocked look crossed her face. "Dieter, you didn't say any more than that, did you?"

"No, no, of course not. But I did have to go and clear the arrangements with Christophe. He was hesitant, but I pushed him until he finally agreed to hire you."

"Push him? What was the problem?"

"Well, Kati, there is one thing I didn't tell you . . ."

"What is it, Dieter? You said you didn't tell them any more about me."

"No, it's not about you, or your background, or anything having to do with you. It's about the hotel."

"What about it?"

"Well, business hasn't been very good. Since de Beaumont has refused to spend any money on renovations, it's starting to look even shabbier. People who do come and stay with us usually visit the Europäischer Hof. After they see how much nicer it is over there, they rarely find any reason to return to the Waldhotel. This has hurt our business terribly, and you remember we were already in trouble to begin with. After all, they have many of our most experienced people now, and it's a first-class operation. So the rumors have been flying that de Beaumont has lost all patience with us and that he's planning to close the Waldhotel and concentrate all his efforts in France. That's why Christophe is so hesitant to hire even one more person. First of all it costs him money, and second he can't even guarantee how long that person will have a job. You see, he does have a conscience. We've had three years to prove ourselves and there's no telling when his father is going to pull the rug out from under him."

"That's terrible news," Kati sighed, shaking her head in disbelief. "Any idea when all of this might happen?"

"No. That's the problem. Everyone is on edge with all the uncertainty. We just try to live day by day. But the morale has suffered terribly because of it."

"I can imagine," she agreed. "Well, it's no more uncertain than my life has been for the past few years. I'll probably fit in just fine."

"I'm sure you will. In any case, it's a job. You said that was what you wanted."

"Oh, Dieter, it is, it is!" she cried, suddenly realizing she hadn't even thanked him for all his efforts. "Thank you, thank you so much." She leaped across the room and hugged him tightly.

"The best news is that you won't be too far away, either. You can come here at night and tell me everything I missed in the dungeon. Your room is only two doors down."

"That's terrific. I can be out of your hair tonight. I'll get all moved in so I'll be ready to start tomorrow morning." Immediately she began to transfer her things down the hall.

"Well, that's everything," she announced a few minutes later. "I guess I'll say good night now and try to get some sleep." She kissed him good night and started for the door. She held the doorknob in her hand when suddenly she turned back to him, a concerned look on her face.

"Dieter, what did you tell them my name was?"

"Funny you should ask," he replied. "Catherine, of course, just as you instructed me. But that's where you left me. No last name, no nothing. I assumed, correctly I hope, that you would not want to use either Becker or Meier, so I picked a lovely French surname for you. I hope you like it." He smiled slyly.

"And what would that be?" Kati asked, realizing how much he was enjoying this part of the conversation.

"Olivier," he announced. "Catherine Olivier. Do you like the way it sounds?"

"Very elegant, I think, Catherine Olivier . . . Catherine Olivier," she repeated, twirling around the room as if she were dancing in a grand ballroom. "Yes, I like it very much. But it also has a secret meaning, doesn't it?"

"Of course. You remember Olivier Dabescat, don't you?"

"I remember hearing about him. I think he had already died by the time I was born."

"Yes, yes, he would have been long gone. I only had the chance to meet him once, with your grandfather. He was really something, a true legend. Olivier Dabescat was the most famous maître d'hôtel the Ritz Hotel in Paris had ever known. He was in charge of the restaurant there for more than forty years. When Karl-Gustav took over the reins after Ludwig died, Olivier came to the Waldhotel to help him get started." Dieter smiled as he recalled the memory of the hotel great. "So, you see, I thought it would be appropriate for you to borrow his name."

"I agree," Kati replied, pleased with her new identity.

"So now, my little one, we have two secrets."

"Yes, we do. And they belong only to us, forever. Promise?"

"Yes, I promise," he said. "Now out, Mademoiselle Catherine Olivier. I'll see you in the morning. Don't be late on your first day."

"Never! Oh, Dieter, thank you again. Good night." She ran across the room and planted one last kiss on his cheek. Then she was out the door. Dieter noticed a spring in her step he hadn't seen since she had been a happy, carefree teenager.

CHAPTER

32

THE MEMO was circulated less than five months later. It was short, almost curt in its tone, and very much to the point. No one who read it would be left with any doubt in their mind about what was going to happen.

In essence, the letter said that due to a management decision, the Waldhotel would be closed at the end of September. It stated further that some employees would be contacted about continuing their employment at the hotel in France. All others would be given an "equitable separation." They would be required to make their own arrangements with the hotel's new owners. It was signed with the scrawly signature of Henri-Etienne de Beaumont.

Kati felt sick after reading it. Another management change, no matter how skilled the new owners were, was going to be hard on the Waldhotel.

"In other words, there is no guarantee that any of these people will have a job after September?" she asked.

"Yes, I'm afraid that's true," Chef Muller agreed. "But you needn't worry, Catherine, I've told you that I very much want you to come with us to France." Yes, he had told her. Many times. He liked the young woman from the moment he saw her walk through the swinging doors to report for her first day of work. Soon he discovered that her talents were wasted in the storeroom, and the minute the opportunity arose, he promoted her to a position as an assistant saucier. There she excelled, and continued to learn another aspect of the process of running a top-notch kitchen. She was extremely capable in many areas. Somewhere along the line she had had the benefit of fine training. She possessed a wonderful, upbeat attitude that was contagious, and beyond her skill; the quality that endeared her to him the most was her enthusiasm. When several of the kitchen staff had fallen ill with the flu and they were left terribly short-staffed, he had watched Kati scurry from kitchen to kitchen, working her hands, and her feet, to the bone. She simply did whatever had to be done to get the meals upstairs. She asked few questions and never complained. She was an asset to anyone's operation, and Chef Muller was not about to let her go.

The Villa Soleil staff would be much smaller than the one at the Waldhotel. He would need someone with her sense of responsibility there even more than he did here. He very much hoped she would decide to go with them.

Still, after repeating many times his desire to have her there, she still seemed undecided. In fact, he thought she was thinking of staying in Baden-Baden, where she could easily get a job at the Europäischer Hof. He decided to throw out a carrot he knew would be difficult for her to pass up. "Catherine," he said, "if you go with us, I promise you that within three months you'll be the sous-chef at the Villa Soleil."

Her face lit up. Sous-chef. That would be a major step up for her, plus it would give her the experience she would need if she ever wanted to open a restaurant of her own.

"Thank you, Chef Muller. I'm grateful to you for that," she replied. "It's a very generous offer. Please let me think about it for a day." That was all she could say. She couldn't unleash all of her pent-up anger, her growing hatred of Henri-Etienne de Beaumont for selling the hotel. He was going to put loyal employees, some of whom had worked for her grandfather for decades, out of work. These hardworking, conscientious people would be out on the streets in just a few more weeks. Inwardly she raged, but she was unable to voice her opinion to anyone other than Dieter for fear that her secret would be revealed.

During the time she had been back at the Waldhotel, she had been extremely cautious about seeing Christophe. Like all the other employees, she had to use the back door to enter and exit the hotel. The first time she realized that she was now forced to go through the back door of her own home, anger overtook her. But gradually, as with all things she was unable to change at the moment, she adjusted. Soon it was only another habit of her daily life.

The first time she saw Christophe after her arrival was purely by mistake. Chef Muller had sent her upstairs to accounting to get a copy of a missing delivery receipt. As she was searching through the stacks of papers, she heard his voice. It was unmistakable. The easily recognizable accent of a Frenchman speaking German. A voice that had always sent a shiver of excitement through her body when she heard it. A voice she had grown to love—and then to hate. She looked up. He stood on the opposite side of the lobby near Dieter's desk. The desk was occupied by the other concierge, since Dieter had gone to Munich that morning. She stood staring at him, paralyzed. When she started to tremble, she grasped the desk tightly. She had gone over this moment time and time again in her mind, preparing for the inevitable. But none of her rehearsals helped her now that it was actually happening. She was completely taken aback by her strong physical response as she clutched the edge of the desk even more tightly. Her knuckles whitened.

He looked much the same as he had when she left. Maybe a little bit older, a few more lines around his lovely eyes. He wore a beautiful navy suit with a striped shirt and tie. He had told her that he always bought his shirts in London.

It looked as if he was trying to handle a guest complaint. He shifted his weight from one foot to the other, thinking about how to deal with the situation. The man he was speaking with appeared to be agitated. As he continued to speak, his voice rose with irritation. When Christophe's attention was distracted by something in her direction, she put her head back down quickly.

"Monsieur de Beaumont, I hope you understand that our entire vacation is being ruined by this," Kati heard the man say. "Please, you must do something about it today. I cannot go another night with the incessant noise. I am here on my honeymoon, and I don't need to tell you that it is certainly not adding to the romantic setting of your hotel. I am also not willing to be moved, so don't even suggest it. I reserved the suite we are in over a year ago simply because of the extra-large terrace. I don't want to leave it," he continued. His tone was lighthearted, but his message serious.

Christophe looked uncomfortable. This guest had obviously put him in a tough position. He was silent for a minute. By the look on his face, Kati knew that he was trying to bide his time, trying to decide what was the best plan of action. Still, she remained uncertain what the man was complaining about. The new wife of the disgruntled guest gave her the answer a minute later.

An attractive young woman exited the elevator and walked toward them. "Hello, darling," she said to her husband.

Christophe introduced himself.

"Hello," she said politely. "I hope you are the key to getting our problem solved. It really is spoiling an otherwise perfect holiday," she said, tugging affectionately on her husband's sleeve. "Constant barking, all the time this dog is making noise. The minute he stops, something else attracts his attention and he starts in again. It is really terrible. Whoever owns him allows him to sleep outside on the terrace at night. He is an awful creature."

"I will telephone the Baroness today and ask her what she can do about the dog," Christophe said at last.

"Fine," the man agreed, "but would you be kind enough to call now, please? Then we can go on and enjoy our day, knowing that the problem has been solved. You don't mind, do you?"

Now Kati knew exactly what the problem was. The Baroness to whom Christophe referred had been coming to Becker's and staying in the same suite for two months every year, ever since Kati could remember. Besides being one of the most devoted guests, she was also one of the oldest. Kati assumed that the woman must be well into her nineties by now. She was an old friend of her Opa's. She had seen her several times over the past weeks being escorted into the dining room by her nurse. She used a cane now and appeared frail. Kati suspected that both her mental and her physical health had declined over the last few years. One of the floor waiters had complained last week that she had indeed lost her mind. She had called room service and ordered an entire meal, only to claim when it was delivered to her room that she had never called. Still she was a handsome old woman, always dressed to the nines when she came down for dinner.

The Baroness always traveled with her dogs. In earlier years there had been two or three. They were miniature French poodles, immaculately groomed and sporting colorful silk bows in their topknots. Kati assumed the others had died, and now she saw one of the boys periodically walking the remaining one. The dog walked with the same deliberate pace as his owner. He was crippled and apparently half blind, for the last time she had seen him, he had stopped dead in the middle of the street and was barking at nothing in particular. The boy tugged impatiently on the leash, but the old creature refused to budge.

The Baroness always reserved one of the largest suites on the main floor. It had a big terrace, used mainly by the dogs. The complaining couple was obviously in the suite directly above hers. It was the most luxurious room in the entire hotel, used a large portion of the time by honeymooners.

Christophe had stalled as long as was reasonable. He hated the thought of a confrontation with the Baroness. But the man was right, and he wanted an answer now. "All right," Christophe agreed, "please step over here with me and I'll telephone the dog's owner."

The three of them started toward the desk where Kati had halted her search for the missing papers. Quickly she got up and went behind the partition that separated the front clerks from the accounting department. She knew she should just go back downstairs and continue looking for the document later, but she couldn't pull herself away. She had to see how he was going to get out of this one.

Christophe picked up the house phone and asked to be connected to the Baroness's suite. Slowly and diplomatically he explained the problem. He listened patiently and finally thanked the Baroness before hanging up. He put the receiver down and shook his head.

"Well?" the man asked. "What did she say?"

Christophe wore a perplexed and, at the same time, amused look. "Well, I am afraid we did not solve the problem," he said. "The Baroness claims that there is no dog."

"No dog?" the woman said in amazement. "Well, she is clearly out of her mind. There most certainly is a dog."

"Of course there is," Christophe said. "Apparently the Baroness has forgotten about him."

"Well," the man said, "if she claims there is not a dog on the terrace, then it must be a wild animal. I am going to report it to the authorities, and I will have the *chien sauvage* shot on sight. Whatever this thing might be, it is apparently a menace and a danger to all of your guests." His tone was stern, but there could be no question that the man was only joking.

At his remark Kati could no longer contain her laughter. When she was able to peek out again, she saw that Christophe also had been unable to maintain his composure. The three of them had broken into uncontrollable fits of laughter.

"I'm so sorry," Christophe was finally able to say once he managed to get himself under control. "I apologize. I promise I will personally visit the Baroness this afternoon and take care of the problem. You will sleep peacefully tonight."

"Thank you, Monsieur de Beaumont," the man had said. He and his wife left the hotel still giggling.

Kati had no idea how Christophe was going to handle the Baroness. But he had certainly dealt with the newlyweds wonderfully, succeeding in turning a potentially unpleasant situation into one that could now be viewed with a sense of compassion and humor. He would still have to confront the issue, but at least now everyone understood what they were dealing with.

Kati returned downstairs with the missing papers, still giggling helplessly, but also with a grudging respect for Christophe's diplomatic skills.

After that she had been close to him only two times. One morning she had agreed to work two shifts to cover for an employee who had resigned hastily after a harsh disagreement with Chef Muller. In keeping with her easygoing nature, she had merely smiled and said, "Of course."

When she arrived prepared to work the frenetic breakfast shift, she was astounded to see Christophe in the pastry area. He wore an apron and was putting the several different varieties of bread into the baskets that were placed on each tray. She stepped quickly into the back kitchen and began preparing the egg orders. Once the activity built and everyone was scurrying like mad, he went to the side of the kitchen and began offering words of encouragement. "Keep it up, everyone," he shouted over the din of the clashing pans and glasses. "Only fourteen more deliveries for a perfect morning." Kati's head rose to watch him. She couldn't believe it. She was at once angry and pleased at what she was hearing. Christophe was using the exact words she used to use when she did precisely the same thing. When he had first joined the hotel, they would both go to the kitchen early.

In the beginning Christophe would watch her as she garnered the troops for the toughest part of their day. Now that she was gone, he copied her routine down to the last word. Her anger subsided. He's been smart enough to continue a routine that was so successful, and obviously he hadn't felt the need to establish a different routine simply to show that he was the new boss. At the same time, holding on to the old tradition must have had an effect in boosting the staff's morale, she thought. Maybe he was as caring as Dieter claimed.

The second time she had seen him was at a meeting Chef Muller asked her to attend. Five or six of them sat around Karl-Gustav's desk, which was now occupied by Christophe. It felt so odd to be seated on the opposite side of her former work space that her hands shook with nervousness as she reviewed the figures. Looking up from the papers she was reading, her eyes locked with Christophe's. There seemed to be a distant flicker of recognition. She wanted to scream out a thousand different things. She wanted to tell him to get out of her grandfather's chair. She longed to go to him and tell him she was back. Her emotions fluctuated between hatred and adoration for him and for the job she saw he was trying to do, and she was overwhelmed by a sense of confusion. Their brief encounter so terrified her that once the meeting had adjourned, she practically ran from the room.

From then on she was very cautious. She tried to avoid being caught in a situation where she was alone with him. It was fairly easy. He was so busy working on the move that he had very little time for anything else, which was fine with Kati. It allowed her to keep her feelings under control and to continue her charade, free of any worries about being discovered by him.

Finally, after much mental struggling, she had reluctantly accepted Herr Muller's offer to move to the Villa Soleil. Dieter had already agreed at once, happy for the opportunity to spend the last few years of his career in a warmer climate. "Maybe I'll like it so much I'll want to retire there," he had said to her. "Come, Kati, come with the rest of us. We'll have some fun. It will be good to be away from here for a while. You can always come back." All of those things were true. But she loved being home so very much. Everything was familiar. Even the smallest things, like spending an hour or two browsing at the small bookstore in town, gave her great pleasure. She had just spent three years in France. Granted, not on the glamorous, chic Riviera. Life there would be entirely different from anything she had ever experienced. Everyone said good things about the Villa Soleil. It was supposed to be beautiful, set up high in the hills overlooking the coast. The restaurant there was well regarded, although it only had one star. Maybe it would be fun. It would certainly have to be better than staying in Baden-Baden and watching what the new owners might do to the Waldhotel. They were Americans, and rumor had it that they were going to turn Becker's into a very commercial operation. She envisioned the Waldhotel being transformed into a Sheraton or Hilton, with automatic elevators and those horrible little foil packettes of shampoo. That would surely be too painful to watch. Nothing could make her go to work for the Europäischer Hof. It would be like deserting her family altogether. Her Opa would not rest peacefully in his grave on the hill if he knew she had gone there. No, she would go to the Villa Soleil. At least there she could still be near Dieter, who loved her so much. Also, even though she tried not to admit it, her admiration for Christophe was slowly growing as she watched him struggle to the very last minute to convince his father not to let go of the Waldhotel. In the end it was a fight he would lose, but she respected him for trying. At the Villa Soleil she would work hard and learn even more about the hotel business. But someday she knew she would be able to return.

On the day before they were scheduled to leave, Kati went once more to the cemetery. Soon she would arrange for her mother to be brought there as well. Standing above the headstones, she repeated her vows. "I promise you," she told the trees and the river. And then she knelt beside her Opa.

The Villa Soleil was as breathtaking as everyone had claimed. The mere beauty of its setting in the hills above the coastline gave it a unique quality that was not available anywhere else. Here one could have the best of both worlds: relax in the quiet charm of the mountains, while only a short ride away was the excitement and glamour of the fashionable Riviera.

Kati investigated the hotel thoroughly. She was curious about the place where she knew her mother must have been seduced into selling the hotel to Henri-Etienne, the place where Christophe had grown up. When no guests were in sight, she walked leisurely around the property. The grounds were meticulously kept, the landscape extraordinary. From a distance she watched pairs of lovers stroll slowly, another couple merely sat at the terrace with a bottle of wine. She wondered if Christophe had left a girlfriend behind when he went away to hotel school. It was indeed a romantic setting. She could see how her mother, not totally in control of her unstable emotions, had been easily lured into making a wrong decision. Especially in the company of the seemingly charming elder de Beaumont. Making the move here meant that she might have to see him sometimes, but she had already resigned herself to that. She made her way to the pool area. It was exactly as both Dieter and her mother had described it. She thought about poor Dominique Robillard, jumping from this glorious vantage point to her death. Her hatred for Henri-Etienne grew.

The exquisite property was enough to make even the most discerning traveler overlook any slight flaws in the hotel's service. And indeed there were many. Henri-Etienne ran a very relaxed operation in comparison with the Waldhotel. "People don't expect the type of formal, almost stiff service that they receive at Becker's," Christophe explained to her once when he had overheard her making the comparison to a coworker. "I think it has a lot to do with the weather and the very relaxed environment on the Riviera. Not to say there isn't room for much improvement, however. We're working on that every day." She hadn't realized that he was close enough to hear her comments. She must have appeared shocked to him when she heard his voice. Once again he stared at her as if he recognized her. She fled the room quickly, claiming she had an errand to run. She felt him continue to look at her as she left. Did he think that perhaps he knew her from somewhere? She couldn't risk turning around and trying to read his thoughts.

Very soon it became evident that Henri-Etienne was turning over the running of the hotel to his son. At last he had devised a way to get him to come home, and he was prepared to do anything to keep him there. Besides, lessening his daily responsibilities gave him more free time to run around all over the Côte d'Azur with any one of his several young girlfriends.

Dieter loved the new surroundings. He knew the area intimately from many holiday trips in his youth. He found the clientele much more relaxed and far less demanding than those in the Black Forest, although some could be equally as nasty and snide. Many of his favorite guests from Becker's also frequented the Villa Soleil when they were in search of sun and a touch of the Riviera. He enjoyed seeing them. Of course they were delighted that even though the Waldhotel remained closed, its new owners not moving with any great speed to reopen its doors, they were still able to see their old friend Dieter at least once a year.

Kati explored the area with the same passion she had investigated Paris years earlier. The entire region was rich in history. On her rare days off she took excursions to the small villages not far from the hotel. The frenetic atmosphere of Nice and Cannes held very little appeal for her. She much preferred the quiet, country atmosphere of the medieval towns north of Vence. She was happy to spend hours wandering in the hills around Grasse, exploring the countless varieties of wildflowers that had made the town world-famous for its production of perfumes. She never tired of the charming walled towns, especially Tourrette-sur-Loup. The village was constructed more than twenty centuries ago on a site that dominated two deep ravines. Looking out from the narrow passageways of the town now populated by artists and writers, she had a commanding view of the valleys beyond. Before her was a sea of shimmering olive and orange trees and a ground cover of violets. Often she would convince Dieter to go with her to one of the small restaurants overlooking the valley for lunch, where they would order a nice bottle of the local wine and one of the many outstanding fish. Afterward they would go to the town square and sit contentedly, watching the old men playing *boules* for hours on end.

"I really like it here, Kati," he would say. "I never thought I could feel so good about a place. I always thought that I could never be happy anywhere else but smack in the middle of the forest. But I've really grown to love this. I'm thinking about looking for a small house here when it's time to retire."

"You're not going to retire," Kati always insisted, knowing full well that Dieter only planned to work one more year before leaving the hotel. "You're going to work until you're a hundred. Besides, what would you do with all your time if you suddenly weren't at the hotel all day?"

He laughed gently. "You'd be surprised what I could cook up. For one thing, I'd go fishing. You may recall, I'm a pretty good angler for an old man."

"Taught me everything I know," Kati agreed, flashing him a warm smile that recalled the days long ago when they had fished together in the lakes around Baden-Baden. She also thought briefly of Rick Adams. "We could use you as a supplier for the restaurant. It's the one thing I'm enjoying most about the kitchen at the hotel. There is such a variety of fish, and each one can be prepared so many different ways—the rascasse, the red mullet, the bass." Her mouth began to water. "I'm learning a lot."

"You'll continue to learn, Kati. You're cut out for the business. I don't know where you'll end up, but I'm certain it will be as the chatelaine of one of the great resorts."

"You have such faith in me. Right now I'm just a sous-chef in a one-star restaurant. I've got a long way to go."

"You'll make it," he encouraged her. "I'm certain of it."

Her favorite excursion so far had been over a weekend when the two of them had decided to drive to Vaucluse. They rented a small Peugeot and headed west, taking the road that cut directly across the middle of Provence. They passed through the *départements* of Var and Bouches-du-Rhône. Once in Vaucluse, they visited the precariously sited castle high above the village. Most of the visitors to the castle believed that it belonged to the town's most famous citizen, Petrarch, but Kati knew from her studies that it really belonged to a friend of his. As she peered out from the thick stone wall into the rugged valley, she recalled all of Petrarch's poems to Laura, the woman who was the object of his unrequited love. In one of his greatest works, she remembered, he claimed to have spent twenty-one years passionately in love with her, and another decade crying for her. His most famous poem recounted the first time he set eyes on Laura in a church in Avignon. Kati felt that way about Christophe. Would their attraction for each other continue to go on from a distance for years to come? On the drive home she was quiet, lost in her own thoughts of what the future would bring.

"Is everything ready yet?"

Kati heard the sound of Henri-Etienne's gruff voice as it boomed across the expansive kitchen. It was already ten o'clock. She had been up since dawn preparing food for him. She turned in his direction and answered him in the most civilized voice she could muster. "Almost, Monsieur de Beaumont. We're just finishing packing the salads and the sandwiches."

"Very well," he grunted. "What about the champagne?"

"The champagne has been placed in the back of the car, sir," answered one of the assistants.

Henri-Etienne and several of his friends were off to the annual auto rally in Monte Carlo, which, since the early part of the century, had traditionally been held at the end of January. They were invited to be the guests of a well-known count, whose imposing villa in the hills offered a bird's-eye view of the difficult concourse, and Henri-Etienne had offered to bring lunch for all of them. His suggestion had been welcomed, and Kati had been assigned the task of organizing the program. Now, placing the elegant food in the baskets, she barely restrained herself from adding a healthy dose of cyanide to the portion marked for the great hotelier.

"Here they are, Monsieur de Beaumont," she announced. He moved toward her to examine the feast. It was not a typical picnic—this sumptuous spread included twenty different cheeses, six different types of bread and crackers, sliced meats of all varieties, quiches, lobster salad, shrimp salad, chicken salad, and a selection of fruits and desserts that would have pleased even the most demanding palate.

His eyes voiced his approval. "Okay, let's get it out to the car. We're running late."

Not a word of thanks. Nothing. It was typical, she reasoned. The man was simply devoid of manners. Totally lacking in the social graces. Except for his always-perfect grooming and impeccable dressing, he reminded her of Monsieur Grifont. She hated the man with a passion reserved only for him. In her heart he was the most terrible of humans—without any morals or scruples. How her mother had ever fallen prey to his supposed charms was beyond her wildest imagination. She marveled at the difference between father and son. Henri-Etienne was coarse. Christophe had a gentle manner. Henri-Etienne felt that yelling at the employees was the most successful way of making them productive. On many occasions Christophe was forced to soothe the ruffled feathers of an employee who had been the target of Henri-Etienne's rage. Christophe preferred to work patiently with each of them in an effort to bring out their very best. She had watched Christophe carefully, although from a distance, both at the Waldhotel and here at the Villa Soleil. As with her situation at the Waldhotel, many of the employees had known him since he was a child. He was fair, and kind, and appreciative of the employees. He had begun a tradition of giving birthday parties for their children, and Kati was often invited to these events. Most of the time she declined, but once in a while she would attend. She watched Christophe with the children. Her thoughts returned to the afternoon they had spent together at Heidi's. It seemed so long ago.

Kati brought her attention back to the present. She was glad that Henri-Etienne would be gone for the day. The hotel was much calmer and seemed to run so much more smoothly when he wasn't around. He was so offensive, chasing his young lovers around the pool, constantly making extra, unnecessary demands on the already overworked staff. If only he would go away, forever, she wished, and then smiled at the unlikely possibility.

Later that afternoon Kati was shocked to hear that her most private thoughts had come true.

"He's what?" she exclaimed, unable to believe what Dieter had just said.

"He's dead, Kati. They recovered the car only an hour ago. He was driving on the Moyenne Corniche. They were almost at the entrance to Monte Carlo when they were hit head on. Both Henri-Etienne and his passenger—I don't know which one of the young ladies it was—were pulled from the wreckage."

"Dead," she repeated, still unable to digest the news. Her first thoughts were of Christophe, for as much as she wanted to believe that she no longer cared for him, she still sympathized with the pain he was going to experience. She wanted to run to him and comfort him in his time of confusion and grief. Regardless of how he felt about his business dealings and the tragedy of his mother's death, Henri-Etienne was still his father.

"Yes, it's a pity," Dieter continued. "I suppose everything will fall to Christophe now. What a burden for him."

"Yes," she agreed, but only with his second point. She was not a hypocrite, and would not allow that Henri-Etienne's death constituted a tragedy in her mind. She was only sorry the guests had not first been able to enjoy the sumptuous lunch she had painstakingly prepared for them.

CHAPTER

33

*T*HE HOTEL prospered under Christophe's direction, as he created a camaraderie among the staff that was far more powerful and effective than even generous raises would have been. The Villa Soleil was alive with a revitalized spirit. Guests immediately felt the warm and caring attitude that emanated from every person with whom they came in contact. Kati's respect for Christophe grew daily as she watched him handle his new responsibilities with the skill of a seasoned professional.

His brother Phillippe came from New York for his father's funeral. During his brief stay he had gladly sold his shares of ownership in the hotel to Christophe. He had never had any interest in the business and was happy to be totally out of it forever. So, with the young and dynamic de Beaumont solely in charge, the small resort hidden in the hills became a force to be reckoned with.

In April the prestigious *Michelin Guide* bestowed a second star on the hotel's restaurant. Kati was delighted to have been an instrumental part of the team that achieved this crowning award for superb French cuisine. Chef Muller had kept his promise to her, and she had been promoted to sous-chef only a month after they had made the move. The publicity that the acknowledgment generated boosted the restaurant's business as well as the hotel's. The timing couldn't have been more perfect.

There was a big celebration when the award was announced. Christophe hosted a party for the entire staff. It was a lovely evening, and the employees were enjoying the rare occasion when they were able to act as guests in their own hotel. The band was playing and everyone seemed to be having a wonderful time, when Kati looked over and saw Christophe start to walk in her direction. She began to shake once again, never having gained control over her body at the sight of him. As he got nearer, the trembling increased. He was heading directly toward her.

"Catherine," he began, "I just want to offer my congratulations. I know you had so much to do with our success." He leaned forward to kiss her on both cheeks. His skin against her face made her feel faint. It was the first time he had touched her since the day she left Baden-Baden. Pulling away from her, he stared hard at her, just as he had the one time in her grandfather's office before they had closed the Waldhotel. His eyes searched her face for some sign of a woman he had known before. He and Kati only drew apart when a voice called out to him.

"Christophe, darling," said the beautiful woman who was now by his side. "Christophe, please, there is someone I want you to meet." The woman was probably about Kati's age, maybe a little younger. She was a perfect example of the best the Riviera had to offer: tall and tanned and dressed in a diaphanous sheath of bright yellow silk. Its color only accented the golden tones of her long straight hair. Kati watched as the two of them walked away, arm in arm. She longed to be the woman by his side. Later that evening she had the misfortune of seeing them drive off together in Christophe's new car.

By the beginning of May, when the film festival opened in nearby Cannes, word had spread about the Michelin rating, and the hotel was booked to capacity. Celebrities, film stars, aspiring actors and actresses of every level of talent flocked to the area in hopes of being seen and admired. It was a mad, crazy time, and Kati was thankful for their protected position up on the hill. The traffic in front of the Carlton Hotel on La Croisette was so heavy that it often took hours to travel just a few blocks. Camera crews, the press, fans, and tourists stood for hours hoping to catch a glimpse of their favorite star.

Kati enjoyed the notoriety the restaurant's achievement had brought. Often she was asked to come out from the kitchen to receive the praise of a table that had especially enjoyed their meal.

One night as she walked proudly through the dining room on her way to a table at the far end, her attention was caught by two couples sitting near the window. Later she realized that she had first looked in their direction because of all the noise they were making. In the intimate, formal room their coarse laughter rang out loudly, and some of the other diners stared at them unabashedly, hoping it would curb their rudeness. The two men at the table were responsible for most of the problem. They were both heavyset and looked as if it had been a great effort for them to comply with the restaurant's rule that gentlemen must always wear jackets. They wore large gold rings on their fingers; Kati was certain that hidden underneath their shirts were heavy gold chains. One of the men was beginning to go bald. In a vain and unsuccessful attempt to cover his shining skin, he had combed his hair upward from his neck and wrapped it around his entire head. The women outdid the men in their display of bad taste. One of them was dressed in a fire-engine-red sequin dress. She had long red nails and a jewelry store's worth of trinkets on her neck, wrists, and fingers. Not one potential limb or digit was left unadorned. The jewels were large and gaudy—lots of gold sprinkled with diamonds. Kati was prepared to write them off as just another group of Hollywood's finest—until she heard the voice of the other woman. Her back was to Kati, but as she passed, she heard the unmistakable sound of her sister's voice. Of course it was Eva-Maria. There could be no mistaking her heavily accented English. The girls had studied English in school together, and their intonations and inflections were almost identical when they spoke. Kati was so astounded by her discovery that she called out "Eva-Maria" even before she had a chance to think about what she was doing.

Eva-Maria was equally surprised. She swung her head around and met her sister's eyes. Kati wore a simple black dress under her long white apron, which, by this time of the evening, was usually spotted and stained. Eva-Maria examined Kati from head to toe. It had been such a long time. After the accident Eva-Maria had come once to the hospital. Sylvie Lazare had contacted her and implored her to visit her sister. She pointed out to her that Kati had no one else in the world besides her, and wouldn't it be nice if she could find an hour to spare? Eva-Maria had sat in Kati's small room, looking uncomfortable. "Hospitals make me sick," she had said. Kati was far too frightened by what was happening to her to appreciate the humor of the remark. Eva-Maria then said something about going out of town with Peter for a month. Kati had felt that it was merely an excuse so that she would not have to visit again. After that Kati had only gone once more to the house on Avenue Foch. It was at the time when she had almost completed her treatments. They had talked for a while, not about anything important. Kati had played with Petra for a few minutes, and then she had left. It was the last time they had seen each other. Until this very moment.

"Why, Kati, whatever are you doing here?" Eva-Maria cried.

"I work here," was Kati's simple reply.

A long silence hung in the air while the others at the table stared at Kati as if she were a creature from outer space. Their eyes wandered back and forth from sister to sister, wondering what would happen next. All Kati wanted to do was leave the table gracefully and quietly, without having to answer any more questions, or speak another word to her sister. But it was not to be that simple.

Eva-Maria must have realized how awkward everyone felt, so she tried to make amends. "Everyone," she said, waving her bejeweled, manicured hand in Kati's direction. "I would like you all to meet my sister, the chef," she added, feeling a need to explain Kati's outfit. "Kati, this is . . ." Kati didn't quite catch the name of the other couple. "And my husband, Charles Palmer." Charles rose slightly, along with the other man. Kati was certain she could hear the clink of their gold chains under their polyester shirts. A husband? Charles Palmer? Charles Palmer the film director? Yes, it must be him. That explained why they were here tonight. At last Eva-Maria had convinced someone to marry her. Kati wondered what had finally persuaded Eva-Maria to leave Peter and she hoped that this man had had the decency to adopt Petra, giving the poor child legitimacy at last. What had happened to Peter?

Kati knew full well she should make her apologies and hurry off to the table that was patiently waiting for her, but she couldn't resist finding out just a little more about all of the changes in Eva-Maria's life.

"It's nice to meet all of you," she said. "I suppose you're here for the festival."

"Of course," Eva-Maria answered. "Haven't you been away from the stove long enough to read the papers? Charles's latest film has been nominated for an award. We're all certain he's going to win, aren't we, darling?" She ran her hand down the side of his bloated cheek.

"That's wonderful," Kati offered. No, she certainly hadn't read his name anywhere. The big American movies that year were *The Godfather II* and *Jaws*. She didn't remember reading anything about Charles Palmer. "I wish you the best of luck. How long will you be staying?"

"Oh, just for a week," the eminently offensive Mr. Palmer answered. "Then I'm going to take your gorgeous sister down to Italy for a few days, before we return to California. Got to get back to L.A., you know, deals to make, movies to shoot."

"Yes, yes, I understand," commented Kati, shocked at the fact that not only had her sister left Peter, but she had moved to Los Angeles as well. She wondered if she had had any more children, but didn't inquire. It was time for her to say good night. "Well, I hope you've enjoyed your meal with us," she said.

"We sure have," the group answered in unison. All except for the other woman, who was reapplying her face powder and bright pink lipstick and looking anxiously around the restaurant, loathe to miss an important arrival.

"That's lovely. Well, I must be going. . . ."

Kati was just finishing her sentence when she heard his voice from behind her.

"Good evening, Mr. Palmer. Welcome to the Villa Soleil."

It was Christophe. He was also making his nightly rounds of the restaurant. Many important members of the film community were dining with them tonight, and he wanted to be certain he didn't miss any of them. "I hope you've enjoyed your meal," he continued. They all nodded their heads enthusiastically. The other man rubbed his fat stomach. Kati wanted to disappear, to slide into the floor, anything. She had to leave the table now.

Christophe's hand reached up and patted her affectionately on the back. "I see you've had the pleasure of meeting our sous-chef, Mademoiselle Olivier. It's really Catherine who is responsible for most of this superb cooking."

Kati just wanted to smile and leave the table quickly before another word could be said. She looked directly at her sister. Her eyes begged her not to say a word. But it was too late. The damage had been done, and Eva-Maria could not let it lie.

"*Mademoiselle Olivier?*" Eva-Maria asked, pointing her finger at the shocked Kati. "What do you mean, Catherine Olivier? This woman's name is Kati, Katharina Becker-Meier. I should know, she's my sister."

Christophe turned to her. They were only inches apart, standing side by side in the crowded, noisy restaurant. But he looked at her so intensely it was as if they were alone in the universe. In that split second all the doubts he had harbored about this woman, all the uncertainty he had felt, the gnawing feeling that he had known her before, disappeared. The realization was stunning in its clarity. He had watched the beautiful girl at work from a distance, admiring her dedication and devotion to the hotel. Each time he tried to speak with her, she had run from him as quickly as possible. After he had convinced himself that it was only an illusion that he had known her before, he decided that she was just terribly shy, though he couldn't help feeling drawn to her. Now, in this moment of painful recognition, he hated himself for not having confronted her long ago.

Her secret had been revealed. Kati turned once again to Eva-Maria. She no longer saw the sister she had once known. The last vestiges of the love she had felt for her withered and died as she finally acknowledged that Eva-Maria could only hurt her. Kati had tried to be a sister to her, to patch up their family differences, to ask so little in return. But now she truly saw the woman for what she had become and for what she had been for a very long time.

After that harsh realization, there was nothing more she could do. Kati stared back at Christophe for a moment longer and then she fled the room. She ran so fast toward the back door that she almost knocked a waiter over as well as a stationary food-service tray. She ran through the kitchen and out into the warm spring air. She breathed quickly and deeply, unable to get enough oxygen into her lungs. She felt as if she was choking, suffocating from the realization of what had just occurred. Damn Eva-Maria! Damn her for not having the decency to keep her mouth shut. She had been so happy, so satisfied with the simple life she had been able to carve out from all the tragedies that had befallen her. She was so glad to be at the Villa Soleil. She had Dieter, her dearest friend, and she had her work. Now she had nothing left but the shame of the lie she had created.

Finally her tears came. She allowed them to flow, for she was alone now and much too upset to hold them back. She kept walking, past the pool and the beautifully landscaped, fragrant gardens, until she reached the end of the terrace. An ancient stone wall, about three feet high, served as both a place for lovers to sit and view the coastline and as a guardrail to protect unsuspecting guests from falling into the deep ravine below. It was from some point along this wall that Dominique Robillard had jumped to her death. Now Kati sat on the wall, looking out at the thousands of tiny sparkling lights of Cannes and beyond. The fog-free harbor was illuminated with the beacons of hundreds of yachts, and occasionally she thought she could hear the sound of music or laughter emanating from one of the majestic boats. She stared out at the water, her tear-filled eyes blurring the images. She blinked several times and tried to bring the coastline into focus. The mild breezes surrounded her, the moist night air comforted her in her moment of abject despair.

"Kati, why didn't you tell me? Why didn't you just come to me when you returned to Baden-Baden? You know I would have welcomed you. You didn't have to sneak into your own hotel through the back door."

The sound of his voice only upset her more. Once again she began to tremble. She remembered all the wonderful times they had shared, the long walks, the talks they had about so many things—the future, the hotels they would run, the children they would have together. She had trusted him so, had wanted to be his friend, be his lover. When she had needed it the most, he had been a dream come true for her, until the nightmare began. Her crying continued and her shoulders shook with her sobs.

Finally she was able to speak, but her back remained to him.

"How could I? How could I have come to you? The Waldhotel isn't mine anymore. I just wanted to be there, to be near the only home I had ever known. I was so lonely, I didn't know what else to do. I also remember that you came to the Waldhotel for the first time under a different name," she added.

"Oh, Kati, my poor darling. How could you stand it? The hotel, your mother, your accident, and now this charade you felt you had to carry on."

She could feel him moving closer to her.

"How did you know about the accident?" she asked, amazed that he had somehow heard about it.

"Dieter told me. At first he didn't want to. I had to beg him to let me know how you were doing. Kati, I never stopped wishing things could have been different for us. I never stopped loving you."

He dared not touch her yet, for he realized this moment might be his only chance to win her back. Now was his opportunity to tell her how he felt.

"I'm sorry too," she sighed softly.

Suddenly his emotions overtook his desire to restrain himself, to move slowly with this woman he had loved for so long.

"Kati," he cried, touching the back of her shoulders lightly with his hands. His hand sent shock waves all the way through her. "Kati, things can be different, I promise. I know you can never forgive me for what my father did, but you must believe I knew nothing about it. Nothing at all. I couldn't forgive him for many things he did to me. Buying the Waldhotel was only one of them. The only regret I have about his death is that we didn't resolve any of those problems before he died. I'm not sure that even if he had lived a thousand years, we could have been friends, but I was willing to try. Now it's too late. Sometimes I think it was a blessing. He had done so many terrible things in his life, had caused many people so much misery. Nothing he did, except for what happened to my mother, was as terrible as what he did to your family. I hated him for it. I hated him because he took you away from me just when we were beginning a life together. Oh, Kati, I love you so much. I've loved you since the minute I first saw you when I arrived from Lausanne. Not a day passed after you left that I didn't think of you. I was devastated when my letters to you were returned unopened. I never walked by the river again after you left. I went out of my way to avoid going there, and to all those places we used to go at night after we'd put in such a grueling day. It was too painful for me to relive those memories. Please say you'll stay with me now. Now that I've found you, I can't ever lose you again. Kati, please turn around and look at me," he implored.

Kati hung on every word he said. She believed he was telling the truth. There was nothing now that he could possibly want from her. Except her love. The love that she had closeted inside her, deep within her most private self. She had watched him from a distance for so long, desperately wanting him without ever being able to admit it—even to herself.

Her crying subsided and at last she turned her reddened, tear-stained face to him. He looked at her in a way that told her it didn't matter to him that she no longer possessed the extraordinary physical beauty she had had when they had first met. She smiled the same warm smile he had fallen in love with, a reflection of the beauty within her, a beauty that remained unchanged despite all the tragedy she had suffered, a beauty that was more touching than ever before.

Suddenly she was in his arms, his strong, powerful arms that she had dreamed about so often. He enveloped her and comforted her, telling her in a continuous whisper how much he loved her and needed her. They stood for a long time, wrapped in each other, neither of them wanting to break the embrace they had each desired for such a long time.

"Oh, Christophe, I love you," she said at last, acknowledging the emotion she had felt for precisely the same amount of time as he. It was almost a physical release to finally tell him, to speak so honestly about her feelings. She looked up at him, his face lightened by the reflection of the full moon. "How did we let this happen?" she implored.

"I don't know. I'll never understand why. I know why you felt the way you did. I can't blame you for that. There was no reason for you to believe me. Except that I was telling the truth. I never once lied to you. Maybe there was no other way for us to finally be together. Maybe all the suffering will only make our love stronger. All we have to worry about now is making up for lost time." He took her in his arms again and covered her mouth with his. His kisses were laced with a passion she had never before experienced. At that moment she wanted to join with him, to give him everything her enormous heart had to offer.

They walked slowly, arms wrapped about each other's waists, toward Christophe's bastide on the hill.

By the time they arrived at the front door of the villa called Ma Joie, they were beside themselves with desire. Christophe fumbled in his pockets for the keys like a schoolboy.

"*Ma joie*—that's what you are to me, Kati, the joy of my life. I'm never going to let you go." They embraced again. He refused to remove his mouth from hers as they passed through the open door.

All at once Kati realized that she was still dressed in her dirty apron with her plain black dress underneath. She began to giggle.

"What are you laughing about, my love?"

"My costume," she said. "It's not exactly the type of outfit I had in mind for an occasion like this."

"Kati," he said, once again taking her in his arms. "I wouldn't care if you were dressed in a sack. I might love you even more, if that's possible." He began kissing her again, kisses that even in her excitement felt familiar after all this time.

The nearness of him was intoxicating. She wanted him to make love to her. For the first time she wanted to give herself completely. She stared up at him, begging him to take her to his bed. He answered her prayers. Slowly he helped her shed her clothes. Once she was naked and lying in his bed, he removed the rest of his things and went to lie down beside her.

"Kati, you are more beautiful than I even imagined. I've waited so long for you." He stroked her hair and shoulders lightly.

Suddenly her thoughts went back in time to the horrible experience in Paris. She sat up in the bed, frightened by her memories and terrified that she might not be able to continue. "Christophe, please, be gentle," she begged him. "I . . . I . . . ," but she could say no more before his fingertips touched her lips and silenced her.

He handled her as if she were a precious jewel. Slowly he explored every inch of her luminous skin. Her shoulders, the gentle slope of her neck, the delicate indentation of her throat. He cupped his hands lightly around her breasts, teasing her tender nipples until they hardened beneath his fingertips.

The first time he touched her face in an area where the scar tissue remained, she shrunk back and turned her head away from him. It was not only her facial scars but the internal scars she bore as well that troubled her now. For a moment she was back again on the floor of the kitchen in the Pension Grifont; her blouse was torn away and the repulsive man was hovering over her. She closed her eyes and chased the terrible vision away. Her resolve returned, as with one powerful stroke she swept the nightmares to the very back of her mind.

"Kati, please, look at me, and don't be embarrassed. I love you. I love every part of you. Your scars are not ugly to me. I'm only sorry that you ever had to suffer. It must have been terrible for you. I only wish I had been there with you. You'll never experience pain again if I am able to prevent it, I promise. Now, please, look at me, lovely one."

She turned her face to him, anxious and hungry and desirous for his touch.

He stroked her and fondled her for what seemed like hours. When she finally relaxed enough to part her legs for him, he entered her slowly. She raised herself up to him, tentatively at first, and then more forcefully.

"Slowly, my love," he cautioned. "We have all the time in the world now. I'll be gentle. I never want to hurt you." Movement by movement he opened her.

Finally she was able to accept all of him. He struggled to hold back his urgent need to climax as he waited for her rhythm to build. At last her movements grew to a frenzied pitch and she threw her head back, moving it from side to side, savoring the experience. So pleased was he to be giving her such happiness that he was able to stop his own pleasure from exploding until the very last seconds of her joy. Then he climaxed with the force of a rocket, pouring his warmth into her with a ferocity he had never before experienced.

"I love you, Kati," he said once more, when his heartbeat had slowed and he had regained his breath. He held her in his arms and brushed away the tiny beads of perspiration from her forehead.

"And I love you, Christophe," she whispered, still elated by the blissfulness of their first experience together. "So very much."

Minutes later they were both wide awake again, their mouths hungry for each other.

"Come," he said, "let's go out on the terrace." They took a light blanket to cover their nakedness. Wrapped in each other, they began to talk about all that had happened since they were last together. For the first time, Christophe spoke of his mother's death.

"Kati, I fought coming back here because of the horrible memories I had of this place. At first after my mother died, I grew to hate her. I just couldn't understand how she could desert Phillippe and me. I hated her for leaving us alone to grow up by ourselves. I could never see how someone could become so dependent upon another human being. So dependent that they could give up their life for them. Then, as I grew older, I began to see the kind of man my father really was. Slowly I understood how she could be driven to do such a horrible thing."

Kati listened patiently, realizing how important it was for her to hear all he had to say.

"When I met you, it was the first time I really wanted to allow anyone to be close to me, to know my secrets. I wanted you to know them because you were so strong, so independent. You had goals that were important to you. You knew exactly what you wanted to do with your life. I watched you struggle every day at the hotel, I saw how you continued against all odds to succeed in restoring the Wald-hotel to its former self. You were determined to do it no matter what."

As he continued to speak, Kati realized how much they had in common. They had both been born into the wonderful, yet challenging world of hotels. They had shared so many of the worst tragedies life had to offer. Christophe had endured his mother's suicide, Kati her father's. Kati had learned to live with the fact that her sister wanted nothing to do with her family. Christophe lived with a similar feeling about his brother, Phillippe.

Their outpouring of emotions drained them.

"Let's go back to bed," she suggested when Christophe's head grew heavy against her shoulder.

The minute they were next to each other, their bodies pressed tightly together under the light covers, their passion for each other rose again. This time when they made love, Christophe was able to be even more patient.

"I need you, my love, I need you so much," he said as he held her and rocked her in his arms until she began to melt into him.

Then Christophe began his exploration of her body, slowly, as if he was touching her for the first time. His hands retraced their earlier steps, once again making her flesh quiver with anticipation. Kati lay on her back while his fingers explored every part of her. She moaned softly and thrust herself up to him. She urged him to enter her, but he was determined to pleasure her completely.

"Please," she cried out, but he continued his exploration. Finally she could stand it no longer. She abandoned herself completely. She arched her body up, her legs wrapped tightly about him. She was begging him to please her in a manner she had only dared to dream of. Her head fell back in exquisite pleasure and she allowed him to take her, to know her deepest desires.

"Christophe," she cried. "Yes, yes, please, my love," she urged him, "I've never felt like this before." His smiling face looked up at her, showing her the happiness she gave him. His enjoyment was heightened when he saw her experience such ecstasy.

Minutes later she turned to him, a mischievous smile on her face. Slowly and cautiously she lowered her fingers around him. His desire for her remained, magnified by the feelings she had shown. She explored his most intimate parts, stroking every inch of his lovely skin with a delicacy that conveyed her love for him. The gentle urging of his hand on the back of her neck gave her the confidence she needed. Her mouth surrounded him. He responded tenderly and frantically, all at once. He thrust himself up to her as she had earlier to him. Finally he could stand it no longer. He raised himself up on his hands and pushed her shoulders away. Gently he turned her on her back. She submitted to his wishes, wanting nothing more than to feel the warmth of his explosion again. Her wish was granted seconds later, for he could wait no longer. He collapsed next to her, holding her tightly against his chest.

Their eyes had been shut for less than an hour when the sunlight poured through the windows. The lace curtains cast shadows of tracery on the muted yellow walls of his apartment.

"I'm afraid to get up," she whispered. "I don't want this to end. It's such a beautiful dream."

"It's not a dream, my love. It's going to be the way our life is from now on. We're going to make love constantly, endlessly. In every location, in every spot we think might be fun. Oh, Kati, it's going to be wonderful."

"What about work?" she inquired.

"Work? We'll fit a little work in when we're not making love. One or two hours a day, at most. I don't want us to become tired."

She laughed and turned over in the bed. The clock indicated it was already after nine. "What about the vegetables?" she cried. "All of the good stuff will be gone, the tomatoes picked over, the berries bruised. I must get down to the market immediately."

"Don't be silly," he calmed her. "You're the lover, and soon to be the wife, I hope, of the owner of this place. The sole owner. No longer will you be shopping for the vegetables. We'll send someone down to get everything you need."

She smiled at this thought. More than anything she wanted to make certain she had heard him correctly. "Christophe de Beaumont, was that your way of proposing to me?"

"Yes, it was. I could make it more formal if you like. How about tonight at dinner?" he suggested, kissing the top of her head. Despite his comforting words, she was still very self-conscious about her scars. He tried to avoid touching the areas that had been damaged the most severely, even as he sensed there were other scars, internal scars that she wouldn't speak of yet. It would take time, he knew, but he vowed to help her heal in every way possible.

"I accept your offer."

"For dinner or for marriage?" he asked.

"Oh, no, it's not going to be that easy. At this point it's dinner only. I have to think about the other."

"For how long?"

"Just until dessert," she said, grinning from beneath the sheets.

CHAPTER
34

ON THE DAY of the wedding they were blessed with the most glorious weather. The wind blew gently across the area by the pool where tables had been set up for the luncheon reception. The temperature reached perfection in the early afternoon, just as the first guests started to arrive. It was a small gathering of only their closest friends. Heidi and Mark came from Munich and celebrated their happiness for Kati and Christophe by staying at the Villa Soleil for a week. Jean-Louis and his wife sent their best wishes, but were unable to come because Clothilde had just given birth to their first child. Sylvie arrived on the morning of the ceremony, delighted to be sharing in the celebration.

"You have no idea how happy I am to see you," Kati said as she drove back from the airport with her. "Ever since, well, you know, ever since my mother died, you've been the closest thing to a mother I've had. I'm so glad you could come." Many were the times over the past few weeks that Kati had longed to have her mother by her side. As she planned the details of her wedding day, she missed sharing the experience with her. At least Heidi had arrived in time to help her make some of the last-minute decisions. "Pink or white napkins?" Kati would ask her best childhood friend as if it was the most crucial thing in the world. "Oh, I don't know, why not the white?" Then they would giggle like schoolgirls, for reasons neither of them could explain.

Tears filled the kind woman's eyes. "Kati, I wouldn't have missed it for the world. You have been like a daughter to me. For a long time, I even dreamed that you might become my daughter-in-law. But it looks as if everything has turned out best for everybody. You're going to like Clothilde. She's a wonderful girl. She makes Jean-Louis very happy. And now, to think I became a grandmother last week. Oh, how the time does pass."

. . .

Kati left Sylvie in her room and went to prepare for the ceremony. She had selected a lovely white cotton dress. It was simple and elegant, and its full skirt would move gently and gracefully in the wind.

"You look beautiful," Heidi told her. "No matter what, a bride doesn't feel like a bride until she puts her dress on. I remember my wedding. Until I put that gown over my head I was just one of the spectators. But the minute I was dressed, I really felt special. Don't you feel the same way?" she asked her best friend.

Kati had to admit she did. It was really her day.

Heidi helped her secure the crown of tiny Provençal flowers she wore in her hair. They finished her makeup and walked slowly down the hill together.

Dieter walked Kati through the long hallway to the terrace, where the guests were gathered.

"I've waited a long time for today," he said, holding her elbow firmly. Kati shook with anticipation. She turned and smiled at him. They could see Christophe standing on the terrace at the end of the long corridor. His face lit up when he saw her. "Kati, I wish you every happiness," Dieter said. She kissed him on the cheek and gave him a hug that told him how much she loved him. As they neared Christophe, Dieter released his arm from hers and offered her to the young man of whom he had grown so fond. No one was more pleased for the couple than he.

They stood together at the edge of the terrace. The air was so clear that they could see all the way to Nice in the northeast, and to the southwest as far as Cannes. The sea was the azure color described in countless poems and captured by thousands of artists over the centuries. The air was fragrant with the intoxicating scent of mimosa.

The mayor of the village, another old family friend, began to speak. Kati had written a good portion of the service. He spoke first of suffering and of life's many struggles. He spoke of honesty and moral goodness. He talked of the couple's unfolding and unending love for each other. When he began to speak about the merging of their families and their histories, Kati turned to Christophe, her eyes wet with the implication of what he was saying. They had endured so much, both together and alone. Surely this day was the culmination of their experiences and the beginning of a new life.

Before he placed the narrow wedding band on her finger, Christophe took her hands in his and recited a short verse by Frédéric Mistral, the region's beloved poet. The poem said eloquently that the three ingredients of love were simplicity, truth, and fidelity.

"These three things I promise you, Kati," he said, giving her the golden token of their precious union.

Kati and Christophe continued to stand side by side on the terrace after the short ceremony. "You have never looked more beautiful," Christophe told her. "And I have never loved you more."

"It's the happiest day of my life," she answered, hoping that the peace and contentment she had known since that night after the scene in the restaurant would continue forever.

Originally they had planned to wait until the fall to be married. July and August were the hotel's busiest months, when the hotel carried a waiting list pages long. But almost immediately after setting a date in late October, they had become impatient and moved it up. There would not be time for a honeymoon now, but Kati didn't object. "I feel as if I'm on a honeymoon every day here. Besides, where else could we go where we'd get such great service?" she had asked.

She was right. Everyone on the staff had been delighted with the new romance. They had begun to treat her as the fiancée of the owner rather than the sous-chef. "Don't do that," she would insist when someone gave her deferential treatment. "I'm still an employee here, you know!" But there were changes, all of them for the better. They moved into one of the largest bastides. The view from their terrace overlooking the entire valley was breathtaking. Every night before they went to bed, they would sit outside, taking in its magnificence. Often they would end up making love on one of the wide chaise longues. Sometimes they would awaken there the following morning, wrapped only in a thin blanket, and each other.

Their guests celebrated with fine champagne and a delicious lunch of *loup de mer* followed by the traditional wedding cake. It was a perfect afternoon. As the sun set behind the hills in back of the hotel and the light shifted every few minutes, changing the color of the entire countryside, Kati felt that all was right in her world. She had married a man she loved more than life itself. Because of all they had shared in the past, she was certain that their bond of marriage could withstand anything they could be faced with in the years ahead.

CHAPTER
35

"$\mathcal{A}$REN'T THEY BEAUTIFUL, Madame de Beaumont?" asked the delivery boy as he showed her the order of fish he had brought that morning for the restaurant. He was the youngest son of a local fisherman from whom they bought most of their fish. He had laid them all out on a large table, lined up like little soldiers waiting for her inspection, beginning with the large turbots and on down to the tiny rougets at the far end.

"Here are some of the finest snappers we've seen this season. Look how firm they are. Their eyes are still bright and shiny, as if they were still alive," he commented proudly, turning a large one over in his hand. He handled them as if they were objects of gold.

"Yes, they are," she agreed. "Fine, they'll be just—" was all she could get out before the nausea overtook her and she was forced to flee from the kitchen to the small bathroom down the hall. She reached the sink just in the nick of time. The young delivery boy stood staring after her, baffled as to what he had done that could cause such a violent reaction to his beautiful display.

It was the third time this week she had been ill. The fish had really done it to her. She couldn't stand the sight of them. Looking at any food so early in the morning just wasn't possible right now.

She stayed away from the kitchen for two days, claiming she had a tremendous backup of paperwork that needed to be attended to. On the afternoon of the third day, she drove into Vence.

Her doctor confirmed the suspicions she had harbored for a month.

"Yes, I would say that around the middle of May there will be a new addition to the de Beaumont family," said Dr. Lascelles. He was a delightful, ruddy-faced old gentleman who had delivered both of the de Beaumont boys. He had hardly been able to offer his congratulations before she jumped from her chair in his office and threw her arms around his neck.

Never was there a happier moment in her life. She couldn't wait a minute longer to share her news with Christophe. She started back to the hotel at breakneck speed and then suddenly came to her senses and slowed down, not wishing for one second to endanger the life of the baby she now carried. The baby who was more precious to her than anything in the world.

Arriving at the hotel, she sped under the canopy and jumped from the car with the engine still running. "Please put the car away, Louis," she yelled to the astonished valet. This kind of behavior was most unlike Madame de Beaumont. Usually she was reserved and calm. Always polite, but never in such a rush as today. Something important must have happened, he thought.

Christophe sat at his desk, as usual buried behind a stack of papers. The sight of his lovely wife standing in his office made him smile with joy. She never failed to delight him with her mere presence. Then he realized she looked a bit disheveled and that she was out of breath.

"Kati, what's wrong?" he asked, his face showing immediate concern that something was the matter with the woman he loved so very much.

"Nothing's wrong," she said, suddenly realizing she hadn't even stopped to comb her hair. It must look very wild from the fast ride in the convertible, she thought. But she didn't care. She was too happy to bother about something as meaningless as her appearance. Right now the only thing in the world that she cared about was sharing the most important news of her life with her husband. "Nothing's wrong at all," she repeated, walking around to the side of the desk. "In fact, things have never been better."

"That's a good report," he said, swinging around in his swivel chair and rising to greet his wife. "What makes this particular day so terrific?" he asked, reaching out and pulling her toward him so that he could kiss her.

"Well, it's not every day I can tell you you're going to be a father," she said, unable to contain her news for a split second longer.

"Kati," he cried out. "Kati, is it true?"

"Yes, it is," she said, giggling like a schoolgirl.

He hugged her tightly, never wanting to let her go. She wrapped her arms around his neck and then slowly slid them down his back.

Her first indication that he was crying was when she felt the convulsive movements against her hands.

She pulled away from him. He turned his face downward. She reached under his chin and lifted his face to hers. Tears were streaming down his cheeks. It was the first time she had ever seen him cry.

"Oh, Christophe, you're not unhappy, are you?" There had been so many disappointments in her life that she was conditioned always to expect the worst.

"Oh, no my love. Of course I'm not unhappy. It's just the opposite. You're going to give me the most valuable gift I could ever have. I'm ecstatic." His tears stopped almost at once, chasing every possibility of gloom from her mind. As they kissed, her only thoughts now were of how she could make the next seven months pass quickly.

She really needn't have worried, for the mild Provençal winter sailed by. Even the famous mistral winds, which could be bothersome and grating on one's nerves, seemed to be less formidable this season.

Her nausea subsided, and once again she was back in the kitchen shortly after daybreak. Her complexion blossomed. Not since long before the accident had her skin looked so glowing and healthy. Her appetite soared, and she embraced her pregnancy with stamina and grace. She kept up a strenuous exercise program, swimming and playing tennis as often as she could. Christophe was constantly cautioning her to slow down, but she saw no reason to treat her condition as anything but a normal, delightful part of being a woman. Eva-Maria had once told her that when she was carrying Petra, she had spent the first three and the last two months in bed, completely miserable. Kati couldn't help suspecting that one's disposition might have a great deal to do with how smoothly the nine months could pass.

Edouard Karl de Beaumont arrived on a rare rainy day in late May. On the way to the hospital, watching the wetness run down the car windows as Christophe drove and she timed her contractions, Kati hoped that the weather didn't portend badly for her child. But after Kati had been in labor for only three hours, the proud doctor, who could now claim responsibility for bringing two generations of de Beaumonts into the world, held the bright red, screaming little boy up for his mother to see.

"Just as ornery and noisy as his father and uncle," he proclaimed.

"He's healthy, and he's beautiful, having inherited the good looks of his mother," Christophe told her as she gently held the sleeping newborn in her arms.

"I'm not going to accept that opinion," she said. "I'm going to wait and see how he turns out. It's really not fair to judge the poor little thing. He's still so new. Let's wait for a couple of days before deciding what we've got here." He knew she was only joking but had to admit secretly to himself that it was going to take a few days for him to take shape. Right now, when he stood looking through the windows in the nursery at the newborns, they all did look very much the same. His son, however, was distinguishable by his healthy quantity of dark, curly hair. It wasn't wispy or stringy like some of the others. Christophe stroked the top of his heavy mane of thick hair. Yes, maybe he could take credit for that feature of this wonderful little creature.

Two days later all three of them sat in the backseat of the Rolls as their new driver Jules drove them back to the hotel. The front seat was piled high with flowers and presents for the mother and the new addition.

"Jules, you can speed up a little. He's not going to break if you hit a bump. I've got him well under control back here," Kati said to the cautious driver. He had traveled at no more than twenty miles an hour since they had pulled out from the hospital's driveway. At this rate, she would have to feed the baby again in the car.

"I'm sorry, Madame de Beaumont. I'm very nervous. I've never carried a child in the car before. I would never forgive myself if something happened to him."

"The only thing that will happen is that you are going to be arrested for driving like an old man," she joked, touched by his concern for their son.

Finally they reached the winding road leading up to the Villa Soleil. Jules never really did push the car to a decent speed. It had taken almost twice the normal time, but she didn't feel comfortable mentioning it again. She was just grateful that they were home at last.

The first thing she noticed when they made the turn into the driveway was the canopy over the front door. It was completely covered with flowers. Not an inch of fabric peeked through from underneath the blanket of color. There were literally thousands of blooms—roses, carnations, violets, marguerites, hyacinth, daffodils, iris, chrysanthemums—all of the glories of the region. It was so festive, so colorful. Christophe smiled when he saw how her face lit up.

"Oh, Christophe, what a glorious idea. What a way to welcome our son home," she cried in delight.

"It's really for his mother," he said. "I think it will be awhile before he appreciates this. Right now, it appears that all he wants to do is eat." Edouard had opened his hungry mouth like a baby bird. He was beginning to scream, using the only method available to him at the moment to communicate his desires.

"You're a hopeless romantic," she told Christophe, "and I love you!"

The canopy was only the tip of the iceberg, for as they drove under the awning, she saw that the entire staff had put on their best uniforms and had gathered together to offer their welcome. About a hundred employees stood side by side and as the car came into view, they began to cheer and wave.

Kati's eyes brimmed with tears. She turned to Christophe, who was smiling, bursting with pride as he was about to show his new offspring to his extended family for the very first time.

Alone in the hospital the night before, Kati had suddenly felt very depressed. Her first son had been born, and there was not one member of her family to share the occasion with her. She was saddened by the fact that Edouard would grow up without ever having the joy of knowing a grandparent. He would be deprived of that special relationship that Kati had treasured so dearly. She allowed herself to feel a certain remorse for the things that had happened in her life, but she put those feelings aside when they had brought the baby back to her for another feeding. Holding him in her arms, feeling his hungry mouth against her breast, was the most wonderful sensation.

Looking down at him now, she was content with the fact that he was blessed with two parents who loved him more than anything in the world. Christophe, Kati, and the baby represented a new beginning. A new generation had been born into the world because of their wonderful union. Maybe he would become a hotelier, maybe not. It really didn't matter to her. As long as he was healthy and happy.

As she looked out of the car window and saw the many people gathered in front of the hotel, their faces full of love for this young being, she felt certain that he was going to grow up in a warm, loving environment, always surrounded by those who cared about him and his well-being. The two-day-old Edouard must have felt it also, for suddenly his crying ceased, and he fell fast asleep, cradled in his mother's arms.

CHAPTER

36

$\mathcal{E}$DOUARD was a delightful child. He rarely cried or was cranky and was content to play alone for long periods of time, fascinated by the colorful mobile suspended above his crib. He would reach up toward it with his chubby fists and try to pull it down. It remained just beyond his grasp, but instead of growing frustrated he would simply laugh and try again.

The sound of his laughter pleased Kati more than anything she had ever known. Her only regret was that she could not spend twenty-four hours a day with him.

"Go on now, Kati," Margarethe would urge her each morning. Once again the devoted nanny had outgrown the family she had gone to live with after she left the Waldhotel, so when she received word of Kati's new baby, Margarethe had written and asked if there was any possibility of coming to work for her. "Nothing would please me more than to come and take care of another generation of your family," she had said in her letter. Kati couldn't believe the good news and she sent word at once asking her to get there as soon as possible. Everyone was delighted that Margarethe was part of their lives again.

"Go on now," she would say, scooting Kati out of the child's room. "After he's bathed and powdered, we'll come down the hill for a visit."

Reluctantly Kati would leave the apartment. Once in her office, every few minutes she would look up anxiously toward the door in anticipation of their arrival. Never had she known such pleasure, such love. Both she and Christophe worshiped the adorable child and devoted every spare minute to him. Watching him grow and develop enriched their relationship tremendously.

"You're such a wonderful mother," Christophe would tell her time and time again. "Not such a bad lover either," he would say, leading her toward their bedroom. After Edouard's birth their passion for each other seemed only to increase, and Kati was not surprised in the least to find out in January that she was almost two months pregnant.

Her second pregnancy did not proceed nearly as smoothly as the first. She was constantly sick. Her morning sickness, which she had experienced for no more than two weeks when she was carrying Edouard, lasted almost into the fourth month. She was constantly tired and often disagreeable. As the baby grew, the increased pressure caused her legs to swell. Her back ached so much that she was forced to lie on the floor in her office several times a day in order to help lessen the pain. She regretted having taken the ease of her first pregnancy for granted.

"You're anemic and you must rest more," Dr. Lascelles had cautioned her during an examination. There followed a long lecture about how each pregnancy was different. She couldn't expect to sail through every one as she had the first. She must stop working so hard, for her sake as well as for that of the child. "Now, do you understand, Kati? I'm giving you strict orders to take it easy. I'm going to call Christophe this afternoon just to make sure everyone is aware of the seriousness of this."

"All right, Doctor," she agreed reluctantly. But there was so much to do at the hotel. They were always booked for months in advance, and even though she had hired someone to replace her as sous-chef, the kitchen still greatly depended upon her daily guidance.

"Now, this is serious, Kati," Christophe said that night. They sat out on the terrace, Christophe sipping a glass of wine and Kati drinking a hot cup of herbal tea. "I want you to slow down. I won't have you running yourself down and becoming sick. You're to rest, just as Dr. Lascelles has advised. I couldn't bear it if anything happened to you." He cradled her head in his hands and looked deep and long into her eyes. "Promise me," he insisted.

She saw genuine concern and fear in his kind eyes. "There's nothing wrong with me. I'm just a little tired, that's all," she said.

"Promise me that from this minute on you'll take better care of yourself. Please, Kati. You mean everything to me."

"Okay, I promise. I'll be a model of moderation. In fact, I'll become a veritable princess," she teased. "Then you'll all be sorry for being so overly concerned about me."

"That's just fine with me. As long as you start feeling better. Now, into bed for you. No more staying up to close the restaurant every night."

She was wide awake and felt fine, but she knew better than to fight him. He tucked her in tightly, wrapping the cover gently around her burgeoning stomach. He rubbed his hands lightly over the blanket.

"I'll be back soon, my love. I just have a few things to finish up." He turned the light out and left her alone in the room as she thanked her lucky stars for granting her such a wonderful man.

By the time July arrived, Kati was feeling better, encouraged by the fact that her delivery date was only a month away. She was so anxious to give birth. She had gained much more weight than she had with Edouard, and her face and cheeks wore the awful "mask of pregnancy," the harmless but unattractive shadows caused by the increase of melanin in her system. In addition to being darker than normal, her skin was dry. She applied tons of the richest moisturizers she could find, and only hours later her face was parched again. Every part of her body felt bloated and swollen. The smallest movement was an event. It had been a long, rough ride. She yearned to have her glorious figure back.

She had given up practically all of her responsibilities at the hotel. They were having an especially warm summer and most of her days were spent by the side of the pool with Edouard and Margarethe. Christophe was forced to bear the additional load left by her absence. She felt a tremendous sense of guilt seeing him work such long hours.

"I'll make it up to you," she said one night as he slipped into bed, exhausted after a sixteen-hour day.

"You have nothing to make up to me, my sweet. All I want is a healthy wife and baby," he assured her, leaning over her protruding belly to kiss her good night.

Kati began crossing off the days on her calendar. She couldn't wait now. Seventeen, sixteen, fifteen . . . only two more weeks to go—if the baby was on time. She feared it would be late. The waiting seemed endless. Her temper was short, and she lashed out at Christophe when he announced that he was going on a trip.

"It's only for a few days, Kati. I promise I'll get back on the plane the minute we finish our business. Please don't be upset. You know I wouldn't leave now if it weren't absolutely necessary," he insisted.

But she was too upset to listen. He continued on with the details. Something about Phillippe's business. He had called and pleaded with his brother to come to New York immediately. Christophe had agreed to go.

"I just hope you'll be back before the baby comes," she sobbed. Suddenly she felt so unattractive, so heavy. Her every move was laborious. She longed to be sexy again. To feel her body against her husband's.

"Of course I'll be back before then. Now please, Kati, calm down. I can't stand to see you so upset."

Christophe took the plane to Paris the following morning and connected to the Concorde flight to New York.

Pangs of guilt overtook his thoughts as he ran through Kennedy, barely making his flight to Los Angeles. What if something should happen to her while he was gone? What if the baby came early and he was not there for her? What if he couldn't pull off the plan as he'd hoped to? Then he had risked everything, lying to Kati. And for what? Dieter was the only one with whom he had shared his secret. That fact soothed his mind. If anything happened, Dieter would know what to do. Anyway, he reasoned, he would be back at the hotel in three days. If his plans went according to schedule, these few hours of worry and concern would be well worth it.

Kati thought the days would never pass. Just as she was taking a nap on the afternoon of the second day Christophe had been gone, the phone rang.

"Madame de Beaumont," said the familiar voice of the hotel's general manager, "I'm so sorry to bother you, but I've got a small problem that needs to be solved at once, and Dieter is out of the hotel for the afternoon."

"It's all right," she assured the young man. In a way she was happy to have the distraction. "I'll come down to the office in a few minutes."

"So you see, I need to give them an answer now if the materials are to be delivered on time," the competent manager finally concluded at the end of his long explanation.

He was right. The remodeling of some of the rooms had to be finished in October. It was a question that really only Christophe could answer.

"Don't worry, Roger. I'll call Christophe in New York and see what he wants to do. I'll let you know what he says."

She went to her office and looked up Phillippe's phone number. Figuring that with the time difference they should be waking up about now, she picked up the phone and dialed the number directly. The crackle on the line told her the call had gone through on the first try. On the second ring a woman's voice came on the line.

"Mr. Beaumont's residence," she said cheerily. Phillippe had long ago dropped the "de" from his name.

"Hello, I'm trying to reach Christophe de Beaumont," Kati said.

"I'm sorry, Mr. Beaumont is not here. This is the answering service. May I take a message?"

Quickly Kati checked the clock. It was only seven in the morning in New York. Where could they possibly be at that hour?

"I'm calling long-distance. Could you tell me when they are expected?"

"I'm sorry," the perky voice answered, "Mr. Beaumont is out of the country. He left for Mexico yesterday morning."

"There must be some mistake," Kati insisted. "Isn't Christophe de Beaumont, his brother, staying at the apartment?"

"No, I'm sorry, no one is staying there. We were instructed to take messages. Mr. Beaumont will return next week. Is there a message?"

"No . . . no . . . there's no message," she said. She hung up the phone gently, every ounce of strength drained from her body.

Mexico? Not back until next week? Christophe hadn't mentioned any of that. He said he would be with Phillippe in New York doing business and that then he would return to France on the first plane out after they were finished. Suddenly nothing made sense to her anymore and she became desperately worried. What if he hadn't even gone to New York? What was he up to? Why hadn't he left more information for them? Where was her husband? She sat at the desk for a long time. Her thoughts ran through the entire gamut of possibilities. Christophe was ill and had gone to seek treatment. Something had happened to Phillippe and he had gone to Mexico to help him. He hadn't told her anything for fear that it would upset her. He had gone away with another woman. Yes, that had to be it. If it was anything else, he would have shared it with her. She looked down over her enormous stomach to her swollen ankles. She felt monstrous—fat, and ugly and tired. Of course, he had to get away for a few days. Kati had been awful to live with during the last seven months. She had been sick and irritable. The days she had felt well enough she had spent with Edouard. And she had been absolutely useless at the hotel. She hadn't made any contribution at all. Christophe was forced to do everything. Now he was taking a break, a short interlude with another woman. Who could blame him, she reasoned? All Frenchmen took a mistress sooner or later, didn't they? Wasn't that one of the cornerstones on which their culture was built? Yes, it was only a brief interlude. Surely he still loved her. But telling herself so didn't make her feel any better. Her eyes filled with tears. She closed the door before anyone could see her. She put her head on the desk and allowed herself a good cry. She was still there, her arms wrapped around her head, when Dieter came in almost two hours later.

"Kati, Kati, what's the matter?" he cried out, running around the side of the desk.

She looked up at him, her face still wet from her tears. Seeing him, she realized he was still her dearest friend in the entire world. "Oh, Dieter, I've just made the most horrible discovery."

She proceeded to tell him the whole story. He listened patiently, trying desperately to decide how best to handle the situation. He had questioned Christophe before he left about what to do if they needed to contact him. In fact, he had begged him to postpone the trip for a little while. At least until after the baby came. But Christophe was as stubborn as his father. He had insisted that now was the time to go. If he was right, everything would work out beautifully. After all, it was all for Kati, because he loved her so much. He had assured him that he would only be out of reach for a day and that he would call as soon as he reached Los Angeles. He had sworn Dieter to secrecy. Now, seeing that the unexpected had happened, Dieter wasn't sure that he could keep his promise.

"Oh, Kati, my sweet Kati," Dieter said, putting his arm around her. "It's nothing like that. Christophe is not with another woman. That I can assure you."

She turned her eyes expectantly toward him. Dieter had never lied to her, even on occasions when it would have been the easiest thing to do. Never had he told her something that was not true merely to lessen her pain. Immediately she felt relieved, for she believed him with all her heart. Unless, of course, Christophe had lied to him also. She refused even to entertain that thought. It was too horrible to imagine that he would deceive them both.

"Well, then, what is it? Where could he possibly be if he's not in New York?"

Now Dieter hesitated. Quickly he tried to calculate how long it would be before Christophe would board the airplane home. Geography had never been his strong point, and under pressure he became even more confused. Was it seven hours earlier or later there? And how many more to California? Two or three at this time of year? Oh . . . he couldn't remember. He would just have to go with the original story and hope it would calm her until he returned. He couldn't possibly mention that Christophe had gone to the West Coast, or the entire plan would be ruined. No . . . stick with the original, he thought. Yes . . . that will be the best.

"He is in New York, Kati. And he is with Phillippe. Phillippe has become involved in some funny business deals. That's why Christophe had to go over there. And until things are straightened out, he wants everyone to think that he's out of town. That's all there is to it. I'm sure everything is going to be just fine. It's only going to take a couple of days. Besides, Christophe promised he'd call tonight. Now, please, Kati, don't get all upset over this. It's nothing."

He could tell that she wasn't one hundred percent convinced, but believing him was her best option at this point.

"Oh, Dieter, I hope you're not trying to protect me from the truth. I'd really rather hear it from you. I think I could handle it better. We've been through so much together."

"Kati, you must believe me, you've made yourself crazy over nothing. Nothing at all. Now look at you. You're exhausted. Go up to your room right now and get into bed. I'm going to have your dinner sent up to you."

"You're right," she sighed. She raised her heavy body up from the desk. "I am so glad you came back when you did. I was going mad with worry."

"Everything is going to be fine. Christophe will be back tomorrow night. Now go and get some rest. Right now the only thing that is important is that baby." He patted her stomach and pushed her out the door. "I'll be up later to check on you."

After she left, Dieter sat down in the chair she had vacated. He had been totally unprepared for what had happened. He scolded himself for having left the hotel. If he had stayed here, he could have answered Roger's questions and none of this ever would have happened. How foolish of him. He had been so tempted to tell her the truth. But that would have meant breaking his promise to Christophe. And spoiling his surprise. Dieter was a man of his word, and nothing short of a dire emergency could make him go back on his honor. He only hoped that Christophe's trip was successful and that by keeping his vow he had not endangered the life of Kati or her unborn child.

CHAPTER

37

WHETHER IT WAS because she was so upset by the phone call or because it was simply time, when Kati awoke the next morning, she was in labor. It was only seven A.M. She tried to fall back to sleep, but the second she shut her eyes, the gripping cramps would strike, waking her more fully each time. She continued to lay in bed for a while, timing the contractions with the bedside clock. She sent Margarethe off to tend to Edouard and ignored the several phone messages that had been pushed under the door.

At first she was angry that Christophe was so far away and that she was having to go through this experience all alone. As the contractions came more quickly, fear replaced her feelings of anger. She needed her husband with her. It was her right. He should be there by her side, holding her hand and encouraging her every step of the way. Several times she had expressed her concern that the baby might come while he was away, but he was so convinced that he would be back in time that she had finally allowed him to go. Not that she could have stopped him if she had tried. He insisted that his brother's problems were of the utmost urgency. Now it was too late. Another contraction swept through her body. There was no doubt in her mind that she would give birth today. Alone, without her husband nearby. She picked up the telephone and called Dieter.

"Well, it's you and me again," she said before her breath was taken away by the sharp pain. "Ahhhhhh . . . ," she gasped into the receiver.

"Don't move. I'm on my way," he said in the most comforting voice. "I'll have the car sent up immediately."

When he arrived, she had dressed and packed and was ready to go to the hospital. She took one look at him and began to laugh. The color had drained from his face. He was far more nervous than she. Dieter could handle the pressure of twelve irate guests all banging on his desk in unison, but the thought of Kati having a baby on the way to the hospital was more than he could take.

"Calm down, will you," she said. "We've been through worse things than this together."

He helped her gingerly into the backseat. His hands were shaking as he held her elbow. "You're, you're not going to deliver in the car, are you?" he stuttered, unable to conceal the panic in his voice.

Kati laughed. "Not a chance. I've got a feeling this is going to be a long one. If the delivery is in keeping with the rest of the pregnancy, we could be at the hospital for days before the baby arrives."

"Well, Christophe will be here tonight."

"You spoke to him?" she asked, amazed that it had not been the first thing he mentioned. Suddenly she realized how terrified he really was.

"Yes, he called late last night. I came up to your room to tell you. I even knocked twice, but you were so sound asleep I didn't want to awaken you. He said everything went fine. He was leaving on a flight from New York to Paris. He gets in just in time to make the last connection to Nice. He's scheduled to arrive tonight at five."

"Oh," she commented, both surprised and pleased at the good news. Maybe in the end he wouldn't disappoint her. She was about to ask more questions when another contraction overtook her. Secretly Dieter was pleased that the contraction had come just at that moment. He had been saved further explanation regarding Christophe's whereabouts for the past three days.

Kati's prediction was correct. She spent the entire morning in labor, her body enduring the rise and fall of pain as the slow process continued.

"The first one was so easy," she said to one of the nurses late in the day.

Her face was stained with perspiration. Her beautiful hair hung in wet strands against her cheeks. She was tired and beginning to worry that something might be wrong.

"It's often that way," the efficient woman commented, not showing a great deal of compassion for a scene she witnessed countless times each week.

"No, no, this is a different kind of pain," she insisted. "I think you should call Dr. Lascelles."

"He just left the hospital," the nurse answered. "He said he'd be back in an hour. Now, please, just try to relax." The nurse left the room.

Kati closed her eyes and prayed that the pain would subside. Minutes later it began again. It was unlike anything she had ever endured. The cramps that began in her lower back and uterus traveled up her spine, gripping every inch of her body along the way. She writhed in the bed, turning her head rapidly from side to side. The sheets were soaked with her heavy perspiration. Her mind began playing evil tricks on her. Once again she was at the Waldhotel, standing at the entrance. A car pulled up under the canopy. When the door opened, Christophe stepped out. Christophe. Where was he now? She needed him. But he got back into the car and it drove away before he heard her. She chased the car to the end of the driveway, but she couldn't catch it. Where was he going? She needed him to be with her. "Christophe," she screamed. "Christophe. . ." The door to her room swung open. In rushed a nurse, followed by Dr. Lascelles and Dieter. She recognized them all, but she couldn't recall why they were running in to be with her.

"It's all right, Kati," the doctor said, pulling back the wet covers and grabbing her hand. He stood by her side, trying to take her pulse. "It's all right now, we're here with you. Everything's going to be fine."

They changed her sheets and gave her some medication. Her terrifying hallucinations ceased, and she was once again back in control.

Finally she had dilated sufficiently to be taken into the delivery room. Dieter had stayed with her all afternoon. After the terrible scene he had refused to leave her side. He had held her hand and made small talk with her until they both just looked at each other and laughed. As she looked at him now, he seemed even more drained than she.

The orderlies moved her from her bed to the gurney. "Easy," they cautioned her. "Easy does it, slowly now." Kati continued to moan with pain.

When they were almost halfway down the corridor, she heard

the sound of footsteps running toward them. She was certain she was dreaming again. Then she heard his voice calling out to her.

"Kati, Kati, I'm here, my love," he said as he reached her side. Never had she been happier to see him in her entire life. They stopped the stretcher and allowed him to kiss her.

"Oh, Christophe, I missed you so. I was so worried about you."

"There's nothing to worry about, my love. I'm home now. Everything is fine. Dieter said you tried to reach me and couldn't. I'll explain everything to you later. Right now I think you're going to be busy having our baby. Now, don't worry about a thing," he said, all the while stroking her wet hair gently away from her face. "I'll be right here, waiting for them to bring you back." He kissed her again before she disappeared behind the imposing metal doors.

After seeing Christophe, Kati seemed to be able to tolerate the pain a little better. It was almost as if she was subconsciously waiting from him to arrive before she delivered. Not more than an hour later she gave birth to a nine-pound baby girl.

"Wonderful! About time there was a girl in this family. For too long the de Beaumonts only had boys," the proud Dr. Lascelles announced, as if to imply he had played an integral part in the determination of the sex of their child.

They had agreed long before that if it was a girl, they would name her Claude Dominique, for Christophe's mother. Seeing the infant for the first time, squealing and squirming in Dr. Lascelles's firm grip, all of the trauma of the last nine months was immediately erased from Kati's memory.

Christophe was not there when they wheeled her back into the room.

"Where is my husband?" Kati demanded of one of the nurses.

"I don't know, Madame de Beaumont. He must have gone down the hall for a moment. I'll try to find him and let him know that you're back."

"Yes, please do that. Thank you. I want to see him now."

"Of course," she said, disappearing into the corridor.

It seemed to Kati as if she was alone in the room for a long time. But her sense of time was distorted after the ordeal of such a long labor. It was probably no more than five minutes.

Long before she saw them, she was aware of their presence in the room. Their unmistakable fragrance filled the air. Finally she spotted them. An enormous bouquet of spring flowers had arrived while she was in the delivery room. Marigolds, zinnias, peonies, delphiniums, and ox-eye daisies, and of course the beautiful dahlias—all of the flowers that used to grow in the garden at the Waldhotel. Whoever had brought them had placed them on top of a dresser against the far wall. There were dozens of them, and each one was a more vibrant, beautiful color than the other. She thought she recognized the brightly colored ribbons wrapped around the neck of the vase. Sonja Fichtl's trademark. No, it couldn't be. Why would she have flowers here from Baden-Baden? Attached to the ribbon tied at the neck of the crystal vase was a small package. Kati strained her eyes to see what it contained, but the bouquet was too far away for her to see it clearly. She lifted her head and tried to sit up, but not an ounce of energy remained in her body.

At that very moment Christophe entered. His smile told her he had seen their daughter.

"She's beautiful, Kati," he beamed. "Was she worth all the trouble she gave you?"

"Every minute of it," she said, holding her weakened arms out to him. "If that's the worst of it, we're in luck."

He walked to the side of the bed and took her in his arms. "Oh, Kati, I love you so much. You are the most wonderful wife anyone could ever dream of having."

She looked into his eyes and told him how she felt about him.

"Did you see your flowers?"

"Yes, I was trying to see what is attached to them when you came in. Who are they from? It looks as if they have the same ribbons Sonja used to put on her arrangements. And what is that around the vase?"

"So many questions. Let me see if I can help you out," he offered. He walked over to the elegant bouquet. He untied the small package and returned to her bedside. He handed her both the card and the box. "The card first," he instructed.

"So they're from you," she said.

"Unless you took a lover while I was gone," he answered with a smile.

The box was heavy in her lap. It remained there while she

opened the envelope. The top of the card was imprinted with the Fichtls' logo. On it was written . . .

"To my beautiful chatelaine, the keys to your lost kingdom. For the past, but especially for the future. With all my love, Christophe."

She removed the lid of the box slowly. She reached in and pulled out its contents. At once she recognized her grandfather's keys. They were all there, the large skeleton that opened the main vault, and the smaller ones that fit the safety-deposit boxes. Every one of them. She held them in her hands, staring at the rusty, antiquated collection that was a symbol of so many beautiful memories of her life at the Waldhotel. The tears flowed freely down her cheeks.

"It's yours again, my love. It's all yours to do with as you please. The Waldhotel finally belongs to you again. I know it took me awhile. I'm glad you didn't lose patience with me . . . ."

"Christophe, oh, I can't believe it," she cried. She pulled him down to her. It was too good to be true. After all the heartache and the tragedy. He had made her dream of owning the Waldhotel again a reality. Their embrace spoke of all the passion and the love they had overcome so many obstacles to share.

When they finally released their hold on each other, she looked into his eyes. She felt ashamed for thinking the terrible things she had only yesterday. He read her mind.

"So, as exciting and as plausible as it may have seemed to you, I was not off on an adventure with my mistress. Rather, I was in Los Angeles negotiating the sale of the Waldhotel with the owners. After I finally found them, that is. The Americans drove a hard bargain, I must say. I've been after them for over a year. I just couldn't understand them. They bought the hotel and then just let it sit there, empty and uncared for during the last three years. They never even opened it after we left. I've no idea what condition it's in. Dieter heard from one of his friends that we've got our work cut out for us."

"Dieter knew about this?"

"Of course I did," he answered, having entered the room just as Kati was asking the question.

She turned to him and began to scold him. "You knew about this? Why didn't you tell me yesterday when I found out he wasn't in New York? You saw how upset I was."

"Kati, I knew you'd be all right," the wonderful, wise old man said. "Besides, a promise is a promise. Now I've kept a promise for each of you and from each of you. That certainly entitles me to see your new daughter right away, doesn't it?"

Almost as if on cue, the nurse entered at that exact moment bearing Mademoiselle Claude Dominique de Beaumont. Kati held her arms out to receive her. She stroked her tiny head and checked each of her delicate fingers and toes one by one. The proud father and godfather huddled over the newborn. Dieter had a thousand questions for Christophe about his trip and the details of the purchase of Becker's. They began talking excitedly. Minutes later they looked over and found that both Kati and Claude were sound asleep. The keys were still clutched tightly in the new mother's hand.

CHAPTER
38

THE RENOVATION of the Waldhotel took almost four years. The time could have been cut in half, but Kati's demand for perfection had reached the level of an obsession. Every detail—the fabrics, the finishes, the furniture—had to meet her exacting standards. If not, the unacceptable goods would be returned to the manufacturer to be replaced or modified.

During the time the hotel had been owned by the Americans, it had sat empty, and no one had even been sent in from time to time to inspect the interiors. As a result there had been extensive water damage from pipes that had burst during an especially cold winter. The main pipe over the Grand Salon had broken, ruining all of the glorious antiques and priceless carpets. The chandelier, once magnificent, had crashed to the floor. Hundreds of its sparkling crystal drops shattered in the fall. The Baccarat factory was commissioned to replace all of them at an enormous cost, since it was a pattern they had not made since the early nineteenth century.

They salvaged what they could, but much of the furniture, and nearly all of the wallpaper and draperies, were beyond repair. Kati spent weeks wading through the archives of the great fabric houses of Italy and France trying desperately to find the patterns that had been used when the hotel was first constructed. In most cases her careful research had paid off, but a few times even she had to compromise her wishes when the cost or time it would take to duplicate the exact thing became unreasonable.

She hired a team of architects and designers whose clear direction it was to remodel the hotel to its former, elegant self while at the same time adding all of the modern conveniences demanded by the most sophisticated traveler. The planning was an excruciating process. Kati was relentless in her quest for perfection. A room facing the river must have thinner net curtains than one with no view facing out to the front; a room with north light was colder than those on the other side of the building and must be furnished in warmer tones. All these things had to be taken into consideration or the new Waldhotel would not be as successful as she hoped. The antiquated faucets and shower fixtures could be taken out, but the bathrooms must stay exactly the same size. The old tile floors could be removed but must be replaced with the finest white marble. The oversized bath towels embroidered with the Waldhotel crest had to be specially ordered from France. The valuable headboards and footboards, some inlaid with ebony and ivory, had to be taken out and refinished. No modern beds with built-in bedstands for her hotel. Lamps, tables, chairs, drapes, cutlery, linens—the list of items to be decided upon was endless.

Kati, Margarethe, and the children had moved into temporary quarters in the building across the street while the hotel was under construction. Dieter took the same room he had occupied for twenty years. "I never realized how much I missed this place until I returned," he said, looking around the lobby. "Now I don't think I could ever leave again. All that talk about retiring to the south was just so much talk. This is home." Kati couldn't have agreed more. Each morning when she came through the door, he was already seated at his desk, hard at work.

Christophe came every weekend to visit his family and check on the work that had been done. Each time he arrived, Kati was bubbling over with things to tell him. He would barely be out of the car before she would grab his arm. "Come," she would urge, tugging at his sleeve like a small child. She would drag him around and show him the progress they had made since his last visit. He didn't have a chance to take off his coat or loosen his tie before he was off looking at a new rug or light fixture. But their love for each other and the children only grew. A project such as this, which could stress even the most perfect relationship, only seemed to make theirs even stronger.

Kati was standing at the entrance to the hotel when the truck pulled in. She recognized the package by its shape the moment the delivery men removed it and began carrying it toward the hotel. Of all the things they had expected—the chairs bought at auction in London for the reception desk, the antique sconces for the newly lacquered walls of the bar, the Victorian rose-patterned carpets for the suites— none was met with more enthusiasm than the crate that was now being carried into the Waldhotel.

"Just put it over there," she directed the men. "Yes, that's right, on the side wall out of the way of the carpenters." Her voice held the concern of a mother watching someone carry her newborn for the first time. "Thank goodness it arrived today. I was getting worried it wouldn't be here in time for the opening," she said to no one but herself.

She waited until that night when she and Christophe were alone in the hotel. They had made another inspection. Kati had busily jotted down on her pad all of the last-minute details that had to be attended to prior to the opening the following week. The dresser drawers in the rooms on the fourth floor had not been oiled, and they did not slide properly; the prints had not been hung in the hallway of the Presidential suite; the towels in the honeymoon suite were neither the right color nor the right quantity; light bulbs were missing in the lamps in the bathroom off the main foyer—all these small but important details had to be corrected.

"Over here, Christophe," she said. "This just arrived today." She found a knife in the pile of the worker's tools and began slitting the sides of the package.

"Here, sweetheart, give me that," he said. "I can't have my wife's nails looking as if she did the construction herself," he joked, although he knew his statement wasn't far from the truth. Never had he seen anyone work so hard and so fiercely. No job was too menial for Kati.

The last wrappings dropped away and they stood side-by-side looking at the portrait.

She breathed a final sigh of relief once she was certain it had arrived without any damage. "I'm so glad it got here in time. I kept calling Jean-Louis and making him check with the shipping company. When I called the last time, he sounded as if he was ready to kill me."

"Well, he can yell at you in person next week when he's here. I'm really looking forward to meeting him."

"Oh, he's wonderful," Kati said. "And Sylvie said she couldn't wait to see you again. I've never met Jean-Louis's wife, but I'm certain she must be lovely. They're bringing the baby, too. Margarethe has already volunteered to watch him."

For a moment, as she stood staring at the portrait of her grandfather, remembering when Christophe had first sent it to her in Paris, she allowed her thoughts to wander. What if she had taken the easy road and had married Jean-Louis? There was never any doubt in her mind that he was in love with her. He still cared for her immensely. But it just hadn't been right. She had only wanted him as a friend, not as a husband or a lover. Kati had waited, at that time not knowing exactly for what. Now she was so glad she had. Her long wait had paid off. Now she had her wonderful Christophe, her beautiful children, and her hotel. Nothing could have been more perfect.

"Kati, are you listening to me?" Christophe's voice broke through her thoughts. Her smile confirmed to him that she had been a thousand miles away. "What were you thinking about?"

"Oh, nothing," she sighed. "Everything, actually. You, the children, my time in France. Oh, Christophe, you've made me so very happy."

"And you me, my love," he said. He led her by the hand, through the darkened halls and into the Grand Salon. Drop cloths still covered the floors, an effort to protect the newly finished parquet. Workmen's tools were strewn throughout the room. Vestiges of the last of the construction work were still evident. Christophe bent down and pulled back a section of the heavy canvas cloth, revealing the thick, Oriental carpet. He sat down and his eyes begged her to join him. Soon they were lying down side-by-side, their arms and legs entwined. Emotions as strong as those they had felt the first night they had walked together through this room and out onto the lawn overtook them. He held her and stroked her hair tenderly. "I love you, my sweet. I'm so proud of what you've done here."

"I couldn't have done it without you," she said. "You've made all of this possible."

"No, I only helped you. You were determined to do it from the day I met you. It's really all yours, Kati. And it will be a great success."

"But it wouldn't be anything without you," she said, taking his face in her hands and pressing her lips to his.

Their kisses were urgent. Kati's excitement was enhanced by the feel of Christophe's clothing as it rubbed against her thin silk dress. He began to undress her slowly, holding her hands together so that she was unable to do the same for him. Once she was naked, lying back on the soft carpet, he kneeled next to her and allowed her to remove his suit. She proceeded as slowly as her anxious hands would permit. She savored every moment—loosening his tie, unbuttoning each button on his shirt carefully, gently pulling down his suit pants to reveal his hardness. Never had she wanted him more. After all their years of marriage, her passion for him had only increased.

"I want you, my darling. Please come to me," she begged as she pulled him down to her. "Christophe," she cried, not wanting to delay their lovemaking another minute. "I love you so."

"I know, my darling, and I love you." He took her in his arms, stroking her softly, letting her excitement build.

"You are the most precious thing in the world to me," he said.

"I love you more tonight than ever before. You've made all my dreams come true."

Their need for each other could be put off no longer and he entered her with the same caution and concern for her that he'd shown the first time they had made love in his bastide at the Villa Soleil.

His face looking down at her, his powerful chest rising and falling with their mutual rhythms, brought Kati to climax at exactly the same time as he. They held each other tightly, swaying urgently, waves of pleasure rushing over and through their entire beings.

"You are everything to me," Kati whispered, suddenly exhausted from the long week. "Yes, everything," she repeated. Then she slept peacefully in his arms.

She surveyed the assortment of clothing scattered about the floor. "What if someone got the dates mixed up and came a week early for the party?" she asked when they awakened later.

"We'd tell them we were having an owner's test run, just checking to make certain everything was all right for the opening," he answered.

They both laughed and suddenly felt very naughty. They had no regrets, and soon they fell back into each other's arms and made love again. Hours later, not more than a few minutes before the arrival of the first workmen, they tiptoed like teenagers across the street to their room.

The day of the opening dawned and still the tables for the dining room had not been delivered. There was to be a seated dinner that night for two hundred guests after the performance of the symphony.

"Get Herr Lockmann on the phone again for me," Kati yelled to her secretary. Kati's own demands for the highest standards had been matched in the carpenter she had selected to make the tables. Even though she had called him repeatedly to remind him of his deadline, he was not willing to compromise quality by rushing. Late yesterday he had admitted to her that he still had four tables to finish.

Christophe was not even there to share her anxiety. He had things to attend to at the Villa Soleil and would not return to the Waldhotel until later in the day.

At three o'clock Kati got word that the truck bearing the precious tables had arrived. She breathed a sigh of relief and went down to supervise the delivery.

"Set one of them up and let's see how it's going to look," she asked the manager of the restaurant. Minutes later the table had been covered with its light pink linen cloth. The new porcelain, a floral pattern by Villeroy-Boch, was a duplicate of that used at the first dinner ever served at the Waldhotel. It was beautiful. The silver place settings shone. The many different glasses would sparkle brightly once the candles were lit. The small crystal vases in front of each place setting would each contain a small assortment of flowers. They would only stand about six inches high so as not to block the guests' view of each other across the round table. Kati stood back and looked at the setup. She tried to imagine how the entire room would look when it was complete. Slowly her eyes traveled to the floor. The end of the skirt was almost three inches off the floor. It left an unsightly dark rim around the base of the table. Something was terribly, terribly wrong.

"Dieter, come in here right now," she yelled out.

He heard her panic-stricken voice. He dropped what he was doing and ran into the dining room.

"Dieter, look what's happened. The cloths are too short for the tables. They look awful. And there's no time to have them resewn. I'll have Frau Mercer's neck for this. Even when all the chairs are in place, they will still look horrible. Oh, what are we going to do?" She turned to him, her face begging him to perform a miracle.

"Wait a minute, Kati," he said patiently. He walked around and sat down in one of the chairs. "It's not the cloths, Kati, it's the tables. They're too high. In his rush to finish, Herr Lockmann must have measured incorrectly."

She looked across the room. Certainly he could not have made the same mistake on all of them. But sure enough, as she glanced slowly around the room, all of the table heights were the same. All three inches too high.

"Get every saw around, gentlemen," she commanded.

There were thirty-three tables. The afternoon was spent cutting down each one of the hundred thirty-two table legs. Kati, aided by every available man, remeasured and cut, while Margarethe and all of the maids stood anxiously by, setting each table as it became ready. When Christophe arrived, he was immediately handed his own saw. Still dressed in his suit, he began cutting madly. At six-fifteen the last table was put in place and the remaining perfectly sized pink cloth was hastily thrown over it.

"Thank you, thank you all," Kati yelled out to them when the emergency job was completed. "I'm sorry to leave you, but I've got to get dressed now."

Kati showered quickly, annoyed to be deprived of her anticipated luxurious bath. "Can you believe that Lockmann?" she yelled out to Christophe as she dried herself quickly.

"It's unconscionable," he agreed, annoyed himself because it had upset Kati. "But they look beautiful now. No one will ever know. You looked terrific with that saw; someday we'll even be laughing about it," he suggested.

"Not just yet. I'm going to wring his neck first," Kati continued as she sat before her dressing table and started her makeup.

Christophe emerged from his shower minutes later and began putting on his tuxedo.

"You're going to look so handsome," his wife commented. "You know how I feel about men in black tie."

"It's only because you grew up around so many waiters. Don't try to fool me, young lady," he teased.

Kati finished her hair and makeup. She went to the closet where her new ball gown was hanging, an extraordinary creation by Yves Saint Laurent. Made of emerald-green satin, its off-the-shoulder style complemented her lovely neckline. She stepped gingerly into the unwieldy garment. "Here, love, please help with this. The zipper is totally impossible," she said, holding the bodice of the cumbersome dress in her hands and shuffling toward her husband.

"Lovely," he said, stroking her bare breasts with his fingers.

"No fooling around, Monsieur," she warned. "This is serious business." He got on with his assignment. "Thank you," she said as she felt the tight-fitting material close around her still-perfect figure.

She walked back to the closet. "Oh no," she cried a second later, her voice signaling despair.

"What is it?"

"My shoes, where are my shoes?" she said, panic now overtaking her. "Where has Dagmar put my shoes?" Dagmar was her new maid. "She promised me she would pick them up this afternoon. But she was helping us with the tables. Oh, I hope she didn't forget. I had shoes dyed this same green color to go with the dress. I have absolutely nothing else to wear!"

"Are those your shoes over there?" Christophe asked, pointing toward the closet on the other side of the room.

"Oh yes," she said, immediate relief filling her voice. "I wonder how they got over there? She must have dropped them off in a rush. Oh well, it doesn't matter, as long as they're here."

"Let me get them for you," he offered. "Sit down, my little princess, and I'll be happy to put your shoes on for you."

She agreed at once to his suggestion. "How kind you are, Sir," she replied, sitting once again at her dressing table. She extended her slender foot out to him. The beautiful high-heeled pump slid on easily. As he placed the other one on her left foot, she felt something in the toe.

"Wait a minute. There's something wrong," she said, reaching down and impatiently taking the shoe from him. She shook it gently. Out fell a piece of jewelry. A look of confusion crossed her face. She took the object in her hand. As she untangled it, she saw that it was a sparkling necklace.

Christophe's face could not hide his pleasure. He smiled at her. "It's a good thing you found your shoes," he said.

"Oh, Christophe, it's the most beautiful thing I've ever seen." Indeed it was. The entire necklace was made of diamonds. There was a round-cut stone in the middle, surrounded by a string of smaller diamonds, patterned in a leaf motif that glistened brilliantly. "Oh, Christophe, it's exquisite," she repeated. She reached over and kissed him.

"I hoped you'd like it. Shall I put it on?"

"Yes, of course."

She turned and faced the mirror. Standing in back of her, he fastened the necklace in place. She looked at her reflection in the mirror. The necklace sat perfectly across the base of her throat. Tears flooded her eyes as the memories of a night so long ago came back to her. "One day, Kati, you, too, will have beautiful things of your very own," her Opa had said as they stood together in the vault, "beautiful necklaces and rings that you will wear on special nights like this." Now her grandfather's prophecy had come true. She cried with happiness, as Christophe gently held her. Silently they thanked one another for what they meant to each other.

"Madame de Beaumont," he said, pulling away from her, "I believe you have a gala to attend." She dried her tears as he offered her his arm and escorted her downstairs to their guests.

Kati concealed her nervousness and tension behind a glowing smile as she greeted many of those attending by name. Sylvie and Jean-Louis had come from Paris, Heidi and Mark from Munich. Margarethe, in a new dress, looked as lovely as Kati had ever seen her. Dieter stood discreetly on the side, beaming with happiness. In the crowd she spotted some of her family's friends—the Lord Mayor of the City, now in his nineties, the kind Dr. Hoeffer who had treated Tilla so well—all of them had come to celebrate Kati's triumph over the toughest of odds. She recognized many of the others, members of the important social crowd who had defected to the Europäischer Hof years before. She was delighted to see that they were back.

The hotel glittered. Everything had fallen into place at the very last minute. She and Christophe strolled through the rooms slowly, anxious to hear the response of the guests. Soon they heard the sound of the bells ringing, signaling that it was time to leave for the performance. The hansom cabs were lined up like little soldiers ready to take the patrons to the performance. Even the horses were dressed for the festivities with their wreaths constructed of multicolored flowers from the hotel's refurbished garden.

As Kati looked down from her seat in the box high above the orchestra, it appeared to her that everyone was enjoying the symphony's brilliant rendition of Boulez's works. However, she could not sit still for more than a few seconds, so excited and worried was she about their first night. At intermission she excused herself and headed back to the hotel. She preferred to wait there until the hansoms returned bearing those who would determine whether or not the Waldhotel would succeed under her caring hand.

"Wait, I'm coming with you," Christophe insisted. "I can't sit still for the rest of this either."

They decided to walk back. The river was calm, its flow barely audible. "It's beautiful, isn't it?" she asked as the lights of the main dining room came into view.

"I'm so proud of you, I'm speechless, Kati. You've done a wonderful job, and it will be a great success," he assured her.

He opened the narrow private gate leading to the back entrance of the hotel and allowed Kati to pass. Inside they could see the waiters scurrying back and forth preparing for the return of the guests. Kati looked up to the top of the imposing stone building that had sat like a corpse for three years. The hotel had such a long, rich history, having been alternately purchased and sold for motives ranging from hope to despair. Now she had brought it back to life.

Three hours later, just as the elegant celebratory dessert of flaming cherries was placed in front of each well-fed guest, the orchestra began to play. To the opening strains of "As Time Goes By," Christophe led Kati onto the dance floor, beautiful in her glorious gown with the sparkling diamond necklace. She was indeed a princess in her own castle. The chatelaine of the new Waldhotel Becker. Silence fell upon the room for a split second before the first guests began to rise from their seats. Soon they were all on their feet, clapping and paying tribute to the woman who had restored one of the grand hotels of the world to its former glory.

The sound of popping champagne corks filled the air and the party began in earnest. Beautifully dressed women and men in finely tailored dinner jackets crowded onto the floor until there was no longer any space to move. Guests wandered from room to room, extolling the beauty of the hotel. Everyone had something wonderful to say about the new Waldhotel.

It was four in the morning when the last guests finally wandered upstairs to their rooms. Christophe had gone outside to say good night to a departing couple, and Kati found herself alone in the silence of the darkened foyer. She sat down heavily on the stairs, wondering if she would ever find the energy to get up again. Her full skirt fell gently around her ankles, the abundance of green silk flowing down onto the stair below.

She looked up at the three portraits hanging on the wall. First she glanced at Ludwig, the founder of the Waldhotel. Then her eyes settled on the portrait of Karl-Gustav, which had been sent from Paris by Jean-Louis. Then she moved to the new one—a lovely image of Kati in a ball gown. Christophe had insisted that she sit for the portrait. "Kati, you're the person responsible for continuing the tradition. If it weren't for you, the Waldhotel would only exist in some obscure book on grand hotels of a former era. No, you've got to be up there next to your grandfather." He was adamant, and after much discussion she had finally agreed. He had also suggested that they hang all three of them, side by side, against the wall facing the staircase. No one could miss the reminder that the Waldhotel Becker was now being run by a third-generation family member. Now she was glad she had given in to Christophe's wishes. She was proud to be there next to her beloved Opa.

.   .   .

"Maman, Maman, there you are." She heard both of their voices at once.

She turned her head around and saw them standing at the top of the stairs. From the sneaky smile on Edouard's face she determined that he had been responsible for waking his sister and convincing her that they should venture downstairs.

"What are you two doing up at this hour?"

"We couldn't sleep. The guests were making so much noise. We wanted to find out what was going on," Edouard said, giving her the answer they had apparently agreed upon in advance.

"I see," she laughed, too happy to see her darling children to scold them for getting up from their beds. "Well, I'm afraid the party is over and everyone is gone, but you can come down here and sit with me," she offered.

"Yes, yes," they agreed in unison. They scrambled down the stairs and sat down next to her, one on either side.

"Maman, you look so pretty tonight," Claude said as she reached up to touch the beautiful diamond necklace.

"Thank you, sweetheart."

Claude looked beautiful, too, with her sleep-filled eyes. Her mother's eyes. She had luminous, milky skin—the same skin Kati had had before the tragedy of the fire. Kati reached out and hugged both their tiny, sweet-smelling bodies close to her. The three of them sat very still for what seemed like a long time. Edouard, the instigator of the late-night caper, fell back to sleep almost at once.

"Maman," Claude said softly.

"Yes, my little one."

"Maman, when I grow up, I want my picture to be up there, right next to yours."

She squeezed the little girl closer to her. "Yes, my darling, that would be wonderful."

Kati glanced up at the portraits once again. It seemed to her that both Ludwig and Karl-Gustav gave her a secret look of approval. She had kept her promise. With the back of her hand she brushed aside a single tear before gathering up her two children and carrying them upstairs to their warm beds.

ACKNOWLEDGMENTS

*M*ANAGEMENT of a great hotel is a very specialized area—it requires dedication and devotion to a constantly changing, constantly trying environment. Maintaining the balance is a juggling act attempted by many, but mastered by few. I was lucky enough to observe, to speak with, and to learn from the very best. My grateful appreciation to the following men and women who have dedicated their careers to the pleasure of those they serve.

At the Brenner's Park-Hotel in Baden-Baden, West Germany: Mr. Richard Schmitz, General Manager; Mr. Wilhelm Luxem, Assistant Manager; Mr. Gustav Treu, Concierge; Ms. Astrid Pokorski, Secretary to Mr. Luxem; Mr. Willy Maier, Doorman.

My sincere thanks also to Mr. Jean-Claude Irondelle, General Manager, Hotel du Cap, Cap d'Antibes, France, and Dr. Stassen, Director of the German Academic Exchange.